The Spaniard's Daughter

Melanie Gifford

PIATKUS

All the characters in this book are fictitious and any resemblance to real persons, living or dead, is entirely coincidental.

Copyright © 2006 Melanie Gifford

First published in Great Britain in 2006 by
Piatkus Books Ltd
5 Windmill Street, London W1T 2JA
email: info@piatkus.co.uk

This edition published 2007

The moral right of the author has been asserted

A catalogue record for this book is available from the British Library

ISBN 978 0 7499 3838 3

Set in Times by Palimpsest Book Production Limited, Grangemouth, Stirlingshire

Printed and bound in Great Britain by Clays Ltd, St Ives plc

ASK

she completed her first novel journalism and publishing, as well Europe, Africa and America, only fuelled her passion fiction and she continued to write copiously in her spare time. The award of a writer's bursary allowed her to concentrate on becoming a full-time author. After spending much of her life in the south of England, she currently lives in Scotland with her partner and two cats.

Melanie is the author of *The Gallows Girl*, also published by Piatkus.

Also by Melanie Gifford

The Gallows Girl

To Gillian, Emma and Ben with thanks.

Chapter One

I had just turned fifteen when I stole my first baby. This was no dark concocted plot on my part. I wasn't much of a schemer, not then. I fell into it the way you might stumble over a pothole in the street. My life had already been thundering to some sort of crisis. It was like watching a cannon fuse burn down. You either tried to snuff it out with your fingers or stood back and waited for the explosion.

Juliana Rodriguez. An olive-kissed name for an orphaned bastard child. Yet my hair was not the glossy, jet-black of the Spaniard but red, a deep burnished copper that sometimes lightened to gold in the hottest days of summer. Some of my guardians' friends remarked that I had a cat's aspect – high cheekbones with a wide, tucked-up smile.

People told stories about me all the time. I knew this, but I'd yet to catch anyone in the act. Sometimes I got close. A pause when I entered the room, a snatch of breath. Conversations were sliced up and folded away. I witnessed it in the street, the coffee house and the apothecary where Catherine bought those foul-smelling potions to soothe her feet. I doubted anyone *knew* very much, but an absence of facts only served to oil busy tongues.

At the time I was naïve enough to think that what they said didn't matter. Gossips were full of the war against the rebels in the Americas. Men were leaving by the shipload. Women wailed as if their husbands were already lost, or tumbled gratefully into the beds of their lovers. No one, I hoped, would notice me amid the chaos.

A stupid notion, on reflection.

Fifteen. Almost a woman. My guardians, Richard and Catherine Worledge, had decided to hold a birthday party in my honour at their town house in Wexborough. Or rather Catherine had decided and Richard, sensibly, agreed. The house was typical of the style of buildings that were sprouting like a rash across the town. Built from a soft, golden sandstone it had just the right number of windows, a pediment above the polished front door and marble steps spreading down into the street. I thought it resembled a slab of not-so-fresh butter sitting on a cobbled dish. It was astonishing, when I remarked on this to Catherine, how her face could deepen to scarlet then pale again in the space of a breath.

'Have you any idea how much that house cost?' her thin, bite-you mouth demanded. I replied that, whatever the cost, it still looked like a butter house to me. She didn't talk for the rest of the day and, unrepentant, I ended up taking supper in the kitchen. It seemed stupid that she should empty her purse on a certain type of building just because someone else had declared it fashionable. It wasn't like a dress that you could wear for a night then throw away after use. But that was Catherine for you.

The party was well underway and I hadn't put a foot out of my bedchamber. Mrs Deever, Catherine's housekeeper, had toiled for three hours turning me into a French poppet. I fidgeted while she smothered me in a velvet gown, pulled a choker roughly around my neck and plastered my chin with thick, sticky cream.

'To hide your birthmark,' she explained. 'Hold still. I've chafed my knuckles once already trying to button up your stays.'

'I have to breathe don't I? Any more powder and I'll choke.'

'You'll just have to put up with it. You know that mark frightens the children.'

'I didn't invite them. They don't care whether it's my

birthday so long as there's enough cake to stuff in their mouths.'

'Your mama says to cover it and cover it I will.'

'She's not my mama.'

A sharp tap on my face with the back of her hand. My teeth clipped the end of my tongue. Needles stabbed into my mouth. Deever waited, testing my willingness to defy her. Better take a slap now, I thought, than have her going off whining to Catherine, who seemed to keep a mental tally of all my supposed misdemeanours. Once I'd notched up a certain amount I'd feel the sharp side of her temper. The servants snitched on me every chance they got.

I let the old hag finish dressing me. Both feet were crammed into satin slippers and her skinny fingers tugged a wig down firmly over my red hair.

'Better,' she declared. 'Everyone will think so.'

I barely recognised the white-faced ghost staring back at me from the looking glass. Deever ushered me out of the room and downstairs to the noisy carnival below. The hired quintet had struck up a merry tune. Guests performed a gavotte on the dining-room carpet. Festivities had spread from room to room, spilling into the hall and filling each alcove with laughter. Catherine, in a wig so tall she had to duck under doorways, passed me among her friends. I felt like an exotic trinket purchased for a guinea at a fly-blown foreign market. Visitors admired me the way they might a fine horse or a remarkable painting. People grinned and pinched my cheeks. I half expected one of them to examine my teeth.

'This one will wed a banker or merchant,' Catherine said, laughing, 'or catch the eye of some country squire.'

When she was finished with me I let go of my lopsided smile and stood quietly beside the parlour hearth. I curtsied at all the gaudy peacocks and did not speak unless spoken to. Later, Catherine put me with the children before returning to her guests. I tried to play party games. I sat infants on my lap or chased them around the room, these

3

giggling bundles of chaos. Older girls had little time for me. They lost themselves in petty conversation while the minutes ticked down, talking and talking without actually *saying* anything. Others clustered their chairs near the open door and cast distracted glances into the hall, hoping to hook a handsome face.

My friends were picked, like a gown, a pair of slippers or a lace-trimmed nightshift. We did the rounds of one another's houses, moved like cards in a game of hazard. I was at that in-between age, bored with childhood trinkets yet not old enough to be allowed a serious opinion. Sometimes I just wanted to smoke, get drunk or fall fumbling into a man's lap like loose women were said to do. The last time I was too rebellious Catherine punished me herself. That night in my distress I wet the bed, which put me in trouble with the servants who had to strip the linen and clean the mattress. I had often been called wilful but in reality thought myself a terrible coward.

Until I heard about the baby.

For nearly two hours I'd played the happy birthday girl and beneath the smile I felt like an exhausted dog. Finally, a harassed-looking maid wandered in carrying a tray of cakes. I caught her wrist.

'Look after the children.'

'Got work of my own to do,' she said, squirming free of my grasp. 'I ain't a nursemaid besides.'

'It's only for a while. I'll make sure you get something from the dining table. A few sweetmeats perhaps, or some party favours. There might be sixpences inside.'

'I'll get into trouble if I'm away from the kitchen too long,' she protested, but there was no conviction in it.

I escaped into the dining room. Long tables had been set up against the walls. Evening sunshine soaked the room in a dim, brassy light. Guests crowded around me. A drink, sherry from the smell of it, slopped over my arm.

Blake, sharp in his head footman's livery, stood over the

4

remains of the buffet. It had taken cook all morning to prepare. The sweetmeats and cheeses had been ravaged, the cakes reduced to crumbs. Blake's eyes widened when he spotted me. Creases appeared in his pinned-on face. His tongue ran along the edge of his teeth.

Birthday trinkets were spread out on the table beneath the window. Guests wandered in, lifted, compared, speculated on who had bought what and how much it cost. Every corner was filled with chattering faces. I felt a pinch on my forearm. One of Catherine's friends leered at me. Her lips were a scarlet gash filled with a jumble of teeth. She muttered something, but the wine had gone to her mouth and I couldn't make sense of the slurred muddle. When I didn't answer she scowled and tottered off in search of a more sympathetic ear.

This was the very cream of Wexborough society. Beached seafarers, retired soldiers and petty politicians – all those who had escaped the war along with wives, mistresses and husband-hunting daughters. Most didn't even notice me. They passed my life between them as if it was a morsel from the buffet table. Each mouth took a bite.

'Richard fought with a business partner because of her, did you know that?' The speaker paused long enough to suck on a sculpted pipe. 'They traded blows on the lawn at the rear of the house. Richard is no brawler or I'm sure he would have killed the fellow, who at any rate was never invited to the house again.'

His companion wafted a feather-trimmed fan in front of her chin. 'The girl is very comely, would be a perfect angel if not for that mark.'

'Yes,' her friend agreed, 'if not for that mark.'

Richard had caught us in the back parlour. I'd been lured inside with the promise of a new game 'all the way from India' that his colleague wanted to show me. He was a crude, thick-set man with spades for hands. It wasn't the 'game' that had upset me the most but my guardian, returning afterwards from the garden with his nose bloodied and dirt streaking his silk shirt. He called me a strumpet and cuffed my cheek. Catherine had to get Blake to escort him upstairs. I cried for an hour.

That was when I first learned how dangerous beauty could be, but I wasn't aware of what might be achieved with this power until much later. I didn't spend much time pouting into mirrors. All I ever saw was 'the mark', the cherry-red smear running from the corner of my mouth to my chin. Not much of a thing compared to a harelip or a face scoured by the pox. I took a good teasing over it, until some bored child at a tea party screamed that I was a witch and had been drinking blood. That got all the darlings into a lather and Catherine took me home in embarrassed disgrace. I spent an hour trying to scrub the blemish off and gave myself a bad rash that stung for a week. The mark ran in my family. Catherine reminded me of that whenever she was in a bad mood. It seemed the only time I ever learned anything about myself was at the whim of her temper.

I fled the dining room. I couldn't fumble anything off the tables with Blake brooding over everything. The maid was going to have to wait.

The study beckoned, a refuge packed with shelves of leather-bound books, though Richard always complained that he couldn't find a decent bookseller. I adored the written word and the places those words took me. Together we travelled the world and through those pages I met long-dead explorers, warriors and adventurers. It was as if I'd been allowed to enter their lives and share something wonderful.

When Richard was out on business or squandering Catherine's money at one of his gambling clubs, I spent hours curled up in his leather chair with a volume open on my lap. On good days the sun threw streamers of light across the mahogany desk. If my luck held I'd find a newspaper, neatly folded. Or one of Catherine's society magazines that Richard occasionally flicked through. When I closed the study door, the Butter House and all its simmering troubles were gone.

Now the door hung open. Richard was perched on the edge of his desk, idly flicking pipe ash on to the carpet. 'Another of my vessels has been requisitioned to take troops to the war,' he declared, gesturing with his brandy glass, 'which in any case we seem in danger of losing. Understand that I attach no blame to the King. Parliament is full of wastrels set on plundering other people's fortunes. Thievery, I call it.'

His friends pursed their lips and nodded. Their hunting dogs' eyes ranged over his books, the family portraits, the silver ornaments littering his desk. Richard was oblivious to this. His voice, taut with passion, carried above the discordant twang of the spinet that someone was trying to play in the music room next door. 'It's no longer a kind world to men whose business is the sea,' he finished.

I met a real sailor once, a grizzled old man with a chipped clay pipe in his mouth and a head full of stories. Catherine had taken me to Richard's offices at the docks. Richard wasn't there and I was obliged to wait outside while Catherine fetched the key from his clerk so she could retrieve some letters. While she fumbled around in the clutter the sailor, who was perched on a crate by the quayside, delighted me by seemingly producing a farthing from my ear. He showed me the scars on his back where he'd felt the lash and bade me touch his hands, which were like old leather after years of blistering work. I could almost smell the faraway places he had been to and imagined tropical winds breezing through his white, thinning hair.

Not like Richard, whose feet never left shore. Richard only ever smelled of brandy and tobacco, mixed with a whiff of the Italian cologne his vessels sometimes brought in. Catherine suffered his indiscretions with a tight smile. Sometimes when she glanced at him across the dinner table, or in the parlour in front of the evening fire, her eyes seemed to darken.

'The business which you claim to care for yet seldom manage because you are too drunk, or too fond of the card

7

table, is mine,' she reminded him once, sewing needle puncturing the fine lace of her sampler in an ugly, erratic pattern. 'You only came into my fortune because your father had sufficient wit to find a fat-pursed spinster to marry his dullard son. My papa only agreed because he wanted me wed before he died. You would not have taken me to the altar otherwise.'

Richard's clothes were always too garish and the earnest expression etched on to his face made him look a buffoon. Despite his affection I felt like a debt he was obliged to pay off piece by piece. Yet if not for him, Catherine would've packed me off a long time ago.

I slipped away from the study door. I was tired and my belly hurt. I hadn't eaten a proper meal since supper the night before. The party might clatter on long into the night. I sent a maid to ask cook for a hot drink to settle me. She went off, scowling.

I retreated to my room. The party wouldn't suffer for my absence. A fresh coverlet had been spread over the bed and a candle flickered in its holder on the dresser. I opened both windows and peered into the deepening gloom. The sun had dipped into the not-quite-night of midsummer. The air was warm, like a gust of heat from the kitchen hearth.

I flumped fully clothed on to the bed and waited for my drink. Footsteps creaked along the passage. I sat up, smiling.

Edward Blake slipped into the room with a friendliness that did not fit him and gently closed the door. The stench of sour wine lurked in his grin.

'Got a sore belly have we? Well, I know a trick that'll put it right.'

Thick fingers fluttered towards my bodice. His nails were polished. They brushed against the embroidered velvet. I edged away. Just enough to put half an inch of muggy air between us. His grin slipped a little.

'Now,' he said softly, but with thorns spiking every word. 'No need to go behaving like that. Not when I'm trying to help you.'

'You shouldn't be in here, Blake.'

'I was Mister Blake last I heard.'

'Mister Blake then.'

'What about you, Miss Juliana? Why are you hiding in here like a frightened rabbit? You should be downstairs enchanting all your fine guests. Mrs Worledge will wonder where you are. If she asks me, what shall I tell her? What do I say? I'm head of the staff. If you go down sick it'll look bad for me.'

'My belly's only sore because I was starved to fit inside this frippery of a gown, besides, Deever says she's in charge.'

The grin tightened. 'No use trying to play the wily politician. I watched you leave the dining room and I saw you running up the stairs.'

'Don't touch me.'

'I only want to rub a bit of warmth into you, Miss Juliana, to settle that poorly stomach.'

'I'll lock the door next time.'

'You haven't got a key.'

'I'll put a chair against it.'

'What, and barricade yourself against poor Ed Blake who only wants to provide a bit of relief?' He shook his head. 'You're a bad 'un. Just like your papa. They stretched his neck. Who's to know what will become of you.'

'What do you know about my father?'

Blake didn't answer. With that jackal's smile, he ran his fingers down the front of my gown. Sounds drifted along the hallway like voices in a fog. I tried to say something else but the words stuck in my throat. He leaned forward. His breath whispered over my face.

A sharp rap and the door swung open. A maid stood framed in the light from the passage, steaming posset in her hand. Blake hauled her back outside. Hot milk slopped on to the carpet. He slammed the door. Through the wood I heard him growling like a dog and the maid bursting into tears.

9

I held my breath. He did not come back. Five minutes I waited, then ten. I couldn't stand it any longer.

Downstairs the party droned on. Someone was yelling. A glass was knocked over in a flurry of exclamations. I stumbled through the house. The hem of my gown dragged on the floor. The wig felt hot and itchy. Some of the pins had come loose and it kept slipping. Nobody seemed to notice me. Only one refuge remained and I made for it now.

The back parlour was an odd, out-of-the-way place built from the remains of an old washhouse that once stood on the site. It lay at the end of a narrow, crook-leg passage ill served by daylight. Richard once thought he might use the room to store his documents but it was too chilly in winter and a chore to reach. These days it served as a graveyard for Catherine's whims. Monstrous dragons, bought when everything Chinese was the fashion, stood guard over a pile of rugs. Old paintings, obliged to surrender their wall space, lay stacked in a heap beside the bare hearth. Mismatched tables and chairs dotted the carpet.

I fumbled through the gloom and squeezed behind the dragons. The rugs made a soft bed and I settled down with my back against the wall. Not a squeak from that tiresome party invaded this quiet place. I drew my legs up under me. Half an hour, no longer, then I ought to rescue the maid from my abandoned charges. She'd be fair spitting by now and would want something better than a couple of sweetmeats for her trouble.

I rubbed my eyes, trying to push Blake out of my head. He stuck to Catherine like a terrier and knew I wouldn't snitch on him. I'd decide what to do about the situation later. Despite my posset ending up spilled over the upstairs landing my belly had settled down to the odd gurgle. A ladleful of broth from the kitchen would fix that.

Outside, through the thin curtains, the last of the day's light leaked from the sky. Everything in the room blurred into shadows. A link boy's torch bobbed past the window and was gone.

10

The door whispered open. Catherine breezed into the parlour, candlestick gripped in one hand. She wasn't laughing any more. She set the candle on a card table and seated herself in the armchair beside the dead fire. A tall woman followed and perched on the high-backed chair opposite. Much of her face was pressed into a lace handkerchief, but not enough to hide the long, hooked nose or the brown mole sprouting beneath her left eye. It was Mrs Sorrell, a spindly creature with a demeanour like sour milk pudding. She often partnered Catherine at Hazard. Air wheezed out of her lungs. She was close to tears.

I pressed myself against the wall and peeked between the dragons' porcelain haunches. Catherine's voice was calm but firm.

'Did you bring the baby here?'

Mrs Sorrell snorted into her handkerchief. 'I had to. Philip will not tolerate it in the house.'

'Very well. I will make arrangements, though Richard must not know. Is it a boy or a girl?'

'A boy.'

'I see. Little wonder Philip will have naught to do with it. To have such a cuckoo in the nest must be an enormous blow to his pride. Bad enough that Jane is his only child. How is the girl?'

'The surgeon was with her throughout the labour. He tells me Jane is weak though will recover. Philip will not speak to her. He was black with anger the moment he learned of the brat festering in her belly and is now threatening to cast her into the street.'

'When did he discover Jane was with child?'

'Not until very late in her time. The girl was always thin. She could likely carry a whole litter and scarce put an inch on around the waist. She always insisted on wearing billowy cotton gowns around the house. We put it down to fancy and thought no more of it.'

Mrs Sorrell dropped the crumpled kerchief on the table

and leaned back against the chair. 'I won't have that thing in my house, Catherine. Philip has locked Jane in her room. She can bawl the walls down and it won't make a whit of a difference. Our entire family has its hopes pinned on a good marriage for that girl and I can't let anything ruin it. Certainly not some wastrel's bastard.'

'Do you know who sired the infant?'

'Adam Fairchild.'

'Oh.'

'What difference does it make? The father could be a bishop or a dockside beggar and the result would be the same. Understand that we are only thinking of Jane. Her position and future happiness. Philip would rather disown her than suffer disgrace. This misadventure could be the ruin of us.'

'Fairchild will not accept the baby as his own?'

A shake of the head. 'He has painted Jane as a cheap whore. Philip can do nothing. Fairchild's friends are too numerous and too powerful and, in any case, he has gone to France for the season. It's no use. The child will have to go. We have no place for it.'

'Where did you bring it? Not to my front door I trust?'

'No, no. I did as your message bade me and had my coachman take it to the kitchen. A shilling tucked into his palm will ensure his discretion. Your maid was waiting for him and took the child. It has been given something to stop it bawling. I have no wish to see it again. It would be best if it had never been born.'

My guardian nodded as if the two women were merely discussing the whims of the weather. 'I think you ought to return home, Alice. If anyone enquires tell them you have a headache.'

'We are beholden to you, Catherine. My family's gratitude can prove extensive.'

'We will say nothing more of this. In the meantime see to Jane. She will get over the child. Philip will forgive her and your household will be at peace. Now if you will pardon

12

me, I have neglected my own guests. Our little package will be safe where it is for an hour or so.'

Mrs Sorrell tucked her handkerchief into her sleeve. 'Your scullery maid is reliable?'

Catherine collected the candlestick and led her guest to the door. 'She knows better than to do anything witless.'

The women slid out of the parlour as quietly as they had entered. The door closed with a soft click. The smell of burnt wax lingered in the air. I waited a few minutes then edged out from behind the dragons. I'd not thought much of babies. Just pink faces that were sick a lot and cried most of the time. One, birthed badly, had killed Catherine's sister. That, so the gossips said, put Catherine off having children of her own for good and Richard had no word on the matter.

I left the room and headed for the kitchen. 'You've a nose for trouble,' Catherine once told me. 'It runs in the family.' Yet I had no scheme or plan of any sort. I didn't think, first I will do this, then this and this. I stumbled along the passage, my ravaged belly forgotten. I'd never thought Catherine a kindly woman. But she'd been talking about getting rid of a baby. A *child*. It wasn't the same as throwing a scrap of rotten meat into the gutter for dogs to scrabble over.

A thin curtain of steam fogged the kitchen. I'd wandered in here often in the past, sometimes with special instructions from Catherine, other times out of idle fancy. I couldn't resist the warmth and rich smells of cooking food. Rarely was it not full of noise and smoke, with huge iron pots hanging from cranes over the fire.

Maggie Burns was up to her elbows in grease from the mountain of dirty plates dumped in the washtub. Strands of limp brown hair hung loosely over her flushed cheeks. She was a parish girl who'd worked for us this past year. Her brow was knotted above tired eyes and she jumped when my shoes scraped on the tiles.

'Why aren't you at your party?' she asked irritably.

I checked for any sign of the cook. Her door was closed

13

and, her work done for the night, she'd likely be asleep. She drank gin in the evening while Catherine turned a blind eye, because she got the best price for meat and her pastries were delicious. I pictured her squeezed into her overstuffed armchair and snoring fit to crack the plaster.

'Where is the baby?' I demanded.

Maggie tucked her hair back under her cap with a greasy finger. 'What baby might that be?'

I shut the kitchen door and grabbed her arm. She yelped. 'The baby!' I pressed. 'Show me where it is.'

'Gerroff. I'm not fetching a beating on your account. Let me go or I'll yell.'

'Is that so? Shall I tell Mrs Worledge about the beef you've been filching from the pantry to sell to that ostler's lad? My bedchamber is right above the kitchen. Twice this week I've watched him slink out of the back door with a packet tucked into his coat. The mistress will have you thrown into the gutter. You'll have to beg or steal. You'll eat stale bread and sleep with rats, and I will not care what becomes of you. I want the baby Mrs Sorrell's coachman brought to the back door. You took it out of his hands. I know it's here and I'll not ask you again.'

She stood in front of the sink, regarding me with those big, frog eyes. Water dripped from her hands on to the tiles. I could almost hear the thoughts clunking around inside her head. Then her gaze flicked towards the pantry.

I strode across the kitchen and yanked on the latch. Hinges squealed as I pulled the door wide and peered into the gloom.

'Fetch a candle.'

Maggie lit one and pressed it into my hand. The wavering light threw distorted shadows across the walls and ceiling. A draught slipped through a chipped windowpane. Sausages hung from hooks, along with onions and various dried spices. Earthenware jars glinted on the shelf and a sweet, cloying smell filled the cramped space.

Stepping inside, I peered past sacks of flour and boxes

of fruit. Something shifted near the wainscoting and I tensed, half expecting to confront the glittering eyes of a rat. Instead the light fell across the pink face of a sleeping baby.

I stooped and held the candle closer. The child didn't stir. Its eyes, so small and yet so perfect I could count the hairs on each lash, were closed. An odd sensation fluttered in the bottom of my stomach. Here was a brand new mind, a new soul.

'Catherine,' I whispered, 'what have you done?'

My unease grew as I noticed the cheap basket in which it lay – an old, dirty thing a tinker might use to sell pegs at a local market. Coarse, stale-smelling linen swaddled the child. Yet Mrs Sorrell was a rich woman with a house that was considered one of the finest in Wexborough.

'What will happen to it?'

Maggie Burns fidgeted in the pantry doorway. 'The wet-nurse has been sent for. She will have the child away before dawn.'

'A wet-nurse?' I turned to look at her. 'It is to be cared for then?'

She pressed her hands against her cheeks and shook her head. 'The woman is bad with children. The baby will die within the week.'

'I don't understand.'

'Seldom does a newborn last more than a few days in the hands of Mrs Skegg. They wither like a bloom in want of water. If the poor mites don't starve then I've heard she puts them in her bed and rolls over them in the night so they suffocate. Then she pays a quack to say the child died of a fever. Saved many a titled family from disgrace, that woman has, and none of the gentry round here will say a word against her.'

I set the candle on a crate and picked up the sleeping child. The swaddling was warm in my hands. I could smell new skin, hear the whisper of soft breath. I'd never held a baby before. 'He's beautiful.'

15

'A pest is what he is, Miss Juliana. You mustn't go soft over him.'

'You wouldn't say that if he was your child.'

'I ain't got time for birthing brats.'

'I heard cook say you have two little brothers and a sister.'

Her gaze fell. 'Aye, that's true enough.'

'Fetch me a cloak.'

'I won't help you. You can snitch to Mrs Worledge about the beef all you like. There's worse things can happen than getting thrown into the street.'

'Fine, I'll get it myself.'

A homespun woollen cloak hung beside the back door. Cradling the baby in one arm I snatched the garment from its hook and wrapped it around myself with my free hand. It smelled of smoke and old grease.

'That belongs to cook,' the maid protested. 'She'll throw a fit.'

'I'm not venturing outside alone in this gown. People will think I'm a harlot. Now open the back door and be quiet about it.'

At first I thought she might refuse, but after a moment she unpegged the latch and eased the door open. The night whispered in. Candles spat and guttered. Maggie's eyes were wide with fright.

'Where are you going? If Mrs Worledge should come looking for you . . .'

'Close the door after me then go back to your dirty pots. I'll return soon.'

I stood on the back step and stared into the dark. Though I knew the town well enough, I'd never gone anywhere unescorted, even if it was only Richard's groom hanging on to my shadow. With the maid watching me I couldn't let my brave face crack now. I hurried into the lane running along the rear of the house. The rectangle of light flooding from the kitchen snuffed out as the door swung shut.

Chapter Two

The baby seemed to grow heavier in my arms as I hurried away from the Butter House, hugging the shadows every time a carriage clattered past. On the main road, orange torches bobbed in a welter of sparks. Summer was a curse upon the link boys, with so little dark in which to hook a customer. The short nights were also enemies of the cutpurse. The narrow alleys behind the fine houses made a fat nest for these leeches. Constables tried to clear them out, but they always came slinking back, blades and clubs greedy for another pocketful of someone else's coins.

I started to run, awkward in my billowing party dress. Cook's cheap cloak kept catching my ankles, threatening to spill me into the dirt. The baby shifted in my arms but didn't wake from its drugged sleep. Only a short distance to the docks. I could smell salt water on the air, hear the current pulling the ships against their ropes. I felt the thrill of spoiling Catherine's plans – of winning a trick over this ice-hearted woman. She'd be angry, and I'd be in trouble, but this was a child's life and any decent man or woman would do the same.

Wouldn't they?

Lanterns had been lit along the quayside, their light reflected in the rippling water. I paused and listened, hoping no one else was about at this hour. A dog barked somewhere nearby, like an old man coughing into his cup.

A breeze caught my face as I slipped around the corner of a warehouse and scampered past the barred doors of the traders' premises. There was the thick oak door of Richard's office, the shuttered windows glaring down at me like blank, wooden eyes. To my left, water lapped against the wooden pilings of the quay. Lights glimmered high up on the ships where the night watch tramped the decks, likely dreaming of bed and a mug of brandy. Planking creaked and dust swirled between the ropes.

Ahead stood a solitary bow-top caravan. Gypsies often came to the docks when the ships were in. They bought up damaged cargo and made what they would of it, turning out trinkets and making colourful clothes out of strips of cloth. I often spied their wagons when I accompanied Catherine to the office. A patch of common scrubland less than half a league beyond the town boundary stone provided good grazing for their ponies – the greys or skewbalds that pulled the caravans along the old drove tracks. Romany women haunted the harbour, selling dried flowers, herbs and wooden pegs.

I held my breath at the foot of the low wooden steps, trying to work out what I would say. Maggie Burns had a distant cousin who was a Romany and she was always prattling on about them. She seemed to find their odd way of life very exciting. I hoped that what she said was true.

Only one wagon, only one chance. Candlelight flickered behind thin muslin curtains. Music twanged softly, each note crisp and clear. A stringed instrument, an old lire or perhaps a mandolin. Sailors brought some over from Italy and they were much in favour with travellers.

I must have made a sound. The music stopped. The caravan shifted on its leather springs and a figure became outlined against the candlelight. The half door whispered open and a gust of rich incense swirled about my head. A face appeared in the semi-darkness. Black plaited hair parted in the centre, a long nose, olive skin spiked with two piercing eyes. Her expression was thick with mistrust. I was a *giorgio*, an outsider.

'I have a little boy,' I blurted, unfolding the warm bundle from the cloak. 'I don't know if the stories about you are true or not, but he'll die if you don't help him. I've heard there's always use for a boy in a gypsy camp.'

I knew how it must have looked. I felt like a mummer in a bad play. The woman did not move from her place on the top step. 'This child, it is yours?' she asked in the clipped tongue of the Romany.

I swallowed hard and held the bundle out. 'Yes.'

Her skirts, stitched together from many colourful panels, rustled as her bare feet descended first one step, then two. 'You're not its mama. You could never give it up so easily if it were, no matter how badly you might want to save it. You don't know how it is to have life in your belly.'

She shook her head. 'I've had girls come to me, some younger than you, begging help for their little ones. Some want a charm or a blessing, others to run away with us. Always they bring trouble in their wake. So tell me, *giorgio*, why should I take this baby and risk a rope around my neck if someone should come looking for it? Why shouldn't I just send you packing off into the night from where you came? You're not poor or desperate. There's no look on your face that speaks to me of trouble, of a household shamed or a papa threatening to kill you for birthing a bastard. You've lied to me once tonight. Who's to say you won't lie again?'

'No one knows I'm here,' I retorted. 'I did lie to you. I haven't birthed this child. I stole it from people who, rather than suffer disgrace, would see it die. There is no time and nowhere else to go. I'd pay you if I had money that was mine to give. I'll get down on my knees and beg if you want. But take the baby. Please.'

I was frightened, I had to admit it to myself. I had no friends among the Romanies. This woman was tall and proud. She wore gold on her ears and fingers. I did not want to cross her. Get a gypsy blessing and prosper for life, the saying went, but a gypsy curse will make you shrivel and die.

'When he wakes he'll want feeding,' the woman said at

last. 'I doubt he'll get anything from you. I can sweeten some goat's milk.'

She took the child from my arms, smoothed back the swaddling and studied his peaceful face.

'He's been dosed. Did you do it?'

'No.'

'Laudanum, I expect, but he'll be none the worse for it. You held him well. Perhaps there is something of a mother in you.'

She turned and slipped back inside the caravan, closing the door behind her. Voices muttered within, then the music started up again, soft and lilting on the night air. In the morning the wagon would likely be gone.

I pulled the cloak tightly around my shoulders and made off through the muggy streets without looking back. When I arrived at the Butter House the kitchen door hung open. Inside, Catherine was waiting.

'You took the baby,' she said. 'You stole it.'

'What you planned was wrong,' I replied, as I had before and again before that. 'It was wrong.'

My throat was parched. A pitcher lay on the shelf by the hearth, pewter ladle protruding over the lip. I wanted to taste cool water, to go to my bed, sink into sleep and forget this dirty night. Accusations had been thrown at me until my ears hurt. The fire died and turned cold, candles burned down to their holders. Maggie Burns sat in the corner, white faced and crying.

I stood in the cook's cheap cloak and faced Catherine. She'd taken off the monstrous party wig. Her hair resembled frayed string hanging loosely around her ears and temples. She was still a young woman but the grey was starting to creep in. Crows' feet cracked the corners of her eyes.

'You will tell me where you have taken it,' she continued in that flinty voice.

'Madam, I will not.'

'You are a stupid girl. Stupid and selfish. Who is to say what damage you have done in your ignorance? Yet you stand there and defy me like some self-righteous hussy who's never had the benefit of a Christian home. You are an evil creature, and you have brought shame upon this household.'

I chuckled mirthlessly. 'How can I shame the likes of you?'

Maggie's hand flew to her mouth. Outwardly, Catherine's expression didn't change, but I saw a hardening in her eyes that I knew well enough. She glanced around the kitchen, at the heaps of dirty plates, the scraps of uneaten food. Empty bottles littered the floor. Some had toppled and spilled their dregs across the tiles.

She took a deep breath and curled both hands into fists. 'Come with me, Juliana.'

I followed Catherine out of the kitchen and down the hall to the lobby. The party had wound up, the guests returned home. A lady's satin slipper sat forlornly on the carpet amidst a dark patch of spilled wine. Catherine kicked it out of the way. Half-empty glasses were clustered on tables and lined up along the drawing-room mantelpiece. Stale smoke clogged the air, mixing with bittersweet perfumes into a horrible, cloying fug.

The study door lay open. Richard was slumped in his armchair, head cradled in his arms, caged by a crescent of empty bottles. Tobacco spillings littered the desk. Catherine barely spared him a glance.

The staircase seemed endless. I counted each step to the top landing. Servants hurried past, trying to tidy up before daybreak. Blake watched me from the bottom of the stairwell, a brass holder with half a dozen candles squeezed in his fist. He blew out each flame until his face faded into shadow. In the semi-darkness his eyes glittered like black diamonds.

Barely a scrap of breath remained in my lungs. My trip to the docks had exhausted me. Both feet hurt and my arms ached from holding the baby. The passage seemed to swim in front of my tired eyes, the candles fazing into orange fireflies that sparked before my face.

Catherine stopped in front of the nursery and gestured me inside. She followed, closed and locked the door. What was passing through her mind? She could control her face the way a dock worker might call his pup to heel.

The nursery provoked no fondness. I couldn't recall ever playing there, or spending happy times under its plastered roof. Gaily painted furniture was mostly hidden beneath thick canvas sheets. Dolls propped one another up at drunken angles on the shelves. The air was stale and flecked with dust.

A bulky wooden trunk sat on the floor beneath the window, its sides coloured with crescent moons. Catherine lifted the lid and took out a hickory tawse.

'Juliana,' she said, 'can you give me a reason why I shouldn't punish you?'

'I stopped you committing murder.'

Her knuckles whitened against the split wood. 'You must tell me where you have taken the baby. I am aware of your reasons for doing it and I don't doubt you thought they were right. But you are just a child and there are things you do not understand.'

I swallowed. My throat felt like tree bark. 'You wanted it dead, I understood that. It wasn't even your child.'

'If word of this indiscretion gets out it could seriously damage us,' Catherine continued as if I hadn't spoken. 'We have gained important favours by helping good people dispose of their errors. A boy child would bring about a situation the Sorrells can ill afford. Tell me what you have done with it and I shall be lenient with you.'

'The baby is gone where you can't reach him. Split that stick across my spine if it pleases you, but I won't say any more.'

'How did you learn about it? At least your stubborn tongue can tell me that. If you've been listening to gossip . . .'

'I heard it out of your own mouth. You were speaking to that awful woman in the back parlour. I was trying to snatch a rest from the party.'

'I dislike it when people sneak around, Juliana.'

'You were doing the same.'

Her face coloured for the first time. The stick shivered between her fingertips. 'You have your place in the world. Other people have theirs. That is the way of things and it is important you learn it. The baby was a . . . mistake. Sometimes mistakes happen and we deal with them the best we can.'

'Was I a mistake?'

'You are a debt. One that can't be paid. As with all liabilities you leech us of our prosperity, more so than any of Richard's tawdry habits. I've spent years paying for your life. I own you as much as I own the horses in my stables.'

'You did not own the baby.'

'Yes I did. That child was given to me to do what was necessary. The wet-nurse turned up at the kitchen door while you were off on your little errand. I had to pay two guineas to be rid of her.'

Catherine dropped the stick on to the rug. 'Enough damage has been done. I won't make a martyr out of you. Pray that the child is not found. Everything you have done tonight could have repercussions.'

'How many other babies have arrived in the night?' I blurted. 'How many other families have you helped? What has been the cost in lives?'

I closed my eyes. The key turned in the lock and a draught wafted my face. When I dared look, Catherine had gone.

My room had been tidied, the bed remade. A fresh candle burned in the holder and a bag of primrose scented the air. A crisp nightshift was spread like a linen ghost across the coverlet.

I sat in front of the looking glass, nudged off my slippers and pulled the wig from my head, letting it drop to the floor in a flurry of white powder. I stared at my reflection. A pale face with drawn cheeks and dark crescents under both eyes stared back. I looked like an old woman.

A lace handkerchief plucked from the top drawer of the dresser wiped the paste from my cheeks. Rubbing hard around my mouth revealed my birthmark in all its lividness. I was sick of masks. Standing up, I tore the gown from my back and let it join the wig on the floor. The nightshift was warm against my skin. I padded barefoot to the open window and leaned out into the darkness. Thoughts about the baby flitted through my head. I imagined him growing up into a young man, good with horses perhaps, and a dusky Romany girl as his wife. Days on the road, nights around a gypsy camp fire with music and the rich scent of roasting hare.

'Be safe,' I whispered.

The sheets welcomed me with a clean embrace. I lay back on my pillows, savouring the comfort the soft mattress gave my aching bones. A moth fluttered across the ceiling, drawn to the flickering light. I yawned, blew out the candle, and surrendered to sleep.

But the night, it seemed, had other plans.

I was dragged from my rest by a figure standing over my bed. A burning taper made a yellow lantern of his face. He snuffed out the light. A draught wafted across my knees as he wrenched off the coverlet and tossed it into a corner.

The door. I had forgotten to bar the door.

I tried to call out. A hand clamped over my mouth. Blake brought his face within inches of mine. His breath was sweet with stolen claret.

'Got you this time, little miss,' he rumbled into my ear. 'Got you good and proper. I was outside the kitchen. Overheard your to-do with the scullery wench. I saw where you went, slipping into the night like a harlot from a lord's house with that little 'un in your arms. I followed you to the docks. It was easy to get away from the house for a bit. And I saw what you did.'

His other hand grasped my leg, the nails scratching the tender skin of my thigh. 'Sometimes you like to play the little lady,' he went on, 'but you're a canny slut and know when to open your mouth and when to keep it shut.'

His grip on my mouth loosened. I gasped for air. Terror and disgust nailed me to the mattress. Had it all been for nothing?

'If I scream they'll put you in gaol for sure,' I whispered, 'perhaps even hang you.'

He let out a low, rolling chuckle, like thunder rumbling over a distant range of hills. 'You ain't going to scream, little miss. Know why? Mrs Worledge has a mind to dismiss Maggie Burns, send her packing into the street without a reference. Perhaps I could persuade the mistress otherwise, perhaps not. Would you like to see the girl begging favours outside taverns? Maybe you don't care either way, but as for that little brat you stole . . .'

'No, don't tell Catherine where it is.'

I felt his triumph. He leaned over and kissed me gently on the forehead, the way a father might a beloved daughter. The hand holding my thigh slid up and plucked at the lining of my shift.

'Do we have a bargain, little miss?' he nuzzled into my ear. 'Two lives for your honour. A fair trade by any measure.'

'Don't hurt me.'

'No need to fret your pretty head. I've no mind to put a brat in your belly. Too many questions. Too much trouble. Your friend Blake just wants a fumble. Not much of a price to pay after what you've done tonight.'

His hands fell on me like a tumble of rocks. Lips pressed against mine. I fought not to choke. Images blurred through my panic-stricken mind. I tried to think of the baby, but all I wanted was to shrivel and die. I felt each scratch, each bruise as it was jarred into my skin. He was cheapening me. And I was letting him do it.

When Blake was finished, when I was left snivelling on

the sweat-soaked bed, he smoothed back my hair and pulled the shift down over my body. I felt like a deer after the hunt, lying torn on the grass with dogs licking the blood from my face.

'Not a word to Mrs Worledge,' he warned. 'Hear me, little miss? There's two sides to every bargain. Two.'

I said nothing as he slipped from my bedchamber. After the doorknob clicked and his footfalls receded down the passage, I turned and buried my head in my pillow.

It could have been worse, I thought.

Blake served breakfast, strutting around the table in his green livery. I pushed food around on my plate with my fork. Catherine tried to make conversation, but the air between us was thicker than the butter on my toast and she quickly gave up. Possibly she mistook my silence for contrition. At least she didn't press me about the baby again.

My body twinged. I'd put on a thick gown with a high neck and long, flowing sleeves to hide the bruises on my arms and upper chest. Catherine had eyed me curiously as I'd limped into the dining room. The day was set to be hot and already the sun was baking the busy streets outside. I mumbled something about wanting to stay indoors. She nodded and let the subject drop. Only later did I realise that she had no intention of letting me go anywhere.

Blake poured tea into my cup. I stared at his white-gloved hand as if it might bite but said 'Thank you,' in a polite voice and did not flinch when he brushed against my chair. He tried to slip me that oily smile. I reached for the cream, struggling not to spill it on the tablecloth.

I doubted that what I had given him – what he had taken – would be enough. My hatred of him had to be stronger than my fear or I'd never know another peaceful night in this house. He'd had what he wanted for now and I'd survived.

Blake often walked through this house as though he were its master. He demanded respect that wasn't his due and, when in the company of his betters, spoke in a cultivated voice that was so false it made me cringe. I never understood why Catherine retained his services. He was lazy, a brute to the maids and rude to tradesmen. Rumour suggested he'd performed an important favour for the family but no one could – or would – say what it was. Blake had power in this household but he wasn't going to enjoy those privileges for ever. Not while I lived.

Richard joined us afterwards in the front parlour. Groggy, shambling, his wig askew and shirt flapping out of his breeches. He'd slept late, the result of drinking enough brandy to put an ox into a stupor. He slumped into his armchair and propped his booted feet on the seat opposite. From the look of him he'd slept in his clothes, and a grizzle of dark stubble coloured his chin. He peered around the room, eyes like two blood oranges. The house had a stale, used smell. 'My friends . . . when did they leave?' he muttered.

Pride was not a word Richard understood, so it meant little to him when Catherine explained that his friends had left quietly after he'd collapsed across his desk. He tried to make a joke of it but quickly sensed the mood, which sobered him more than coffee or salts.

'I did not see much of you, Juliana,' he said. 'I gather there was something of a commotion in the kitchen.'

A twinge of alarm passed through me, but Catherine lied. She told him I'd gone outside and got carried away staring up at the night sky.

'You know what a dreamer she is,' Catherine said wryly. The 'commotion' was put down to some broken plates. A maid was being disciplined.

Richard reached over and squeezed my hand. His fingers felt limp and cold. 'That's Juliana,' he chuckled. 'Head's always full of fluff.'

'Will you go to the office today?' Catherine asked carefully.

Richard smiled and rubbed his eyes. 'Yes, yes of course. There are important matters to attend to.'

But he would be drunk again before noon.

I rose and brushed the creases out of my thick gown. 'I think I should like to go to the park, after all.'

Catherine did not look up from her lap, where a half-finished sampler sat in a tangle of coloured thread.

'You, my dear, shall not stray from this house.'

My incarceration lasted a week. During those long, sultry days I stayed out of the kitchen and as far away from Blake as the walls of the house would allow. Each night I listened for his footsteps in the passage, flinching at every creak as the bones of this large building settled. I couldn't sleep without the coverlet pulled over my head, and often woke, straining for air, in the small hours.

I had the parlour maid hunt out the key to my bedchamber and locked the door. Blake seemed to be biding his time, waiting for another, bigger bite of my particular apple.

Gradually my bruises healed. I glimpsed Maggie Burns a couple of times when she was sent up from the kitchen to collect dinner plates. She was waxen-faced and mostly stared at the floor. Once, she caught me watching her and turned away as if she'd been slapped.

Whispers followed me. They fluttered through walls, up and down stairs, into dark corners. Sidelong glances took bites out of my nerves.

There's Miss Juliana. The child stealer.

I wore circles in the carpet pile with my restless pacing. I haunted the maids, not wanting to find myself alone anywhere with Blake. They put a jolly face on my intrusions but it soon became irksome and Catherine told me to leave them alone. I was too afraid to go into the study by myself, rereading the few books I kept in my room until I knew them almost cover to cover. All day I was itchy, hot and irritable.

Catherine, at least, found something else to occupy her interest. A new circulating library and coffee house had opened up near the Corn Exchange and she visited almost every day, often dressing elaborately for the occasion. All kinds of volumes came back stuffed into her reticule and I don't think she read a single one. Besides, there were more than enough books in Richard's study.

Of Richard himself, I saw very little. He was aware that something had happened between Catherine and myself, though he never remarked on it. He was away most days, leaving early in the morning and often not returning until well after dusk. Catherine and I spent many evenings facing one another across the dinner table, eating silently.

Catherine, for all her quiet manner, seemed very taken with herself. Her eyes were bright and lively. She would laugh to herself at odd times as though suddenly remembering something funny. She didn't seem to mind if Richard was out. I wondered if she had a beau, perhaps a gentleman she'd met at the coffee house. Whatever reason had brought about her change of mood, she chose not to tell me about it. I was happy enough with her good humour.

I had another reason to be thankful. Blake sometimes accompanied Richard during those long hours away from the house. When Richard dashed back home, Blake at his heels, to change his shirt or fetch papers from his study, it was hard to tell who was master and who was servant. Blake dressed so grandly, and swaggered about like a country squire.

Once, very late in the evening when I was too restless to sleep, I crept downstairs in search of some milk. A light shone from the open door of the study. Blake was inside, dressed in Richard's embroidered burgundy waistcoat and the riding jacket with the high collar. They were a poor fit; Blake was at least half a foot taller than his employer and thinner, but he sat like a lord in the leather armchair with a pipe in his mouth and a curl of blue smoke veiling his face. An open bottle of port stood on the desk. Manservants had been thrashed for less but I recalled the way Blake watched Richard. I forgot about my glass of milk, went back upstairs and locked my bedroom door.

Later in the week, Catherine relented and decided to take me with her to the circulating library. Thick, boiling clouds had rolled in from the sea, stacking up on top of one another like loose heaps of dirty cotton. The air cooled and carried specks of rain. Sharp gusts of wind rattled windows and whistled around the house.

Catherine bundled me into my best cloak, drawing the neck string tight. I felt like a ten-year-old. Outside, the town was a clamour of barking dogs and noisy traders. Carriages trundled past, lanterns rattling. I had to hurry to keep up with Catherine, whose long legs took her down the street in great, effortless strides. She clung to my hand the way she might a dog leash. Richard had taken the coach and Catherine refused to use the gig. It was old and creaked terribly, no matter how much grease the stable lad slapped on the axle. We could have hired chairs, but I was happy to walk with her. I enjoyed the fresh air and the tang of salt on the breeze blowing in from the harbour. I laughed as a street trader accidentally tipped over a slop bucket, causing passing ladies to squeal. I dodged potholes as we crossed the road, jumped cracks in the pavement and yelped with delight when the stagecoach rumbled past on its way to Bristol.

Catherine indulged my mood, and even paused to buy me a sweetmeat from a travelling vendor. It felt as if I'd been shut in that stuffy house for years. I was so glad to be outside I would've done anything to please her.

The new circulating library was housed in a former apothecary, the ghost of which lingered in the dated paint-work and Latin names inscribed above the doorframe. Shelves which had once held vials of powders were now laden with leather-bound volumes of all shapes and sizes. Pressing my face against the window I could see more inside, hundreds more, stacked in every corner. Tall paper towers reached towards the beamed roof and open boxes spilled their contents across the floor.

I fought to contain my excitement as Catherine opened the door and ushered me inside. A mixed scent of musty paper and hot, rich coffee filled my nostrils. A low archway opened into a room furnished with a dozen or so lace-covered tables dotted with newspapers. Patrons sat in high-backed chairs and sipped out of china cups. Some leafed through books or chatted quietly.

A lady and her daughter looked up when we entered. The girl was a smaller reflection of her mother. Same colour gown, identical bonnet a daffodil saucer perched at an angle on her plaited hair. I remembered her from my party. She'd sat near the door, her face slack with boredom, and refused to take part in any games. Her mother leaned over and whispered something in her ear. The girl smirked.

I longed for the books, but obediently followed Catherine's impatient tug on my arm as she shepherded me over to a low counter. Behind it stood a short, stocky man with tufts of white hair poking from the edges of his wig. He beamed at us.

'Good day, Mrs Worledge,' he declared, displaying a set of wooden teeth which protruded grotesquely over his bottom lip. 'Hot coffee and a good book provide the perfect remedy for inclement weather, is that not so?'

Catherine giggled like a milkmaid and mumbled something about how a twinge in cook's gimpy leg suggested it might brighten up later. Glancing at the darkening clouds outside, I thought cook would be as well to cut her leg off if that was the best forecast it could manage. But now the proprietor was peering across the counter at me.

'I see you have brought young Miss Worledge,' he gushed.

I stared at the sloppily tied cravat hugging his fat neck. 'I beg your pardon, sir,' I blurted, 'but my family name is Rodriguez.'

The whole coffee house caught its breath. In a corner,

somebody laughed. Whispers rippled around the room and then settled back into the quiet drone of conversation.

Catherine muttered an apology, though I didn't see what she thought she had to be sorry for, and pulled me to a table beside a bay window. A serving girl brought coffee then returned holding a platter heaped with cakes.

I sipped my drink, relishing the strong flavour. Much better than cook's watery tea. I picked up a cake and crammed it into my mouth. It was fresh and hot. Melting butter dribbled down my chin. I laughed at my reflection in the window.

My guardian said nothing. She wouldn't look at me. I was still conscious of other people's eyes darting our way, of the exchanged whispers. I poked my tongue out at one stony-faced lady who recoiled as if she'd been struck.

Catherine's face turned red above the rim of her coffee cup. She tried to read one of the newspapers but it was obvious she couldn't concentrate. Finally, she excused herself and disappeared into the back of the shop, presumably in search of a privy, or a secluded corner where she could cool her temper.

I lifted my cup to take another sip and became aware of someone standing over me, the girl who'd been chatting with her mother. She regarded me with wide blue eyes.

'My mama says you have tainted blood.'

I put down my coffee cup. 'What did you say?'

'Your blood is tainted. That stupid mark on your face proves it.'

I stared at her for a few moments, hot coffee rolling around inside my mouth. Then I did something that no one, myself included, expected.

I hit her.

Chapter Three

I don't know exactly what happened. It was as if my hands flew off the ends of my wrists before my brain had a chance to react. I remember feeling astonished at seeing my fingers in a flapping frenzy around her cheeks. The rest of my coffee tipped over her satin-bowed dress. She threw a screaming fit, grabbed a handful of my hair and hauled me out of my seat. I kicked her shins. She let go and I pushed her out of the way. She fell over another chair, caught the tablecloth on the way down and dragged everything on to the floor.

Catherine appeared, tight-faced, at my side. Sputtering apologies and cake crumbs to the girl's mother, she took hold of my arm and propelled me towards the door. My skin hurt where she pinched it and my eyes were watering because of what that strumpet had done to my hair. Out in the street, Catherine's expression warned me to keep quiet. No stroll back to the house this time. She summoned a chair and crammed us both inside. Her bony knees dug into my backside as the sedan jiggled along the road. The bearers were red-faced and puffing by the time they brought us to our front door. Catherine dismissed them without a tip, ignoring their sullen looks. Charity was the last thing on her mind. She didn't take me upstairs to the nursery but into the parlour. Right away I knew we were going to have one of *those* conversations.

'What an appalling scene,' she began. 'You disgraced me in front of everyone. First you were impertinent to Mr Ruddlewade. Then you start brawling like some street urchin with Mrs Parkhurst's daughter. I never know what you're thinking, Juliana. I cannot fathom your mind at all. Now we shall be the talk of the whole town.'

'The girl was rude,' I protested, 'and the coffee shop owner was wrong to call me Miss Worledge. What was I supposed to do?'

Catherine paced the carpet, clenching and unclenching her fingers. 'Worledge is your name and you'd best not forget it if you wish to lead a peaceful life in this house. Rodriguez is not suitable for the daughter of a respectable English shipping family.'

'I am not your daughter. Take away my name and I'll have nothing left.'

She halted. Livid red spots returned to her cheekbones and spread across her face. 'My husband brought you into this household. He saved you from the gutter and gave you a home. You had a criminal for a father and your mother was little better than a harlot, yet you sleep under my roof, sit at my table and take comfort at my hearth. How can you call that nothing?'

'You never talk about my parents. Whenever I ask, you order me to hold my tongue or go to my room. I can't mention it without scratching your temper.'

'Everything will be explained to you when you come of age. Believe me, you will wish you had never broached the subject. Think on that before you spite me again in public. There is a limit even to Richard's charity.'

She wrenched open the door and stormed into the hall. I didn't want to cry, but my face cracked open like old dough. 'Why did you take me in if I'm such a burden?' I called after her.

'Why . . .?'

As thunderclouds boiled over Wexborough, so I weathered my own storm. Forbidden once again to leave the house, I tucked myself away in the back parlour with whatever books

I managed to filch from Richard's study.

Catherine took her meals alone and stayed out of my way, which suited me. I'd had enough of her sour face and moods that changed from fair to foul depending on her whims.

Clouds hung in the sky like rolls of dirty sackcloth. Rain fell in sheets, hissing on windowpanes and swamping the road outside. Thunder rumbled. Lightning cut the sky in two with bright spears.

I scampered into the empty dining room, which boasted the tallest window in the house, and watched as each flash painted the sky with fire. Street hawkers had been driven under cover. Shops barred their doors as rain turned gutters into fast-flowing rivers.

I was eager to throw open the window and scream into the clouds, to feel the thunder pummel my ears and taste the sweet rain on my lips. I wanted to dance in the downpour with my hair flapping around my cheeks. I was alive and I adored it. I relished the rush of blood in my ears, the feel of air sucked into my lungs, the tingling in my fingertips as if I had touched the very core of the storm. I felt as if nothing could hurt me.

The weather broke after two endless days, leaving the town looking washed and new. The air had lost its clammy feel. A warm breeze tickled in off the hills behind the town.

Catherine decided she couldn't stay away from her precious circulating library. The house was too quiet. Richard was away almost all the time now. Sometimes I heard him stumbling through the door in the small hours when the summer heat robbed me of sleep. Blake waited up for him, laughing whenever Richard bumped into something and sent it clattering to the floor. That laughter felt like a demon running its fingers down my spine.

Catherine pinned a bonnet to her hair and put on a fat pearl necklace. Against her pink skin, it resembled a row of gleaming teeth. She wore a light summer gown with a scandalously low neckline, trimmed with taffeta bows. Tight corsets gave her the waist of a girl ten years her junior. A coloured feather dangled from the brim of her hat.

She was like a child with a new scarf or fairing from the market. 'Fetch me a sedan,' she ordered a footman. When it arrived she was out the door in a breeze of rich cologne. I watched from the parlour window as she squeezed her petticoats into the chair and tapped on the door. The bearers set off, dodging puddles the returning sun hadn't yet managed to dry out.

I was sitting by the window when, less than an hour later, she returned.

Anger pulled Catherine's cheeks as tight as drum skins. The chair had barely touched the pavement when she had the door open and was out, brushing aside the helping hand one of the bearers tried to offer her. She tore open her reticule and threw a handful of coins into the dirt before storming up the front steps. I heard her shoes clattering on the hall tiles followed by a muffled exclamation from the maid.

'Juliana!'

Catherine could always sniff me out when her temper was hot. I stood with my back pressed against the window as she blustered into the room. Her bonnet was torn off in a shower of pins and hurled into the corner.

'Everyone knows.' Each word was a barb dipped in poison. 'My reputation lies in tatters.'

She pulled off her gloves a finger at a time. Her mouth was a thin gash. 'They were all talking about me. My name was thrown around that coffee house as if I wasn't even there.'

She slapped the gloves on to the table. 'Do you know what is being said about me, Juliana? More to the point, my dear, darling girl, can you imagine what they think of you after that commotion the other day?'

They could call me the devil's daughter for all I cared. I just wanted to push myself through the glass and run up the street as fast as my trembling legs would take me. I didn't want to fight with Catherine again. I was sick of fighting.

Now the bows were coming off, torn from Catherine's bodice so that they littered the floor like dead butterflies. She ripped off her necklace. Pearls scattered across the rug. 'I warned you that you can't just behave any way you like, especially not in public. Mr Ruddlewade told me to my face that I was not to bring you to his establishment again. I was forced to pay for the damage you inflicted on his crockery. Right in front of those smirking women. "I will have my compensation now, madam," those were his very words, "or will be obliged to inform the magistrate".'

I couldn't hold my peace any longer. 'Why does it matter to you what those people think? They only care about themselves and their precious gossip.'

'That gossip could cost us dear,' she snapped back. 'Those women have husbands, Juliana. Men who have money invested in Richard's business. And what of me, if I cannot walk the street without stares and whispers following me like a pack of hounds? The whole town is probably aware of your little escapade. I don't dare show my face socially again.'

Catherine paused. Her breath rattled in her throat. She stared at the mess on the floor, then at her ruined gown, as if only just realising what she'd done.

'Promise me that you will heed every word of mine from now on and be obedient to my wishes without question.'

I shook my head. 'When you make that sort of promise, there always comes a time when you have to break it. Then you are sorry and you hate yourself.'

Catherine sighed. With that one sound I knew I was lost.

'I want you out of my house.'

'It's Richard's house.'

Contempt replaced the fury in her eyes. 'Don't play the fool. It was never Richard's.'

*

That night Mr Worledge returned early. He'd contrived to win at cards and threw a scattering of coins across the dining-room table.

'Thought I'd try a hand or two before coming home.' He beamed. 'You should have seen the look on those rogues' faces when I trumped the lot of them. Told you good fortune would smile on me. It'll be a new bonnet for you, Catherine, or perhaps a brooch if you've a fancy.'

He leaned over. Brandy fumes wafted into my face. 'And how about a bunch of ribbons for your pretty head, eh, Juliana? Mustn't forget the other lady of the house.'

He fixed me with the bemused, foggy look that had squatted on his face so much of late. The pitiful collection of coins gleamed on the tablecloth. I thought of the I.O.U.s littering his study desk, made out to the very men he had so proudly taken a pittance from tonight, and I went on eating my dinner.

Much later in the night, Richard and Catherine had a storming row. A grumbling stomach had taken me to the kitchen in search of bread and hot milk. I listened at the parlour door as they yelled at one another like children quarrelling over a broken toy.

'The girl is no good,' Catherine declared. 'She has cast a shadow on this house from the day you brought her over our threshold. Well, I have had enough. I will suffer that petulant, cherry-streaked face of hers no longer. If this is how she will meddle in my affairs now, what calamities has she in store for me in the future?'

Richard's voice: 'Girls at that difficult age are by nature precocious. It is the same for all parents of young ladies.'

'She's no lady. Did you see the way our male guests eyed her at the party? No, I don't suppose you did. You were too engaged in entertaining your drunken friends to notice much of anything. That girl was a trap for men from the day she bawled her way into this world.'

'Catherine . . .'

'Oh, what would you know of women, you farmer's sop? You would still be up to your knees in horseshit if I hadn't brought you into your fortune. If you are a man it is only because I have made you one. I will not have that harlot's daughter defy me in my own house as if she were my flesh and blood instead of some baggage you were tricked into taking as your own.'

The chink of a decanter. The gurgle of liquid poured into a glass.

'Indeed,' Richard continued, voice splintering, 'what kind of man am I with a wife who cannot bear me a child? I took Juliana partly because you wanted a daughter and we have strived to raise her as such. Yet you have chained her, heart and soul, and suffer despair because she does not think as you do.'

'I wanted a daughter, yes. Not some changeling who haunts my waking hours, makes me look a fool in public and treats our good English name as if it was something despicable. She sleeps under our roof but never thinks of herself as one of us. Where does that leave your precious manhood, Richard, when your adoptive daughter would rather be laughed at in the street than permit herself to be called Worledge? No, she must go. She must learn to be a lady or I won't admit her into my home again.'

In the hallway and the lower rooms, the servants closed down the house for the night. Candles were snuffed, curtains drawn, fires damped down. Nobody spared me a glance, though I knew they were listening keenly. I wanted to shrink back into the powder-pink walls and let the shadows swallow me up.

'I shall send her abroad,' Catherine said now, 'with a governess to curb her surly moods and teach her the value of manners as well as respect for her betters. Juliana will have that time in which to redeem herself, or finish up in the gutter she seems so hell-bent on calling her own.'

'You can't send her away,' Richard countered. 'I promised

him, Catherine. I gave my oath that I'd keep her under my roof and see she wanted for nothing.'

'What does it matter to you, a drunk who uses his time to waste my money?'

'I have my honour. If nothing else, I still have that.'

'Your honour lies at the bottom of a brandy bottle along with your wits. Leave the thinking to those that have a mind to do it. I am bound by no promise of yours, least of all one made to a convicted murderer. Think on that the next time you fudge a hand of cards.'

They argued some more, but Catherine had already bested him and Richard was merely trying to salvage pride. I slipped away from the door and started fumbling up the stairs to my bed. Catherine's words gnawed at my mind. I had nothing of my mother's. No picture or scrap of lace. No memory. Was it her red hair on my head, or my father's? Did I see through her eyes, or his? And the birthmark – whom did I have to thank for that?

Someone was watching me from the bottom of the stairwell. The candles in the hall had been extinguished, but a puddle of light splashed across the tiles from the open study door. I paused, nerves straining. I could hear him breathing, a rasping edge to each lungful of air. A tiny circle of orange glowed as he drew on a pipe, and fragrant smoke drifted past me towards the shadowed roof.

Instinctively I moved nearer to the wall. He chuckled and slipped back into the darkness, leaving a hint of cologne in the air. I recognised the sweet, fruity smell as one of Richard's favourites.

But Richard was still in the parlour arguing with his wife.

I scurried up the remaining stairs and along the passage to my bedchamber as fast as my flapping nightshift allowed. Once inside, I closed the door, fumbled for the key and turned it in the lock. My throat was dry and I felt sick. The stink of pipe smoke clung to me like leprosy. I wanted to throw my windows wide and suck in the night air, let it

40

wash over me like a soothing balm. But all I could see was *his* face. I kept the casement fastened, pulled the curtains across the face of the moon and wriggled under my bedclothes.

I was to be gone from the house within the week. Richard would not look me in the eye or say a word in my defence. Deever oversaw the packing of my belongings into a pair of enormous, leather-clad trunks.

My new keeper was quickly engaged. On the day I was due to leave she turned up at the house in a gown the colour of ashes and a bonnet like an overcast sky. Even her face had the hue of dead flesh. Only her hair, which was the colour of rich mahogany, seemed in any way lively, though her expression when she greeted me was as unforgiving as her apparel.

'So this is the girl?' she said, eyeing me.

Mary Morgan was her name, and I was obliged to curtsy to her in front of the servants. Catherine ushered us both into the parlour, where I endured the coldest cup of tea that had ever wet my tongue. Miss Morgan coughed a great deal and smelled vaguely of garlic. She nibbled at her scone, wearing it down to the size of a pebble with her busy lips. Pleasantries were exchanged with Catherine in clipped sentences as though someone had taken shears and snipped away at each word. I kept stealing glances, trying to guess this dusty woman's age. Years of scowling had cut furrows into her forehead, yet she had the pink hands of a girl.

Catherine had booked our passage aboard a small packet boat called the *Lucky Maid*. The captain was one of Richard's men. I'd never met him, though knew he had a reputation for giving short shrift to passengers. Livestock and chattels were his business, not a pair of fragile women, but his vessel was bound for Belgium and there wouldn't be another for some days.

I was to share a cabin with Miss Morgan, into whose

41

charge I was immediately placed. My luggage was already on its way to the docks. Richard had gone out and the servants had better things to do than see off the 'little viper' who was responsible for their mistress's foul moods.

Catherine lingered beside the front door. Was this goodbye or good riddance? My stomach was in knots at the thought of the journey ahead.

'Well?' she said. 'Have you nothing to say for yourself? No final words before you go? Making eloquent speeches was never a problem for you before, Juliana. Why so silent now?'

I drew my shawl tightly around my shoulders and climbed down the steps to the waiting gig. Summer was slipping away and the wind whistling down the street carried the first cool breath of autumn.

The *Lucky Maid* was a squat looking vessel of weathered timber. Eyeing her from the dockside, I wondered how anyone could dare venture out to sea on such a modest ship, let alone trade cargo in foreign ports. She sat low in the water like a featherless duck, the gaudy figurehead grinning down at me with chipped eyes. The harbour breeze was thick with the smell of sour fish and canvas. Men rolling barrels up the gangplank leered at me.

'Wait here,' Miss Morgan instructed. 'I will go and speak to the captain.'

As soon as she was out of sight I edged away from the quayside. Dock workers swarmed around stacks of barrels and crates, struggling to get them loaded. Pedlars hawked goods. Carts and carriages trundled past in endless succession. The rich rubbed shoulders with the lowly as both jostled to board vessels bound for places I'd only read about. A troop of soldiers marched past to the tune of drum and fife, looking grand in their scarlet uniforms. How many would lie dead before the war in America was over? Did the same thought cross their minds as they walked in perfect step beneath those fluttering banners?

I kept half an eye open for gypsy wagons, but they'd likely be at the other side of the harbour where ships were unloading. I arrived at Richard's offices. The door was locked, the windows shuttered. The building, once proud with a carved sign above the entrance, now looked drab and unwelcoming. Cream paint was beginning to flake off the walls. Moss had taken hold under the eaves and was spreading in a dark stain. On the upper floor the fastenings on a shutter had worked loose, letting it swing wide.

A tall hat bobbed through the crowds. Mr Littlejohn, Richard's business associate, hove into view. He was in an uncommon hurry for a man who was prone to falling asleep at his desk – something Richard had always joked about over dinner.

I checked to make sure Miss Morgan hadn't reappeared then went after him, dodging tradesmen and beggars. He stopped and turned at the sound of his name.

'Miss Juliana,' he declared, peering at me with his muddy eyes. 'A long time since I've had the pleasure of your company. Too long, I think.'

Some people are born old. I couldn't picture Mr Littlejohn as a boy. Age clung to him like a tight pair of breeches. He grinned mawkishly, baring fake teeth that stuck out over his bottom lip. The fingers and thumb of one hand danced along the end of his walking stick, beating out a restless tattoo.

'Richard has not been to the office?' It was more statement than question.

Mr Littlejohn removed his spectacles and rubbed them on the hem of his cotton waistcoat. 'It's been more than a month now. I have my hands full trying to keep the business afloat and our investors are losing patience. I don't know what concerns keep Mr Worledge away from his office, but if he does not minister to pressing affairs soon then my efforts shall have been wasted. I have tradesmen baying for my blood, excise men at the door and ship crews threatening mutiny. Yet my warnings go unheeded.'

He coughed. Spittle flew from his mouth. 'I can manage for a while longer, but there are important decisions that only Mr Worledge can make. When I receive instructions they are sent by letter and that man of his, Blake, keeps turning up and barking orders as if he was the one trying to put shillings in our employees' pockets.'

He took out a snuffbox, flipped the lid and took a generous pinch. After a moment he sneezed, shaking a cloud of powder from his wig.

'You must forgive me, Juliana,' he continued, eyes watering. 'I mustn't burden you with the problems of trade and commerce. A man forgets himself when matters weigh heavily on his mind. What brings you to the harbour today? You're not alone I take it?'

'I'm being sent abroad with a new governess. The trip is to better my education. To teach me to be a proper lady.'

'This is rather sudden.'

I nodded. 'We are travelling aboard the *Lucky Maid*. My new guardian is talking to the captain.'

'Sailors are a superstitious lot. Out on the ocean they will look for bad omens in everything. It might pay to be . . . discreet.'

'Do you mean my birthmark?'

'Indeed, forgive my impertinence, but you may wish to powder your face.'

'Thank you for your concern, but I've been in hiding long enough.'

'Quite so. How long will you be gone?'

'I'm not sure. A year. Perhaps two.'

'A long time for a child to be away from home.'

'I'm hardly a child, Mr Littlejohn.'

'Even less so when you return. We must talk then, Juliana.' He tapped me on the shoulder with his cane. 'There are important matters to discuss which concern you and you alone.'

I was about to ask him what he meant when Miss Morgan billowed along the quay front in her coffin-clothes.

'I have to go,' I told Mr Littlejohn. 'I promise to speak to you when I come back.' I squeezed his arm and ran off to join my new guardian. She glanced doubtfully at Richard's colleague but made no comment as she led me back to the *Lucky Maid*. Halfway up the gangplank I paused and looked back. Mr Littlejohn, once Richard's closest confidant, was scuttling back towards the harbour wall, holding his hat against the breeze. People put their heads together and laughed as he passed, though he was a well-known figure around the docks and there was no malice in it. A final look at the shuttered offices, then I fastened my cloak before climbing up the last part of the gangplank to where Miss Morgan waited.

Chapter Four

If the wind was brisk around the docks, it was howling on the open sea. Waves smacked against the planking of our ship, showering the deck in brittle spray. I'd never been on any kind of boat before and wasn't sure I liked the way the floor kept moving under my feet. Panic gripped me when the shoreline disappeared, swallowed up by the grey mist that even the strongest wind seemed unable to clear.

Miss Morgan refused to come out of the cramped cabin we shared. I often heard her retching into the basin at the side of her narrow bunk. I spent as much time on deck as I could. Once I'd come to terms with the heaving seas, I felt genuinely free for the first time in my life. Gulls screamed in my ears and wheeled like white kites above the masthead. The open air salted my tongue and the wind whipped my hair about my cheeks.

The ship's first mate clapped me on the shoulder and told me, winking, that I had good sea legs. 'Must have had a seafarer in your family,' he remarked, scratching at the puckered scar that seemed to split his face in two. 'You can always tell them that do. They take to boats the way fish take to water.'

Breakfast was taken with Captain Henry Lockhart, a sallow, bitter man who seemed to have taken up sailing as a result of ill fortune either in love or business. His cabin was a shrine to the life he had apparently once known, all gilt-edged books and silver tableware.

'Having women on board is a nuisance,' he declared,

carving his meat into tiny squares. 'Some consider it bad luck to carry passengers on a merchant vessel. Can't say I'm superstitious myself, but Mrs Worledge must be in a hurry to get you to Belgium if she put you on my boat.'

What we knew of Lockhart we learned from the crew. Sailors it seemed were full of stories, each more fantastic than the last. I never knew if they believed their own yarns or were merely teasing us, but they lightened the journey and made Miss Morgan forget her queasy stomach. There had been times at the breakfast table when her face turned to buttermilk. She picked at her food while both the captain and myself ate heartily.

Time pressed heavily upon us. The fog chased us over the water and enveloped the ship in a clammy shroud. Nothing to see except a circle of featureless ocean around us and nothing to read except the Bible, which was the only book Miss Morgan had brought with her. I had been allowed none as they took up too much space in my luggage. My sense of freedom had evaporated. Instead of enjoying a great adventure, I spent hours curled up on my narrow cot, watching the lantern swing from its hook on the ceiling. Everything familiar was gone. My stomach turned in slow flips that had nothing to do with the swell of seawater against the *Lucky Maid*'s hull. My entire world had been crammed into the trunks I'd brought from Wexborough. I felt neither brave nor clever, and there was no way off the boat. I gave in easily to tears, usually when Miss Morgan braved the deck to take some air. Often I wasn't even aware of the reason. Catherine's temper? Blake's unwelcome attentions? The worst aspects of the Butter House receded into a vague mental fug. I pined for my room, Richard's books, the park – everything about the noisy, clamorous town I'd left behind.

You've hardly been gone at all, I reasoned, yet in allowing myself to be sent away I had suffered a defeat. I felt shamed, guilty, a dozen other things. I *had* to be a bad person, surely, or none of this would have happened?

47

Sometime towards evening Miss Morgan overheard one of the sailors crack a ribald joke to his friend and she suddenly burst into laughter, her face as red as a field of poppies.

Settling down for the night in our cramped quarters, I asked her to tell me what she had heard. The mask fell back at once.

'Say your prayers then go to sleep,' she told me, 'tomorrow we will reach land and be off this wooden tomb. I am weary of the way it pitches like a carriage on a potholed road.'

But just before she blew out the candle, a smile crept back across her lips.

Rain was hammering down by the time *Lucky Maid* groaned into the crowded port and the crew made her fast against the quay. I leaned over the rail and viewed the grim scene before me. This dirty, grey place that stank of sewage and rotten fish, where buildings were crumbling and the locals went about dressed like beggars, had no place in the beautiful leather-bound books of Richard's study.

Miss Morgan and I exchanged glances. I'd heard she was well travelled but perhaps things had changed since she was last here. I was reluctant to leave the wooden planking of the *Lucky Maid*'s deck. The crew was already beginning to unload the cargo. This was just another harbour, a place to work and then move on. They had not been banished.

A gloved hand slipped into my own and squeezed my fingers. Miss Morgan's face remained as stern as the flagstones of the dock. 'I will see if I can find a carriage,' she said, 'though forgive me if I come back with nothing better than a cabbage cart and an old donkey.'

My long exile began badly. For the first few days it would not stop raining and the bad roads frayed our nerves. It was a dull, colourless world we viewed from the window of our jostling carriage. We drove between fields that stretched for miles over flat land without a single hedge, populated by scarecrow people dressed in filthy rags who stared at us as we rattled past.

We slipped over the border into France. Though in an enemy country, we were regarded as a pair of harmless English fancies who would breeze away again like the wind that swept the south coast.

Everywhere, the poor, crippled and desperate littered the roads. There was no respect in their dirty faces, only a sullen animosity. Our coachman used his whip liberally to clear them from the lanes. Miss Morgan pulled down the blinds. 'Don't look at them,' she told me. 'There are many angry people in this part of the world, and anger can lead a man to forget his place.'

I settled back into my seat. I had already noticed how the rich lived in this country. We had passed their magnificent chateaux surrounded by gardens filled with fountains and flowers. Nowhere before had I witnessed such a vast gulf separating rich and poor.

The miles rolled on in a daze of jolting roads, cold days and restless nights spent in flea-ridden inns. Even the best of these seemed populated by tiny, tooth-laden demons intent on chewing our tender English flesh. In one memorable establishment the roof leaked, dripping water on my bed for hours on end. When I moved the leak seemed to move with me, until I gave up and woke the following morning with a damp nightshift and snivelling nose.

At the next place we stopped, the landlady's smile died on her lips and she flapped her hands in the air before slamming the door in our faces. Our coachman, Jacques, who had learned English from his sailor father, held a shouted conversation with her through a half-shuttered window.

'It is the red mark on *l'enfant*'s face,' he explained when he returned. 'She thinks the child has the plague and will not let her into the house.'

Miss Morgan and I spent that night in the coach while

49

Jacques slept underneath with a pistol tucked into his coat. Thankfully it did not rain again.

And so it went on. One inn looked pleasant enough but harboured a barky little dog that never shut up, not once, all the time we were there. I hated the food, the water smelled and tasted strange, and I could not master the singsong language no matter how patiently Miss Morgan tried to teach me. We visited crumbling castles and canals, took in some sagging French towns where tensions seemed to simmer beneath the shoddy façades. She told me of the country's history while I yawned and pined for the greener, friendlier fields of England.

Days turned into weeks and still my new guardian's cautious enthusiasm did not dampen. She called me Miss Rodriguez throughout, never Juliana. Only once did she address me as Miss Worledge.

'Don't call me that,' I growled. 'Don't you ever use that name, not in England, not here, not anywhere.'

The mistake was not repeated.

We had been advised to stay away from Paris. 'A hotbed of pestilence,' was how Miss Morgan described it, and I was told that we would not be visiting Spain, though I was given no reasons why. Instead we left Jacques at the coast and took a boat from Brittany southwards to Portugal, where Miss Morgan went down with some sort of ague in a Lisbon guest house, leaving me fretting for days with nothing but the view from the window and a simple-minded maid for company.

Then it was on the water again, through the Straits of Gibraltar and onwards to Marseilles. The land changed now as we delved deeper into Europe, from rolling vineyards to lofty mountain peaks. I took in opera in Vienna, chamber music in Salzburg and fell asleep in a museum in Prague. Weeks turned into months and the seasons paraded past in a succession of summer greens, autumn golds and crisp winter whites.

Every night after supper Miss Morgan sat down and took writing paper together with some quills from the small black valise that always accompanied our luggage. She set down word of our travels, and my progress, in her neat hand. I don't know how many of those painstaking epistles made it back to the shores of England, or whether any were received in return. We seemed to be on the move all the time, like leaves blowing in a restless autumn wind.

Finally, we travelled south again to Italy. Dark-skinned men pinched my skirts and made me feel like a queen while Miss Morgan blushed violets. We ate delicious food dripping with oils that brought spots out on my face. I could feel history instead of having it crammed into my head. A land of kind weather and ancient ruins. People with dancing hearts sang and squabbled in the space of a breath. Everyone talked with wild, excited gestures whenever anyone was willing to listen.

In Florence, we rented rooms in a three-storey house near the River Arno. The building was owned by a florid-faced dowager and her pregnant daughter, Elizabetta, who grinned at everything. Her belly was as enormous as her smile and she heaved it about as if it was a bundle of laundry. I hadn't thought it possible for a human body to swell to that size. Expectant ladies in Wexborough spent the last weeks of their confinement in the privacy of their chambers. They did not strip the linen from beds or hang out washing while humming tunes around a mouthful of pegs. The girl was not married but no one seemed to care, which was surprising in such a papist country. Any one of the half-dozen or so laughing, impudent young men who delivered goods to the back door could have put her with child. They all treated her with equal affection.

Every morning I had to wake up to that grin when Elizabetta waddled in to open the curtains. Thinking her insolent, I complained to her mother. In stuttering English, the dowager explained that her daughter was born grinning.

51

Deformed face muscles had frozen that smile on to her plump cheeks and she would take it to her grave.

'Men think she is good for anything. How can they take no for an answer when she is smiling at them all the time?'

Miss Morgan conducted my lessons on the terrace overlooking the river. Hours were spent learning Latin, which I picked up quickly, and Italian, which I didn't. A local instructor schooled me in dancing and social etiquette. Where the money for that came from I don't know. Miss Morgan paid it, with a po-face, out of her seemingly bottomless reticule. Wasted money, as my feet would not go where I wanted. I tripped, stumbled and fell flat on my behind. Just as well I couldn't understand my teacher's exasperated remarks when I trod on his toes or elbowed him in the midriff.

One afternoon I returned from sketching on the riverbank to find the house full of screams. I peered through an open door. Elizabetta was spread-eagled on an enormous bed, her thick legs splayed. The room stank of sweat and hot linen. A bald-headed man, stripped to the waist, squatted between her knees. I thought, what in God's name is going on? Did a secret brothel run within the ochre-coloured walls? The man offered encouragement. Blood smeared his chest. The dowager, who stood behind the chair, grasped her daughter's hands. Elizabetta heaved and spilled out something small and wrinkled. A thick sausage-like cord tied it to somewhere deep inside her. Spasms rippled along the girl's flaccid thighs. She groaned and heaved again . . .

The next thing I knew I was on my back in my bedchamber and Miss Morgan was applying wet linen to my forehead.

'Was I sick?' I whispered.

She nodded. 'You made quite a sight sprawled across the tiles. The dowager's son brought you upstairs.'

'They must think me a fool.'

'A little weak-kneed perhaps. In any case, Elizabetta is delighted with her baby daughter.'

'I'll never let a man touch me,' I declared.

'If the right man does the touching, you will want it with all your heart,' Miss Morgan replied.

I tilted my head to look at her, but she wrung out the linen and said nothing more.

Two streets away from the apartment, Miss Morgan discovered a small, tree-ringed park and took to walking there for half an hour each morning. Tired of listening to the baby's bawling, I asked my guardian if I might join her. To my horror, I found the place overrun with children.

'The park is a favourite haunt of mothers,' Miss Morgan informed me. 'Toddlers like to play on the lawns. This can be a dusty town. Grass draws them like water.'

After a few minutes strolling amid the trees, we took a bench by the fountain and talked for a while. Miss Morgan named all the plants, and commented on the architecture of the surrounding buildings. She would not tell me anything about herself, despite my gentle promptings. It was almost as if the sun couldn't penetrate the dull clothes she still wore. I noticed, however, that her gaze never strayed far from the children. Even on our route between the house and the park, she snatched thief-like glances at other people's babies.

Next morning, under the trees, a poppet-faced girl left behind a strip of lace, which had become snagged on one of the rose bushes. Miss Morgan worked it loose and tucked it into her sleeve. Many times over the next few days I caught her with that strip in her hand, running her fingers over the material.

I was changing. In half a dozen months I had turned from a scampering child into a bundle of lank, swinging limbs. Spots ravaged my face. As soon as one died another three took its place, usually somewhere horribly visible like the end of my nose or middle of my brow. My beautiful hair of deep burnished copper turned stringy and awkward despite hours of determined brushing.

'I need new clothes,' I told Miss Morgan, while struggling to squeeze into one of my old gowns. Everything was either too tight, too short or both. I was conscious of the way my body pushed against the material, of the shoes that felt like satin vices.

'You must have a new dress,' she agreed, appraising me. 'Something sensible and hard-wearing. I shall take you to the dressmaker's tomorrow.'

'You need something too.' Her grey dress was wearing at the elbows and the hem was frayed. A button was missing from the top of her bodice and another two were working loose. 'You'd look pretty in a blue gown with wide, white bows.'

Miss Morgan looked down at herself and her pale cheeks turned a shade of pink.

As promised she took me to a dress shop the following morning. The proprietor, a hawk-faced woman who spat English in a carving-knife hiss, stood by as Miss Morgan ordered a plain grey gown for herself and the most uninteresting jumble of cloth ever stitched by human hands for me. I suffered the indignity of being measured and tried not to flinch when the drab material was draped over my shoulders.

'I must slip out for a while,' Miss Morgan told me. 'Stay here. Don't wander.'

The second she was out the door I pulled off the sack she'd bought me and dropped it on to the floor. 'I'm not a beggar or milkmaid and I won't dress like either,' I declared.

The proprietor's eyes flicked over the discarded garment. 'What would the young lady suggest?'

Two women, sisters from the look of it, were standing near the window poring over some material. They were too engrossed to notice me. I pointed to the younger girl. 'I want to look like her.'

'Will cost extra. More than your friend has given me.'

I had an allowance set by; money Miss Morgan had provided which I'd never had cause to spend. 'I will pay you.' I tried to sound confident. 'And when I have chosen a gown for myself, we will pick something for my guardian. That grey thing she ordered belongs in a nunnery.'

I chose swiftly. A rose pink gown with a low, square neckline, fitted bodice and pagoda sleeves trimmed with taffeta bows. I decided to forsake a bonnet in favour of a square of gauze worn over a powdered wig. This, the dressmaker assured me, was very much in favour with well-to-do Italian ladies and sure to catch the eye of any gentleman.

For Miss Morgan we selected a pale blue gown with an embroidered bodice, sleeves and a looped skirt. The sort of thing the wife of an English vicar might wear for a tea party.

'Still, it is not the sort of garment I can imagine madam wearing, modest as it is,' my adviser remarked dryly. 'She does not seem the sort.'

'She is,' I assured her. 'She simply doesn't know it yet. Say nothing and deliver these to our apartments. It will be a surprise for her.'

I wriggled back into my old gown. When my guardian returned I waited innocently as the dressmaker informed her the garments would arrive in two days.

'Good,' Miss Morgan said. 'I have met the most charming English family. We have been invited to a party in celebration of their eldest son's birthday. The garments will arrive just in time.'

How nice, I thought.

The package was delivered at the end of the week. Miss Morgan threw a fit when she saw what I'd done, but she put on the blue dress and let me wear my new gown. She sat tight-lipped as we rode in a hired carriage to the party. The event was held in a large house near the centre of town, owned by a friend of Mr Thompson, the gentleman whose son's birthday we had come to celebrate. After a flurry of introductions, Mr Thompson made small talk with Miss Morgan. He complimented her on her dress and she blushed a deep scarlet, thanking him with the voice of a mouse.

At the dinner table, I sat and picked through my food. Boiled meat, vegetables, potatoes dripping with butter. None of the colourful Italian delicacies that had enslaved my stomach these past few weeks. Most of the other guests were English and they had a lot to say about themselves. Mr Thompson's eldest son was a swaggering nineteen-year-old who bragged as if he'd been born to it. He seemed to assume that one smile was enough to burst the heart of every girl in the room. I stared at the bits of food rolling around in his ever-working mouth and thought how the local men would laugh at his bluster.

The younger brother, a callow, lean-faced youth called Roderick, nudged me under the table. 'Come with me,' he whispered. The dancing had started and most of the guests had taken to the floor or were in the drawing room smoking or drinking port. I had been enjoying a glass of wine that was too large for my own good and felt light-headed. We slipped from the room and Roderick led me by the hand up a flight of stairs and then another until I stood with him, heart beating like sparrow's wings, on a darkened landing. Only a streak of moonlight through the window in the far wall lit our faces.

'This part of the house is not in use,' he whispered. 'No one ever comes here.'

'I will be missed,' I told him, pretending not to notice as his arms curled around my waist like warm-bloodied snakes.

His face was only an inch from my own. Words whispered across my cheek. 'Not yet.'

In the peaceful gloom we exchanged breathless kisses. At first the bad memories rushed in. Blake's bruising fumbles. But Roderick's touch was soft and left my mouth tingling. He held me gently and I tasted bittersweet wine on his lips.

We remained like that for several moments, saying nothing while he drank me and I in turn became intoxicated by his warmth. But when his hand strayed towards my bodice I let go of him and stepped back.

'No, Roderick,' I said gently.

Confusion rippled across his face. I was afraid that everything would be spoiled but he smiled and took my hand again. We scampered back downstairs to the noise. Miss Morgan was lingering on the edge of the dance floor, clapping along to the music. On impulse, I grabbed her arm and hauled her into the middle of the floor.

'Dance with me,' I cried.

It was too late to resist. We were the oddest couple in the room, all feet and no grace, but Miss Morgan laughed and let her hair fall loose. When the hired quartet had finished playing, everyone applauded.

In the carriage home, Miss Mary hummed to herself while I sat clutching the posy of flowers Roderick had slipped into my hands. He told me his family was once more on the move, this time to Rome where his father had some business interests.

Nothing mattered for now. Miss Mary caught me watching her and smiled. She had drawn more than one admirer at the party and her eyes were full of secrets.

'Did you have a nice time, Juliana?' she purred.

I gazed at the flowers. 'Oh yes.'

Weeks merged into one another. We hardly noticed. Summer rolled around again and baked the streets with hot, golden sunshine. We travelled the country, enjoying beauty wherever we found it and discovering treasures in both likely and unlikely places. I could flirt with the local lads so outrageously that it was often I who turned their cheeks red. I had all the music, books and art I could want.

Miss Morgan wore ever more flattering dresses and kept her dark hair around her shoulders instead of scraping it up into ugly coils. A letter arrived for her during a month-long stay in Genoa. As soon as the messenger had gone, she scurried plum-cheeked to her room. She never told me who'd sent it but I guessed it was not Catherine.

Next day, while savouring the wares of a boisterous local market, she treated herself to a satin neck choker inlaid with a marble cameo.

'You must think me terribly vain,' she said apologetically.

I laughed and helped fasten it around her neck. 'Now you are fair game for any Italian prince.'

'Any man can be a prince,' she replied, 'as long as his heart is good, his love sincere and his head firm upon his shoulders.'

Soon the golden days had to end. My penance was over and England beckoned. We spent our last night on the terrace, listening to the sounds of the night as moths chased one another around the lanterns. In the distance, a man's voice raised in a lilting melody that tingled the nerves. I wonder if he sang to his lover, if he was saying goodbye.

'I shall miss this dear place,' Mary said. 'And you, Juliana. You most of all. You are not the creature Catherine painted you.'

I squeezed her hand. She gave a weary smile and closed her eyes. Light flickered across her eyelids. The distant song ended on a drawn-out note and the silence that replaced it seemed intense. We had become such friends over the days and weeks that it seemed the grey-faced woman I first met in Wexborough could not possibly have existed.

'I wonder if I shall ever wed,' I sighed, thinking back to Roderick and that moon-silvered landing. 'Did you ever come close?'

'Now there's a notion. I think one husband is enough in a lifetime.'

'You are married?' I gasped.

'I was, a long time ago when I was young, almost as young as you, Juliana. My father arranged the union and used up half his fortune to settle a good dowry on me. I was the last child in the family to be wed and I daresay Papa was keen to be rid of me. I was always a burden on his patience. My new husband only wanted money and an heir, but I loved him. I was an age to love anyone. My belly put paid to those fancies. I was barren, so my husband divorced me. It took a year and a ransom in lawyers' fees to do it. When the papers were signed I treated it like a death, wore black and mourned. In the end I became a governess to be near children, even if they were other women's children. It is an acceptable profession for one in my position and I do not have to rely too heavily on my father's charity. But all I ever wanted, and still want, is a child of my own. The ability to make life is the most precious gift a woman could possess.'

I swallowed hard. 'Do you know why Catherine sent me on this trip with you?'

She opened her eyes. 'I never question the motives of my employers. It is not my place.'

I shook my head. 'You more than anyone would understand.'

I stood on the quay in my pretty Italian shawl, a frown cracking my face as Mary busied herself checking the luggage. Our modest collection had grown in the course of our travels but I felt like throwing it all into the sea.

The weather, as if sensing our mood, rolled thick clouds across the sky. Specks of rain pecked my cheeks and a stiff breeze whirled around the harbour. A flurry of dust snatched my hair and filled my mouth with grit.

In a moment we would board the ship that would take us back to England. The *Sally Anne* was a merchant vessel that usually brought trade goods from the South Seas. It had been fitted with cannon to ward off the Corsairs that still

59

plagued large areas of the Mediterranean, so the shipping agent had delighted in telling us. I found the idea of being boarded by a band of heathen cut-throats hopelessly romantic, but Mary soon toppled my fantasy.

'They would sell you into slavery, or hang you from a rope and set your hair alight,' she told me. 'Better to jump overboard than fall into the hands of those rogues.'

Our captain was a broad-shouldered Scot by the name of McDermott. He wore a beard the size of a bush and ran his crew like a team of horses. His deep voice boomed out curses and a hefty boot sought the rump of any seaman guilty of slacking.

As our baggage was taken on board the men kept stealing glances. One crossed himself after accidentally brushing against me. Mouths were full of whispers.

'Superstitious rabble,' McDermott said dismissively. 'They don't like that red smear on your face, lass. They should look at their own ugly faces. 'Twould make their mothers nervous.'

'I don't want to cause trouble.'

'Pay them no heed. You'll be treated well enough once we've put to sea.' He clapped me on the shoulder. I tried to smile but the sense of unease stayed with me and grew as the *Sally Anne* slipped its moorings and headed towards open water.

Someone kept watching me. A grizzled sailor with piercing green eyes and candle-wax hair cropped so close I could see the pink of his scalp. He did not cross himself, or turn to papist beads, or make the sign against the evil eye with his fingers. His gaze chained me to the deck, even as he worked. When he was perched in the rigging I could feel him looking down on me. When he scrambled below, I knew I was in his thoughts.

Less than a day out of port, the clouds broke apart and the wind died. All around us the sea was as flat as a blue china plate. Sails hung from the masts like empty canvas sacks. McDermott cursed the skies in some impossible dialect and sent out a rowboat to try to tow us into useful weather. The gentle dollop of oars dipping into water mingled with the creak of the towrope as we inched across the glossy millpond.

I turned away from the rail and there was the watcher, standing like a white-haired ghost I'd somehow conjured out of the decking. He marked me with that dagger gaze and his chapped lips peeled back from his teeth. He possessed the rough-cut countenance of an Englishman but when he spoke it was with the lilt of a Spaniard.

'That mark on your face,' he said. 'I've seen it before, dreaded it all my years on the sea. You're his daughter. No one but his kin could carry the stain.'

We were alone. He could put a blade to my throat and no one would know. I pursed my lips and tried to sound confident. 'I don't know what you mean,' I told him, hiding shaking hands in the folds of my skirts. 'It's just a birthmark.'

He shook his head. Corded veins stood out on his neck. A hand caught my chin. I tried to pull away but he held me firm, his finger tracing the red smear from the corner of my mouth to my jaw line. 'Nay, young lady. 'Tis far more than that. You're Manuel's. You bear the mark.'

I opened my mouth without any notion of what to say. Fear cut me to the pit of my belly. This was not some fanciful sailor's yarn spun to earn a coin from impressionable passengers. Something lurked in this man's face that warned me I was only a whisper away from learning some dreadful truth. I wasn't certain I wanted hear it.

A hatch opened behind us and someone called. The sailor turned away. I stood knock-kneed as he clambered down the hatch to join his unseen shipmate. After it closed I remained beside the rail for a few more minutes, but he did not reappear.

When I felt calm enough, I went below. No luxury of a

cabin this time but the sailors had rigged up a curtain in the corner of the hold. Hammocks stitched over and stuffed with canvas provided mattresses, while the first mate had lent us his bowl and looking glass. Dried fish, fruit and barrels of wine surrounded our makeshift quarters, as well as boxloads of expensive Italian drapery bound for the fashionable London shops. The smell was a little too potent for my nose but Mary seemed not to notice, or be troubled by it if she did. I found her sitting up on her pallet reading from a leather-bound book with a title written in Italian. Her lips worked soundlessly as she tried to improve her skills at the language. Thinking of England with its endless rain and sour-faced merchants only filled me with gloom.

Mary glanced up from the page when I sat down opposite, smiled and went back to her reading. I said nothing. I had a feeling my business with the watcher wasn't yet done.

Darkness fell over the water in a hushed blanket. Mary had fallen asleep early, lulled by a calm sea, which was much kinder to her queasy stomach. I paced the deck, cloak wrapped tight, watching insects circle the flickering lanterns. The boat hugged the shore, close enough for swarms to be drawn to the soft light.

Most of the crew was below apart from the pilot, the watch, and a small group of seamen rolling dice beside a guttering candle. A breeze of words carried on the night air. Someone chuckled when he had a lucky throw, followed by the envious curses of his fellows.

'What's your name?'

I flinched. The watcher peered at me through the gloom. His bare feet had made no sound on the wooden planking. 'What's your name?' he asked again. Rum sweetened his breath. The scent of salt and stale tobacco clung to his canvas breeches. 'Tell me what lie you live under.'

'Juliana Rodriguez,' I said in a little-girl voice.

His eyes widened. They glimmered like jet under the drifting stars. 'So he gave you his name? He must have been taken with you. Or perhaps it was your mother who charmed him.'

'I never knew my parents.'

He laughed softly. 'No surprise there. Few were acquainted with Manuel Rodriguez 'cept at the end of his sword and fewer still who lived to remember. The name Manuel the Bloody came from his scarlet mouth and his appetite for spilling other men's gizzards. He was a Spanish nobleman, robbed of his inheritance by the pretty young whore his father took to his bed. She bore his bastard and took Manuel's fortune, so the lad turned to plundering the shipping lanes. He raided holds, strung crews from their own mastheads and claimed the lives of any passengers, noble or commoner, that had the bad luck to be on board.'

He hawked and spat over the rail. 'No man could catch Manuel the Bloody. In the end, the Spanish king gave him a letter of marque to plunder foreign vessels legally, as a privateer. But the English sprung a trap and hanged him for piracy just the same, in a place called Antigua where he sometimes holed up to spend his booty. Many would dance on his grave.'

'Why are you telling me this?' I demanded. 'What do you want? Do you take pleasure in tormenting me with these gory tales of the past?'

He leaned forward so that his face was inches from mine. I matched his stare, though it chilled me to gaze into those bottomless eyes. 'Any man – or woman – has a right to know who they are and where they hail from. Maybe you have a destiny. What I tell you now might help you pick the right path. It's your due, nothing more.'

He straightened. I was trembling and it had nothing to do with the cool breeze wafting across the waters from the dark, huddled shore.

'I knew Manuel,' he continued. 'I served on one of his ships. For years I butchered for him. I helped spend his stolen gold, shared his harlots and drank myself into the gutter. And I dodged the noose for betraying him. Not that you have to believe me, mind, but the sea is my witness. Sometimes sleep doesn't come easily and I see that mark, bright even against Manuel's sun-beaten skin. I hear him laughing, telling me to settle my dues for turning him over to the English. That debt is now part-paid, and I'll wager every Spanish doubloon or English guinea I've stolen in my life that his blood is your blood, just as his mark is your mark.'

'Who was my mother?'

A hatch slapped open. Mary's sleepy head appeared. The sailor slipped into the shadows. Soft footfalls trailed across the deck.

'Juliana, what are you doing up here? I heard voices. Who were you talking to?'

I glanced over the rail. The black bulk of the shoreline had faded into the distance. Around us, I felt the thick swell of the open sea. 'Just another seaman with a head full of stories.'

Next day the wind picked up. We had fair sailing all the way to England. When I returned to the Butter House, Catherine was waiting, and it was not long before I stole another child.

Chapter Five

'You look like a whore,' Catherine accused. 'You smell of cheap scent and too much wine. Where did you get that dress, and who smeared rouge on your face?'

I held my tongue and waited while she circled me like a hunting dog. Every so often she reached out to pluck at my bright Italian gown and her mouth curled. I forced myself not to flinch at the touch of her bony fingers. There was a great deal I wanted to say but this was not the right time.

It had proved an inauspicious homecoming. Our ship had docked without incident. A rented gig and pair had brought us and our dust-coated baggage from the harbour and deposited us outside the front door. The Butter House looked mostly unchanged, though the step was in need of a brickbat and the curtains were drawn.

Catherine herself admitted us. She hunched over as she walked. Her slippers whispered like dried leaves on the carpet. She seemed so small, or perhaps it was just that I had grown. Tired lines scored her gaunt face.

'Painted ladies, both of you,' she continued. 'Miss Morgan, your services were engaged on the strength of your reputation. I had hoped you would provide a steadying influence on Juliana. Prove to me that I was not mistaken.'

She sat us both down, in our travelling clothes, while our luggage lay unpacked in the hall. Mary was obliged to describe our trip in detail. Catherine hung on to every word. I was not allowed to interrupt. I wanted tea, or perhaps some water. I was permitted neither. When Mary was finished, sparing neither the truth nor my blushes, Catherine nodded as if nothing my guardian said had surprised her.

'It seems you omitted a great deal from your letters. Your father will hear of this.'

Mary folded her hands together and matched Catherine stare for stare. 'I am afraid, Mrs Worledge, that I have passed the stage where my father's attitudes are of any concern. Miss Rodriguez has learned a great deal during our travels abroad and behaved magnificently. You have every cause to feel proud.'

'Rodriguez is it? The girl has addled your wits. Leave my house before I have your bags thrown into the street. You can expect no further fee or reference. As for you,' she stabbed a finger at me, 'tidy yourself up then join me in the withdrawing room.'

Catherine shuffled off, leaving me in the parlour with Mary. I embraced her, not as a teacher, but a dear friend. She promised to write though we both suspected it was unlikely we would see one another again.

'I don't want any more of her money,' she said, spilling tears into a crumpled handkerchief. 'Be careful around that one, Juliana. Her mind is full of bitterness. Don't let it poison you.'

'Don't go back to wrapping yourself in those awful mourning clothes,' I countered. 'I should have made you leave them in Florence.'

She laughed a little, despite herself, then picked up her luggage and walked out the front door. A chair would take her to the coaching house, where she could catch a stage home. Only when the door closed did I begin to realise how much I would miss her.

My bed sported a new coverlet and a fresh pile of linen was stacked on the dresser. Both windows were thrown wide and a warm, late-summer breeze brought in the scent of roses from the gardens across the way. My luggage was already unpacked, the gowns hung neatly in the wardrobe, other garments folded and placed in drawers. I opened the top of the dresser and took out Miss Mary's parting gift: the Bible she had carried with her across Europe. I ran my fingers over the leather cover, worn smooth with handling.

I won't forget you.

Feeling hot and dirty from the journey, I began to undress. A hip bath had been brought from the kitchen and filled with steaming water. I slipped into the scented liquid, luxuriating in the way it soothed my tired flesh. I pampered myself until the water turned cold. After a brisk towelling, I rummaged in the dresser. I fancied a silk petticoat next to my clean skin and a light taffeta gown.

I frowned. Some of my underclothes were missing, the very best from Italy. I checked each drawer, the bottom of the wardrobe, even under the bed.

What had I done with them? I'd seen to the packing myself, since our Italian maid could not be trusted with the delicate silks. Exasperated, I threw on a robe, strode on to the landing and called for a maid. The girl who came running was a stranger, a loose-haired creature with crooked teeth.

'Who are you?' I demanded.

'Nancy, miss.'

'How long have you been here?'

'Nigh on six months.'

'What happened to our usual housemaid?'

'Don't rightly know, miss. I was a parish girl when the mistress took me on.'

'Some garments are missing from my luggage. Do you know what has become of them?'

'Mr Blake took care of the trunks. Told me to mind my business when I tried to help.'

Blake. That name still put shivers down my back. Too much to hope that he might have caught some terrible fever or been trampled by a runaway horse. Fate was never that kind.

'Where is Blake now?'

'If you please, miss, I think he's gone to join Mr Worledge in town.'

'And where in town might Mr Worledge be?' I pressed.

'Ain't my place to know or say, miss.'

Fuming, I let her go and made my way downstairs. The house was gloomy and deathly quiet. I expected to find Catherine in the parlour, but it was empty. I checked the other rooms. No sign of her.

I frowned. Things were missing. Small things. Trinkets that Richard had brought from abroad, a couple of paintings, the bust that glowered from its pedestal beside the front door. Dust coated most of the furnishings.

Finding Maggie Burns still working in the kitchen was a relief. 'Mrs Worledge dismissed most of the servants,' she explained, 'and took on an orphan girl because she was cheap. Poor soul can't look after such a big house by herself. Mr Blake is rarely here and the stable lad has his hands full as it is. Still, the mistress doesn't seem to mind. Hardly anyone comes calling these days.'

'What about Mrs Deever?'

'Had a to-do with Mr Blake over who was in charge of the household. She complained to Mrs Worledge and was thrown into the street. I never thought I'd see that woman cry.'

Maggie stirred the pot of soup she had bubbling on the stove. She looked much older than I remembered, with a streak of grey running through her fawn-coloured hair. The kitchen was a jumble of pots and pans, many in dire need of cleaning.

'Where is cook?' I asked.

'Her back gave out and now her son's looking after her in Chichester. Don't think he's too pleased about that seeing as he has a wife and brats of his own to feed. I look after the kitchens now.'

'Is there no one to help you?'

'The maid's clumsy and I don't care for her much. Was there anything else you wanted, miss?'

*

68

Catherine and I dined alone that evening. She pushed food into her mouth and chewed while her eyes appraised me. She had spent the afternoon in town and on her return we had sat in the withdrawing room while she tested me on my lessons. I spoke perfect Latin and managed a few lines in Italian without stumbling over the words. I quoted poetry and Greek philosophy, described the magnificent palaces of France, talked of paintings and sculpture. I said nothing about a white-haired sailor with piercing eyes who spoke of a pirate with a mark on his face the colour of blood.

'You have returned to England in good time,' Catherine remarked. 'We have been invited to a society ball at the new assembly rooms in Duke's Park. It will be a good opportunity to see how you conduct yourself. You have grown, Juliana. Many young men, I am sure, will take more than a passing interest. Try not to disgrace me.'

'How is Mr Worledge?' I asked. 'Will he greet me before I retire?'

Catherine flicked her hand. 'Richard is engaged in what he does best. You might see him within the hour or the week. In the meantime you will need a gown for the ball. Something respectable, not those harlot's rags you brought back from the Continent.'

'They are the height of fashion,' I protested.

Catherine waved her fork. 'I will not tolerate anything frivolous. You are at a size now where one of my old gowns might fit.'

'I don't want one of your smelly old dresses.' I threw down my knife. It clattered on my plate and splashed gravy across the tablecloth. 'I want something of my own.'

I fled the table, knocking over my chair as I scurried out of the dining room and up the stairs. Catherine called after me but I covered my ears with my fists. When I reached my bedchamber I slammed the door and threw myself on to the bed. How stupid to think that things might have changed. Catherine was as sour as ever. She had brought

69

out the gutter in me in no time at all. I wished I was back in Florence, amidst the flowers with a friend who listened and cared about what I thought and felt. I remembered Mr Thompson's young son, the kisses on the shadowed landing that sent the first quiver of love coursing through me. I desired that feeling again, wanted it to fill me and never go away. I despaired of spending another moment in this strange, dead house.

Morning found me in a contrite mood. I was eager for breakfast, so I let Catherine scold me before taking my place at the table.

'Why have you sold some of the things in the house, and dismissed most of the servants?' I asked, attention fixed on my plate.

She answered without looking up. 'Your education was costly, Juliana. It was necessary to make sacrifices. All the more reason for you to be grateful.'

Richard arrived home at noon the next day. I barely recognised the husk that stumbled into the hall, hat dripping with the rain that had fallen most of that morning. I greeted him alone. Catherine had grown a headache and taken to her bed for a nap. His eyes widened when he saw me. He opened his mouth to speak then paused as if he had forgotten my name.

'Juliana . . .' A hoarse whisper. 'Is that you?'

I curtsied and his thin mouth cracked into a smile. 'Welcome home,' he said. 'How long has it been? Let me see . . .'

His brow furrowed and I felt I could stand there for ever while he struggled to remember. He tried to say something else but fumbled the words.

'Over a year, sir,' I told him.

'Really? That long? Let me embrace you.' Arms circled my waist. Under his clothing I could feel bones. He shivered. A papery mannequin whose hair had dried to wisps. It hurt to look into his eyes. Watery and bloodshot, they could not seem to focus for more than a moment at a time. Grime encrusted the neck of his shirt, the cravat was badly tied and his shoes, once always polished until they gleamed, were scuffed and spattered with mud. He felt so fragile I feared he might snap him in two. He straightened and gazed into my face, brushing a wayward strand of hair from my forehead and tucking it behind my ear.

'What a beautiful creature you have become,' he sighed.

Then the man I hated more than anyone else in the world stepped back into my life. Sharp as a pin in a fine coat and breeches, he made an entrance like the squire of a grand house returning to his property. On catching sight of me, he smiled a cat's smile and his tongue slipped across his lips. He said nothing, no word of greeting or deference, but his eyes flicked over me as if they were knives. Instead of taking Richard's hat and coat he threw his own over the balustrade and strode past me into the study. He helped himself to a glass of port while Richard struggled out of his own jacket. Having taken a leisurely sip, Blake rang for the maid. She came at a run and curtsied. He gestured towards Richard. The maid nodded and led him away. He mumbled to himself, one set of restless fingers entwined in the folds of his cravat. His other hand pulled a soiled kerchief from his pocket. Something fell out – a tattered, ink-stained paper. I waited until the maid had helped Richard upstairs then I picked up the note and smoothed it out. It looked like a page from a dairy. The handwritten scrawl was barely legible and meandered over the page, but I managed to decipher the jumble of words.

It was an I.O.U. made out for a staggering amount of money. Richard's signature was scribbled on the bottom. I looked up to find Blake watching me. A moment later he closed the study door.

Later that afternoon Catherine took me into her bedchamber – a light, billowy place furnished with white lace and mahogany – and stood me in front of her tall looking glass. I was now her height, with a full figure and thankfully clear complexion. She opened her wardrobe and rummaged through her dresses. Some half dozen were selected, held up against me then laid across her bed. A couple of faded bonnets followed together with some gloves and whalebone stays.

'You may make use of these until I am able to obtain suitable replacements,' Catherine told me.

Dismayed, I stared at the jumble of garments. The bonnets were dusty, the gloves falling apart and the gowns ungainly monstrosities that would bury me beneath layers of crushed velvet. 'Miss Morgan paid a small fortune for my own gowns,' I muttered.

'Frivolous Italian fancies are not suitable for respectable English society,' Catherine answered, holding a muslin wrap up to the light. She nodded and added it to the pile.

'But I chose them myself.'

'Are there not enough harlots in this town without you wishing to parrot them? Now take off those gaudy rags. There is much to do today and I am short on patience.'

'I will not.'

Catherine blinked a couple of times. Quick as a cat, she grasped my bodice and tore the front of my dress open. Breath whooshed out of my lungs. Expensive silks ripped apart under her claws as though made of paper. Coloured bows were strewn across the carpet.

While I stood in my petticoats, Catherine picked a gown off the bed and thrust it under my face. 'Put it on,' she ordered, 'and do not argue with me again. I want you dressed decently for supper.'

I skulked back to my room like a scolded pup, Catherine's gown held tightly against my bared chest. Both wardrobe doors hung open and the inside was empty. I pulled open the drawers on my dresser. Everything was gone.

I slammed the drawers back into place and sank to my knees. Pain spread through my hands. I uncurled my fingers.

My nails had dug sharp crescents into both palms.

I had no choice. I stood, pulled off the remnants of my ravaged gown and slid into the clothes Catherine had given me. The dress was an ungainly looking thing ideal for frumps and old women, not a girl who had returned from Europe wanting to light up the town. Two of the fastenings were broken and some of the embroidery had worked loose. I pinned everything together and regarded myself in the looking glass. I resembled a withered old maid.

I turned the mirror to the wall and went downstairs to the kitchen. I needed to talk to someone. Anyone. Maggie was nowhere to be seen, though steaming copper pots hissed angrily from their hooks above the hearth. The pantry door was open and I heard someone cough. I crept up and peeked around the doorframe.

Blake was squatting on a barrel, head bent, his back turned. I must have made a sound because he jerked to his feet. His cheeks were flushed, his eyes a livid blue. In his hand was one of my petticoats. It slid out of his grasp and on to the floor.

'Welcome home,' he said, before pushing past me. A moment later the kitchen door slammed.

Once I'd gathered my wits about me, I picked up the undergarment, took it into the kitchen and threw it on to the fire.

I was not safe from Blake yet.

Richard left the house again that evening. He stumbled down the front step and into a carriage, which immediately set off up the street. I watched from the door, wondering if I would see him again that night.

Blake remained behind. I heard him enter the study, then the clink of a decanter. A moment later, Catherine's slippers shuffled across the hall. The study door closed. A key turned in the lock.

I hurried into the parlour and stuck my head behind

Catherine's writing desk. The Butter House had its tricks. Little twists of sound. Corners that gathered words like a vortex of autumn leaves and sent them spiralling around the masonry. This spot was a favourite eavesdropping haunt of mine, especially when I thought Richard and Catherine might be discussing me. I once had a nasty moment when Mrs Deever caught me on my knees with my ear pressed against the plaster. I mumbled something about dropping a hatpin.

'You'll likely find it there, I'm sure,' she'd declared.

'Would you care to help me look for it?'

'Church is the only place you'll see Ellie Deever on her knees.' And that had been the end of it.

It was a tight squeeze. Catherine's voice was low but carried clearly. 'More drink?' she admonished. 'You are becoming as bad as he. You would do well to keep a clear head and your wits about you. One cannot be complacent, even when dealing with fools.'

Blake's laughter rumbled through the stonework. 'If I dunked my head in a barrel of brandy and didn't surface for a week I still couldn't match the stomach of your beloved husband.'

'Never speak to me like that while in the house,' Catherine's voice hissed like hot coals in snow. 'I have warned you before. You are taking too many liberties. Learn patience.'

'Patience?' Blake's voice cracked. 'You enjoyed your comforts while I squatted in gaol with the rats. Even after my release the best you could do was let me become lackey to that fop. He took your business and squandered your money while I had to empty his pot and put his dinner in front of him every day.'

'Better that than the Tyburn gallows. Richard saved you from the hangman.'

'Aye, Catherine. For that reason alone I have not pressed a pillow over his drunken face, or scratched his throat with my razor.'

'Everything will turn out as it should. In the meantime you are too audacious with your airs and graces. People think it is a whim of Richard's to dandy you up and let you smoke his tobacco. But soon they will begin to wonder. Once the tongues start wagging there will be no stopping them.'

'It's your money, Catherine. Yours and mine.'

'Yes, money tied up in the shipping company. Father never suspected Richard would try to gamble away our lives. If he continues the banks will foreclose. You'd do well to remember that.'

'I ought to be the one with the fine carriage and the comfortable seat in the gentleman's club.'

Catherine laughed. 'You are no gentleman, nor could any fortune mould you into one. Be grateful for what you have. It is infinitely preferable to the gutter.'

'You are a whore and a witch,' Blake retorted. 'Just like that redheaded foundling Worledge took under his wing.'

'Stay away from Juliana. She could still cause problems. Stealing that baby proved what she is capable of.'

'You think I'd hurt your little treasure pot?'

'I still don't like the way you look at her. No good can come of it. She is poison, that one. Whatever you do she will eventually turn it to her own purposes. Save your lechery for the bawdy house.'

They talked some more, shifting the conversation on to more trivial matters. When Catherine entered the parlour she found me in an armchair with my face in a book. 'What are you doing here?' she demanded, eyes narrowing.

'My bedchamber was too hot,' I replied with wide-eyed innocence. 'I came downstairs to read.'

She appraised me for a few moments, then her face relaxed. 'You move like a ghost sometimes, Juliana. One day your pitter-patterings around this house will land you in trouble.'

*

Supper that night was eaten in silence. Catherine and I sat at opposite ends of the table. Between us, a cluster of half-spent candles spat hot wax. Shadows leapt across the walls like living things.

Blake had apparently risen above such menial things as serving food. Instead the stable lad brought our dinner. His name, I learned, was William. He was an awkward, gawky lad with a missing tooth and an impudent smile. He tried to keep a straight face while serving my soup but I caught his eye and winked. His grin had me silently rejoicing. I was determined to find allies anywhere I could.

'Get me the key to Richard's bedchamber,' I instructed him the following morning.

'But miss, I've been told that no one's to go in there save Mr Worledge himself.'

'He is out for the day and possibly half the night as well,' I countered. 'His manservant is in the study helping himself to the port and Mrs Worledge is off buying a new hat for the ball. The maid has spare keys to all the rooms and she won't give any of them to me. She's too afraid of being punished. You, I suspect, will have better luck.'

Another gap-toothed grin. 'I just might.'

'Sixpence if you succeed.'

'You're on.'

I passed through to the kitchen and sent Maggie out to the pump, telling her I wanted a bath. She moaned that the stew would spoil if she wasn't there to keep an eye on it. I dug in my heels and made her take the biggest pail, knowing it would take an age to fill and that Maggie, who was a good two inches shorter than me, would struggle to haul it back across the yard.

Left to myself, I took the money jar out of the plate cupboard. I fished out a sixpence, tucked it into my sleeve then replaced the jar. These were petty funds kept for the occasional errand. Maggie never kept a note of its contents. She couldn't write, or count beyond her own ten fingers.

I slipped William the sixpence during afternoon coffee. He pressed a brass key into my hand. I fingered the cool metal, eyeing Catherine as she bit into a sweetmeat. She had returned from town in a sour mood, unable to find any bonnet that took her fancy.

'The streets are filthy,' she complained, 'and my feet fit to drop off.'

She declared she would take a nap after coffee. I feigned sympathy and agreed it was a good idea. The moment she disappeared upstairs, I collared William and warned him to keep the maid occupied while I took my own liberties in Richard's room.

'Won't be a problem,' the lad boasted. 'I reckon Nancy has taken a shine to me. Daresay I could keep her in the washhouse for as long as need be.'

'You are too clever for your own good, William.'

He tipped me an insolent wink. 'Glad you see it that way, miss.'

Exiled from Catherine's bed, Richard kept his rooms at the opposite end of the passage. This corner of the house was a trap for the north winds that frequently blustered around the brickwork. Weak light seeped through a narrow window that overlooked the courtyard and stables beyond. A musty air of neglect hung over everything.

I fumbled the key out of my sleeve and pushed it into the lock. It turned with a click and the door swung open. A few paces into the room, my slipper knocked against something. It rumbled across the floorboards and fetched up against the foot of the dresser.

I stooped to take a closer look. An empty bottle. I picked it up and sniffed the open neck, wincing at the odour of stale brandy. Other bottles, a great many bottles, lay strewn across the floor, piled on top of the trunk at the foot of the bed or gathering dust in crooked heaps in each corner of the room. A glass menagerie of greens and browns – even a broken-handled clay jug that a beggar might use to glug cheap spirits.

Careful where I put my feet, I moved deeper into the mess. The smell of alcohol clung to the furnishings. Loose bundles of clothing were tossed haphazardly over chairs or draped over the end of the bed.

No one's to go in there, William had said.

No one to change the bed linen or brush down the rugs. No maid slipping in early to throw open the windows and let in fresh air.

I opened the wardrobe and peered inside. Everything was in disarray. Mismatched garments were bundled together or lay where they had fallen. Shoes were crammed on to the shelf, some so tightly that the leather had been squashed into ugly shapes. Scraps of paper littered the cramped space. When I picked one up it flapped open like a dirty handkerchief. I spread it out against the wardrobe door, read it then picked up another. This one was torn from a tradesman's ledger book. The next was written on fine vellum bearing the crest of Richard's shipping company. Everything was scribed in his unsteady hand. All were I.O.U.s.

I searched his jackets, his waistcoats, even the pair of breeches poking out from under the bed. The pockets were stuffed to bulging with ink-smudged notes.

'Richard, what have you done?' I whispered.

I crammed the papers back into his pockets and, dodging the bottles littering the floor, turned my attention to the dresser. The mahogany top was lost under a layer of dust. Dirty plates and cutlery were caked with the decaying remnants of a meal. An ashtray brimmed with spent tobacco.

I pulled open the top drawer. More empty bottles. More I.O.U.s. The thick air of this filthy room clogged my throat. Richard was damned and there was no one to try to save him.

Except me.

Chapter Six

'Stop fidgeting, Juliana. We are almost there.'

'This dress is choking me,' I complained. 'It itches and smells like a horse blanket. No one will dance with me.'

'No one is likely to if your humour does not improve. Gentlemen are attracted to a smiling face, not the vanity of a pretty gown. Find some cheerfulness and the dances will follow.'

It had proved very difficult to smile at Catherine these past few days. I glared at her as she settled back in her seat. We had enjoyed a gentle journey through town, the rented carriage inching along the busy evening streets. Catherine had restored her features with the aid of thick powder and a rash of coloured patches. My birthmark was likewise buried. Her rented gown of crisp green velvet contrasted sharply with the drab sack in which I sat and suffered. What other treasure had disappeared from the Butter House to pay for this extravagance?

The Dovecote Assembly Rooms were housed in an imposing lump of a building funded by a merchant who made his fortune importing coffee. Stepping down from the carriage, I took in the warm sandstone and the rows of windows framed in white wood. Lanterns, resembling tiny coloured moons, lined the outer courtyard. Liveried footmen swung open the front doors as we approached. Catherine whisked me past their starched faces and into the muggy interior.

The sweltering press of bodies was intense from the lobby

inwards. Everyone seemed to be drinking or talking. Pipe smoke clung to the ceiling in a blue fug. The gentle strains of music filtered through the hubbub, adding elegance to the chaos.

Catherine grasped my hand and herded me towards the end of the hall. She nodded and smiled greetings at strangers. My gown drew a few curious glances but there was far more eccentric fare to catch the eye. Monstrous headdresses were topped with wax fruit or fleets of tiny wooden ships. Over-size bows looped across skirts, or hung from the back of gentlemen's wigs like huge velvet moths. It was a place of caricatures. Rouge-mouthed gargoyles with white painted faces, or satin-clad nymphs flitting among the throng, dispensing giggles like party favours. I anticipated meeting the hostess of this spectacle but Catherine seemed disinclined to seek her out. Did it even matter whose party it was?

We squeezed through an oval atrium papered with chat-tering dandies and into the main assembly room, a chamber filled with music and heady scents. Guttering candles were reflected a thousand fold in the chandeliers suspended above my head. Marble busts set into alcoves high in the walls added to the grandeur.

The floor was alive with dancing couples. Brisk melodies were thrummed out by an orchestra perched on a curved balcony above the entrance doors. Other guests clapped along to the melodies, or waited in hope of finding a partner.

Someone waved to Catherine from the far side of the room. 'A business matter,' she confided. 'Too pressing to let slip. Go and meet some of the other young ladies. No doubt they will be eager to make your acquaintance.'

Finding myself dumped amongst a gaggle of strangers left me feeling awkward. Catherine had already disappeared into the crowd. I cast about for a refuge. Refreshment tables had been laid out against the wall opposite the balcony. I picked out a path through the throng and made straight for the punch bowl. A serving wench in fancy dress poured me a generous cup. She was got up as old Queen Bess and looked quite sharp in a red wig and ruff. Two gulps and I was grinning like a simpleton. I let my gaze rove around the room, taking in the faces and letting their talk rumble around me. Much was said about the American war, a conflict that brought victory then defeat, then victory again, and seemed set to drag on for ever. Nothing had been gained. Good men were dying while other nations threw in their lot and the number of widows grew with the passing months.

Those who had returned from the battlefields spoke of how bravely they had fought. They described wounds just serious enough to earn a discharge home, and talked of heroism whilst other men nodded and scratched their chins. These sages were the dregs, the ones the war would not have. The old, the gout-ridden and the cowards who'd used up fortunes to buy their way out of duty.

Gossip travelled like a breeze through summer branches, whispering into every nook and alcove. It was very powerful, this tide of words. Every busy mouth found an eager ear. Names were tossed around and discarded. In five minutes I heard enough scandal to fill a book.

Two people in particular lay at the core of all this talk. Cecilia Fortescue and Adam Fairchild, the latter always mentioned with a slight catch of the breath as if the very words were poison. 'Who is this Mr Fairchild?' I asked the serving wench. 'Is he here tonight?'

The girl looked startled that I'd spoken to her. I smiled reassurance. Her eyes narrowed and she leaned across the table. 'There, by the door to the gentlemen's room. The fellow with the dark hair and no powder on his face.'

'He's as bad as they say?'

'Since you ask, miss, there isn't a gentleman here tonight who wouldn't like to see him dead.'

The notorious Adam Fairchild was holding court in a shadowed alcove beneath the gallery, surrounded by a gaggle of laughing women.

'He's ruined marriages and sired bastards by the score,' the girl continued. 'Pretty ladies are treated like cattle but would die for a smile from him.'

'You are making it up. I never knew a servant who didn't like to colour a good tale.'

She looked at the floor. 'As you like, miss. I was only telling you what most good people already know.'

I arched my neck to see above the bobbing heads. Fairchild stood no taller than most of his audience. He was not possessed of a strong build or countenance that would stop a heart beating. One might say that his nose was over-long, jutting over his top lip like a granite outcropping, or his eyes too close together. Black, curly hair clung to his scalp and tumbled reluctantly down the back of his neck where it was shackled by a velvet bow. A scar pinched his right cheek, lending his face a lopsided aspect that proved unsettling. When he smiled, which he did infrequently, his bloodless lips twitched as though the gesture was foreign to him.

But a few seconds staring at Adam Fairchild taught me that here was a man who did not rely on a pleasant face. He was possessed of a dark, brooding charisma that dominated the room. The sort of allure that could make a leader or devil of a man whatever his physical aspect. I could almost taste danger, sense the threat of a wolf let loose among lambs.

Despite myself, I felt stirrings inside me that I did not entirely dislike. I caught my breath as his charcoal eyes swept around the chamber, settling on me for only a moment before moving on. People seemed to wilt under that brittle gaze. My tongue dried in my throat. These feelings were different to those I had experienced with that boy in Florence, but every bit as powerful.

Someone pawed my sleeve. I dragged my eye away from Fairchild and faced Catherine. She was out of breath and red spots burned above her cheekbones. A man of indeterminate age stood at her side, regarding me with eyes like poached eggs.

'Juliana, I want you to meet someone,' Catherine gushed. 'This is Mr George Proudlove. His father is a clergyman and once ministered in our parish. George remembers you from early childhood and is keen to renew your acquaintance.'

'I was just a lad myself,' the newcomer confessed, 'though if I may say so, I have very fond memories of you.'

I took his measure, searching for any recollection and finding none. He had a curious flat face, a smudge of flesh for a nose and a demeanour that reminded me of a crumpled rug. An oversize cravat sprouted across the front of his shirt and spilled over the edges of his waistcoat. Unbidden, he took my hand and planted a kiss between the knuckles. His mouth felt like a fish freshly hooked the river. I tried to pull away but he did not let go.

'I would consider it an honour if you would dance with me,' he continued, while Catherine watched us carefully.

'I don't dance.'

His fingers tightened. Pain flared through my hand. 'You are too modest.' He smiled and it was like a pit opening up in the ground. 'Your charming guardian tells me you have had lessons in Italy. It's not often that I am able to attend a ball in town. Even less that I should encounter such delightful company. I shan't take no for an answer.'

I glanced at Adam, but he was lost in his whimsies and Proudlove was already leading me on to the floor. Very well, I would give him a dance. A dance cost nothing.

The music started up and we worked through the first gavotte. Proudlove stumbled about the floor like a dog with three legs. I grimaced when the heel of his shoe landed squarely on my toes.

'You are uncommonly fetching,' he murmured into my ear as we applauded the orchestra.

'And you, sir, are disarmingly forward for a clergyman's son.'

83

He laughed as if I'd made a jest and waved a hand around the room. 'My parents frown on dancing and other such frivolities, but I am not of the cloth and therefore free to indulge myself more or less as I please. A generous tithe to his church ensures my father turns a blind eye. Another dance?'

I ached to be away, but he kept me on the floor for two more pieces. My head was ringing with his endless chatter, and the music was beginning to grate. In the end he let me go only because he claimed to have important matters to take care of. Stumbling back to the refreshment tables, I vowed to dance with every other man in the room rather than let Proudlove touch me again. Catherine thankfully was nowhere to be seen. Also absent was Adam Fairchild.

The maid had changed. A fat girl in an angel's outfit thrust a dish of hot tea into my hands. I savoured the drink, rolling its rich flavour around my tongue before swallowing. When I looked up from the dish, a young woman had joined me at the table. One look and I realised I had just met the notorious Cecilia Fortescue. Her sins had been laid bare by a hundred wagging tongues. A spirited, self-indulgent and very pregnant magistrate's daughter with a beguiling smile and eyes that seemed to fix on me whichever way her head turned. From what I'd overheard she was the scandal of the town, flaunting her swollen belly at all the fashionable parties just to spite her father, whose respectability she slighted at every opportunity. Cecilia often turned up uninvited and unaccompanied, but no one refused her entrance. The identity of the child's father was a secret she kept to herself like a sheathed sword.

At first I was treated with indifference but, sensing a kindred spirit, she quickly mellowed. I was fascinated with the way she treated all those disapproving faces with light-hearted contempt.

'Were you forced to wear that?' she said, eyeing my gown. 'I thought so. Some mothers insist on making identical poppets of their daughters.'

'Catherine Worledge is not my mother.'

'Old sour face? I'm not surprised. I could never imagine her putting up with the inconvenience of actually having a child.'

I spluttered into my teacup and dropped it on to the table. Cecilia watched me, grinning. I guessed she was very late into her term, at least eight months if my memory of Elizabetta in Florence served me right, and she carried herself as if proud of her condition. As she spoke, voice twittering like a nightingale's, she absently patted her rounded belly. Without warning she grasped my hand and laid it on the swelling.

'He is kicking,' she remarked gleefully. 'Can you feel it? I daresay he is dancing along to the music.'

I pulled my hand back as though it had been bitten. A curious fluttering sensation tickled the back of my throat.

'You get used to it soon enough,' Cecilia laughed. 'Have you ever handled a newborn baby?'

'Yes,' I replied. 'I have.'

She regarded me shrewdly and I wondered what, if anything, she knew about me. There was no time to reflect on it. Despite the scandal surrounding her, Cecilia did not want for dance partners. Time and again some nervous male plucked her out on to the dance floor. Men seemed to partner her to upset wives or sweethearts. Perhaps it was drunken bravado or they did it for a dare. She returned each time flushed and breathless, her eyes glinting.

'Did you see the look on Emma Branton's face when I had her husband in the gavotte,' she chuckled. 'Or the way Mary Smythe glared needles when her dullard of a fiancé couldn't stop talking to me at the end of the dance, then tried to steal a kiss.'

'Does it pleasure you to hurt people so?'

She tucked a loose hair back under her wig and smiled as though I was an ignorant child. 'Oh no, Juliana. They love to hate me. When they go home they will forget their own indiscretions and talk about what a flirt I was, and how I scandalised everyone by monopolising their husbands. They will pray for my soul and take to their beds with an easy conscience.'

'What about the child? Have you no thoughts for its welfare? All this dancing . . .'

But she only laughed and pecked my cheek before being whisked off by another eager partner. I also had my share of time on the floor, but only when Cecilia was already taken. Other than that, I found myself claimed by the old or ugly. Or meek little boys the other girls would not look at. No one to my knowledge succeeded in provoking jealousy from a loved one by dancing with me. If I could, I'd have ripped off Catherine's old gown and burned it on the spot.

When Cecilia returned at the interval she caught the look on my face. 'It's a dangerous game, Juliana,' she confided. 'It takes skill to humiliate our noble friends. One new to society mustn't scratch too deep, or she might find her claws drawn and clipped.'

'Is that a warning?'

'A little advice for the future.'

I didn't answer. Instead I went to fetch us both a drink. The smoky air had left my throat parched. Catherine was not visible anywhere in the room. Adam Fairchild, however, had returned wearing a change of clothes and carrying a silver-topped cane. His menage clustered about him once again. In the course of the evening, Cecilia had hardly affected to notice him. Now, as if reacting to some unspoken cue, they glanced at one another through a gap in the crowd. I caught it on my way back from the refreshment table with a glass of fruit punch in each hand. Their eyes locked for only a moment before returning to more immediate business. In that instance Cecilia spilled all her secrets.

I thrust the glasses into the hands of a startled footman, spilling punch over the front of his shirt. 'Anyone can become his doxy,' I told Cecilia. 'I will prove it to you.'

I elbowed my way between the guests and pushed into his grinning circle. I was his height and able to look him evenly in the eyes, though my throat felt full of rocks.

'Would you favour me with a dance, Mr Fairchild?' I cooed, using the most seductive voice I could muster. ''Twould be a shame to let such fine music go to waste.'

Someone tittered. Adam's dark eyes blinked and the corners crinkled into hundreds of tiny folds. There was something oddly loathsome about him. He was a dish with an undertaste, an apple with a worm lurking just beneath the glossy red flesh. But I willingly put my neck in the noose. I could not help myself. I was standing on the edge of the precipice and being pushed.

He flicked his gaze over me the way a butcher might pass a knife over a shank of meat. 'What an interesting dress.'

He pressed a wine glass to his lips and looked away. With a few words he had cut out my heart and thrown it to the dogs. His admirers laughed openly. I tried to leave the circle but stumbled over an outstretched foot. Recovering myself, I fled into the outer rooms, cheeks burning. I had tried to play the game and ended up a common fool.

I slunk to the entrance of a long, rectangular chamber. Smoke clouded the light from hundreds of guttering candles. The area was dotted with tables, each surrounded by men playing cards. Servants flitted expertly between them, serving drinks, lighting pipes. Beneath a set of tall, heavily curtained windows not more than a dozen paces from where I stood, I spotted Richard's ashen face. Beside him sat the grinning caricature that was George Proudlove.

I stepped forward. A footman's hand restrained me.

'You may not come in here, miss. 'Tis for gentlemen only. The ladies' parlour is further down the passage.'

'That man,' I indicated Richard, 'I need to speak to him.'

'Those guests have left instructions that they are not to be disturbed. I will be happy to convey a message once the game has ended. Now if you please . . .'

I wandered back down the hall, hunting for Catherine. I found her in an alcove with a boy half her age. She laughed like a merry young thing. Rouge smeared both cheeks and her wig sat at a drunken angle. The boy whispered something then nibbled on her ear. Catherine yelped in delight and slapped her thigh, sending her wedding ring tumbling from her scrawny finger. She didn't notice me though I stood within touching distance.

I stooped and picked up the ring. Catherine's foppish friend slid an arm around her waist. I weighed the cool metal in the palm of my hand, running the edge of my thumb along the inside. Something had been engraved there once, wearing down with the years.

Slipping the ring into my reticule, I weaved past revellers towards the front doors. I stood in the lee of the entrance, swallowing warm air in long, tearful gasps. I had come here to conquer and ended up the court fool. I debated whether to walk home. The carriage was not due to collect us for hours. Nearby, a link boy idled beside the boot scraper, his torch sputtering in the moth-speckled night. A stiff breeze whipped the treetops and clouds pondered overhead, underbellies turned silver by a low-slung moon. My imagination populated the darkness with robbers, no doubt lurking just beyond the rectangle of light spilling from the doorway behind me.

I turned back inside. I would wait in the hall until it was time to go home.

'There you are.' Cecilia appeared in a whisper of skirts. 'I thought you'd gone for good, and just when this party was really beginning to liven up.'

'Grown tired of being pampered by your men?' I mocked. 'Or are you saving yourself for a final bite of the apple?'

'Hmm, if not melodramatic then that was certainly poetic,' Cecilia observed. 'It's only natural that a kicked dog should want to snap back. Here, this will help divert you.'

From the bottom of her reticule came an engraved silver box. She prised open the lid. Inside was light brown powder.

'A potent brand of snuff,' she explained. 'Perfect for clearing an overburdened mind. Care to try some?'

'From an admirer?'

'Of course. I told him I was sick of flowers so he brought this. I was astonished at his initiative. I think of him whenever I sneeze.'

Cecilia took a pinch, spread it on the back of her hand and snorted it up each nostril. I followed suit.

'It is very strong,' she warned, 'and might take time to get accustomed to.'

I thought the top of my head was going to explode. I clutched my nose and doubled over. Tears streamed out of my eyes. I sneezed so hard I bit my tongue. Cecilia was beside herself with laughter, but then she sneezed too and that set me off again.

'Let's go back to the ballroom,' she said, struggling for composure, 'and see if we cannot tease a final dance or two out of those dullards before the night is over.'

The journey home found Catherine in a sober mood. Perhaps her dandy had found younger fare. Or the wine might be wearing off and her head was paying the price. Outside, thickening clouds had smothered the moon. The only light was the bobbing will-o'-the-wisps of the carriage lanterns.

Catherine's face was in shadow, but I could sense her watching me. Desperate to break the silence, I spoke first. 'I saw Richard.'

No reply. Paper rustled in the swaying darkness. Perhaps a note from her young beau, though she could not hope to read it.

'I saw Richard,' I said again. 'He was playing cards with a group of gentlemen. He looked very ill, but I was not allowed to see him.'

'You are mistaken,' Catherine responded, tongue as smooth as a viper's. 'Those rooms are always busy and full of smoke. It could have been anyone.'

'But . . .'

'It was not Richard.'

Her words grew jagged edges and her thin knuckles cracked as she pressed her fingers together. A full minute passed before she settled back against her seat.

'George Proudlove was very taken with you,' she said finally. 'He has asked if he may call. I have invited him over this Saturday.'

'I don't remember him.' The lie tripped off my tongue.

'He danced with you.'

'Many men danced with me, most of them badly. He was just another face.'

'A face with a good deal of privilege behind it. Mr Proudlove has a country house, extensive lands and a father in the clergy. You would do well to start thinking about your future, Juliana.'

I leaned across and pressed Catherine's wedding ring into the palm of her hand. 'And you would do well to consider your own.'

As soon as the carriage drew up outside the Butter House I clambered out and dashed inside. Scooping a candlestick from the hall table, I tripped up the stairs in a flurry of skirts, my shadow dancing in the bobbing light. Catherine had taken away the key to my bedchamber and Nancy was in and out as she pleased. But it was the only space in this mostly loveless house I could call my own.

Pulling up a stool, I sat in front of the dresser and regarded myself in the looking glass. My appraisal was honest and painful. What I saw staring back at me was a creature without life or spirit. Only in my eyes was there a spark, something that Catherine's old clothes could do nothing to disguise.

I pulled off the wig in a shower of white powder and wiped the paint from my cheeks. Beneath the dull mask was the girl who had so handsomely bloomed in the Italian sun.

My skin had cleared, my hair was a rich copper and my eyes as bright as diamonds.

I wanted back the rouge and the fine Italian perfumes. Most of all I wanted a dress. A real dress, not some hand-me-down sack. And I determined to get it, whatever the cost. Never again would any man dismiss me with a glance or unkind word.

I smiled at myself in the polished looking glass, remembering Cecilia's swollen belly, the laughter we had shared.

But first there was Richard.

I wanted to save him but not because of love. My motives were entirely selfish. I did not know how many secrets concerning my past were locked up in this house, but I felt sure that my position was safe only for as long as Richard lived. He spent much of his time indoors now, too ill or drunk to go anywhere. He rose late and, when he emerged from his bedchamber at all, chose to sit in the study surrounded by his books. There he drank bottle after bottle whilst Blake played the humble servant and brought in more whenever Richard called for it.

Then Blake disappeared for a while. Catherine continued her visits to the library and salons. I seized upon this brief opportunity, not realising that my most formidable enemy would prove to be Richard himself.

I tried to help him. Swearing the maid to silence, I watered down the brandy, but Richard noticed and smashed the bottle against the study wall. He continued to drink as if filling his body with poison could somehow clear his mind, would help him make sense of his crumbling world. He squatted in his chair behind that huge mahogany desk, bills and I.O.U.s spread out in front of him. A dazed, almost amused look sat on his face, as if he did not understand what was happening to him or what to do about it. Talking achieved nothing but a slurred jumble of words. He neglected to change his clothes. Servants glanced at one another behind his back.

I never returned to the study in those terrible days. All its former magic had slipped down Richard's throat along with the port and brandy. A pall of tobacco smoke clung to the furnishings.

His illness spread through the house. I began to find more and more empty bottles. In the end I didn't even have to search before stumbling across them. I lined up a dozen on Richard's desk while he sat there, slack-jawed. He swore in his slurred tongue that he did not know where they had come from. I explained how I had found some in the hall outside his bedchamber, others in the privy or littering the path outside the back door.

'I do not know what you mean, Juliana. Pray stop haranguing me. I am very weary.'

Anger? I was too afraid for him, for myself, to be angry. I was losing the battle. He was slipping away from me like a thief in the night. He was almost always sick, retching for minutes on end, even when his belly was empty. Bile flecked his lips.

I asked Catherine to send for a surgeon, but she waved me away and went back to reading her letters. 'No one is to be summoned to house without my approval,' she warned. 'Richard has shamed us enough. Do you understand, Juliana?'

I understood perfectly. Richard was killing himself, or being murdered, and there was nothing I could do to stop it. To stop them. He was falling into the pit and I was afraid. I became irritable and snapped at everyone. Exhaustion circled my eyes with dark rings. Next time I looked in the mirror I saw someone on the verge of being broken. The image frightened me, so I resorted to lies for protection. I wrote letters to Mary Morgan and Cecilia, and filled them full of happy thoughts even as tears blurred my tired eyes.

Catherine and I were like two feral cats edging on one another's territory, ready to bare claws and fangs if either stepped over the mark. She was the mistress of the house, but we had learned how to prick each other. In that sense we were equals.

Over coffee, she turned the conversation to George Proudlove, mentioning him at every opportunity as though determined not to let him slip from my mind even for a minute. She watched me constantly. After a few days I found it hard to keep my temper. I even started to have bad dreams about the man, populating my nights with visions of his round, grinning face.

Letters arrived at the house, which Catherine zealously pushed into my hands. All the seals were broken, and they were all full of nonsense. Rambling paragraphs bored me with news of his estate, his parents, and admiration for me that, he declared, knew no bounds. He reiterated his desire to call and once enclosed a shiny guinea as 'a gesture of goodwill'. Did he think me a harlot?

'You must write back,' Catherine gushed, hovering around me like a bluebottle until I had read every last word of these tiresome missives. 'He is a good man from a fine family. You need to repay his kindness, Juliana.'

Later, I gave the guinea to William and instructed that any letters not from Mr Proudlove should be handed directly to me. Catherine was not to be told. He brought two, still sealed, and crumpled where he had stuffed them into his pocket. One was from Cecilia inviting me to tea. The other was from Mary Morgan. She was being courted by a widower called Ernest Pettit. He'd had his eye on her for a while but Mary had been too smothered in her own gloom to notice.

'I am sure he will propose within the week,' she wrote, 'and an early wedding is likely. He has been making certain arrangements that he believes I do not know about. Such a sweet, naïve man! My only sorrow is that such a union would not be graced with children. Ernest's wife died in childbirth and the baby did not survive. However, we will find solace in our books and our mutual affection. I know that you will give us your blessing.'

It gladdened my heart that love should have found my friend after she had believed herself abandoned by it, gladness that turned bitter as I thought of the lies I would have to tell her in return. I did not want her to be concerned about me, or spoil her happiness with tales of my own misfortune. I pushed both letters under the rug and went to find Catherine. I wanted out of the house and was willing to make up any excuse. As it happened, she provided one for me.

'You have had another lovely letter from George,' she said, smiling at me from the parlour couch. 'He is in town on business and has asked to call. I have sent a messenger to his lodgings and anticipate his arrival a little after one o' clock. I expect you to receive him warmly.'

'You have no right to read my letters,' I told her. 'Whoever they are from.'

'Nonsense. As your guardian it is my duty and I shall continue to do so until you come of age.' She regarded me from beneath her thick eyelashes. 'Or you are married.'

She took some coins out of her purse and dropped them into my hand. 'You are spending too much time flapping around Richard. Go and buy yourself some fresh rouge to make yourself presentable to Mr Proudlove. And cover up that mark.'

Catherine offered the use of her carriage but I said I would walk or take a chair. I did not care for her driver watching my every move. In the street I hailed a sedan and gave the address Cecilia Fortescue had penned on her letter. It took me to the house she shared with her father, a lumbering block of a structure surrounded by stone walls and rumble-tumble gardens.

Cecilia's papa was a gruff, learned man with a stooped back and a ring of silver hair framing his face. He treated me with polite reserve at first, but I was at my charming best and he soon mellowed. Cecilia greeted me with a kiss and we sat in her parlour with two steaming dishes of tea.

Whilst the clock on the mantelpiece dragged its hands through the hours, we exchanged gossip whilst avoiding the one subject that was close to both our hearts. More than once I felt she was working up to telling me something, but the maid would come in, or she'd lose her nerve, or something else would occur to distract her. When it had gone three o' clock I took my leave with a promise to visit again. As we embraced, the swell of her belly pressed against me and I fancied I could feel the child moving inside.

Catherine was in a terrible rage when I returned unrepentant and without the rouge she'd sent me out to buy. She wished all the ten plagues of Egypt upon my head for making poor George wait and then not turning up to greet him.

'He is not my friend, my beau or my kin,' I told her. 'I have no wish to see him today or any day. If you are so taken with George then why not wed him yourself since you seem so determined to become a widow.'

Dishes of cold tea littered the withdrawing room table and George's cologne hung in the air like a bad memory. The door hung open. In the hall, Nancy was on her knees trying to scrub the floor.

'George wants your hand in marriage,' Catherine told me flatly. 'He has agreed to settle a handsome sum on you.'

'More money with which to poison Richard?'

'That is his choice. Women can rarely interfere in male matters, less so when it involves their own husband.'

'So am I little better than a horse or pig a farmer might sell at the town market?'

'You will benefit the most from this. I can think of no better match for a daughter of mine.'

'Daughter? I am a member of your family only when it suits, Catherine. You have told me about George's house and lands often enough. What a rich pie to dip your finger into. Is this what you have been grooming me for, why you took me to the ball? To parade in front of him? How well you have planned it.'

Catherine didn't answer. She strolled over to the mantel-piece in a whisper of skirts and returned with a small, satin-covered box, which she held out to me. 'George wants you for his wife,' she repeated. 'Here, wear his ring. He planned to give it to you himself, but has grown weary of bending to your whims. The banns will be read and you will be Mrs Proudlove before the season is through. Do your duty by me, Juliana.'

'Is there no end to this?' I said quietly, staring at the box. 'You would have everything of Richard's and now you intend to meddle with my future. Very well, if George is to wed me then he must formally propose. I do not deal with a go-between; he must snare me himself. We shall see if he is man enough at least for that.'

Chapter Seven

I was helpless in the face of Richard's self-destruction. His creditors, tired of being fobbed off with excuses, sent messengers to our front door in ever-greater numbers. Most were content to leave with a few guineas and a promise of more, but one man brandished a fistful of I.O.U.s and threatened to see the magistrate if his dues were not settled in full. Blake, who was always on hand when there were debts to be paid, leaned forward and grumbled something in his ear. The man's face turned as white as fresh bread and he stumbled back down the steps. The I.O.U.s flurried out of his hands. Later they were torn up and fed to the kitchen fire.

The wine merchant, however, received prompt payment and the following day arrived with a cartload of clinking bottles. I went out to meet him and, while petting his bony draught horse, begged him not to deliver any more. He laughed and told me it wouldn't make any difference.

'Can't stop a man drinking if he has a mind to,' the merchant explained. 'More'n enough taverns to keep 'im happy if he can't get none at home. I don't aim to let no alehouse or gentleman's club get any o' my business.'

When I was not looking out for Richard, I dodged George. I burned his letters and tore the heads off his flowers, littering the carpet with fractured blooms. He was in town for a week and took every opportunity to seek me out, wearing ever more outlandish clothes in his efforts to impress. Always the perfect gentleman in front of Catherine, he stammered and blustered when left alone with me.

97

'What does he want with me?' I asked, exasperated after one such visit.

'It is understandable that a single gentleman of some means would wish to call on an eligible young lady,' Catherine replied.

'I didn't ask to become the object of his affections.'

'Do you consider yourself so unique that you can pick and choose? Peasants do that and they breed like undisciplined curs.'

'George is pushing into my life as if he has a right to it. He grinds me down like a pebble on a bad tooth.'

Despite my attitude, he remained persistent. On Monday he left in a temper. On Tuesday he greeted me like an old friend. On Wednesday he found courage in the bottle. A few swigs of brandy and he blurted out all his plans. Catherine had given her consent. I would become George's harlot, only the word he used was 'wife'.

'You would make me very happy,' he slurred, fumbling his empty glass.

'What of my happiness?' I countered, 'or does that particular balance not enter into your accounts?'

He smiled, trying to put some charm into it. 'I would do everything within my power to ensure that happiness.'

'Then do not pester me with dead flowers, badly written letters or unwelcome proposals made over the rim of a brandy glass. With no choices I can never be happy, under this roof or yours.'

'Your guardian, Mrs Worledge, has said . . .'

'Richard Worledge is my guardian,' I corrected. 'Speak to him before you try to steal my life.'

On Thursday I overheard George talking with Catherine in the drawing room. They tossed my name back and forth as if playing a game of shuttlecock.

'This is becoming a bore, Catherine,' George said. 'Can't the girl be made to see sense? A good father would have beaten the reluctance out of her. I would be home with my dogs and she with my heir in her belly. I grow weary of playing games just to pander to her pride.'

'All part of the courtship game, George,' Catherine soothed. 'Be patient. Even a rock wears away with time.'

'Time is a commodity I cannot afford to squander, madam. I have stayed overlong in this wretched town already. Bring her to reason, or my patience will go the way of my temper. All I need is a legal consent and she is mine. Are you sure your husband cannot be made to sign? Is there no other way?'

Catherine laughed. 'You are too greedy to let Juliana go. While Richard lives she is under his protection. Drink may have befuddled his mind but he is all too aware of her worth.'

Silence fell between them. Then George grunted. 'Very well. I must conclude my business soon. Other matters demand my attention and my estate goes begging. I shall return a week today. I need not remind you, Catherine, that you also have a considerable investment in this enterprise. It is in both our interests to succeed.'

I sought refuge with Cecilia. I called on her in secret while Catherine was at the library or the new literary circle she had joined. I never directly mentioned George Proudlove, though with her connections Cecilia must have known he was in town and spending a great deal of time at Catherine's house. But she was as circumspect with her own affairs as she was with mine.

'What will become of the child?' I kept asking. She always responded with a beguiling little cut of the lips and turned the conversation to something else. Cecilia was not a creature of this world. Watching her, seated on the parlour couch beside me with the sunlight turning strands of her hair into bright fingers, it was easy to believe that she was a ghost or a dream, which would fade from sight with only a chuckle, like music tinkling on the wind, to remind me that she had ever been there. We gossiped, spun yarns, listened to each other's stories. But her secrets remained locked away in some inner place. Getting her to talk about Adam Fairchild was akin to drawing a nail out of a stout oak with your teeth.

On the third Saturday of the month I found Mr Fortescue waiting for me in the hallway. I'd tried a few hands of whist with Cecilia but the baby was pressing heavily and she'd retired for a nap. Everything she did required great effort and her rosy complexion had been replaced by a pallid, sickly look that reminded me too much of Richard.

'Don't fret so, Juliana,' she'd said, regarding me through puffy eyelids. 'It's just a touch of the vapours.'

She summoned the maid to help her upstairs. I saw myself out, but her papa stopped me at the front door.

'I would have words with you, Miss Rodriguez,' he said, tugging on his neck cloth. The ring finger of his left hand was missing, and his expression as he eyed me was unreadable. He sat me down in his oak-panelled study in a leather armchair that almost swallowed me whole. I waited while he poured himself a glass of brandy. He stared out of the window for a few moments, as if the answers to all the world's conundrums lay in the streets outside. Finally, he seated himself opposite me, his desk an expanse of polished wood between us, and spoke, steepling his fingers beneath his chin.

'You must tell her to get rid of it,' he began. 'I will not have a bastard take my name and sit at my table.'

He paused. I didn't say anything. He swallowed a mouthful of brandy and slapped the glass down on the desk. 'For months I've watched her belly swell. I have had to suffer the derision of others while she pushes her way out of my affections. Do you know who the father is? No? Well, I doubt you would tell me even if you did. A gentleman would already have embraced his responsibilities. A man without honour is not worth knowing.'

He picked up a framed etching from the corner of his

desk. A portrait of his wife, I guessed. Cecilia told me she'd caught some terrible sickness while in India and had taken weeks to die. All Mr Fortescue's money couldn't save her and he'd not ventured abroad since. Even now he stared at the etching as if he could will her back to life. Grief ploughed his face. I fancied that if I touched his cheek I would find it as cold and unyielding as iron.

'You are Cecilia's only genuine friend,' he continued, replacing the etching. 'Her peers are too concerned with their reputations to willingly become involved with her. I love my daughter but I am a pragmatic man. Someone has poked her for a marriage dowry, or to press me financially over the child. Either way, they want a cut of my fortune. I cannot permit that. It would open the door for every libertine in the county. I am not cruel, Miss Rodriguez, but she must dispose of the child. You must convince her.'

A clock chimed somewhere deep in the house. Mr Fortescue checked his fob watch, made an adjustment then returned it to his waistcoat pocket.

'What if I was to take the baby?' I said.

He eyed me shrewdly and lit a pipe, filling the air above his head with rich blue smoke. 'How will you accomplish this? You are hardly at an age to legally adopt.'

'I know a respectable person in want of a child. You won't see or hear about it again.'

'You can assure me of that?'

'Yes.'

'And you wish payment in return?'

My fingers curled into fists. 'Not payment. A favour.'

'Pray continue.'

'I need a dress. Something Italian with an embroidered front and a sprinkling of bows. I have an important assignation and my guardian's household budget will not stretch to anything she considers frivolous.'

He nodded. My fingers relaxed.

*

I rode a sedan chair home with the smile of a witch painting my face. When I arrived at the Butter House, Maggie Burns was squatting on the front step bawling her eyes out. Behind her, the door hung open. The first fallen leaves of autumn gusted into the hall in a flurry of red and gold.

I stepped out of the chair, paid the bearers with a sum Mr Fortescue had given me and hurried over. 'Maggie, what's wrong?'

'Mr Worledge is dying,' she blubbed. 'He's been drinking all night. Bottle after bottle, and always screaming for more. William has gone to fetch the surgeon but I doubt he could get here in time even if he sprouted wings.'

She buried her face in her apron. I shook her. 'Where is Catherine?'

'Shut in her bedchamber with the door locked. She says there's naught to be done.'

I gritted my teeth and ran past her into the bowels of the house. A terrible sapping heat choked the study. The windows were shut tight and the fire stoked into a roaring, spitting demon with a bellyful of sparks. Richard's legs poked out from beneath his desk. He had fallen from his chair and lay with his shoulders propped against the polished globe that dominated the corner of the room. A vast world mapped out in faded reds and greens on which Richard had shown me the faraway places visited by his ships before he spun it into a blur of colour.

At first I thought he was dead. His eyes were open and fixed. Then I heard a drawn out sigh – a sound filled with pain. I knelt beside him. The carpet was a swamp of spilled drink, broken glass and bottle corks. Richard did not seem drunk. He had gone beyond that. He spoke as if his mind had been detached from his poisoned body the way a quack might lop off a gangrenous limb. He regarded me with a dreadful clarity, his eyes staring into my own with a child's innocence as if he could not fathom what he'd done to himself.

I was no doctor. I didn't know what part of him had broken, had finally given up under a swill of brandy. The life was slipping out of his body as if some devil had tapped into him and was draining his spirit away.

'I kept my promise.' Each word climbed painfully out of Richard's throat. 'You held on to your name.'

His lips broke apart in an agonised smile. 'The only thing in which Catherine failed to get her own way. She was sour for years because of it.'

'What promise? What vows have you made, Richard? And to whom?'

A coughing fit wracked his body. Blood flecked his chin. 'Manuel,' he wheezed. 'Your father, Juliana. God help me . . .'

I gripped his shoulders, my knuckles white against his green velvet jacket. 'Forget my father. I know about him. Who was my mother, Richard? Catherine is a soulless woman who will tear my life into pieces. You must help me. There is no one else.'

His face turned a dreadful pallor. A spasm coursed through his chest. He kicked out, splitting his shoe on the edge of the desk. He whispered two words as the last breath rattled out of his lungs.

'Littlejohn knows . . .'

I rose and backed away, staring down at his supine form. In the hearth, a log split open and spat a shower of yellow sparks into the chimney's black mouth.

A rustle of satin. Catherine filled the doorway. Pastry crumbs ringed her mouth.

'You let him die,' I accused.

'Did you try to help him up?' She stepped into the room. 'Did you run to fetch water? Hold his hand? Offer comfort?'

I looked away. 'You never loved him. Not from the day you married or even before.'

'How could I? He was forced upon me, thrust into my life by a man greedy for a fat dowry and a wife for his

103

doltish son. Richard was grateful that I never hated him. I felt too much pity for that.'

'Thrust upon you the way you would force George Proudlove on me?'

'Selfish as always, even as you kneel beside the man who succoured you. Make the best of it, Juliana. Worse things could happen to a young woman in your position. Marriage will bring respect and a roof over your head.'

'Provided I pander to my husband's whims?'

'Perhaps you will prove clever enough to turn things your way. Richard was never my master.' She eyed the body of her husband. 'Now don't you think you ought to find something to cover him up?'

Richard was buried with little fuss amidst the brambles and lop-sided tombstones of the town cemetery. He had no surviving relatives. A scattering of mourners coughed into their handkerchiefs. A persistent drizzle had fallen all morning, deadening the parson's voice.

I bawled most of the way through the brief ceremony, despite Catherine pinching my arm. She'd borrowed a black dress from a widow friend because she did not want to spend money on a new mourning gown. I had to make do with more of her old clothes. A strip of black velvet knotted above my elbow was the only mark of respect permitted.

My tears dried abruptly. Mr Littlejohn stood on the other side of the cemetery, mopping the drizzle from his brow with a crumpled handkerchief. He appeared shorter and thinner than I remembered. His clothes were a battered hodgepodge of fading colours and frayed cuffs. I tried to catch his eye but he stared at the open grave.

Muddy water was already swilling around Richard's coffin. The parson snapped his prayer book shut, a signal for the gravediggers to pick up their shovels. The mourners immediately started to drift away, some hurrying to their coaches as the clouds darkened further. A few stopped to

104

offer Catherine their condolences. While she went through the act of the stricken widow I slipped away from her side and pursued Mr Littlejohn. He strode down the path towards the gate, coat flapping, tricorne pulled over his forehead. I caught up with him as he reached his hired sedan chair.

'Mr Littlejohn, I would speak with you, please.'

He shrugged me off, clambered inside and slammed the door. He made to signal the bearers with his cane, thought for a moment then leaned out. His nose twitched as though he could scent some terrible threat in the air, one that had nothing to do with the blackening clouds.

'It is not good for us to be seen together,' he warned. 'Come and see me at the shipping office. No, that'll likely be locked. Go to my residence in Brook Street. I will meet you there.'

He slumped back in his seat, tapped the roof of the carriage and was off, leaving me standing on the path with his calling card clutched in my hand.

'What business did you have with Richard's colleague?' Catherine demanded as our coach rumbled back into town.

I spluttered something about wanting to thank him for coming. 'Richard had so few real friends,' I added.

She eyed me carefully. I saw the questions, the poisonous thoughts brewing in the dark cauldron of her mind. 'Are you sure that is all? He seemed in an uncommon hurry to be gone.'

'I daresay he wanted out of the rain.'

'Stay away from that man. He is an old fool with a head full of nonsense. Mr Worledge involved him in the company as an act of kindness. He felt it his duty, a debt to an old acquaintance. I am under no such obligation.'

She was quiet for a few moments. 'From now on you are not to address me as 'Catherine'. I no longer consider it appropriate.'

'Yes, Mrs Worledge.'

She nodded. 'Many things will change now that Mr Worledge has died. His obligations were further reaching than you can imagine. Promises were also made that, as far as I am concerned, perished with him. We will discuss some of these later.'

That afternoon I watched as every scrap of Richard's existence was stripped from the Butter House. His clothes were given to the parish, his books crated and taken away to be sold. His private chambers were cleared and his bed shrouded beneath white sheets. Nancy scrubbed the floors and walls then burned sulphur so that even the scent of him was driven out.

Alone in his study, I gazed at the rows of empty bookshelves. The desk had been removed along with most of the other furnishings. My steps echoed on the bare floorboards. I was torn between a sense of loss for the only guardian I'd known, and an urge to seek out Mr Littlejohn. He claimed it wasn't safe to be seen with me. Safe for whom?

I dressed sombrely for dinner – really I had little choice – and made my way to the dining room as the last afternoon light faded into the blue-greys of evening. Blake was perched in Richard's chair, a glass of red wine by his hand and serving dishes spread out in front of him. He was peacock pretty in the finest velvet and satin. His dark, lank hair was swept back behind his head and secured with a large bow. A silk cravat tumbled down the front of his embroidered waistcoat.

I frowned. The fit was too good for Richard's clothes. Where had Blake obtained them? He lit a pipe and settled back in the chair. Catherine sat opposite. She smiled and dabbed her mouth with a napkin. Her gown was spotless, all sparkling whites and blues. Her teeth glimmered in the candlelight. She looked genuinely happy for the first time in years.

William took away their soup bowls. Blake waited until the boy returned with a platter of meat and a fresh bottle of wine. It was as though Richard's debts were so much waste paper, and all the precious items that had been sold to try to pay for them were of no consequence.

I was drawn into the flickering pool of light. Gold glinted on Blake's finger. He wore Richard's wedding ring. His hands were a smooth, pale pink with neatly trimmed fingernails. Yet he handled his wine glass like a town bawd.

Catherine spotted me and laid her fork beside her plate. 'You are late. How long have you been standing there?'

My voice sounded small in the high-ceilinged room. 'I want to dine in the kitchen.'

'What?'

'I won't sit at the table. I'd sooner starve.'

Blake burst into laughter and had to push his napkin into his mouth to keep from choking. 'She'd rather eat with the servants, would she?' he said, recovering. 'Our company doesn't suit, then?'

'You *are* a servant,' I reminded him.

His mirth turned to anger in a wink. He made to rise from his chair but Catherine stilled him with a raised hand. 'Very well,' she told me. 'Perhaps a little time in the kitchen might teach you something about managing a household. A useful skill in a new wife. I'm sure George would agree.'

And, with a tilt of her head, I was dismissed.

Maggie Burns didn't utter a word of complaint when I appeared in her kitchen with a grumbling belly. She sat me on a stool, piled a trencher high with leftovers and left me to get on with it. Next day my bedchamber was left untidied. When I collared Nancy she squirmed out of my grasp.

'Let me go,' she howled. 'Mrs Worledge says you've to do it yourself.'

So I struggled upstairs with bundles of linen, made the bed, brushed down the rug and caught a faceful of smoke when I tried to kindle the fire. Blisters quickly sprouted on hands that felt clumsy and awkward. The simplest tasks became a challenge.

Thankfully, William still ran errands for me. When I spoke to him his cheeks often turned radish red. He would find a stammer from somewhere, his blush deepening as his words fell over themselves in an effort to escape his mouth. Nancy's disgust was palpable.

Within the week, a gaggle of wintry-faced lawyers descended on the house, sporting old leather bags stuffed with papers for Catherine to sign. I couldn't eavesdrop as Nancy had been keeping an especially sharp eye on me these past couple of days, as if at any moment I might disappear into a closet with William. When Catherine saw the men to the door, a look of grim satisfaction sat on her face. I recalled the I.O.U.s and waited for an army of creditors to arrive and slice up the household, but no one came.

Blake was out most days, slipping from the house like a thief and not returning until dusk. Everyone was full of talk.

George Proudlove returned to Wexborough at the end of the week and promptly invited himself to dinner. He seemed in high spirits and greeted Catherine like an old friend. I was ordered to resume my place at the dining-room table.

When it came to eating and trying to talk at the same time, Mr Proudlove was an artiste. He had kind words for Nancy, and tipped William handsomely for the mere act of delivering the roast duckling. Unsurprisingly, it was left to Catherine to condemn me.

'You will wed Mr Proudlove at the end of the month,' she said. 'The ceremony will take place in his local church.'

George nodded eagerly whilst stuffing his mouth with carrots. He dropped his fork, grabbed my hand and crammed a ring on to my finger. The gem was as big as my knuckle but had a cheap look to it and the silver band pinched my flesh.

'There,' he declared. 'Now we are betrothed.'

I sat and let my dinner grow cold while they divided my life up like buccaneers sharing a trunk of booty. I could sense Catherine's triumph. After dinner, George signed the papers, sealing my future with ink and wax. He had bought me the way he might a horse at a market and there was nothing I could do about it.

At the end of George's visit, I was pushed towards the front door to bid him farewell. He paused on the step, the wind catching his coat and flapping it out like crow's wings. He leaned towards me and pressed his lips against my cheek. I recoiled. George was unfazed.

'A first kiss for the soon-to-be blushing bride,' he said. He buttoned up his coat, bid Catherine good fortune and let the night swallow him up. All that remained was the orange glow of smouldering tobacco where he'd emptied his pipe into the gutter, but his scent lingered on my skin.

Back inside the house, I tied on an apron and helped the servants clear the table, the very table at which I'd dined. After lugging a pile of plates down to the kitchen I rinsed my face in dishwater and rubbed it dry with a linen rag. No use. I could still smell him, and his ring wouldn't budge no matter how hard I tugged. Even smearing my finger with a dollop of fat from the turnspit failed to shift the cursed thing.

That's how I stood, by the leftover vegetables, squeezing back tears. I'd held them in so often lately I thought my insides must be swimming, that I'd start to leak through my nose and ears, perhaps the pores of my skin.

George might have my hand in marriage but he'd not stain his bed sheets with my blood. I'd wear his ring, but no heir of his would swell my womb.

I had no illusions about losing my virginity. Catherine had given me the 'wifely duties' talk and seemed dismayed that I wasn't as shocked as she thought I'd be. But I'd heard the parlour whispers among the older girls at the tea parties I'd attended. Cecilia Fortescue didn't get pregnant just by wishing a child inside her belly. Men became fathers by doing more than smiling at a girl in a comely way. I'd heard about blood and pain. I knew how horrible childbirth could be, that you 'might die'. But I'd listened to the other stories too and knew there were ways to stop it.

109

So who was to deprive George? William? No, his intentions were always good but his will power would crumble in front of Catherine. It would sour Nancy for good and ruin him, even if he had the wit to know that his manhood was meant for more than just piddling through.

Our coachman? He was an idle oaf with a foul temper. Rumour said a dose of the pox had nearly cost a kitchen maid her life when she grew too enamoured of him.

Over the next few days I appraised every man with a whore's eye. Finally, salvation arrived in the shape of a dirty-faced brute called Moses Cripps.

Chapter Eight

He turned up at the kitchen door with bloody shank of beef thrown over one shoulder. Rain hammered down, but he wore nothing other than a rough pair of canvas breeches, a linen shirt open to the waist and scuffed leather sandals. He pushed into the kitchen warmth. Steam began rolling off his soaking clothes in lazy wisps that curled towards the ceiling.

I coughed on my breakfast and stared. Milk trickled from my open mouth. His arms were smeared with grease, his hair – long and raven black – lay slick against his skull. He threw the shank down on the kitchen table. Bone shattered. Lumps of gristle showered on to the floor.

'Here's your beef for the week, Maggie,' he rumbled. 'A good cut, just 'cause I'm so soft on you.' He looked more beast than man. A thatch of black hair sprouted across his chest and down to his navel, where it clustered at the waist of his breeches.

'Pagan out of his wits again?' Maggie asked from her place at the fire.

'He is that,' the visitor laughed. 'Won't see him out of his bed till Monday morn, I reckon. They've done keepin' his pew over at Queen's Church, seein' as how he never turns up for Sunday service.'

Pagan was the local flesher, an enormously fat, almost spherical man with a belly like a church bell and a thick beard smoking his chin. Since taking myself to the kitchen I'd caught a string of tales about this notorious drunkard.

He employed a number of men to do his carting and carrying, freed criminals mostly so he could pay them less.

Footpad? Smuggler? Moses had the eyes of a hanged man. A smell, a heady mix of butchery and sweat clung to him like a shroud. He turned those eyes on me. 'Who's the wench?' he asked Maggie, wiping his hands on his breeches. 'A new maid? I thought that flint-eyed mistress of yours was keeping a tight purse these days?'

'Mind your mouth. Juliana was in Mr Worledge's charge.'

'So what's she doing in the kitchen eating off a wooden trencher? Not much of a lady if you ask me. My ma was buried in a better gown than that dusty old thing.'

I couldn't find a word of reply anywhere in my head. Suddenly he lunged towards me, teeth bared. I shrieked and scrabbled backwards off the bench. His laughter was like river water pouring over a lip of rock. I sat on the floor, fuming. Maggie laughed too. 'Come back day after next, Moses,' she said, wiping her eyes with the corner of her apron. 'Mrs Worledge wants a cut of ham and cook needs some bacon.'

'Got plenty o' bacon already,' he declared, squeezing the maid's behind. She squealed and batted at his thick arms until he let her go. She paid him with money out of her jar. Still laughing, he strode back out into the rain. A cart and dray horse waited in the street. Moses vaulted on to the driver's seat and kicked the animal into motion. He glanced back into the kitchen before the doorframe cut him from view. He wasn't looking at Maggie, but at me. The rain pummelled his skin, crisscrossing his chest with wet stripes.

I could have bludgeoned him to death with his own shank of beef for the way he'd dismissed me. I resented his familiarity with Maggie, his easy, rolling gait as though walking around the very world posed no great inconvenience, and his words which had run roughshod over us both. I thought of those muscles and stared at the lump of beef that lay, leaking blood and rainwater, on the kitchen table. I imagined him picking it up and tearing it to shreds with his bare hands.

Maggie closed the kitchen door and tried to straighten her mobcap. She regarded me for a few moments, her eyes round and shining. Her fingers fumbled on the cap. Perspiration spiked her face, though the fire had not yet been banked for the night's cooking.

'Mind yourself around Moses Cripps,' she laughed. 'It's only a bit of harmless mischief but he forgets his place sometimes.'

'Does he have a wife?'

'Aye, and she's a hard woman at that. Bear it in mind next time you fix your eyes on the crack of his shirt.'

That night I went to sleep with the smell of raw meat still in my nostrils. I awoke, tired and irritable, to find myself sent to the market with Maggie. We walked along thronging streets, skirting puddles and gutters brimming with refuse. The market was a squeeze. Everyone seemed to be yelling. I fidgeted while Maggie fussed over everything, discarding a parcel of flour then choosing another that to my eyes looked exactly the same. Nothing she saw was right, nothing quite good enough to grace the kitchen. When she was finally satisfied, her purchases barely covered the bottom of her basket and my feet were fit to drop off.

'It'll be a carriage for you when you wed Mr Proudlove,' she remarked as I hobbled along, desperately trying to avoid her swinging basket. I was too tired to think of any sensible reply and my belly was rumbling. It was already past noon. The rains of the past few days had lifted their wet skirts and gone elsewhere. Puddles shrivelled and the mud was baked into cracked flakes.

A carriage was waiting in the lane outside the stable yard when we arrived back at the Butter House. On top sat a po-faced coachman, stiff in a green coat.

'Hello, who's this?' Maggie remarked. 'I've not seen that carriage round these parts before.'

Entering the kitchen we discovered a lady's maid sitting

113

at the table with tears smearing her face. 'Miss Rodriguez,' she said, getting up off the bench, 'you must come at once. Miss Cecilia's birthing has started, but the child is lying badly in the womb. The midwife says it is cursed and will not touch it. Mr Fortescue has sent for a surgeon but Miss Cecilia is asking for you. We are all afraid she will die.'

'I don't know anything about birthing children.'

'Please, miss, she needs a friend.'

So I found myself riding in a fine carriage much sooner than Maggie Burns or myself had anticipated. The driver ran the team at a cracking pace. However, when a couple of vegetable carts blocked the street the shouting match he had with their owners drew a jeering crowd. A good half-hour passed before we were underway again.

The maid's face was a pudding of tears. She took her sodden handkerchief away from her face long enough to tell me that her name was Emily. 'There had been birth pains before,' she blubbed, 'but they always came to nothing. The child was not due for another two weeks. Miss Cecilia doesn't know what to do. She lies in bed screaming fit to frighten the devil and spilling blood over the sheets.'

I grasped her wrists and tried to calm her down. 'Has anyone else called at the house? Mr Fairchild perhaps?'

She gawped. 'No, miss. None have called save the midwife.'

Mr Fortescue was waiting in the hall. 'The worst is over,' he told me.

'The surgeon arrived? He took care of her?'

He shook his head. 'Our usual surgeon was nowhere to be found. Ten guineas bought a quack who scratched like a dog and stank of gin. No reputable doctor would come, no matter what fee I offered. They are all afraid of bringing scandal upon themselves, and their good names are apparently worth more than the life of my girl.'

'And the child?'

He sighed. 'It will live, whether through a miracle or a curse I cannot yet tell. My daughter has birthed a bastard boy with a thatch of dark hair and a chubby hand dipped into my fortune. What is it about these libertines that allows them to worm their way into young women's hearts with such ease? Not one possesses an ounce of decency. I loved Cecilia's mother. Loved her from the day we were first introduced. She was the only girl I courted. These rakes collect conquests they way some men display duelling scars. Honest daughters are made deaf to their fathers' concerns, and are blinded to these wastrels' lack of scruples. You can say to a girl: "Look at his bastards, look at the broken hearts – at the families' hearts", and off they'll go, at the flick of a whisker, to soil themselves at these creatures' hands. An irresistible poison, Miss Rodriguez; a foul brew from which they willingly sup. The more they have, the deeper they fall. Where is the sense in it?'

'Perhaps there is no sense to love.'

'Love has naught to do with it. This is wilful degradation. Cecilia is so moonstruck by this man she is incapable of making proper choices. Well, by God, I'll take the hook out of her mouth.'

'May I see Cecilia?'

He waved in the direction of the stairs. 'Yes, for whatever good it might do. The surgeon had to cut her to get the baby out, but she's of strong stock like her mother and will survive to shame me once again. Emily will take you to Cecilia's bedchamber. I cannot go in there.'

As I passed him, he laid a hand on my shoulder. 'We had a bargain, Miss Rodriguez. I trust you will remember it.'

Cecilia's bedchamber was a billowy temple of pale cream linen and lace-trimmed curtains. The windows were flung wide, permitting a breeze to waft about the room like a mischievous spirit.

'Please wait outside,' I instructed Emily. 'I wish to talk with Miss Fortescue alone.'

'But . . .'

'Do it.'

I thought she might try to defy me, but after a moment's thought she stepped back into the passage. A quick check ensured that she was not lingering by the keyhole then I secured the door and hurried over to the bed. Cecilia lay swaddled in a white eiderdown with a wet cloth pressed against her forehead. Sweat coated her face. Both eyes were closed and she seemed unaware of my presence. How tiny she looked, so fragile in this huge bed. The linen had been changed, but the air was coloured with smells. I sat beside her and found her hand. Her fingers curled around mine, the flesh clammy. Her eyes fluttered open and her gaze settled on me.

'Juliana.' Her voice cracked like twigs in a fire. 'Where is he? Why is he not here?'

I tried to summon a smile. It dried on my face. 'He is not coming. He was never coming. For all your wiles, you were foolish to believe otherwise.'

Cecilia's eyelids fluttered. I could not be sure she had heard me. Her breathing was harsh and the skin around her mouth pinched.

'A son. I have given him a son. If he could not love me then I hoped at least . . .'

She drifted off again into that semi-dark place where the hurt seek refuge. I released her hand and rose from the bed, absently wiping my fingers on my gown. Out in the hall, Emily was nowhere to be seen. I caught her coming back up the stairs.

'Where is the baby?' I demanded.

She halted on the steps. 'Cook took it into the kitchen to clean it. The doctor left right away, and Mr Fortescue won't come out of his study.'

'Has Cecilia held the child? Does he have a name?'

'No, miss. She wouldn't look at it. The doctor dosed her with laudanum and she's been asleep most of the time.'

'Very well, I'll see you get five shillings if you can keep

116

your mouth shut. Bring the baby to the stable yard then forget you ever saw him.'

'I can't . . .'

'Cecilia doesn't want motherhood; anyone with half a wit can see that. This will not go hard on her. She knows her papa will forgive her and she can continue to live under his roof.'

I hurried downstairs and barged into Mr Fortescue's study. I demanded a hired carriage with a dependable coachman and a strong team of horses, plus expenses to cover additional costs. He had the sense not to ask questions, dropped a purse into my hand and sent a footman to the nearest coaching house. A post chaise and team rumbled into the yard barely half an hour later, just as sunset turned the sky molten gold. Emily pattered out of the kitchen door with a linen-wrapped bundle. I tucked the purse into her apron pocket, told her to split the contents with cook, and took the bundle into my arms. Emily turned to go but I called her back.

'Not a word of this to anyone,' I reminded her. 'No kitchen gossip or idle chitchat with the other servants.'

She curtsied. 'Yes, Miss Rodriguez.'

'Good. Now go and sit with Cecilia.' I laid the sleeping child on the seat inside the coach then climbed inside. I had no intention of looking at the child if I could help it. The shape, the feel, the smell was too familiar.

Thunder rumbled over the sea. A blanket of cloud rolled in from the west, dragging a storm towards the coast. The pretty sunset was drowned in a boiling mass of purples and greys. Metal-clad hooves sparked on the yard. The driver clutched his hat as a gust of wind swirled around the corner of the house.

I leaned out of the window and told him where I wanted to go.

'A two-hour drive at least, miss,' he replied. 'And that's only if we're blessed with clear roads.'

I glanced at the darkening sky. 'Hurry.'

Across town, traders packed up stalls and battened

shutters. People scampered home, clinging to their bonnets while dogs barked into the rising wind. We stopped at the posting house near the end of the new turnpike. Another man climbed aboard armed with a gun. Muffled words were exchanged, a coarse laugh cut the gloom, then a whip cracked and the carriage lurched forward. An hour later and it was dark. Flickering coach lamps glowered like blinking eyes in the cool air, throwing distorted shadows across the trees now bordering the road.

The baby shifted in my arms. I prayed an empty belly wouldn't wake him up and start him bawling. I'd forgotten to ask Emily if cook had managed to find a wet nurse or put milk down his throat some other way. Holding him close, I kept whispering: 'Don't be afraid,' over and over. Outside, the night was a black cavern of swirling air. The carriage was buffeted on its leather springs. In the distance, lightning fired the sky, followed a few moments later by the low rumbling of the dragon's belly. In the dim light of the lamps, the trees were whipped up into a shivering fit.

I fiddled with the blind. Broken. On the roof, the coachmen shouted across at one another, the words stolen almost instantly from their mouths. Suddenly, the sky split apart with light. The carriage lurched sickeningly. A whip cracked, the world straightened. The coppery taste of blood filled my mouth where I had bitten my tongue.

Not one other soul did we meet on that long road. The storm increased in ferocity, as though the very elements of nature were coming after me to claim back what was taken. Only once did the baby open tiny, bleary eyes to look up at me from inside the folds of linen. He felt safe in my arms, I was sure of it, despite the howling gale outside.

'You won't be hurt, I promise,' I whispered, as the first of the rains began to fall.

Soft lights penetrated the murk as we clattered into the village of Afton Vale, leaking through shuttered windows and spilling from the mouth of a tavern. Lightning flickered,

118

revealing a collection of dwellings clinging to the sides of a low hill. A church steeple poked a sharp finger into the tortured sky, weather vane spinning a mad dance on top of the spire.

I pushed open the door as the carriage halted and stumbled on to the verge. The wind sang about my ears in a wailing chorus of lost souls. It plucked the edges of my cloak with unseen fingers and slapped my hair about my face.

'Wait here,' I called up to the coachmen, their faces white moons in the storm light. One clambered down to settle the horses. I wrapped the baby in a fold of my cloak and hurried up the hill towards the church. A mud puddle sucked off one of my shoes and swallowed it greedily. My eyes were full of rain.

I struggled up a steep, narrow lane, houses crowding in on either side. My feet scrabbled on the slick cobbles. My lungs ached by the time I reached the lich-gate of the church. I paused to catch my breath before limping past the moss-blackened tombstones of the churchyard and into the clump of trees beyond.

The house was exactly as described. A former parsonage, modest though comfortable looking, with sagging eaves and ivy straggling up the front wall. I banged on the painted oak door. A chair scraped across floorboards. Then came a woman's voice, hesitant, enquiring.

'Who's there?'

The wind tore the words from my throat. 'Juliana. Juliana Rodriguez. Open the door.'

An iron bolt squealed and the door sighed open. She stood framed in candlelight, a hearty fire crackling in the hearth behind her. A flash of lightning lit up her face. She had filled out a little, her features losing many of the harsh lines that had always made her look so gaunt. Her hair was different too: all bunched on top of her head and dripping with ribbons. A hint of rouge warmed her cheeks and I picked up the sweet scent of cologne, even in the restless air of the porch.

119

'Hello Miss Mary,' I said, shifting the bundle in my arms.

Her face went through entire seasons of emotions. 'Come inside, come inside at once. What are you doing here? On a night like this?'

I stumbled into her parlour, dripping a trail of rainwater across the floor. Mary held out her arms to embrace me. I thrust the baby into her startled grasp.

'There, a child for you. The child you always wanted. Take care of your new son, Miss Mary.'

'It's Mrs Pettit now.' She unwrapped the linen bundle. Her jaw slackened when she spied the baby within. 'Juliana, what have you done?'

'Saved his life and given you something more valuable than a pretty dress. I have taken him from somewhere he wasn't wanted to somewhere I know he'll be loved. Look after him, please.'

'Has he no parents of his own? Did they not want him?'

Standing soaking in my dress, I told her the whole of it. I did not sit down, or even pause for breath. She listened in that patient way of hers, head to one side, glancing occasionally down at the child as if unable to believe it lay in her arms. Years of frustration fell from her face when she stroked his smooth, white chin.

'What will I say to Ernest?' she asked when I had finished.

'He is your husband?'

'Yes, the wedding was very quick and simple. No relatives on either side, just a couple of villagers for witnesses.'

I tugged a handkerchief from my sleeve and wiped the rain off my face. 'Tell him what you will – that the child was a foundling left on your doorstep.'

She shook her head. 'He won't believe it. He knows how desperate I am.'

'He has no wish for a son? Someone to take his name?'

Mary gazed at the child. 'Every wish in the world. It is what he has always wanted, even though he will not put that desire into words out of respect for me. But I can read

120

his heart. We could tell everyone that the child is a parish orphan. They would understand that.'

A draught shivered down my back and gusted around my ankles. It wheezed across the floor, sucked the smoke back out of the chimney and set the candles guttering in their holders. My wet clothes tightened their clammy grip on my body.

Mary beckoned. 'Warm yourself by the hearth, at least until the storm blows over. I have some milk to give the baby.'

I shook my head. 'A hired carriage is waiting. Close the door when I'm gone and forget you saw me tonight.'

'Things are still not well with you and Mrs Worledge?'

'No, not well. Best if you did not write for a while. Catherine likes to read my messages. So far I've managed to sneak letters past her but I can't tell how long my good fortune will hold.'

I noticed how naturally she held the child, how comfortable they were with one another. 'God bless you, Juliana,' she said, 'even though I don't know whether you're a devil or an angel.'

'I certainly need someone's blessing tonight.'

Slithering back down the hill, I found the coachmen sheltering in the lee of the tavern, supping hot broth fetched from the kitchen. 'Landlord reckons he has a nose for the weather,' the man with the gun told me. 'Says this storm will blow itself out within the hour.'

The carriage was turned and within minutes, Afton Vale was receding into the murk. I pushed my face into my hands and cried until my cheeks stung. I felt sick with nerves and utterly alone. A dry patch on my gown marked where I had held the child. I fingered the material while trying to weigh the rights and wrongs of what I had done. Outside the carriage, the storm rumbled further inland. The wind slackened and the thunder banged its heavenly drums over

121

someone else's house, someone else's children. I whispered questions into the night but the darkness held no answers.

At the driver's insistence we pulled into a coaching inn. I could not begrudge it. Both men were soaked through, the horses badly in need of rest and fodder. I spent the remainder of the night on a straw bed. I would've gladly slept in a barrel for the sake of some peace.

Nevertheless, I had the men out of their beds at dawn and on the road again with barely a pause for breakfast. Arriving in town, I ordered them to drop me off two streets away from the Butter House and handed over the remainder of the money Mr Fortescue had given me. 'Not a word to anyone about last night's trip,' I warned.

Both men nodded. A click of the reins and the carriage rattled off. I dawdled on the way home, hoping Catherine hadn't missed me. I was oblivious to the busy throng of the street. Finally, I crept through the kitchen door and made my way through the house in a slither of still-damp petticoats.

Cecilia was waiting for me in the parlour.

'You took my baby,' she said, heavy weights hanging from each word.

She was seated in Catherine's armchair. Dark circles bruised both eyes and her thin lips were dry. Animosity glowered from her face.

'You should not be out of bed,' I told her. 'It is too soon.'

Her feet shifted beneath the thick cloak that swaddled her body, smaller now that the new life within had gone. 'Your stable lad let me in. Mrs Worledge is not here. Neither is her odious manservant. It seems you were not the only one with business in the night.'

I sat opposite and clasped my fingers together to stop them trembling. 'Did the maid tell you?'

'Yes, but only after I'd threatened her with the street.' She sighed bitterly. 'I don't suppose you will tell me where you took him?'

I shook my head. 'Leave him alone, Cecilia. You don't want him. Enjoy your parties then go and marry an earl or some fluff-headed fop. The baby has found a good home, I promise you that much. Your papa thought it would be for the best.'

'Papa has disinherited me more times than the sun has risen. He always forgives me, whatever my sins, because I am the only woman in his life, the only reminder of the wife he loved. Also, like all foolish men without a son and heir, he hopes my dowry will buy a respectable name. 'Twould make no difference if I lay with every thief and beggar in the south of England. A good match is favoured over any reputation, however scarlet. We all have reputations, don't we, Juliana?'

I felt my tongue turn to lead. A mirthless laugh fell out of Cecilia's mouth. 'We are alike in many ways, you and I. We don't enjoy being told what to do. We both want to shock, to indulge in whims that will outrage a society that in itself is full of outrageous people. It amused me to be associated with you, and I perceived you had a similar interest in me.'

'This is not a game, Cecilia. Or a whim to colour my standing in the eyes of stupid, arrogant people. I thought only of the baby. He's not something you can tuck away in a cupboard whenever you fancy attending a concert or masquerade.'

'He would have been looked after. I enquired about a nursemaid.'

'Your papa was determined he had to go. I could not stand by and see him become a parish boy or sold off to a sweep.'

'So you befriended me because you wanted my child? I suppose you have always wanted it, even though you might not have realised it at first. I noticed the way you kept looking at my belly while drinking tea on my couch. I could sense your mind asking questions, asking whether I had any love for my unborn child or, perhaps more importantly, the father.'

She closed her eyes for a moment. 'Yes, deny it as much as you like, I know of your desire. How does it feel to have your blood burn, to have someone constantly in your thoughts and not be able to push him out, even when you suffer for it?'

'I don't love anyone.'

'This has naught to do with love. I told you we had much in common, Juliana. So now I daresay I'm expected to forget all about the baby and go and make the proper match desired, provided anyone with a decent name will have me? Well, there are some things I cannot forget. I felt every second of that birth. I've never known pain like it. It seems as if a part of me has been torn out and can't be put back. Perhaps you would do well to remember that, child stealer.'

She coughed. Tremors shivered through her body like curtains rippling in a breeze. All her magic, all her charm, had gone, drained out like fine wine poured through the tap of a barrel. No longer the sylph, the coquettish young tease who held sway at parties, holding court amidst an assembly terrified of her social executions. She had lost her power.

I stood up. 'Let me see you out. I presume you have a chair or carriage waiting?'

Cecilia fumbled under her cloak and handed me a linen-wrapped package bound with string. 'Papa asked me to give you this. It seems you and he are better acquainted than I realised. He has good cause to feel pleased with you. I suppose I shall have to behave now there is no one to promise me the world.'

'Adam?'

'He brought me down further than he ever humbled you, Juliana. He has not replied to my letters. Messengers have been turned away at the door to his club or told he is not at home. He will never be at home. Not for me.'

'Yet you are still besotted with him?'

Cecilia didn't answer. She trod carefully to the door and put a hand on the knob. Then she turned. 'I hear you are

124

to wed George Proudlove. Let us hope marriage proves kind to you. I thought you were my friend. It seems I was wrong about a great many things, but the greatest mistake you will make is believing you know how many times a man can hurt you before you are able to let him go.'

After Cecilia had left, Maggie Burns called down the passage from the kitchen. 'Your Miss Fortescue, she and the baby are hearty? Seems a mite soon to be up an about.'

I nodded. 'They are both well.'

'I daresay Mr Proudlove won't approve of you having friends such as her.'

I sighed and turned towards the stairs, Cecilia's package under my arm. 'On that account he has nothing to fear.'

I entered my bedchamber and closed the door. Satisfied that I would not be disturbed, I laid the package on the bed and tore at the string. The linen took an age to unravel. I was frantic with anticipation as the last of the wrapping unwound on to the floor. Revealed was an armful of velvet cut and stitched into one of the most alluring gowns my starved eyes had feasted on. I held it against me. A river of gorgeous material tumbled down to my feet. A queen. I would look like a queen.

I viewed my reflection in the looking glass. This was a garment to send the imagination flying. With it, there was nothing I could not achieve, no one I could not have if I set my mind to it.

'Fair bargain, Mr Fortescue,' I whispered. A smile cut across my lips as if slashed by the glinting blade of a buccaneer's sword. Tomorrow. Tomorrow was the day the meat carrier came.

I rested for the remainder of the afternoon and slept soundly that night. I rose with the sun and, yawning, laid out my new gown on the chair before starting to plan. I spun a cautious web, aware that I lacked the experience or sophistication to entice men as effectively as Cecilia. But my innocence could, in itself, prove my best weapon.

125

'A man likes nothing more than to deflower a maiden,' Cecilia once told me. 'Virginity is a challenge, and once claimed it is gone for ever. I swear most of the libertines who haunt Wexborough's assembly rooms keep a tally of their conquests, of the girls they have turned into women, and the wedding nights they have ruined when the groom discovers he was not first past the gate, as it were.'

The house was mine. Catherine had left word with William that she had gone to visit George at his estate and would not return for at least another day. Nancy, idle milkmaid that she was, malingered in bed and as a result Maggie was up to her ears in dirty linen. I sneaked into Catherine's bedchamber and plundered her dresser, determined to turn myself from a strawberry-faced doe to a royal consort. I filched her scent, dipped into her jewellery box and clouded my face with her powder. Dressing was difficult without help but my time in Florence had taught me a trick or two. A necklace for the final touch then I checked myself in the mirror, running my hands over velvet loops and bows, turning this way then that. No wig, I decided. I wanted him to see my hair, to run his fingers freely through it.

'How could any man resist you?' I declared.

How indeed?

The hands of the hall clock kissed noon. Maggie had gone to the washhouse with a cart groaning under mountains of laundry. That ought to keep her hands in water for two hours at best. William was cleaning out the stable and no tradesmen, save one, were expected at the door for the remainder of the day.

It was going to happen. It was *meant* to happen.

I paced the kitchen, wringing my hands and stealing nervous glances out of the window. My ears strained for the lazy clop-clop of hooves on the packed gravel road. I would meet him here, in this grease-stained battlefield of copper pots and pans. The best terms a kitchen slut could offer.

126

Chapter Nine

Moses Cripps was not a man who bothered to knock on doors. He pushed his way into the kitchen with the same bare-chested crudity I'd witnessed a few days before. The door was left to swing on its hinges as he slapped a muslin package stained with fat on to the table top.

'Maggie, where are you?' he growled. 'I've a mind to squeeze your plump arse.'

He sniffed around the room, dark eyes taking in the empty hearth, the sacks of flour, and the vegetables strung from the rafters. Then his gaze settled on me. 'Why, if it isn't the little kitchen girl. For a minute I thought I'd stepped into a bawdy house. What brings you in here dressed like that?'

The folds of my new gown rustled as I crossed to the door and dropped the latch. 'Maggie has business elsewhere today.' I turned to face him, my back pressed against the hard oak. 'And I have some business with you.'

I knew how to stand, how to move my body and bring the heat into his cheeks. My instincts were strong, my desire easily overpowering my fear. Hands on waist, hips thrust out, chin raised. Just like the harlots on Marlborough Street.

Cripps's voice rumbled at the back of his throat. His eyes glittered. 'You playin' games with me? Didn't anyone ever warn you that little girls ought not to toy with grown men?'

I swallowed. 'I am woman enough for you. If you think you are man enough for me.'

He towered over me. I was forced to stand on tiptoe just to meet his gaze. A smile bent his lips. He could bat me out

127

of the way as easily as flicking a fly off the table top. 'Look at you, quivering like a rabbit with a ferret nipping at its tail. This ain't a parlour game. I don't want you running upstairs bawling to your mama just because I've ruffled your feathers. I get plenty of offers, from ladies as well as their maids. Why should I bother with a pup like you?'

'Because you will be my first.'

'So that's it?' Laughter rolled up his throat and spilled out of his mouth. I blushed, feeling all the more the child before this brute, and angry at my own weakness. Fumbling, I locked the kitchen door and tossed the key into a corner. One of us was a prisoner, but who had trapped whom? Palms sweating, I waited him out.

'How old are you?' he asked.

'Old enough to marry. Or take a lover if I choose.'

'Choice is one thing you ain't got. Not any more.' He bent towards me. My nostrils filled with his smell. He opened his mouth and ran his tongue across my eyebrow. A low moan escaped my throat.

'Aye,' he whispered, 'young as you are, you're woman enough.'

I kept touching myself in wonder. When I stood naked in front of my looking glass the little girl was gone for ever. The woman gazing out of the glass was confident, smiling. Already dark bruises were forming where Moses had handled me but these were the marks of passion and I would let them flower in their own way.

Behind me on the rug was a pitcher and ewer. I had washed my insides thoroughly. Perhaps that would be enough. Perhaps not. I folded up the Italian gown and slipped it under the foot of my bed. Then I fastened Catherine's scratchy old dress and glanced again at the figure in the mirror.

My body. All else having failed, my body would get me what I wanted.

*

Next day Catherine returned with a new bonnet and a gaggle of chattering friends. Talk over tea was all about the war and how the king's armies were being defeated by rebels in league with the French. The Americas were all but lost. I was brought into the parlour and paraded as George Proudlove's prospective bride. I had no idea who these people were or where Catherine had found them. She was full of plans for the wedding. I felt as if someone else entirely was getting married.

Released, I fled the room and spent the rest of the morning sulking at the kitchen window, watching next door's cat chase a few sluggardly birds around the square patch of garden. Later I sent William to the flesher's shop with a message for Moses Cripps to deliver more meat. I was still touched by the boy's enthusiasm to please me, despite having a sweetheart of his own.

During that endless afternoon, I invented every kind of excuse to stay in the kitchen, lingering by the back door long after William had returned from delivering his message. I offered to help Maggie but my heart wasn't in the work. Disgusted, she threw a dishcloth at my head and told me to keep out of her way. I strained my ears listening for the lazy clop of the butcher's horse, but apart from the excited squeals of children in the street, the day remained quiet.

Laughter filtered down the passage as Catherine's guests outstayed their welcome. Maggie was forced to go out to the washhouse with a large bundle of linen. Nancy was still in bed coughing her wits out. Left to myself, I found the kitchen oppressive. I glanced at the vegetables Maggie had asked me to cut before losing her temper, and thought I might still give it a try. I sensed her irritation wasn't only due to my clumsiness but so far she had avoided my careful promptings.

I needed to snatch some fresh air. Putting down the kitchen knife, I opened the back door and walked straight into Moses Cripps.

'Been waitin' for me?' he grinned darkly.

'Did you bring the meat?'

'Might have done. Does it matter?'

'I didn't hear your cart.'

'Don't need it for this sort of delivery. No fancy gown today?'

'I don't need that for this sort of service.'

He chuckled. 'That's my lass . . .'

I ran up the stairs to my bedchamber, intent on cleaning myself up before Maggie returned from the washhouse. The door hung ajar. I always closed it before going downstairs.

I crept inside. The room was gloomy, the curtains half drawn across the open window. The air was thick with tobacco smoke and the cloying scent of cologne. Someone was watching me from the shadows beside the bed. Blake. He sat, legs crossed, on the small armchair. He grinned, his teeth leaping out of his face like pearl daggers.

I fumbled back against the door and felt it close behind me. Stupid. I had not seen Blake since Catherine had returned and I'd assumed he was elsewhere on some business or other. To find him lurking in my room knocked the breath out of me. Instinctively my hands folded across my breasts.

The smile deepened. Nothing in the room appeared to have been disturbed. 'What are you doing here?' I demanded. 'You have no business coming into my bedchamber.'

He rose from the chair in a single, fluid movement, the velvet of his embroidered waistcoat whispering against his silk shirt. No one could mistake him for a footman now.

'On the contrary,' he purred. 'I have some pressing business with you, Miss Juliana.'

He held something in his hand, a hand laden with rings that glinted even in the dim light. A folded piece of writing paper. He waved it lazily in front of my face. 'This message is for you. The delivery boy was about to bring it to the front door. I was able to catch him. He swore the note was urgent and had to be given to you straightaway.' Blake shrugged. His feigned expression of ignorance painted a nightmare on his dark, crooked features. 'However, it seems you were busy.'

'Give me the message then get out.' I snatched at the paper but Blake flicked it out of my reach.

'There you go, playing the fool again.' He sounded bored, almost disappointed, though undercurrents rippled beneath his assured exterior. Before I could move, he seized my wrist, prised open my fingers and pressed the sheet of paper into my palm. He ran his other hand through my hair, nails scraping my scalp. Then he sniffed, nose twitching like a rat's. 'You smell of a rutting. Someone's had your skirts up, my pretty lass.'

'Let go,' I cried. 'Get off me. You'll never be as good a man as your master. Richard might have been a drunk, but at least he was a gentleman. You can wear his clothes, drink his port and smoke his tobacco but you belong in the gutter with the rest of the offal.'

His grip loosened. I pulled my hand away and backed to the far side of the room, glancing round for something I could use as a weapon. He was too strong for me, but perhaps I could startle him long enough to run.

'Whine all you like,' Blake jeered. 'You stink of lust, and with your wedding to George Proudlove not two weeks away. I care naught for your innocence or lack of it. You could bed the whole of Wexborough and Proudlove would still marry you. He takes whores with as much relish as he loses at cards. I'll wager you have the pox within a week of becoming his wife. If you haven't got it already.'

Blake grasped the doorknob, twisted it and pulled open the door. Then he was gone. I examined the letter he had thrust into my hands. The wax seal was broken and the page clumsily refolded. I smoothed it out and read the small, neat script.

131

Juliana, there is little time and I fear for my life. I have not heard from you since our encounter at the burial and it is vital that we speak. Hurry to my home and we will discuss matters there. Time is short.

Your servant, M Littlejohn.

I crumpled up the paper and tucked it into my sleeve. In the graveyard that day Mr Littlejohn's eyes had darted around as though expecting some unseen nemesis to leap out and confront him. For me, slipping out of the house was becoming more difficult. Catherine held me on a tight leash while she concocted her awful wedding plans. Flowers arrived from George, basketfuls of them – elaborate displays of lilies and white roses. My bedchamber resembled a garden gone wild. I starved the blooms of water, plucking a single flower from the wilting bunches to wear in my hair while Moses Cripps tupped me behind the oat sacks.

Meanwhile the dressmaker arrived to measure me for my wedding gown. I was also made to rehearse the ceremony with our own local parson and William standing in as the groom. Why did George want me for a wife? Of all the prospective brides his position and privilege could have bought, why me? Catherine hadn't settled any kind of dowry as far as I was aware.

Gossip breezed through the servants. Glances were exchanged at the kitchen table, knowing looks passed from seat to seat like a flagon of bitter wine. Maggie had an idea, of course, and perhaps William also suspected the truth. The look he gave Moses one day when ordered to help unload the cart was as cold as a winter's gale.

Maggie grew sullen. Moses no longer flirted with her. He and I grew careless in our passion and Maggie caught us in the pantry, limbs locked together. She would not talk to me for hours afterwards. 'Don't get a bastard in your belly,' she said finally. 'Moses won't care. If you need a wise woman I can tell you where to go.'

Nothing passed beyond the kitchen door. No one was keen on George Proudlove. But whatever I did meant nothing as long as Blake pushed his way into my life as he pleased. He had gone to ground again, disappearing on one of his mysterious errands, but I kept expecting to find him grinning from some shadowed corner.

Still I was denied egress from the house. Catherine checked on me at least twice an hour, sometimes more. Though I had not seen George since being forced to dine with him that memorable evening, his family called. I was introduced to Mr Proudlove senior, an out-of-town parson crowed up in a black shovel hat, woollen hose, sturdy buckle shoes and a cloak still powdered with the dust of country lanes. A fat gold ring clutched the middle finger of his right hand.

'Show respect to Mr Proudlove,' Catherine instructed. I dipped a curtsy. I'd already been warned that he bore a facial injury but it was hard not to stare. A hole split the right side of the parson's face just below the cheekbone. Through it, gums glistened wetly, and a row of yellow teeth stood like jaundiced sentries. Breath wheezed in and out, turning his speech into a rasping drawl that sounded like pebbles rattling in a wooden bucket. The thought of his long, bony fingers touching me invoked a cold shudder.

I was presented to his dough-faced wife, Marjorie, and a clingy, wide-eyed girl called Charlotte. I thought she might be a niece or godchild, but learned that she was in fact their daughter. She looked about five years old.

Parson Proudlove perched on the end of the drawing-room sofa, thin legs clamped together. Grey eyes flitted across the furnishings as though trying to winkle sinners out of the woodwork. When offered refreshment, he declined tea and asked instead for brandy. William brought the bottle and the parson poured himself a generous measure, which he downed in a single gulp.

'The girl looks like a two-guinea trick out of a bawdy

house,' he said, gesturing at me. 'George needs good breeding stock, a plain woman to teach him a little humility as well as the responsibility of raising an heir. Vanity has no place in a God-fearing household.'

Catherine pulled her lips into a smile. 'Juliana has been well educated. I invested a great deal in her tutelage.'

Proudlove flicked his hand. 'It does no good to stuff a woman's head full of nonsense. What use are fripperies so long as she can bear her husband healthy sons and run a household capably? And obedient – she must be obedient, one of the most important qualities in a wife.'

'You need not trouble yourself on that account,' Catherine purred. 'Juliana will do as she is bid.'

She glanced at me, her face a nest of threats. I bit back my tongue. They talked some more. I was not invited to sit down, or offered any tea. Parson Proudlove spoke directly to Catherine, pausing only to refill his brandy glass. For a clergyman he seemed overly ambitious, openly discussing his plans for rising through the church hierarchy. His wife nodded, then nodded again, continually stirring her tea as it grew cold.

I moved to the window and watched two noisy dogs chase each other around the street. Broken shadows fell across the huddled town buildings. Behind me, the parson droned on. I heard a forced laugh from Catherine followed by a nervous chuckle from Mrs Proudlove.

A tug on my skirts pulled me from my reverie. The little pale-faced girl stared up at me. I wondered if she ever smiled, if she even knew how to smile.

'Are you going to be my aunt?' she said, each word precisely formed by her tiny mouth. An intelligence beyond her years seemed to lurk behind those wide brown eyes.

'Yes,' I replied. 'It appears so.'

Charlotte leaned forward and whispered: 'Do you believe in unicorns?'

I stroked the back of her small hand with my thumb. 'I

134

am sure there are magical places filled with all sorts of wonderful creatures, places where people are always happy and nothing bad ever happens. But we can't always go to these places. We can only dream, and try to make the best of what we have here.'

I let go of her hand. 'Don't you have any friends or toys to play with? A favourite doll perhaps?'

'Papa says dolls are ungodly, and that the boys and girls in our village are the children of sinners.' She tilted her head to one side. Brown curls brushed her cheeks. 'Will you come to stay with us after you are married?'

I shook my head. 'I will have to go and live with your brother in his own house. Perhaps I will see you when we come to visit.'

A frown creased her forehead. I could sense the child-thoughts tumbling around behind her dark eyes. 'You won't stay with George,' she said. 'Not for long.'

Quiet settled over the Butter House. The Proudloves had left for their parish in Dinstock – a market village some twenty miles outside Wexborough. Catherine was upstairs enjoying an afternoon nap. I had business elsewhere.

The last time I saw William, he was squatting on an upended bucket rubbing oil into a carriage whip. Maggie was sorting out the larder. A rat had got in and she was determined to catch it. Nancy, threatened with a thrashing from Blake, had made a remarkable recovery and was cleaning out the dining-room hearth.

I had no money for a sedan chair and lacked the nerve to steal any more from Maggie's jar. I changed into a plain gown and bonnet, slipped out the front door and hurried along the street. With luck, people would think I was a maid chasing an errand. I didn't want to think about what might happen if I was spotted out of doors without permission. Catherine's naps were notoriously heavy but I'd already taken too many chances sneaking out of the house.

Torrential rain had carved ruts into the gravel road. Mud and refuse choked the gutters. I tried to watch where I put my feet, at the same time snatching glances at the clock on the front of the corn exchange. Brook Street lay midway between the Butter House and the harbour, a narrow thoroughfare ending in a square where the old customs and excise building once stood. It took half an hour of squeezing through busy streets before I arrived, exhausted but glad to be out of the Butter House's stuffy confines.

A long street of ill-matched buildings stretched in front of me. Chimney pots jostled for space on top of brick stacks, which looked ready to tumble at the first breath of wind. Stone-faced houses bore the scars of countless winters. Walls were pitted, gutters choked with weeds and old leaves.

I tightened Catherine's shawl around my shoulders. Seagulls wheeled overhead, raucous cries cutting the afternoon air. In the near distance I could hear the bustle of the harbour and the gentle shifting of water as the tide crept up the wooden pilings of the quay. Richard's office was nearby. I was heartsick at the thought of going anywhere near it. I was too frightened of running into Blake, too unsure of where he spent his time when off on one of his mysterious errands.

I found the house. Narrow, squeezed between a draper's shop and a coach house. Curtains were drawn across the windows and the green-painted front door was splashed with dirt from the street. I had knocked twice and was thinking of leaving when, through the wood, I heard a cough. Then a voice muttered something.

Bolts scraped in their brackets. A key was pushed into the lock and turned. The door opened a crack and a bleary eye peered out.

I had met Edith Littlejohn only half a dozen times during my childhood, but she was not the sort of woman one forgot easily. As well as a bellowing laugh and a potato face cracked with smiles, she was possessed of bright, shiverme eyes that held you as she moved and spoke, gesturing with butterfly hands. Eyes in which a challenge lurked. A challenge not to find anything decent or beautiful in even the most ordinary things.

I had not admired her for her humour, which was as expansive as her generous girth, or her seemingly boundless patience, but for her ability to treat life's calamities with amused contempt. She put trivial problems in their rightful place and handled more serious matters with an optimism that inspired faith in everyone.

Edith strode through life whilst others scurried. She never pinched my cheek, patted my back or admonished me to be a good girl. She listened to everything I said as if I was a great philosopher or the wisest of sages. And in all the talking not once did she dismiss anything I said. Instead she taught me to see things differently, to try to look at things through someone else's eyes. Often my convictions – the childish truths that I held to be absolute – shifted. Life was no longer always a 'yes' or a 'no' but a 'maybe' and a 'perhaps'. Black and white blurred into greys, and then glorious colours. Everything came to be possessed of beauty in its own subtle yet wonderful way. Even in the most squalid of Wexborough's rubbish-choked back streets, she told me, children could be heard laughing.

Now Mrs Littlejohn's eyes were dull and blood-ringed with crying. Garments hung loosely from her shoulders. A handkerchief was pressed against her blotchy face, a face that looked as if it had cried for a lifetime, cried until the colour had been washed out. She regarded me vaguely, her other hand trembling as it fingered the streaks of grey infecting her black hair. I had stepped back without realising it.

'What's happened?'

She waved me inside. I followed her down a wood-panelled passage thick with the stench of soiled linen, food gone cold and rugs too long in want of a beating. It took a while for my eyes to adjust to the gloom. I found myself in a parlour filled to the seams with ornaments. Dozens of china-faced dolls peered down from their shelves with dark, glassy eyes.

'Sit down,' Mrs Littlejohn muttered. 'You shan't stay long, but I've not the strength to keep to my feet.' She slumped into a squat armchair while I perched on the couch opposite. A half-full glass of what looked like canary lay on the table beside her, alongside a plate littered with scraps of food. I shivered. Cold grey ashes spilled out of the fireplace. A heap of logs lay untouched in a wicker basket. Apart from Mrs Littlejohn's wheezing chest and my own rapid breathing, the house was a cavern of silence. On the mantelpiece above the dead fire, a clock sat with its hands frozen. 'I've been expecting you, Juliana. A pity you couldn't have come sooner.'

'Where is your husband? At the shipping office?'

She regarded me with those sore, tired eyes. 'Michael is dead, buried amongst beggars, whores and murderers. His body was stitched up in a canvas sack and dumped in an unmarked pauper's grave in a corner of the town cemetery. I couldn't see his face, couldn't say goodbye. Nothing remains of him.'

I was robbed of words. From their vantage point the dolls stared down impassively.

'I was told he had taken his own life,' she continued after a time. 'His body was found floating face down in the water beneath the quay. The boatmen who fished him out claimed they found an empty gin bottle in his jacket pocket. Barely out of the sea and he was buried in the ground. No church service for a suicide. Soon the accusations began. Michael was held to have mishandled Mr Worledge's accounts, embezzled funds, helped smugglers in return for a portion of the cargo – all sorts of nonsense.'

She wiped her cheeks. 'The magistrate said he must have jumped off the quay. My husband had a weakness for fine tobacco and the odd hand of cards but he was no drinker. He hadn't the belly for it. Someone must have killed him. Stole his life the way Catherine Worledge stole everything Michael had worked for. Don't tell me you weren't aware of it, Juliana. Don't insult his memory.'

I gestured helplessly. 'Mr Littlejohn sent me a note to tell me he was in fear of his life. Apparently he had important information he wished to pass on to me, something about my past, but I couldn't get out of the house. Catherine would be furious if she discovered I was here. She tells me nothing, makes plans behind my back and treats me as a marriage chattel. I haven't put a foot inside the shipping office for nigh on two years.'

I covered my face with my hands and squeezed both eyes shut. I pictured Mr Littlejohn floating in the rubbish-choked waters of the harbour, his face eaten by fish.

'I was sorry to hear about Richard,' Edith said, leaning back in her chair. 'Some men aren't born to be strong. Odd how they seem to attract a certain type of wife.'

'I couldn't help him. I wasn't strong enough either.'

'Oh, settle down. Start crying and you will have me in tears again. Enough have been spilled in this house already. This has been a strain on everyone, what with Mr Worledge's drinking and Michael having to run the business virtually single-handed. Trade went from bad to worse. He had too much tied up in the company. When the books wouldn't balance the bank foreclosed. Michael was already a broken man before his murder. A clever legal web means Catherine Worledge can sit untouched in her fine town house. She is welcome to it.'

I searched her face. 'Why would anyone want to kill your husband?'

Edith grasped the arms of the chair and pushed herself to her feet. I moved to help but she waved me away. 'This will only take a few moments.'

She rummaged behind a bookshelf stuffed with loose

documents, ledgers and bundles of rolled-up parchments. 'If you want to hide a tree, put it in a forest,' Michael once told me. Ah, here we are.' She returned with a bound sheaf of paper and dropped it on to the fireside table. My name was written in a barely legible scrawl across the top page.

'These papers have been a stain on our lives,' she continued, tapping the bundle with her middle finger. 'I can't remember how many times we argued over them – squabbled like two unruly children. Michael never once hinted at what they might contain, though he never kept any other secrets from me. Only his wish that they be handed over to you has prevented me from tossing them into the sea. A simple bundle, but weighed down with years of anguish. I give it to you out of cowardice. Destroying these papers would not be enough. Only when they are in your possession will I truly rid myself of the wretched things. Michael made me swear not to mention them to anyone. He considered himself partly responsible for you – agonised over your treatment at the Worledge house. I was too much the obedient wife to defy him.'

I stared at the package, at the clumsy knot in the string. 'What will happen to you? Why haven't any friends called? You can't sit here by yourself.'

'I am the widow of a bankrupt suicide. It is worse than harbouring a pestilence. Friendships that took a lifetime to build unravel in less than a day. I will lose my home and everything in it. The wolves must have their meat. Perhaps that's for the best. Every object, every corner of this house carries a memory of my husband.'

Edith tapped the bundle again. 'This has already driven someone to murder. You must get out of Catherine Worledge's house. Whatever it takes, whatever you have to do, leave as soon as you can.'

Chapter Ten

I hurried back through town, the sheaf of documents pressed against my chest. I was conscious of how light the package was, how fragile the knowledge contained within its pages. Mr Littlejohn had said, in his note, that the time had come to learn about my past. Could my life so easily be set down on a bundle of papers?

I skirted the market square and headed downhill, stumbling on the odd loose cobble. Leaving Mrs Littlejohn alone had proved upsetting.

'Don't fret over me,' she'd said, squeezing my hand. 'Michael lives while I hold his memory. No one can murder that.'

'What will happen to you? Where will you go?'

'I have a sister in Plymouth. A spinster with a decent house and a few guineas in the bank. I'll go and stay with her, try to build a new life for myself in the years that are left. Catherine Worledge and her lawyers can fight over the scraps I leave behind.'

A clock chimed the hour. I coaxed further effort from my aching legs. The tall chimneys of the Butter House poked up into the hazy afternoon. The package slipped and I clutched it tighter in my sweating palms. I'd had to fight the impulse to tear it open. The words inside could change my life if what Mr Littlejohn hinted at was true. But I couldn't risk anything in the open streets. Too many eyes and ears.

Outside the house, I checked Catherine's window. The

curtains were still drawn. I was so intent on what I was doing that I didn't hear the rapid approach of footsteps. A rough push between my shoulder blades. I tumbled over in a flurry of skirts and my head smacked against the dirt. Pain exploded in my skull. The world filled with reds and yellows. I lay gasping like a landed fish, the package still in one piece beside me.

'There's payment for your services, whore,' a voice spat.

A small, flint-faced woman stood over me. Patched and faded garments hung from her wiry frame and leather-bound wooden clogs poked from beneath the frayed hem of her gown. Hatred simmered in her eyes.

'Who are you?' I coughed. 'What do you want?'

'Mary Cripps is my name, and I'm tellin' you to leave my man alone. He can't get you out of his head, talks about you all the time as if you was something special.' She nudged me with the toe of her clog. 'I was the one he took to the parson, who bore his sons and shares his bed. I ain't giving up what little I got for the likes o' you.'

I dragged myself up on to my elbows. I was afraid she would hit me. The entire side of my face ached like a rotten tooth. The street was unusually quiet but I spotted the town constable hurrying towards us. I don't know if it was just coincidence or whether someone had alerted him. Mary Cripps caught sight of him too. She spat into the gutter beside me and scurried off.

The constable helped me up and thrust a handkerchief into my fingers. 'What happened, miss? Was that creature trying to rob you?'

'A misunderstanding. I don't want any fuss.'

'As you like, miss, but footpads are getting bolder in this district. War always brings the rats out of the gutters.'

I mumbled thanks and fled round the back of the house, praying that Catherine hadn't been awaked by the commotion and chanced to look out of her window. Maggie caught me at the kitchen door.

'An accident,' I muttered, shoving past her.

'Catfight more like,' she retorted, pursing her lips. 'That's quite an eye you've got there. You weren't supposed to leave the house.'

'Don't you have work to do?'

'I might, but that face needs sorting first. Your eye'll likely end up as black as a rotten apple. It's swelling up even as I watch. I can put a poultice on it, but for now you'd best go upstairs and see Mrs Worledge. She's awake and been calling for you this past quarter hour.'

'Do you know what she wants?'

Maggie shrugged. 'I don't reckon she's in a right mind to know anything.'

First I stopped by my bedchamber and, for want of a better place, shoved the bundle of documents beneath my pillow before hurrying along the passage to Catherine's room. She was still in bed, propped on a half-dozen pillows. Someone had opened the windows and curtains billowed out on soft currents of air. On the bedside table a laudanum bottle sat next to an empty sherry decanter.

Rouge smeared her face. It covered her hands, the pillows, the top of the bedspread. She grinned amidst the scarlet. It sliced her face open. She held out both arms and my first thought was: She's going to kill me. She's wanted to for years.

'You wished to see me, Mrs Worledge?'

She held out her arms. 'Come here and keep me company.'

I was pulled on to the mattress and cradled against her breast. Cool fingers stroked my forehead. She seemed not to notice my injured eye but instead held up a looking glass in front of her own face.

'Am I not becoming for a woman of my years?' she said, running a fingertip down the line of her jaw. 'Look, my cheeks are as pink as rosebuds.'

I didn't know what to say. Catherine held the mirror closer. She released me and pinched her painted skin. 'I

143

must make sure I get enough meat. There is nothing better for enriching the blood and putting the colour back into a lady's complexion. Too little and I might fall prey to some ill humour. I must send a message to the flesher's.'

I sat with her for a few more minutes but she said nothing else. Eventually she flopped back on to the pillows and was instantly asleep. I backed away from the bed and left the room as discreetly as I could. That put paid to any fears that Catherine might have observed me from her window. Whatever drunken vapours had taken hold of her, fate had granted me grace yet again. I returned to the kitchen so that Maggie could sort out my eye. I didn't mention Catherine. I sat twitching on a stool while some foul-smelling concoction was pasted to my tender flesh. The injury wasn't as grave as I'd first feared. Maggie handed me a herbal drink – mother's old recipe of course – and a strip of soaked linen to quell the throbbing.

I returned to my bedchamber and closed the door. My pillow lay on the rug. Mr Littlejohn's package was missing. I snatched up the pillow. Nothing beneath, nothing under the bed or on the table beside the dresser. The window was fastened, just as I'd left it, and my wardrobe doors closed.

My belly churned as I caught his scent: French cologne, stale tobacco, ruby port. The papers. He had my papers. He would notice that the binding was intact, know that I hadn't read the contents. Whatever secrets lay within were now his and likely Catherine's also. I started towards the door then hesitated, the pillow a crumpled feather bundle in my hands.

Perhaps to Catherine they were not secrets at all.

'Where'd you get that eye?' Moses demanded.

In the dim silence of the larder his fingers roved over my face. I flinched but his touch was as tender as a child's. He traced the outline of the bruise, his other hand cupping my chin.

'I fell and hit my head,' I told him.

144

'Aye, and I'm the next pope. Somebody's smacked you one, and I want to know who. Don't hold out on me.'

I pulled away. Blood thrummed in my temples. 'Blake. Mr Worledge's former manservant and now Catherine's lackey. He beats me if I do not grant him favours.'

'Favours?' Moses's eyes darkened. 'What favours are these? He been snatching at your petticoats, girl?'

I stared at my feet. 'He can do what he likes and I have no say in it. If he touches me again, I'll die.'

'No,' he said. 'Not you.'

I took a deep breath. 'I am also affianced to Mr George Proudlove, a country squire. The wedding will take place at the end of the month.'

Moses spat on the floor. 'You slut, why didn't you tell me this before? I could be hung in chains if we're caught.'

'I was forced into it. Are you going to turn coward on me?'

He grabbed me by the shoulders and shoved me against the cracked plaster wall. 'You'll belong to no one else, I swear. Let the cursed ceremony go ahead. Let this man steal your name. I'll take you in your wedding gown on the very day you utter your vows. I had you first and you'll always be mine. In the end you'll come back to me.'

'And Blake?'

Cripps released his grip and stormed out of the larder. A moment later the kitchen door slammed.

That evening I was once again instructed to take supper in the dining room. Catherine was at the head of the table; Blake sat opposite. I was perched in the middle, staring at the fruit bowl. The tablecloth was showered with half-chewed food as Blake shoved forkful after forkful of beef into his mouth. When he paused long enough to take a gulp of wine, a sly smile creased his mouth.

I nibbled my own meal with the manners of a mouse. When Blake leaned across the table – because he lacked the patience to wait for William to fetch the gravy – something fell out of his waistcoat pocket on to the buttered peas. Blake was very casual about fishing it out and wiping it clean with his napkin. A silver fob watch with a delicate flower pattern engraved on the case. Most unusual – the sort of thing a macaroni or similar eccentric might wear. Mr Littlejohn had possessed one like it. Blake caught my eye across the sputtering candles. We understood each other.

Afterwards, Catherine asked me to sit with her in the parlour and choose some hymns for the wedding. I feigned a headache and retired to the kitchen. No respite there, either.

'I know about Miss Cecilia's child,' Maggie Burns said.

'How?' I replied, genuinely startled. 'You rarely put a foot outside this kitchen.'

'I heard it from a marrow seller, who picked it up from a stable hand, and he got it from Mr Fortescue's cook. In this town everyone knows who you are and what your business is. You can't hide.'

The night wrapped dark hands about the house. An unseasonable chill drew cold fingers across the windows. William banked the fire and drew the curtains tight.

Before seeking the warmth of my bed, I took my courage in my hands and joined Catherine in the parlour. She was seated at her writing desk. Final invitations to the wedding littered the green vellum, addressed to people I didn't know. The ceremony was only a week away.

'I do not want Blake at my wedding,' I told her.

Catherine didn't look up. 'Mr Blake has proved indispensable to this family since Richard's death. Of course he will attend.'

'You may have elevated him to master of this house,' I persisted, 'but he does me no favours and I will not suffer his presence. Do this for me and I promise not to cross you again.'

She put town her quill and turned in her seat. 'Explain yourself.'

I swallowed. 'Blake is a brute. He frightens me. Invite him and you will have to drag me into that church and tear the marriage vows from my throat. I mean it, Catherine. You can force me to marry George but I will not countenance that usurper grinning at me from the pews.'

Catherine was silent for a second. Then she picked up the quill, bent her head and started scratching ink across paper again. 'Wedding nerves,' she said carefully. 'Fortunately Mr Blake is not disposed towards sentimental occasions and will think no ill of missing the ceremony. I shall instruct him to remain here.'

I curtsied. 'Thank you, Mrs Worledge.'

The week blurred into a frenzy of preparation. My few chattels were packed away and Catherine's old clothes cleared out of my wardrobe to make way for a new selection of garments, courtesy of my husband to be. Maggie wanted to give the cast-offs to the parish, but Catherine was appalled at the idea.

'Have beggars and wastrels strutting about in my dresses? I'd sooner see them burned,' she declared.

I sliced up the velvet confection Mr Fortescue had provided and fed it to the kitchen fire. I had no need of it now. The hook was firmly in the fish's mouth. Twice Moses Cripps arrived at the kitchen door and on both occasions I was ready, parading in my new dresses, always sure that my perfume was strong and my bodice a little too loose. I also ensured that one of the servants was also present.

'You, out,' Moses ordered Maggie when he found us picking at a basket of sweetmeats together.

'No, Maggie,' I purred. 'Stay. I enjoy your company.'

She looked from one of us to the other, uncertainty colouring her face. Moses, hands balled into fists, said nothing.

It rained on the morning of my wedding. A leaden sky turned my gown the colour of ashes. My hair was coiled beneath a wig, my face smothered in powder to hide my birthmark.

147

I looked lovely. No denying it. Servants hovered around me like wasps around jam, goggling at my dress. I was unaccustomed to flattery and I would be a liar if I said I didn't enjoy the right sort of attention, but I did not want to look pretty. Not for George. I'd sooner go to the wedding dressed in old sacks. Catherine tried to appoint herself maid of honour but I talked her out of it, suggesting that she might put the younger girls to shame. She wore a monstrous wig packed with wilting blooms. Her eyes were glassy with laudanum.

Whilst waiting for the carriage I took a sip of wine, then another. I could not stand in front of a parson in my right mind and vow to love, honour and obey. When the ribbon-bedecked landau arrived, I sucked on a lemon to freshen my breath and tried not to totter up the step.

'You look a little peaky,' Catherine remarked. I told her it was nerves. A virgin's anxiety over her wedding night. Rain drummed on the landau's raised roof. People went about their business. Not many noticed a bride in a shadowed carriage, in the wet.

The journey seemed interminable. Catherine kept a firm grip on my arm. Was that for support or to stop me running away? 'As you will not tolerate Mr Blake, who will give you away?' she said in my ear.

'You planned that he should do it?'

'Who else is there? William?'

'One of George's friends will suffice. He does have some, doesn't he?'

I was ushered into a strange church the way a criminal might be bundled through the prison gate. I was fool enough to think that I might be married by Nathaniel Proudlove, but George's estate edged into the neighbouring parish and this was the site he had chosen for our betrothal. Strangers filled the pews. Heads turned, eyes settled on me. No Marjorie, no little Charlotte with her face full of day dreams.

Catherine handed me over to some fellow in a scarlet army tunic, a smile curling her mouth. George waited at the end of the aisle. A bent, toothless parson stood beside him with a prayer book clutched in his hands. I appraised my husband-to-be with a clarity I had not enjoyed at our previous meetings. I noticed how short he was and realised I did not know his age. Though his cheeks were smooth, wrinkles lurked in the corners of his watery blue eyes. A fat belly strained against the silver buttons of his waistcoat and a wig, sharp as a raven's beak, perched on his head. I had never seen him without one, had no idea what colour his hair was, or whether he had any hair at all. He had chosen a yellow jacket that looked sickly next to my white gown, and the folds of his neck were buried beneath the frilly layers of his cravat. A sword hung from his waist, though I had not known him to be either soldier or seaman. Not once did he look at me throughout the entire ceremony. Behind me, women coughed, men shifted their feet and a baby bawled its heart out. George pressed a silk kerchief to his nose and grimaced.

The parson's voice droned on, countenancing me to be a good and obedient wife. I spoke when he told me to, repeated whatever words he uttered and felt a bite of metal as a second ring was pushed on to my finger. I took the vows that were to condemn me, whispering so the parson had to lean closer, and wincing at the stink of Madeira on his breath. I did it all. I did it because I wanted away from Catherine. I craved freedom from her plots and petty schemes, from under the workings of her blood-drenched hands. A small price in exchange.

A few final words then I was no longer Juliana Rodriguez but Mrs Proudlove. George's wife. His wet lips on my cheek sealed our pact and he took my arm to lead me back down the long aisle. Catherine's expression of triumph was at odds with her heavy black mourning gown. She was like a girl at a party.

Sitting behind her, like a cat with a mouthful of cream, was Adam Fairchild.

I stumbled. George caught me before I went sprawling.

149

His grip on my arm was tighter than needed. I pulled my mouth into a smile, even though my stomach flipped over.

Who had invited him? Did he attend all society weddings, harvesting hearts like some dire reaper even as brides promised themselves to someone else? When did he arrive? Why hadn't I spotted him before?

I was glad to get out of the church. The grey clouds had broken apart, letting the weakening autumn sun cage the churchyard with beams of light. Jabbering women wet my cheeks with insincere kisses. Fingers plucked my dress, filched blooms from my corsage. I felt smothered.

'Who are you people?' I demanded. 'What are you doing at my wedding? I never invited you.'

'We don't need your invitation,' a girl in a lemon-coloured gown shot back.

'I was the one getting married.'

She laughed. 'Makes no difference.'

As if at a given signal, guests drained away like melt water. Reins snapped, gigs and coaches were turned and sent trundling down the road. Catherine stayed back, gossiping with a tardy cluster of women. I searched for my new husband. He was on the churchyard path, deep in conversation with Adam Fairchild. George kept fiddling with his cravat. His cheeks were a bright pink.

I tugged on Catherine's sleeve. 'My stays have come loose,' I fibbed. 'A minute inside the vestry and I shall have them fixed, if the parson will allow.'

'Very well, but be quick about it. Do not keep your husband waiting.'

I dipped an awkward curtsy and swished towards the vestry, skirts dragging on the grass. Drawing near, I heard George spit and bluster while Adam regarded him with a face like flint.

'I have married the wench. You will be paid, sir, and at a handsome rate of interest. A man's wedding is no occasion on which to come debt collecting.'

'See that you do pay, George,' Fairchild replied. 'There is much grumbling about you in town. Were it not for my intercession the dogs would already have been let loose. I suspect your integrity has been stretched even further than your pocket.'

George paled. To my horror he started dribbling. 'Yes . . . Yes, I am grateful, Fairchild, don't doubt it. But we must tarry awhile. The girl is not yet of age.'

'Any bank would gladly offer credit, given the circumstances.'

'Another loan? The estate is already . . .'

Adam spotted me and silenced George with a raised hand. 'Mrs Proudlove, should you not be with the ladies?'

I favoured them both with my sweetest smile. 'Mr Fairchild, I have been a bride barely ten minutes and already you would seek to draw my husband away from me.'

Adam relaxed. The makings of a smile fluttered across his lips. He bowed. 'I doubt I could coax any man away from your side for long, madam.'

'Nevertheless, it must be an important conversation.'

'Simply man's talk. Politics, property matters, that sort of thing. A bore for you, I'm sure.'

'Well, if you gentlemen will excuse me, I must go and thank the parson for the wonderful service.' I swept past them. Fortunately the vestry door wasn't locked. It was made of good English oak and once inside I closed it tight behind me. I was reasonably sure that neither Adam nor George believed I had heard anything of significance but I dared not stretch my luck.

I took a few deep breaths. No sign of the parson. A tall looking glass was set into the alcove opposite. Papery leaves crunched under my shoes, blown inside by autumn winds that were already colouring the trees in shades of red and gold.

I regarded my reflection. Flushed cheeks, visible even under the powder. Eyes a little tired looking. What had

Fairchild been talking about? Why did George look so afraid?

A flicker of movement in the corner of the mirror. I turned, expecting to see the parson. Instead, Moses Cripps stepped out of the shadows. 'Quite the blushing bride, ain't you?' he growled.

'How did you get here?'

'Got a horse and cart, ain't I? That shire's a strong beast. Could haul me to London if it had a mind. Maggie Burns told me where you were getting wed. An easy journey. Nobody noticed me. I was just another tradesman on the road.'

'What do you want? You have no business at my wedding.'

'I've got plenty business.' He stepped in front of the door. 'I have as much right to be here as any man, more so than some.'

Cripps dominated the cramped vestry. His eyes cut into my skull. 'I saw everything from here. Stood and watched you promise your life away to that fop. So now you're a lady and can't be doing with a common working man. Well, before long I reckon you'll ache to have me lying between your knees again.'

'You have no right . . .'

'But I do have a right, Miss Rodriguez, or is that Mrs Proudlove now? You and me had a bargain, remember? A covenant. And I've seen to my side of it.'

He took something out of his pocket and tossed it on to the table. It fell amid scattered prayer books and old sermons. A silver fob watch with an engraved case. 'Now it's time to keep your side,' he finished.

'What have you done?'

'What you wanted. He won't beat you again. Too much of a fancy for himself, that one. It's always a man's undoing.'

'Moses, tell me what's happened.'

'Easy enough. I followed him down to the harbour. He's

152

always there after dark, stripping out some offices. Decided he wanted a piddle. Caught him behind some crates and, bang. Just another body in the water.'

'You weren't meant to kill him, just scare him off, perhaps give him a few bruises. You'll hang. We both will.'

'Anyone who beats a woman like that deserves the life knocked out of him. Don't try to say you didn't want him dead. Why else did you tell me? Why else parade that black eye? What man could hold his temper when faced with such a thing? Now give me what I came for.'

'No.'

Moses hooked his fingers over the front of my gown and pulled. My bodice burst open like a seedpod.

'I could scream,' I warned. 'My husband is just outside the door.'

'You could but you won't.' He pushed me up against the table. His mouth was inches from my ear. 'You want me. Your tongue might spin lies to fool the devil, but your body gives you away.'

With the strength of a bull he ripped off my dress the way he might flick a moth from a candlelit wall. His big frame trembled. 'Now you've got no virgin's gown to hide behind. No harlot's slammerkin either.'

He pushed me to the floor and fell on top of me. My nails tore in to his neck as he split me open. I cried into the dust and dead leaves. My back ground against the stone tiles.

'Is this too much to ask?' he growled. 'I should tup you from now till doomsday for what I've done.'

The wig came off my head in a shower of pins. Moses buried his face in my hair. His tongue wriggled against my scalp and a low, animal noise issued from deep inside his chest. Fire built up inside me and seared through my veins. I stopped fighting him, stopped thinking, just gave myself up to the hot tide of pleasure. This was the stuff of deep, black sin.

Finally, he grunted and pushed me away. I lay supine on the floor, gazing up at him. My eyes took an age to focus. He fastened his breeches, making no move to help as I struggled, weak-kneed to my feet.

'Come away with me,' he said. 'I could give you an honest life.'

'You have a spouse. Where's the honesty in that?'

'You can't refuse me.'

'Why? What are you going to do? Abduct me? Spirit me away somewhere and use me as you want? Am I nothing better than one of your shanks of meat?'

For a moment, Moses said nothing. I wondered if he'd understood. Then his face split into an ugly leer. 'As you like. I ain't got any more use for you. I've had all I want. Women are the same – all fine and headstrong until they get a taste of a man, then they're no different from any sixpenny tart plying her trade around Wexborough harbour. I can come back for you any time I want. You're my whore.'

I shrank away from him. Moses went on cramming his shirt into his waistband. I was being dismissed, tossed aside like a worn-out straw doll.

I shouted for help at the top of my voice. I shrieked until my lungs ached, then picked up the biggest prayer book I could find and hurled it through the vestry window. A jagged shower of stained glass exploded outwards. Shouts carried from the churchyard, followed by the sound of running feet.

Moses stared at me open-mouthed. The vestry door was flung open and men tumbled in, Adam Fairchild and George at their head.

'What in God's name . . .'

I jabbed a finger at Cripps. 'That animal tried to rape me.'

A whicker of steel and Adam had the tip of his sword pressed against Moses' throat. 'It wasn't like that,' the meat carrier spluttered. 'The wench is lying to spare herself shame.'

154

I sobbed gustily, as fine an actress as any that had tripped out on to a stage. 'He delivers beef to Mrs Worledge's house. He has been trying to gain my favour for weeks and grew angry when I refused him. He followed me here, tore off my wedding gown and threatened to snap my neck if I tried to struggle. He has already confessed to murdering Mr Blake. He boasted about the crime right in front of me. I thought I was going to die.'

'Damn you,' Moses roared. 'You'll choke on your own lies.' He grunted as Adam jerked the sword tip. A trickle of blood ran down Cripps's neck and dripped on to his shirt.

'Another word from you,' Fairchild warned, 'and I shall carve out your throat.'

George took me by the shoulder and lifted my chin with his fingertips. His face was devoid of tenderness. 'Did this man poke you?'

I met his eyes. 'No, sir. I am as pure as God would require of any bride.'

He relaxed and let go of my chin. Moses roared again and lunged towards me, heedless of Fairchild's sword. Adam, taken by surprise, was knocked aside. Before Cripps could touch me, a pair of coachmen caught him by the arms. They were burly fellows, accustomed to handling difficult horses. They marched him, stumbling, towards the vestry door.

'There was something else, witch,' Moses bellowed. 'Something other than a fancy watch. Blake had papers, important-looking papers. Pagan the flesher taught me to read a bit. I saw your name on them.'

He said more but by now he was outside and his words were swallowed up in a babble of curious voices. My belly felt as if it had been cast in lead.

Adam resheathed his sword. He picked up my dress and handed it to me. His voice was as smooth as milk. 'Apart from the damage to your gown, you say he did not touch you?'

155

'No,' I replied warily. 'I was able to draw your attention before he had a chance.'

He glanced at the shattered window. 'You certainly managed that. It seems strange, however, that you were able to slip his clutches long enough to do so. He is an uncommonly large fellow, yet moves as quick as a wink.'

'I bit him.'

'An ox of a man, in the heat of passion? I doubt he noticed. Did you see how those coachmen struggled to get him out the door?'

'What are you getting at, Fairchild?' George blustered. 'Are you questioning my wife's honesty?'

'I merely suggest that in the excitement the facts may have become juggled.'

I drew closer to George. 'My mind is not addled, sir. I managed to struggle free, as I told you. Count my injuries if you are still not satisfied. I like neither your manner nor your insinuations. You were keen enough to put your sword to his throat.'

Adam bowed. 'You are not on trial, my dear.'

Catherine appeared with a blanket from her carriage and wrapped it around my shoulders. 'Cover yourself up, Juliana. You look shameful.'

I was ordered to wait in the vestry. A constable had been sent for. Adam took Catherine outside. George sat with his head in his hands. In the alcove, my reflection gazed out from the looking glass. My copper hair seemed to have turned the colour of dried blood.

Chapter Eleven

A great deal of that day's events have fallen out of my head, or been pushed, or cut out. A shocked mind's desperate efforts to save itself. Perhaps they are gone for good, no matter how much I try to pull them back. That might be for the best.

Yet other things remain vivid, as sharp in my memory as the moment they happened. Moses, his hands bound, yelling as he was bundled into the back of his own cart and driven away. Catherine screaming when informed of Blake's murder and rushing home to see if it was true. The parson fussing over me, laying a reassuring hand on my brow, my knee, or any other part of my body he thought might need succour.

I remember mouthing replies to seemingly endless questions, though I cannot recall what was asked or what I said in return. The parson's wife clothed me in a gown hurriedly fetched from her own wardrobe. The fit was poor but in my befuddled state I made no complaint. A surgeon was also summoned, a keen bloodletter whose remedy for any ill humour was to open a vein. I would not let him near me. This wasn't the first time I'd collected a few bruises.

Declared fit enough to travel, I was helped into George's carriage. We journeyed in silence alongside the turnpike road. My new husband would not look at me, choosing instead to sit and scowl out of the window. We stopped at a coaching inn as sunset painted the sky with streaks of fire.

George spent most of the night downstairs drinking with some friends who had ridden out from his gambling club. I was left in the care of the innkeeper's wife. She spent hours in an armchair soaking up the heat from my bedchamber fire.

Perhaps George was afraid I might try to climb out of the window, or the shock of the day would wear off and I'd throw a shrieking fit. The woman offered no help with my injuries, which had all subsided into one dull ache.

Eventually her fat head lolled on to her shoulder and she began wheezing like a pair of leaky bellows. I huddled myself for warmth and gazed around the narrow bedchamber, trying to salvage some hope out of the ruins of the past few hours.

The papers. Moses Cripps had found the papers. And I had watched him carted off.

At just after midnight according to the mantel clock, George stumbled into the room. He barked his shin on the edge of the door and cursed. The fat woman woke up and he sent her squealing from the chair.

Alone with my new husband, I managed to manoeuvre him on to the bed and, grunting, pulled off his boots whilst he leaned over the side of the mattress and retched. He stank of brandy. It reminded me too much of Richard. Getting the rest of George's clothes off proved impossible. I left him on top of the coverlet and climbed into bed. At some point during the dark hours he wriggled between the sheets, fumbled with his breeches and made me his wife. Afterwards he fell asleep with both legs sprawled across mine.

The following day, George sat over breakfast with a splitting head and an expression that could sour milk. 'I examined the sheets of our bed,' he said, forking trout into his mouth and swallowing. 'There was no blood.'

My own food congealed in my throat. 'I beg your pardon?'

'They were clean. This morning when you were taking air in the yard, I returned to our room. The maid had not yet changed the bed linen. There were no bloodstains.' He put down his fork. 'You were not a virgin when I came to you last night.'

158

'You were drunk,' I countered. 'You couldn't manage.'

'I know well enough what I could and couldn't do. You were no fresh little maid. Someone's broken you in, stolen what's mine by right.'

'In the vestry . . .'

'You claimed that fellow *tried* to have you. In God's name you said you were pure. That was your word. Pure. You've been tupped like a bitch in season. I could name you whore and throw you into the ditch.'

'Will you?'

He pushed back his chair, got up and walked away from the table.

'I had been attacked,' I called after him. 'I was hurt. What consideration did you give to that?'

I fingered my wedding ring and listened to the rain pounding on the carriage roof. The coach lurched on the rutted track. The driver spouted oaths above the steady pummelling as he fought to keep the horses in check. Beyond the window lay a washed-out world of grey. Flat fields stretched away under a lumpen sky, the soil dark and sodden.

I sat alone in my dry enclave. George had ridden ahead on a hired mare, his face petulant, his cloak flapping from his shoulders. He had tried to reason with me, tried to suggest that perhaps a fall from the saddle had resulted in the apparent loss of my maidenhead. 'Such an easy thing to happen,' he'd said, trying to keep his voice light.

'I don't go riding,' was my response.

So began my life as the wife of a country squire, taken from the town I knew to a sprawling estate. Locals spoke in a strange, rolling tongue. You could look for miles and not see another house, just acre upon acre of farmland rolling to distant wooded hills. My new home, Milton Manor, was a pillared block of buff-coloured sandstone. Much of its face was smothered in ivy, half-buried windows winking at me

159

from within their green prison. Neat but unremarkable gardens spread out from the gravel drive, flowerbeds slicing into the lawns like the spokes of a wheel. Behind the house and stables, a modest orchard of two dozen apple trees had thrown down a scattering of unpicked fruit to rot in the grass.

That first day, I was met at the door by the housekeeper who curtsied and addressed me as Mrs Proudlove, a name that stuck uncomfortably in the throat. The staff lined up in the marbled hallway to greet me. They bowed or curtsied as I passed along their rank, and I sensed their eyes on me. George was not present. I was informed that he had changed his clothes and was in the middle of a nap.

That night, on an immense bed in a high-ceilinged room, he claimed me again. I was squashed beneath his heavy, thrusting body. Sated, he rolled over and lay on his back, gasping. A sheen of perspiration coated his face. I waited, damp, wrung out.

Presently he slid off the bed and pulled on his breeches. 'You're a cold bitch,' he spat, scraping his hair into a tail behind his neck. 'I'll have an heir from you as my duty demands, but tupping a pig would give more pleasure.'

He slammed the door on his way out and did not return that night. I lay amidst the rumpled bedclothes and watched the last flickers of the dying fire play across the ceiling. My cheeks were damp but some time passed before I realised that I was crying.

George had visitors in the morning, local gentry who had come to offer congratulations and sniff out his new bride. Mostly they were polite, if curious, and guarded in what they said. Wives and daughters put their heads together and whispered.

Afterwards I took George to task over the matter. 'Those women who came to the house today,' I said. 'They were gossiping about me.'

'Country folk are a superstitious breed, whatever their station,' he replied without looking up from his newspaper. 'Some are put out by the mark on your face. 'Tis harmless nonsense and you would do best to ignore it.'

'Are you sure that is the only reason?'

'I am sure,' he said, taking a sip of port.

Half a hundred candles hissed and spat hot wax in an iron holder suspended from the ceiling. The bad weather had continued, turning the day into a twilight sludge.

'The man who attacked me at the church,' I continued after a moment. 'What will become of him?'

'As far as I know he was taken to Dunsgate gaol, where he shall no doubt be hung. The case is cut and dried. Your attendance at the assizes is unlikely to be required.' George glanced at me over the top of his paper. 'Some questions may arise but no one will doubt your word. I shall see to it.'

Later, George told me he was going riding. He kept an ageing nag, which he laughingly called a hunter, and spent a couple of hours each day plodding around the grounds. My husband was not a man of the land. Though his estate included some good grazing with extensive wheat fields and a modest amount of livestock, I quickly discovered it was other people's hard labour that kept things running. As for George himself, there was always another card game.

One morning, tired of staring listlessly out of one window after another, I offered to go walking with him. 'Just a stroll around the beech tree,' I suggested. 'I'd love to smell the autumn air.'

'I would hate to think of any further calamities befalling you,' he replied. I did not offer again.

Days merged into one another. It was hard to tell one week from the next. The manor was a cathedral of a place compared to my Wexborough home. Passages were endless, ceilings impossibly high. I had to ask directions to every room. Servants fluttered around like ghosts, not a flicker on their wooden faces. I wasn't allowed to do anything for myself. If I wanted coffee, it appeared on the table beside me. If I sneezed, a clean handkerchief was waved under my nose. I began to miss the warm times, helping Maggie Burns in the kitchen, or just delving into a pot of soup that I'd had a hand in making. I felt like a guest in a strange lodging house.

George never spent a whole night with me. Business took him away for days at a time, except that I knew his business was cards and his time spent at one of his town clubs. My experiences with Richard had taught me all the signs. On each occasion, George returned from these trips with a hard face and locked himself in the smoking room for hours, not seeing or talking to anyone.

During his absences, I spent hours by the parlour window sewing crude samplers with fingers that were never meant for needle and thread. I ached for a hot kitchen hearth. To the staff I was always 'madam' or 'Mrs Proudlove'. Never 'Juliana'. Never a friend.

No one of my acquaintance ever called to the house or wrote to me. From Catherine I heard absolutely nothing. I had no idea if Moses Cripps really had murdered Blake. Despite his crudity he hadn't struck me as a killer. George never broached the subject and I had no desire to submit myself to any more of his turnabout questions. It seemed as if our lives were severed from the rest of the world. Even Parson Proudlove never took the trouble to visit. I often thought of Charlotte and her unicorns, remembering those round, dark eyes.

'My father is much taken up with matters of the spirit,' George explained irritably when I remarked on the parson's absence. 'His is a large parish with an ever-wayward flock and he cannot spare the time to journey the breadth of the county for the sake of social niceties. He is getting on in years and coach travel seldom agrees with him.'

'Is that why he did not attend our wedding?'

George buried his face in a book.

Desperate for company, I followed my nose and slipped downstairs to the kitchen. I found none of the cosy familiarity that had made Maggie Burns's kitchen so endearing to a girl in the mood for toast and a tall yarn. A cavern of a room was divided along its length by a long oak table. A gaping, soot-ringed hearth yawned from the opposite wall. Above a pile of blood-red embers, a turnspit was cranked by a panting dog running endlessly in a wheel hung from the ceiling. White-washed walls, studded with hooks, cathedralled above me.

Servants sat clustered around the far end of the table. They gaped at me as I stood dithering in the doorway. The men were playing cards, a practice that George had forbidden among his staff. A minute of silence stretched out between us.

'Clumsy of you not to leave a lookout,' I said. 'Go on, finish your game.'

A sallow-skinned man seated at the end of the table picked up the cards and dealt them out. I recalled that he was Samuel, George's gamekeeper. He had the better of his fellows judging by the heap of pennies beside him. He quickly stripped everyone of their remaining stakes then gathered the cards into a neat pile before tucking them into his jacket pocket.

'Is there something we can do for you, madam?'

'I am merely looking over my house. I thought there might be a back door to the stables through these kitchens.'

Samuel pushed himself away from the table and gestured me to follow him. I walked past the other servants and waited while he drew the bolts on an arched oak door. A slender man, tall, with long arms and an easy-going gait. Hair, so black it almost glittered, was scraped back into a tail behind his neck. Other, thicker hair sprouted from the backs of his hands.

'Going riding, madam?' he enquired as I slipped past him into the yard. 'If so, you're hardly dressed for it.'

'Less of your insolence . . .' I began, turning back to face him, but the door had already closed behind me.

*

If I couldn't be a part of one world then I would force my way into the other. It was impossible to continue like this, a nothing person drifting in a strange house with a husband I hardly saw. So I wore my gowns, painted my face with fine French rouge and joined the giddy whirl that was country society – an endless round of tea parties and glittering balls.

George treated my new-found enthusiasm with suspicion but I was telling the truth when I explained that I was bored. If I was to be a squire's wife then I would play the part with conviction. What did it benefit me to sit at the window all day and stare out at the rose beds?

So he took me to his parties, reluctantly at first. I smiled at the proper times and exchanged pleasantries with strangers who warmed to me as I flattered and fawned my way through those darkening autumn nights.

Recalling all that Mary Morgan had taught me about lady-like behaviour, I joined the women in their parlours. Although curious, they were wary of this newcomer in their midst and questioned me, in polite roundabout ways, about my background. Of course everyone had heard of the wife George had brought out of town and talk soon turned to what had been fashionable in Wexborough when I was last there. I also proved to have a willing ear, which cracked the ice on their tongues in short order. Gossip poured out. It seemed there was nothing they would not tell me. A secret passed in confidence was safe for less than a minute before the whole gaggling herd knew about it. I simply repeated everything I heard, careful not to add anything of my own. No one seemed to notice and when I told someone the same story twice at two parties in the space of a week she laughed both times and declared it a scandal, though it was getting to be an old scandal by then. I was as much a subject of gossip as anyone else. A few people hinted that stories had wafted out of Wexborough as if blown on a bad wind. I wouldn't bite their baited hooks, so they tried other ways to unsettle me.

'The younger girls are afraid of you,' one hostess remarked. 'They think you will play cuckold with their husbands.'

I twitched my mouth into a semblance of a smile. 'I am a married woman, no thief of hearts.'

She slapped her fan into her palm. Her mouth was crammed with badly fitting porcelain teeth. She spat through each sentence. 'Marriage is a means by which women gain a well-fed belly and roof above their heads. You don't wear pretty jewels or ride in an expensive carriage by remaining a spinster. Matrimony allows men to put an acceptable face on their passions. It is a useful arrangement.'

'What about love?'

She laughed as if I had said something foolish. 'You are a wife yourself, my dear. You should know the answer to that one.'

Once he realised that I would not disgrace him, George was pleased with my rapid acceptance into the social fold. When it was our turn to entertain guests I became the perfect hostess. Visitors left the house complimenting George on his fine choice of a spouse.

'You are a good girl,' he told me in the aftermath of one such evening. 'I must say there were times when I thought you an awkward cuss but I am glad to see you settling into your role.'

I lowered my eyes and curtsied. 'I seek only to do you credit, sir.'

'See that you continue to do so.'

But George held other entertainments, gatherings to which I was not always invited. A small card circle visited the manor for his amusement, often involving a few members of the local gentry and, unusually, one or two of their women. These games of faro or whist were informal and the stakes never rose above a few shillings. If someone was unavailable I was asked to make up the numbers but I had no talent for the game. I fumbled the cards, missed my call or picked the wrong hand. My humble stake was plucked away from me in a matter of minutes.

'I should not let your wife play too often, George,' one of his friends smirked, 'lest she bankrupts you.'

'I don't find that remark amusing,' George replied, fingering his neck cloth.

'Really? You need a sense of humour given the way she handles the cards.'

Everyone laughed. My cheeks blushed roses. William Loxborough was my tormentor's name, a wine trader and owner of extensive farmlands bordering our own. I had encountered him at a couple of local tea parties where he had treated me with polite indifference. He was a squat man with a face that resembled a turnip freshly pulled from the soil. On his head sat a monstrous brown periwig that was at least a century out of fashion and he snorted fat portions of snuff from a silver box kept in his waistcoat pocket.

Accompanying him was a brace of giggling young women called Elspeth and Harriet, whom he loosely described as his nieces. I recognised them from my wedding, where they had chattered through the service. Loxborough regularly slapped their thighs or squeezed their plump behinds, chuckling through blackening teeth whenever one or the other squealed. George had invited them to stay the night and Loxborough decided to retire early. His 'nieces' took themselves into the parlour and plundered our sherry.

On retiring, I found that the maid had forgotten my nightly posset. I was halfway down the corridor when I heard giggling coming from Elspeth and Harriet's bedchamber. They'd neglected to close the door properly and my ear was drawn to the narrow crack.

I was eavesdropping like a common servant but this was my home. The girls were half drunk. I heard the chink of glass. They'd likely smuggled a decanter into the room.

'That girl is such an effort,' Harriet declared. 'Did you see the way she handled those cards? Why do you suppose

George married her? She reminds me of the gypsy wench who brings the fish baskets each Friday. Do you suppose she has money?'

'She must do,' Elspeth replied, 'though I don't know if George has seen a whisker of it. All kinds of stories are circulating about her.'

'And as for that red streak on her face, you'd think she was poxed. Someone ought to put a horse's nosebag over her head.'

Both dissolved into giggles, then Elspeth asked: 'Will you see George later?'

'He asked me to come to his chamber at eleven, when plum-face is asleep. He keeps to his own bed, understandably. I have been promised sweetmeats and a night I shall not forget.'

'You'll end up nibbling on more than sweetmeats, I think. Supposing plum-face finds out?'

Laughter. 'Supposing she does?'

I huddled in the dark silence of my room until the clock in the downstairs hall struck the hour. I hadn't yet grown accustomed to the peace of the country. No barking dogs, drunks mouthing oaths or carts rattling past at all hours of the night. Sounds here were amplified. A creaking floorboard often jerked me into a clutching wakefulness.

Now, outside in the passage, the whisper of slippers, muted laughter and the sound of a door gently closing. I slipped out of bed, reached for the doorknob. My hand hesitated. I knew George slept with whores. It was something all gentlemen did, apparently. As his wife I was expected to accept the situation without complaint. But this was worse. I was being usurped under my own roof. I remembered the way William Loxborough had poked fun at me when I picked up too many cards, or put the wrong one down at the wrong time. Harriet and Elspeth, their eyes full of contempt as they flicked secret messages at one another behind their fans. And laughter, always more laughter for George's cloddish wife.

I swung my door open and flapped down the corridor in my nightshift, seeking the satisfaction of bursting into George's bedchamber and catching him, bare-buttocked, between Harriet's fat thighs. I'd scream 'Adulterer' and stir the entire household. All the servants, even in the furthest reaches of the manor, would hear me. I imagined parliament granting me a divorce. George would be shamed, his fortune leeched.

I got within five paces of his room when a hand caught my elbow. 'Where do you suppose you're going?' Elspeth purred.

She was in her dressing gown but lacked the gritty, puff-eyed look of the freshly wakened. Sherry tainted her breath. Her eyes glittered in the light from the candle sputtering in her hand. I had no idea where she'd sprung from.

'This is my house,' I said, shaking my arm free. 'I am not answerable to you as to what I do in it.'

I moved towards George's door but she slipped in front of me. 'You are not to go in there.'

'Get out of my way.'

She didn't budge. The hint of a smile passed across her mouth. 'Go back to bed. That is the best place for you.'

In a breath I felt I could curl my fingers around her neck and squeeze until her black heart burst. Blood pounded in my ears. She waited me out. Pale breasts rose and fell beneath the smooth material of her dressing gown. No need to say any more. Confidence crawled over her face like a nest of ants. My fury lay in knowing that she was right, that I would do nothing – could do nothing. Physically, Elspeth was bigger than I was, though I believed I could fight like a cornered tomcat if it came to it. But the thought of finding George tupping that obnoxious slut made my belly squirm. Barging in would only bring a bucket load of trouble down on my head. I had put in too much effort chipping out a tenuous foothold in this slippery household. Elspeth, the smug bitch, knew it.

Like a scolded child, I returned to my room and did not

emerge again for the rest of that long night. Loxborough and his party left early the following day with a promise to return in two weeks' time. There was no mistaking the look of triumph Harriet flashed me. Elspeth had told her everything, I supposed. I pictured them giggling about it over their morning coffee.

George was his usual self during lunch and only nodded when I said I felt unwell and wished to walk around the gardens. My stomach tumbled like a butter churn leaving me in no mood for a confrontation. The fresh air did little to cheer me up and my mind was a cauldron of black thoughts as I crossed the stable yard towards the kitchen. Perhaps a cup of hot milk would settle my belly.

As I reached the door, Samuel the gamekeeper stepped out, pulling his felt tricorne over his ears. He acknowledged me with a nod and strode off in the direction of the gardens. I ran to catch up, struggling to match his long gait. 'Samuel, wait. I would have words with you.'

He halted and pulled off his hat. 'What might I do for you, Mrs Proudlove?'

I paused to catch my breath. 'You are not a local man,' I managed to say. 'Are you?'

'No, madam. I am from Newfoundland, though I have not seen my home in nigh on twenty years.'

'Where did you learn to play cards? You took the kitchen staff for a tidy sum.'

He immediately became cautious. 'I picked it up.'

'Do you cheat?'

He blinked a couple of times. 'A man has no call to cheat if he's clever enough. I don't call being clever cheating. Cards bought me my freedom and I owe them my life. I take care to use them right and they look after me.'

'Cards saved your life? I don't understand.'

He looked me up and down, though there was no disrespect in his manner. I sensed that he was debating whether to tell me any more. 'I daresay you wouldn't,' he said at last, 'but then you didn't spend two years rotting on a prison barge for a crime you didn't commit.'

'Crime?'

Samuel glanced at the sky. Gathering clouds heralded another afternoon of rain. 'You must forgive me, madam. I've prattled on too long.'

'Do you have a room in the main house?'

He eyed me curiously. 'I sleep in the gamekeeper's cottage at the edge of the woods. Keep a better ear out for poachers that way. The estate used to be plagued with them until I took this post.'

'What do you do if you catch a poacher?'

'I break his leg.'

'That is barbaric.'

He shrugged. 'Better than packing him off to Dunsgate treadmill. Any man sent there for more than a year at a stretch often comes out in a sack and poaching in these parts carries a two-year sentence. Most of the county magistrates are landowners who don't take to having their game plundered, whether the thieves are starving or not. Some have laid gin traps that could lop a fellow's legs off. You won't hear many complaints about my methods.'

'This cottage of yours? Will you take me there?'

His expression hardened. 'Excuse me, madam?'

I laughed. I could not help it. He waited me out, eyes like flint beneath the brim of his tricorne. 'I've no mind to do something foolish in a garden hut with a gamekeeper more than twice my age,' I spluttered. 'There is something else I need. Something far more important.'

'May I ask what that might be?'

'Revenge.'

The gamekeeper's cottage was a stone box smothered in thick fingers of ivy. On the far side a row of trees stood like sentries, a vanguard for the woodland beyond. Good hunting country with plenty to tempt the poachers Samuel had mentioned. In summer this corner of the estate would be alive with lush greenery and buzzing insects. Now a carpet of dry blackening leaves rustled underfoot as Samuel led the way up a flagged path, pushed open the door and motioned me inside. I had to stoop to enter and wrinkled my nose at the deep, musty scent that hung beneath the beamed ceiling like an invisible fog. Half a dozen rabbit skins were strung from the rafters like executed felons. Canvas sacks bulging with secrets filled every corner. A hunting rifle mounted on pegs stood guard above a sooty fireplace and a coarse wooden table was littered with books.

I heard a scratching noise. Samuel noticed my expression. He reached under a bunk and drew out a brass cage.

I recoiled. 'A rat.'

'No, a ferret. Good for rabbiting.' The animal reared up against the bars, nose twitching as it regarded me with bright, button eyes.

'Revenge is a dark business,' Samuel continued, nudging the cage back under the bed with the edge of his boot. 'I don't know why you seek it, nor do I wish to. This job is all I have. If I lose it . . .'

I unclasped a pearl necklace from around my throat and dropped it on the bed. A wedding gift from one of George's wealthy friends. Samuel eyed it without comment. Gamekeeper or not, he would have some idea of its worth.

'I want to learn how to play cards,' I told him. 'Every trick you know.'

He nodded. 'I can show you, but you'll need a stiff face and a good eye to make it work.'

'I have two weeks in which to master the game. Teach me and the necklace is yours. Can you do it?'

He tilted his head. 'How badly do you want to win?'

Day after day I sat in that tumbledown cottage while Samuel flicked cards one way and then another, calling up kings or knaves, hearts or diamonds seemingly at will. He was an

171

easy man to warm to. Once he accepted that I was serious in my intentions, and that it wasn't some 'lady's whim', he seemed to relax.

'Get a feel for the game,' he told me with a wink. 'Sense when the hand is going your way or when it's turning against you. Don't hold the cards like slabs of wood but here, like this. They won't burn your fingers, only your pocket if you don't play wisely.'

'I can't know what the other players are holding,' I protested. 'Luck isn't something I can call to heel whenever it suits.'

'No, but you can read faces. It can take a man a lifetime to master himself, to give nothing away in either tone or gesture. Few manage it and those that do usually move on to better things than the card table.'

'Read faces?'

Samuel shrugged. 'Can't you tell when someone is pleased or angry with you simply from the way they look?' He didn't wait for an answer. 'People give all sorts of things away. The key is to watch your opponent, not listen to what he's saying. Is he sweating? Does he look worried or triumphant? Are his eyes darting around even though his face is a picture of confidence? Be discreet but watch for nervous habits – plucking at hair, rubbing thumb and forefinger together, reaching for a drink every few seconds even though the glass is empty. It doesn't matter what cards you hold. If you're afraid to take risks you can't win. Success hinges on pretending to have something you don't, something better than the other player. Twist his mind, punch holes in his resolve, make him believe with such certainty that he won't dare to try to match you. Don't trust to luck, she's too fickle. Make the cards work for you. Pride will keep your opponent in the game.'

Samuel held my fingers and showed me how to manipulate the cards in a way that would confuse and beguile the eye. He was a patient man; quiet, always evenly spoken.

He cajoled where necessary and served up encouragement whenever I showed signs of mastering these tricky printed oblongs. Whilst he was out on his rounds, I sat in the parlour and practised until my fingertips turned numb. Needlework lay abandoned as I turned the cards again and again, wincing every time I fumbled or dropped one on the floor.

Going to the cottage was never a problem. Because the other servants liked and respected Samuel, they kept any gossip to themselves. George was always in Wexborough, or out riding, or napping in his study. He rarely visited my bedchamber and so far nothing stirred in my womb.

By the end of the first week I felt ready to try a proper game. Three times running I was beaten. Samuel laughed when I discarded my best card and tried to play my worst. No malice lurked in his humour, but I cat-hissed and threw the cards on to the floor.

Samuel knelt and picked them up. He placed the deck on the table in front of me. 'It's not your ignorance of the game that will beat you,' he explained, 'but your temper.'

'You think this is just a game?'

'The rules are the same, whatever your reasons. So we'll start again, and this time you'll keep the cards on the table top where they belong.'

'Promise you won't laugh at me again.'

'Do something stupid and I'll laugh until my breeches split. It won't be any less than you deserve. Listen, learn, and don't make any more mistakes.'

'Tell me, Samuel, what did you do to warrant imprisonment, whether unfair or not?'

He fingered his jacket cuff. 'You have to realise that I'm from a proud family. It was with pride that I fought for the British against the French, though neither had any business waging war on my land. And it was a British general's wife who accused me of trying to violate her when I wouldn't pander to her fancies. All of this is common knowledge. I've made no secret of it.'

I said nothing. My heart was in my feet.

'In the barge I was surrounded by Frenchies,' he continued. 'Prisoners, all of them, and half starved or fever-stricken because of their wounds. I was afraid they'd try to throttle me in my sleep but I was no Englishman. Though none could speak a word of my tongue I made better friends there than I ever found in a line of red-coated soldiers.'

He cleared his throat. 'They carved model ships out of rat bones, using other bones as tools. Strands of hair fashioned the rigging. One man traded a boat with the turnkey. Got a deck of cards and taught me backstreet tricks. I'd managed to smuggle some gold aboard, stuffed it up my behind if you'll pardon me for saying so and used that to lure the barge master into a game. Staked my freedom against it. I won. I had to win. At first I thought he wouldn't let me go but what was one less prisoner? He could say I'd died and been thrown overboard. My country was a changed place and I a crim-inal, so I used the gold to buy passage to England. And now, proud that I was, I work as another man's servant. If I ever feel hard done by it, the cards don't let me forget. Now that's enough tales from me. Let's get back to the game.'

With each hour my abilities grew. One afternoon, amidst a downpour that had the cottage roof leaking like a piece of muslin, I gawped at the cards in front of me and realised that I had won.

He smiled, gathered up the deck and tucked it on to a shelf. 'You're ready,' he said.

I shook my head. 'Not quite.'

I had been finding out as much as I could about William Loxborough, this fellow who thought himself so high above others that he could insult another man's wife to his face and laugh about it afterwards. I invited the local scold, Mary Christchurch, to come and take a glass of canary at the manor. Miserable Mary as she was known, whose face could sour milk and who would gladly sell her mother's soul for news of a good scandal. I poked in the dirt, stirred up the ashes of Loxborough's past and plied Mary with drink until her tongue damned him.

'He has a child on the way, did you know that?' she asked, coughing into her glass. 'He's gone and given Elizabeth Huxley, daughter of the local magistrate no less, a swollen belly. Her husband has been off fighting in America these past two years.'

'When is the baby due,' I asked, keeping my tone light.

''Twas due a week ago. The child is sitting awkwardly in the womb and the local quack fears it will be a difficult labour. I do not think the poor woman wants to live. Her papa has threatened to pack her off to a comfort home if she does not publicly name the father.'

I nodded. I had already learned that Loxborough had a reputation for chasing the wives of absent men.

'I think Lizzie fears her husband's anger more than anything,' Mary continued. 'She has threatened to smother the baby if Loxborough refuses to accept responsibility, yet he will not allow it be given over to the parish. I think he wants the poor mother dead.'

I plucked the top from the decanter. 'More canary?'

The moon stared brittle light on Loxborough's coach as it rattled to a halt in front of the manor. George met them in the hallway. A breath of chilly air whispered through the open door. Something was brewing, like a dark concoction in a pot with the lid about to burst.

Loxborough greeted me with a hearty laugh. I tried not to flinch as Elspeth and Harriet pecked my cheek. I felt as if their kisses had branded me and the scent of their cologne turned my stomach. George was showered in their affections. He slid a hand around Harriet's waist and squeezed.

'Best not get too playful, George,' Loxborough chided. 'More than enough time for games later.' He regarded me. 'Is that not so, my dear?'

175

I dipped a curtsy and kept my eyes on the floor. 'I am looking forward to it.'

The two girls dissolved into giggles.

Dinner was mercifully brief. Everyone seemed keen to have it out of the way. Elspeth and Harriet kept glancing at me and nudging one another. Afterwards the men joined us in the parlour and talked a little business but their minds were on other things. 'What say we have a hand or two of cards to put us in good humour for the evening?' Loxborough said. 'And you, my dear Juliana, must join us again. The game would be so dull without you.'

Faces turned towards me, lips parted, teeth glimmering wetly in the soft light, eyes bright with anticipation.

'I would be delighted,' I said.

'Splendid. Simply splendid.' Loxborough rose from his armchair and exchanged a look with George. My heart was in my throat as I followed the others into the withdrawing room. A card table had already been set up, waiting like an executioner's block. I turned to Harriet, who had taken hold of my arm.

'Shall I begin?'

'Uncle always starts the game,' she retorted. 'Do not worry, Mrs Proudlove, your turn will come soon enough.'

'No, let her try,' Elspeth laughed. 'We can wait while she picks the cards up off the floor.'

I took my place at the table and fingered the deck. The cards felt cold, their edges knife blades ready to slice my pride into strips.

Treat them with respect, Samuel's voice said in my mind. Never forget.

I pretended to fudge the first hand. Everyone watched with quiet confidence, exchanging amused glances as I pushed more coppers into the centre of the green-topped table. Loxborough matched my stake, as did the others, and chuckled as he shoved an oversized pipe between his teeth. 'Let the entertainment begin,' he announced.

I won the first game in less than a minute and plucked his stake from under his bulbous nose. He stared, thunderstruck, at the empty space on the table where his money had lain, then dismissed me with a flick of the hand. 'Beginner's luck favours even you, m'dear. Enjoy your pennies while you have the chance, for a pittance is all you shall win from me tonight.'

I played again, glanced at each of my opponent's faces and placed two shillings on the table. Loxborough laughed uproariously. 'What's this? You want to up the stakes? George, your wife has lost her wits. A glimpse of good fortune and already she would have herself out of the game.'

He matched my stake. Others threw in their money. I won again and then again, upping the price each time. Suddenly no one was laughing any more.

'How high are you willing to go, Mr Loxborough?' I asked, leaning over the table and staring into his blood-tinged eyes. 'Shall I tell your friends that you were beaten by a woman who had barely touched a playing card as little as a month ago? I am sure the news will carry well around the ladies' parlours and perhaps the gentlemen's smoking rooms as well.'

'Juliana . . .' George warned.

'No, damn it,' Loxborough snapped. 'Let the wench play. I'll strip her of her paltry winnings and wipe the smugness of her face, watch and see if I don't.'

A flick of the cards proved him a liar. Shillings were replaced by sovereigns, followed by guineas. I emptied his purse, his jacket and the pockets of his satin breeches. I took the gold rings from his right hand and the fob watch out of his waistcoat. My pile of treasure increased as his face grew darker. Harriet's silver bracelet and cameo choker became mine before I put her out of the game for good and I relieved Elspeth of a gold brooch even as she begged me to let her keep it because it had belonged to her grandmama.

George sat, white faced, sipping glass after glass of port.

A cloud of blue tobacco smoke choked the air above his head. Twice he had tried to stop the game and both times Loxborough waved him away. Soon, only two of us faced each other across this green battleground. Discarded cards lay like dying soldiers. I could barely move for the pile of money and trinkets in front of me. Loxborough's eyes played Judas. I let him win five guineas then plucked them back in the very next turn. This sweating, heap of a man was mine to play with, his obnoxious nieces backdrops to his destruction.

'Another ten guineas,' I demanded, after winning again.

He scratched deep into his pockets then searched them a second time. Finally, he produced a crumpled wad of notepapers and asked for quill and inkpot, which George handed him. Painstakingly, he began to write an I.O.U. I snatched the paper out of his fingers and ripped it to pieces.

'I am not one of your gambling-house fops,' I told him. 'I don't want paper promises. Ten guineas are what you owe and I will have the coins in my hand now. Either that or winnings of my own choosing.'

He stared at me as though facing a demon that had prophesied his death. 'Well, it seems your wife has been leading us all a merry dance these past few weeks, George,' he said shakily. 'I wonder what other talents she keeps hidden.'

I rapped the surface of the table. Port slopped over the green baize. 'Talk to me. I am the one who has beaten you. Pay or suffer disgrace.'

He laid down the quill and tucked the notebook back into his jacket pocket. His fingers shook. In the hearth, a log burst apart in a shower of sparks. On the couch, Harriet sobbed in her sister's arms. Elspeth glared at me as though she would see me burned at the stake. I matched her with a choice look of my own and she turned away.

'Very well,' Loxborough coughed. 'If my word as a gentleman does not suit, what winnings do you demand?'

'Your unborn bastard. The one you forced into Lizzie Huxley's womb.'

Chapter Twelve

'Your actions beggar belief.' George paced the parlour carpet, his boots threatening to wear a path in the thick pile. 'I introduce you to society and this is how you reward me, by humiliating a close friend and dragging my family name into disrepute.'

He paused to clatter among the decanters and pour himself a drink – a generous measure of brandy, though it was well before noon. 'I had high hopes for you, Juliana, especially as you seemed to be settling in. All this talk of wishing to become a dutiful wife – I have met many devious men at my club, men who would strip a fellow of his fortune with the same ease as they draw breath, but your capacity for deception would humble even them. Tell me where you learned to play cards like that. Have you always known and all these weeks of fudgery merely another deceit, another lie?'

He gulped his drink. Half dribbled down the front of his shirt. He wiped his mouth, banged down the glass and filled it again. 'Why'd you do it, eh Juliana? You've never met Elizabeth Huxley. Why give a ha'penny for what happens to her brat? It could be stillborn. Then where will all your tricks and contrivances have got you?'

I pushed myself deeper into the armchair. My eyes were full of grit, my brain begging for sleep. It had been a long night. Arguments, threats, banging doors and broken friendships. But I had won. Loxborough would not be back. His bastard child would be delivered into my arms the day it was born. I had picked up all my winnings from the table and thrown it in the face of her uncaring lover. 'Give this to Elizabeth Huxley,' I'd told him. 'Get her the best midwife you can find. Do that much for her.'

Loxborough left before daybreak, hauling his coachman out of his bed in the stables and forcing him, still in his nightshirt, on to the driver's seat. George went to see them off, trying to placate his precious friend's temper and at the same time console Harriet and Elspeth, who had turned into a pair of spitting cats. What would they say about plumface now over the rims of their sherry glasses?

While George blustered around outside I slipped upstairs to my bedchamber and barred the door but he had not followed. Some hours later I crept into the withdrawing room to be told by a bleary-eyed housekeeper that my husband had gone riding. At least I knew that to be the truth. His riding clothes were damp from the early drizzle and smelled of horse. A crop was tucked into the leg of his boot.

'I was already aware of your penchant for other women's babies,' he continued. 'I bore the wagging tongues in the hope that I might turn you into a good wife. I can only assume you had other goals, namely to humble William and make a donkey out of me.'

I sat up straight in the chair. 'The same way you have allowed me to be humiliated? I know what you were up to last time, George, and it wasn't teaching that tart Harriet how to play whist. If you want me to start playing the decent wife then it's time you behaved like an honourable husband.'

George sat down then stood up again. He pulled the crop from his boot and slapped it against his palm. 'Harriet is a good friend.'

'How many other such friends are there? Have you already taken an entire gaggle of whores to your bed in the name of such friendship? You don't love me, George. You'd sooner spend a night between some strumpet's legs than waste a minute of tenderness on me.'

He jabbed the crop at me. 'Have a care not to test my patience, Juliana. Plans have been made for that baby. You cannot propose to bring it into my house.'

'What plans? By whom?'

He fumbled his brandy glass. It thumped on to the rug. 'What does it matter? I don't want it across my threshold. I won't hear of it.'

'Fine, as long as Loxborough honours his debt.'

'He is a gentleman.'

I laughed. 'If he was a gentleman he would have no debt to settle.'

George whipped the crop across my cheek. I screamed and banged my head against the back of the chair. My eyes watered with the pain. I put my hand to my face. Blood coated my fingers in a crimson glove.

'Learn your place,' George spat.

I sprang to my feet, grabbed an inkpot from the writing desk and hurled it. George was too startled to react. The pot caught him squarely in the chest, spattering his silk shirt with dark fluid. 'Don't you hit me,' I snarled. 'Don't you ever lift so much as a finger to me again or I swear I shall have a knife out of the kitchen and murder you in your bed. I am not some beast you can thrash at your leisure.'

He dabbed at the mess on his shirt with his handkerchief but only succeeded in spreading the stain. 'Vixen. I would have you dragged from the axle of my carriage if it was not for . . .'

He swallowed the words, gulped air and turned red about the cheeks.

'If it was not for what, George?' I prompted.

He dropped the blackened handkerchief and thumped out of the room, slamming the door behind him. A puddle of ink spread out from the spilled pot.

I pressed a square of lace against my injured cheek. 'If you will not tell me, then I shall find out.'

*

My husband left on horseback that afternoon, a travel bag buckled to the saddle. He did not tell me where he was going and refused to discuss anything else. I surmised from the housekeeper, as she put a fresh dressing on my cheek, that he intended to spend a few days in Wexborough and then ride on to Bristol. Everyone was aware that this was more than a simple domestic argument. Servants were always eavesdropping. Maggie Burns used to be a terror for gluing her ear to the parlour keyhole.

I wrapped a cloak around my shoulders and flushed Samuel out of his cottage. 'Can you drive the gig?' I asked him.

'Where might you want to go, madam?' he replied, wiping breadcrumbs and slivers of cheese from his mouth.

I slipped a shilling into his hand. 'Dunsgate gaol. Don't tell anyone.'

The prison was a former cattle barn that had been walled off from the road. It frowned from the slope of a boulder-studded hill on to the scattering of hovels that comprised Dunsgate village. The journey had taken a little over an hour. Sight of the gaol did nothing to quell the grumbling unease that had been stewing in my stomach. The moss-spattered stonework seemed to leech colour out of the surrounding land. Narrow windows had been punched into the walls at irregular intervals. As the gig laboured up the bumpy track I thought I saw a white face peering out at me.

Samuel halted the carriage outside the gate. 'Have a care, madam. This is a filthy place. The stench could knock down a horse.'

'You can wait here. I won't be long.'

'Good. I've no notion to find myself inside any kind of prison again, even as a visitor. But if you're not back out in twenty minutes, or I hear you yell, I'm coming in anyway.'

I thanked him and passed, shivering under a sweeping stone arch. How could men and women survive in such a place? In the muddy yard beyond, a turnkey waddled out of a wooden lean-to. He eyed my clothes and spat into the dirt. 'Are you lost, miss?'

I pulled my cloak tighter. 'Take me inside,' I threw sixpence at his feet. 'Now.'

He led me inside the barn and down a passage lined on either side with makeshift cells. Others had been built into the old hayloft above my head. 'Why is it so quiet? How many prisoners do you keep in this hole?'

The turnkey chuckled. 'Never a time when Dunsgate ain't full, miss. The walls have been reinforced. They're six feet thick in places. Swallows up sound. Snuffs it like a candle. No one but your cell mates will ever hear as much as a cough.' He caught my expression. 'Ain't so bad here, miss. It's cool in summer and I keep a big fire stoked in the winter months. Walls keep in the heat. Looks horrible, I know, but folk like to think that prisoners are suffering.'

I waved him on. Uneven flagstones scattered with straw caught my feet. At the back of the building was a cramped anteroom with a bench, squat desk and brazier. 'All right, miss,' the turnkey said. 'What can I do for you?'

I told him.

'Cripps? Moses Cripps? The turnkey nodded. 'Aye, he's here, though there's talk of taking him to the public gallows at Tyburn. Magistrate reckons our hanging yard's not good enough. He attacked a girl on her own wedding day, though he says she wasn't worth the dirt he spread her out on.'

I arched an eyebrow. 'Let me talk to him.'

'I ain't allowed to let anyone see the prisoners.'

'Family must visit, surely?'

A loose-lipped grin revealed the blackened stumps of teeth. 'You family?'

I slapped coins on to the table. 'Here's two shillings that says I am.'

He scooped up the money and pocketed it. 'Sixpence a minute,' he said. 'That's how much time you've got. Fair bargain I'd say.'

'Very well, but I want to speak to him alone. Bring him here; I won't go near those cells. And no listening at the door.'

'Be it on your own head, miss, though I doubt you'll have much trouble from Moses Cripps.'

Keys jangled as the gaoler plodded to the door. I sat on the bench and waited.

'I knew you'd come running back to me,' Moses said. 'Though it ain't really me you want, is it?'

He looked leaner but still well muscled. A beard clung to his chin. Chains bound his wrists and ankles.

'Put some respect in your voice when you speak to me,' I said.

'What would be the point of that, seeing as you already have me where you want me?'

I took a deep breath. 'The papers,' I blurted. 'Where are the papers?'

A hollow laugh. 'Your precious bundle is safe. I reckoned you'd be after it soon enough.'

'I have influence now. I could buy you out of here, put you on a boat to Ireland. You'd never fear prison again.'

'Oh yes, a squire's wife, but you're still just a whore in a velvet gown. I'd sooner hang than skulk out of my own country at a harlot's behest.' He gestured at his surroundings. 'It's not as bad in here as you might suppose. Harry, the gaoler, is a decent man. Him and I have an understanding. I get clean straw, food in my belly and my clothes in the washtub once a week. You'll get your papers though. I've got a price right enough.'

'Name it.'

Metal chinked. In the torchlight, Moses's eyes were two black slugs. A grin split his face like a fissure opening in the earth. 'Maybe I'll let you stew awhile. Or I might get the rope before I decide to tell you. That would be justice of sorts.'

Before I could answer, the turnkey appeared to take Moses back to his cell. There was nothing I could do. I hadn't another farthing on me. When he returned I let him escort me to the gate.

'Get what you came for?' he asked.

I pulled off my gold wedding ring and dropped it into his palm. George would never notice. 'Don't let Cripps die.'

With George away from home and no friends calling, the hall seemed emptier than ever that week. I tried to catch up on my needlework, I read books or old newspapers. I took endless walks around the gardens, sometimes in the pouring rain.

'You'll catch a fever, madam,' the housekeeper warned, when I struggled through the door one morning like a half-drowned puppy. 'Then it'll be bed and the doctor for you.'

I changed and spent the next hour in front of the parlour fire. A fair had come to the district and I had given most of the servants leave to go and enjoy themselves among the stalls, jugglers and dancing bears. Not so long ago the prospect of mummers and tumbling acrobats would have excited me. Now, after all those brash parties, I favoured solitude.

That Thursday, while the tents and wagons of the travelling troupe still speckled the common land with noise and colour, a baby was delivered to the kitchen door. Elizabeth's Huxley's daughter. My winnings.

'How is the mother, do you know?' I asked the coachman.

'She had a hard birth, but survived,' he said.

I summoned Samuel, who had no belly for the fair, and instructed him to find a home for the child amongst the travellers. 'I don't want to see it again, or touch it. Twice I've suffered when obliged to give someone else's baby away. I am the worst kind of thief.'

He scratched his ear. 'I don't understand. From what I heard, you won the child fairly.'

'I stole it, just like the others. But you wouldn't know about that, Samuel, unless you've been hearing other stories. I've stolen it as surely as if I'd snatched it from its mother's arms. Lizzie Huxley had no choice, of course. The baby's irresponsible father and her own papa saw to that. But what if she spends the rest of her life chewed up with remorse? At least Loxborough was someone she could hate, somewhere to focus the pain. Now she has the agony of knowing that her child is alive but out of reach. What will it look like? When will it cut teeth, take its first steps? What are its fears, joys, hopes? Lizzie carried it in her womb, yet it will never know her. This is almost the same as murder, Samuel.'

'You are too hard on yourself.'

'You think so? Each act carries its own consequences. I can only weigh them to suit myself, to ensure I get the better of someone who has crossed me. I profit out of other people's misfortunes.'

'Then you would make a good banker.'

I laughed without mirth. 'My ledgers would be full of human lives and every account overdrawn. Who could balance my books or settle my debts? You think I've saved a life. All I've done is spited my husband and made more enemies. I daresay I ought to be glad. It's what I wanted.'

Samuel rode out with the baby that afternoon and returned empty handed two hours later. 'I found a family who were glad of the child,' he informed me. 'The man does tricks with horses, an honest-looking fellow who lost his own little girl to a fever barely three months ago. There's a wife and elder daughter to look after it and the fair's making good money. I explained that the baby had been orphaned, which is true in a sense, and everyone seemed happy enough.'

'Thank you, Samuel.'

He smiled. 'Thank *you*, Mrs Proudlove.'

*

George returned from town the next day, much earlier than expected. He'd barely shaken the rain from his cloak before summoning me to the withdrawing room. 'I want an heir,' he said without preamble. 'Whatever devilries you've been up to in order to prevent it must cease. You will discharge your wifely duties and provide me with a son. He will be named Nathaniel, after my father.'

I gawped at him. A child had been ordered the way he might tell cook to prepare a beef supper. 'I . . . I am not a brood mare,' I stammered. 'As to whether any baby is a boy or girl, it is hardly in my hands.'

'A son,' George muttered, his jaw set. 'It must be a son. That mark on your mouth, does it run in your family?'

'I believe so.'

'Curse the devil that any brat of mine should be birthed which such a disfigurement. Can it not be removed somehow?'

'A brat, George? Is that what your child would be to you? Not a son or daughter?' I appraised his flushed cheeks, his frightened, glassy eyes, and realised what he was doing. 'You want to put a baby in my belly to silence me,' I accused, 'to force me to behave. You are afraid that word of what happened with Loxborough will slip out and you are looking for an excuse not to take me on social calls. Do those disgusting people mean so much to you that you intend to chain me with pregnancy? Or is there even more to it than that, George?'

He tore off his riding gloves and tossed them on to a chair. 'I am weary from my journey. Tomorrow night I will come to your bedchamber. Try to make yourself presentable.'

'No,' I quickly replied. 'It is my time of month.'

'You are lying,' he sneered. 'The maid checks your linen. I believe you are not due for another week. We will see if I cannot poke some of the coldness out of you.'

I supposed I was being unfair to George. Every married

man had a right to a son. Yet all the next morning I behaved as a woman under a death sentence. What if I was barren? What if I couldn't give him what he wanted? I'd mostly taken care with Moses. A bit of fireside gossip with Maggie Burns had taught me how to do that but George had lain with me a few times and nothing had come of it. Perhaps he'd disown me, or have a bastard with a mistress and name that as his heir.

In the end, my mental wrangling was all for nothing. My husband broke his neck.

George had decided to go on a solitary canter around the grounds. He took a new chestnut mare Samuel had bought for him at the horse market and set off, with bottle and bread, to make a morning of it.

When it was past noon and he had not returned, Samuel and two stable hands went to look for him. His cooling body lay at the foot of the hedge he had tried to jump. The horse was cropping grass a few feet away.

Samuel broke the news to me as the men brought George's corpse into the parlour and withdrew, hats in hands. He was laid out on an old door that had been propped against the stable wall. A piece of canvas covered his face. Though Samuel tried to stop me, I snatched it away. I wanted to make sure that George was dead, know that it was not some cruel trick he had decided to play on me.

Death made a horrible spectacle of him. His neck was twisted at an angle and a smear of dried blood at the corner of his mouth parodied my birthmark. Mud caked his right cheek, his once immaculately tied hair had worked loose and become a tangled nest of dead leaves and grass. It was difficult to believe that this stiffening carcass had ever drawn a living breath.

I dropped the canvas back over his head. 'Put him in the ground as soon as you can,' I said.

Parson Proudlove arrived in a hired chaise to bury his

son. After the ceremony he spared no words of kindness or comfort, merely nodded before climbing back into his carriage. The servants were all in tears. I was both touched and surprised at this expression of grief for such a bully of a man. Later I discovered that they had not been paid in two months.

Lawyers descended on the house like flies on carrion. Looking like so many vicars in their black coats, they had me sign a series of documents that meant nothing to my dizzy eyes. I did as they asked, if only to be rid of them, and held my peace while they addressed me as Mrs Proudlove throughout, giving emphasis to the name as if it was some sort of special title. Despite their respectful manner, my immediate future was made clear to me. I was to be tossed out on to the drive like a piece of old furniture.

After the lawyers had clattered off down the drive in their dark-panelled city carriages, creditors arrived in droves to tear up the estate. So many creditors I thought that George must be in debt to every man in the county. I could not see how there would be enough to pay them all.

'Your husband was too fond of cards, madam,' a banker from Wexborough informed me as he eyed the paintings lining the stairwell. 'A man ought not to play the tables lest he can afford to back up poor gamesmanship with proper security.'

A pair of labourers shuffled past carrying my chestnut writing desk. They manhandled it out of the front door and on to the back of a wagon, where it was covered with sacks and tied down with hemp. Everything movable in the house went likewise. By late afternoon a caravan of carts and dray horses had pulled most of my wealth down about my ears and spirited it off.

Amongst the throng of buzzards squawking over the remains of my marriage, I spotted a familiar face. 'Mr Fairchild,' I greeted him. 'Where there is a carcass, one inevitably finds a worm.'

He put down the silver candlestick he had been examining and peered at me through gilt-edged spectacles. They had no glass in them, I noted.

'Snappy little widow, aren't you?' he purred. 'I am here for my cut of the pie. Hold your temper and it might amuse me to leave you a bauble or two. The next time you beg a dance at least you'll look the part.'

I swallowed. 'How much did my husband owe you?'

He picked up a salver, squinted at it then dropped it on to a pile of other items. A manservant bundled them into a canvas sack, which he hauled outside. Adam favoured me with a smile. Despite my anger, it had me quivering at the knees. 'George's debts ran much deeper than his losses at the card table. Money was not the only thing he was careless with.'

He cupped my chin in his fingers. His skin was cool and smooth. There was a time when I would have died for that touch. Instead I stepped away. His hand flopped back to his side. For a moment he looked disappointed, then the smile slipped back. 'I wonder if George really knew what he was doing when he married you. It's obvious that his death isn't going to break your heart.'

'And Cecilia Fortescue? What about her heart? Have you forgotten her as readily as you decided to abandon her child?'

'Cecilia has apparently lost her taste for parties.'

'So I should imagine.'

'She had no proof that I sired her brat. That was an act of fancy on her part. It was widely known she had a number of admirers.'

'I suspect, sir, that where you are concerned there is never any proof.'

'In business that would prove a virtue.'

'Is that how you regard people. As "business"? Was George "business"? Am I?'

'You've no right to talk about such matters,' Adam said.

'I heard about the Loxborough bastard. The whole county knows. Ordinary lives never generate gossip. It's those of us with a sharp edge, who soar above the dull and common, that keep the tongues wagging.'

'Why *did* George marry me, Mr Fairchild? We both know it was not for love.'

He tugged a calling card from his waistcoat pocket and slipped it into my hand. 'Come to my club in Wexborough. Show that to the footman at the door and he will bring you to my private chambers.'

I tore the card in two and let the pieces fall to the floor. 'I am not your whore.'

The smile turned sour on Fairchild's lips. 'You may have cause to regret that remark.'

'I doubt it.'

'Indeed? A homeless, penniless widow standing proud on her dead husband's bankrupt estate? What an amusing notion.' He started to walk away, then turned as if just remembering something. 'Oh, bye the bye. That man who attacked you on your wedding day, what was his name again? Ah yes, Cripps. Word has it that the fellow escaped from Dunsgate gaol. Slipped right past the gaoler and made off in the middle of the night. I'd say those were the actions of a determined man, wouldn't you?'

He did not wait for a reply. Perhaps my expression told him all he needed. Moses was loose. A murderer. My lover.

I hurried upstairs, squeezing past half a dozen sweating workmen who were coaxing George's four-poster across the landing. In my empty bedchamber, I fastened all the windows and locked the door before collapsing on to the bare floorboards. I remained huddled like that for the best part of an hour.

By the end of the week, my new life in the country was over. The house was gutted, the land sold off piecemeal, the servants dismissed.

The funeral passed in a blur. On my last Sabbath at the local church, people looked the other way when I took my place in the family pew. After the service, they hurried off.

'A terrible loss,' the vicar blurted. 'You must try to accept your new position with dignity. A sad affair, most sad.' He waddled off, shaking his head. Alone, I waited under the lich-gate as the first rains of the day began to fall.

I had lodgings at an inn, paid for with savings I'd managed to smuggle out of the manor. As soon as I returned I tore off my mourning dress and put on the only other luxury I'd been permitted to keep, a travelling gown in duck-egg blue. Powder went on my face, rouge on my cheeks. I packed a cloth bag with the handful of items that were all I had left in the entire world. Then I did the only thing I could.

I went back to Catherine.

I had already forgotten what a noisy, dirty place Wexborough could be. The market clamour and bustle of tradesmen mingled with the rattle of wagons going to and from the harbour. Children jostled me, street hawkers thrust wares under my face. My nose was thick with the scent of acrid smoke and rubbish.

The stagecoach had dropped me outside the corn exchange, a good half-mile from Catherine's house. I hadn't so much as a penny left to hire a sedan, so I'd hefted my bag and set off down the street. I was uneasy about turning up on Catherine's doorstep like a stray dog, so when I arrived I skirted around the side of the Butter House and into the yard, hoping to have a word with Maggie Burns before facing my former guardian.

Most of the rain clouds had been blown inland by a teeth-chattering wind gusting in from the sea. The sun was too weakened by the onset of winter to afford much warmth, yet no smoke swirled from the tall chimneystacks of the Butter House. My footsteps echoed on the cobbles. Stable doors hung open, hinges creaking in the wind. Inside, the horse stalls were empty, the straw swept up and lying in an unkempt pile in the corner. Harnesses had fallen from their hooks on the wall. There was no sign of William, no indication that a living soul had been here for days.

I returned to the yard. The water trough was rank and nearly empty. I skirted around it and checked the rear of the house. My bag lay where I had dropped it. Most of the upstairs curtains were drawn but a single bedroom window lay half-open, drapes shivering in the stiff breeze.

I scooped up my bag and made for the kitchen. The door was off the latch. I nudged it inwards with my foot. A stench of spoiled meat assaulted me. Pressing a handkerchief over my face, I stepped inside. 'Maggie? Maggie are you there?'

Nothing. I stepped around the table. It was littered with dirty plates, the mouldy remains of food. Pots were piled high in the washing tub. A stale odour hung over everything. I opened the inside door and hurried along the dark passage. The house was cold enough to prick my skin with goosebumps. I listened. Nothing. Not even the tick of a clock. Every door hung open, the rooms beyond swaddled in gloom. I checked each one, slipping like a ghost from parlour to drawing room to dining room in the space of two dozen frightened steps. Repeatedly jerking the bell sash achieved nothing.

I returned to the parlour and opened the curtains to let some light into this mausoleum. The windows were filthy. Thick dust shrouded most of the furniture though a few items, perversely, were sparkling clean as if polished only a moment before. I became aware too, of a curious symmetry about the place. Everything had been laid out in a careful pattern. Ornaments stood like sentries in an unbroken line along the mantelpiece. The armchairs and sofa were arranged in a perfect semi-circle. Even the rotting apples in the fruit bowl had been stacked according to size.

This house, whatever its faults, had always been a place more lived in than looked after. 'Comfortable,' was how

Richard once described it, 'like an old pair of shoes you can slip your feet into without thinking about it.' Now every picture was straight, every cushion standing to attention.

I left the parlour and hurried into the front hall, shoes beating a tattoo on the patterned tiles. At the bottom of the stairs I halted, aware that someone watched me from the upper landing. With great deliberation, a figure began to walk down the staircase towards me.

Blake.

The hallway swirled in a blur of black and grey. I clutched the balustrade to prevent myself sprawling across the floor. It had all been a sham – a terrible lie. Blake was not dead. Moses had not killed him after all. He was coming to get me.

I recognised the cream hose with gold tassels. The black velvet breeches. His favourite embroidered waistcoat. I slumped to my knees as he stepped into the dim light seeping through the crescent window above the front door. I had no defence, no words with which to confront this horrible spectre.

But the face peering at me from beneath the brim of a velvet tricorne was Catherine's.

'Well, if it isn't the pretty wench,' the figure rasped. Catherine's voice, but low and horrible, with a knife twist to each word. The way Blake used to talk. She wore his blue satin solitaire which was two sizes two big and hung around her neck like a noose. Other garments hung from her in baggy folds. This close, she resembled a shrunken doll.

Without warning, her arms slithered around my neck and she crammed her lips against mine. Her mouth was a pit of dreadful tastes, of dirty teeth and bad food. I spat out her poisoned tongue and pushed myself away. Clawed fingers scrabbled at my bodice. 'Come now, pretty one,' she slurred. 'Why so coy? Here's Ed Blake with a sweet word to whisper in your ear.'

'You're not Blake. He's in the ground, rotting.'

I was dimly aware of someone thumping on the front door and voices shouting through the thick oak. The Catherine-thing advanced towards me. Like a petrified cat that's all hackles and spit, I backed away across the chequered tiles.

'What's this?' the Catherine-thing demanded, eyes glinting like badly cut sapphires. 'You have naught to fear from me. As gentle as a feather in the wind, I am.'

Hooked fingers reached out. I kicked out blindly. My flailing foot caught her knee and knocked the legs out from under her. She smacked on to the tiles, the tricorne spinning off her head and fetching up against the bottom stair. I crammed a fist into my mouth. She had cut her hair – shorn it almost to the skin in places. Patches of pink scalp mottled the back of her head.

The banging on the door increased. The voices grew more urgent. The Catherine-thing was getting up, blood gushing from her nose. I fumbled for the knob and prayed the front door wasn't locked. The brass twisted in my sweating palm and the door swung inwards. On the step stood Marjorie Proudlove, George's mother – and beside her, a pair of hefty-looking bailiffs. Without a word, the men brushed past me into the hall and took hold of the Catherine-thing. She was carried, screaming, into the street and bundled into a waiting carriage. A carriage that had no windows.

Marjorie helped me to my feet. The eyes in that doughy face were as hard as flint. 'You must come with me, Juliana,' she said. 'You must come now.'

195

Chapter Thirteen

'Her mind has gone,' Marjorie said, slamming the carriage door. 'It has been rotting for weeks, like an apple turning to brown pulp. I tried to catch you at the manor, to warn you not to come here. When I arrived, boards were already being nailed over the windows. I didn't expect you to leave so abruptly.'

I stared at my knotted fingers as the carriage rumbled out of Wexborough. 'Where are those men taking Catherine?'

Mrs Proudlove wiped her cheeks with a linen handkerchief. 'Bedlam I expect. There'll be no curing her. I realised that yesterday when I called on her to talk about George.'

Catherine had been sitting in Richard's study, piles of torn-up bills littering the desk in front of her. 'She had spent hours ripping them into tiny pieces,' Marjorie continued. 'Paper lay everywhere – on the floor, the shelves, spilling out of her lap. I tried to speak to her, but she took a pair of scissors out of the drawer and began cutting off her hair. She called me a stupid old woman, a country clod and even,' Marjorie's cheeks flushed, 'a parson's cheap doxy.'

She pressed the handkerchief against her nose. 'I asked after the servants. Catherine told me they had all been dismissed, that she could run the house by herself. I don't think she'd eaten or bathed for days. When I tried to take the scissors from her she lunged at me. Luckily her shin caught the corner of the table or those scissors would have ended up between my ribs. I ran from the house, my ears full of obscenities, and went directly to the magistrate. As it turned out there was no shortage of witnesses to testify to her growing lunacy.' Marjorie clasped my hand. 'It was provident that I returned when I did.'

I peered out of the window at the streets I had walked so hopefully less than an hour before. 'She thought she was Blake, Richard's dead manservant. She wore his clothes, tried to talk in his voice. For a moment I even believed it was him.'

'Edward Blake was Catherine's brother, did you not know that?'

I turned my head and stared at her. 'No. How could I?'

'He was a thief and trickster bound for the gallows. Catherine spent a small fortune to buy his pardon and employed him as a footman. George told me about it on one of his rare visits to the parsonage. He was sodden with brandy and too eager with his tongue. I can readily believe it. Catherine Worledge always enjoyed mastery over men, even her own kin. I knew her as a wilful young woman who could spit and curse like a common tinker when someone crossed her. She loved Blake with a dark, twisted passion. Little wonder she lost her wits when told he was murdered.'

'Catherine made a servant of her own brother? A brother she loved?'

'It was not the love of a sister for her sibling, Juliana. This was something unnatural and heavy with sin. George laughed as he told me how Catherine used to take Blake into her bed when Richard was gambling or lying senseless with drink. They shared the same mind, the same black heart. Don't think ill of me for telling you this. You need to understand.'

I leaned back against the carriage seat and closed my eyes. Marjorie offered me salts but I shook my head. The sun ran fingers of light across my face. Soon, the bustle of town was replaced by the whisperings of open meadows and the creaking murmur of wooded lanes.

'Where are you taking me?'

'You married our son and are therefore our responsibility. You'll come to live with Nathaniel and myself in the parsonage at Dinstock. My husband is a pious man and intends to have you work for your keep but it will be honest work befitting a widow.'

'I was a squire's wife. You cannot expect me to become a scullery wench or a milkmaid.'

A snatch of breath. 'Pride is a sin. You must realise that you now have nothing in the world save what we, in God's good grace, provide. Raw knees are better than an empty belly, so treat Nathaniel with respect and accept his judgement with good countenance.'

I opened an eye. Marjorie was fumbling with something. A prayer book, the leather cover cracked and the pages well thumbed. Perspiration hung in a dewdrop from her top lip. 'You owe me nothing,' I said. 'I do not know exactly why George married me and since you did not see fit to attend either our wedding or his funeral I can only suppose you cared as little for him as he did for me.'

Marjorie closed the book and dropped it into her lap. 'George? I cried for him, but it was like the loss of a distant cousin. He was never really my child. I lost him heart and soul before the first hair tufted his chin. The boy was always frivolous, always given over to whims and fancies. Notoriety was food and drink to him but he lacked the will to bend the world to any purpose. When I first saw you with that rich hair and the scarlet mark on your face, I believed he wanted an ornament, a flesh and blood trinket to show off at those godless parties. I would have tried to warn you but who listens to a parson's wife?'

I turned back to the window. 'I think he wanted me for something else. You know what that "something" is, but you won't tell me. You're too frightened. You've been afraid since the day I met you in Catherine's parlour and probably long before. Perhaps I'll never find out. As a Christian woman, I doubt your conscience grants you much peace.'

Marjorie didn't answer. She prised open her prayer book and buried her face in its pages. Did her husband beat her? No obvious marks coloured her face or neck. Of course that meant nothing.

Events had exhausted me. The rocking of the carriage brought on a dreamless sleep. I woke, stiff and riddled with cramp, as sunset burned the sky. We halted outside a low wooden gate almost smothered by a privet hedge. Beyond sat a drooping cottage made soft around the edges with ivy. Moss-speckled thatch hung from sagging gables. Square windows peeked out from ochre-painted stonework. A trellis supporting the bones of last summer's sweet peas clambered up one wall. In the near distance a brook gurgled over some rocks.

Marjorie stepped out, shaking her skirts. I followed her into the deepening dusk, trying to rub some life into my tired legs. An enormous cedar tree spread green arms across the pebble path that led to the cottage's front door.

'Very pretty,' I remarked, desperate to say something.

Marjorie glanced about her. 'These days I can't always give the garden the attention it deserves. Perhaps things will improve.'

Charlotte peered at us from a downstairs window. The intense frown, which had intrigued me in Wexborough, rippled across her forehead. I waved but she did not return the gesture. When we stepped inside, I heard feet slapping across the stone floor and a door closed somewhere at the back of the house.

Children could be jealous. Did Charlotte regard me as an interloper, a near-stranger breaking into her family circle? If so, could I win her over? I was not the most tactful person on earth and the child was clever. Would she regard any gift as a bribe?

My new bedchamber was little bigger than a cupboard, but much more welcoming than the palatial chambers of my former home. I regarded with bemusement the old dresser with a tarnished looking-glass mounted on top, the chipped silver oval throwing shattered reflections around the room. Instead of a four-poster, a single bed, sagging in the middle, hugged the wall opposite the door. A wardrobe with creaking doors took care of my few remaining possessions.

Well, it was better than being left destitute on the road. A window cut a bright oblong into the sloping ceiling. It looked out over the back of the house. Instead of sprawling, scissor-clipped lawns, thick woodland sprouted out of a dark loam floor. A flash of silver marked where the brook tumbled down a few feet of rock. Perhaps it held stickleback or trout. A square of coarse grass marked out a drying green and a log pile squatted under the eaves of an old stable.

'We live simply,' Marjorie informed me when I joined her in the kitchen half an hour later. 'No servants to pander to you here, only a village girl who scrubs the place twice a week and helps with one or two other chores. Earn your keep and I'll treat you as my own.'

'Where is Mr Proudlove?'

'Nathaniel is helping the parson of a neighbouring parish, who can't perform his duties on account of a belly upset. When my husband returns he'll want to meet you again, so you must make yourself presentable. No powder and no painting your cheeks with rouge.'

'Yes, Mrs Proudlove.'

'You must call me Marjorie, except when at church or in front of guests. Remember that you are Mrs Proudlove too.'

She waddled from the room and returned a few moments later with a black linen dress draped over her arm. 'Put this on,' she instructed. 'The fit looks good and it will serve for now.'

I stared at the garment. Another old dress. Another gown the colour of the grave. I made no move to take it from her. Marjorie caught my expression. 'You are in mourning for your husband,' she explained. 'The next few weeks will be hard. You will hear things, cruel things, from gossips who can't hold their tongues. George was known around these parts and not well liked. He had a good head for business once. His dealings made him his fortune; his excesses at the card table lost it. Gambling had a greater hold on his heart than I ever did and his ruin emptied more than just his own pocket. Some people will look for any reason to slight you. We must do what we can to lessen the injury. Please wear the dress, for Nathaniel's sake if not your own. He is very conscious of his position in the parish and hopes to better himself in the eyes of God and his peers.'

She was almost pleading with me. I took the dress. Marjorie beamed as if I was a favoured child. 'Supper is at eight,' she breezed. 'The clock on the landing will tell you the hour. Tomorrow I will take you into Dinstock. You will be happy here, Juliana, I know you will.'

I know you will, I mimicked after she had gone.

During the night, heavy rains washed the countryside. I spent hours trying to get comfortable. Water needled the windowpane, slithered down the roof slates, gurgled into the butt outside the back door. Sometime towards daybreak the weather eased up. The sun poked a bleary eye from between threads of cloud. The morning had a fresh, sharp taste and everything looked new.

Marjorie draped a muslin cloth over an enormous wicker basket and, humming a bright tune, led me through the front gate and into the lane. Charlotte had gone to the local miller's house to keep his daughter company. 'I need fresh bread,' Marjorie told me, 'and we must get you an apron to wear about the house.'

Her mood was infectious and I hummed along with her. As we skirted the ruts that dragged long, waterlogged trenches into the soil, I learned something of the local area and the people who were, ultimately, my masters.

'The land hereabouts is owned either by Matthew Jane

or the church,' Marjorie explained. 'The Janes are a farming family and have roots in this part of the country that stretch back generations. Squire Jane, along with his wife Lady Elizabeth and daughter Emma, live at Dinstock Hall not three miles' walk from here. The house boasts one of the finest stables in England. Squire Matthew is a keen horseman and you'll spot him riding across the Downs most days of the week. Wheat and cattle, that's how he made his money. Honest money it is, too.'

My shoe sank into a puddle. I groaned. Marjorie seemed not to notice and ambled on, swinging that great basket back and forth. 'You may find you have something in common with young Emma,' she continued. 'She is a flighty girl and not keen on marriage, much to her father's vexation. But she has a good disposition and will snare herself a fine husband.'

'Perhaps she doesn't want to get married,' I suggested.

Marjorie laughed. 'All girls want to get married.'

Hedges on either side of the lane fell away and fields stretched for miles in every direction. Clusters of farm buildings sat like grey warts and an occasional tree spread wooden fingers to the sky. I had never seen so much empty space, even during my time at the manor. I watched breathless, as scudding clouds chased their own shadows across the earth.

'At harvest time all you could see was an ocean of wheat,' Marjorie said, 'as if God had gilded the soil. The men used to sing as they worked the fields. Plenty of jobs for everyone. People came from all the surrounding villages to work for Squire Matthew. Afterwards there was always a big end-of-summer fair with dancing and singing. Nothing sinful, mind.'

I tried to picture smiling field hands dancing in a smoky barn to the tune of a cheap fiddle. And lovers stealing into dark corners to exchange whispered secrets away from the noise and merriment. 'It sounds wonderful,' I remarked. 'Don't these things happen any more?'

'No, not any more.'

'What brought an end to it?'

But Marjorie was keeping that one to herself too. For a simple parson's wife she was a pot of secrets. Ahead, the lane broadened into Dinstock village. We stood aside to let a flock of sheep scurry past. A surly-faced drover in a smock and felt hat swished a stick above the backs of the bleating animals. He eyed me curiously as he passed.

Dinstock was a pigsty. No flagstones or cobbled roads. Muddy lanes were punctured with swollen puddles. A few looked fit to swallow a person whole. A ragtag collection of thatched cottages ran the length of the largest street. To the north, a market cross stood forlornly near the junction of two roads and, frowning over the scene, was a tavern called The Wheatsheaf. Stables dominated the opposite end of the village along with a smithy. Beyond, almost hidden by a copse of sycamore trees, lay a squat, grey-stoned church with a square tower. Parson Proudlove's church.

Marjorie wanted to visit the baker's so I asked if I could have a wander around the village. She nodded, already lost to the smell of the hot ovens. I crossed the street, avoiding the worst of the mud. A wagon lumbered past, dray horses snorting hot steam into the crisp, early winter air. I passed a dressmaker's, whitewashed walls streaked with ochre dirt. Next door was a wine merchant, then a flesher. Finally, to my delight, I discovered a small bookshop tucked away like an afterthought. This was the last thing I expected to find in a farming village, though I supposed it must supply the libraries of the better houses in the district. I pressed my nose against the glass and drank in the friendly sight of leather-bound volumes. Bibles and religious texts mostly but there were some essay collections and a little verse.

Another reflection joined mine in the window. Then another. I turned. A loose gathering of urchins took my measure as if I was a horse they were about to steal. They had approached with the stealth of thieves and did not utter a word between them. Though barefoot for the most part, one wore clogs, another a pair of scuffed leather sandals. Something in their eyes spoke of more than just curiosity.

I edged away from the window and hurried back along the street. The group followed, matching my pace. I stumbled, trying hard not to run. Other faces peered from cottage windows, adult faces.

The first pebble struck me on the shoulder, sending a flash of pain down the length of my arm. A second clipped me on the cheek. A third whisked past my right ear. Abandoning dignity, I hitched up my skirts and fled down that filthy road as fast as my frightened feet would take me. I splashed through puddles, lost a shoe to the mud and stubbed my toe against a half-buried rock. Muck spattered the hem of my black gown. Hair fell about my face in tangled coils.

'Strawberry mouth! Strawberry mouth!' my tormentors chanted, pelting me with stones and lumps of horseshit. An old woman eyed me from the door of her cottage as though I was a harlot being dragged through the streets from the back of the hurdle.

'Let me inside, please,' I begged.

'We don't want the likes of you here,' she replied coldly. The door was slammed in my face.

I don't know where I found the strength to go on. I thought I would run myself right into the grave. The jeering gang pursued me all the way to the bakery. I tumbled into Marjorie and clung to her. Within seconds the children melted into hedges and gardens. Marjorie lifted up my head, checked my face and neck. 'You're going to bruise,' she said. 'No other harm done. Gypsies camp on the common ground for the winter and their children are fond of a bit of mischief. Nothing to be too concerned about.'

'It's not just the children,' I said. 'It's everyone.'

I tried to tell her about the faces at the windows, how the old woman had shut her cottage door in my face. Marjorie didn't seem to be listening. She took me back to where I had lost my shoe and fished it out of the mud whilst I kept stealing glances up and down the length of the street. 'I shouldn't have let you go off on your own,' she said. 'A black dress, that birthmark. You're a stranger. Locals are superstitious.'

As we made our way back to the parsonage, the wicker basket stuffed with eggs and fresh bread, I clung to her arm. In the kitchen, I washed my face and tried to shake dried mud from my gown. 'Why all these gypsies?' I asked. 'Where were the village children?'

Marjorie wiped her hands and emptied the basket. 'Most of them need to work in order to support their families. There's little time for games. It has been a hard year. The value of everything has fallen. Farmers are struggling. Do not take today's events to heart, Juliana. No one has much to smile about.'

I retired upstairs and shut myself in my room. Daylight eased into the grey muzziness of dusk. As the landing clock struck five, I heard a tap on my door. A girl, not much younger than me, entered holding a candle and a wooden trencher. A bite of supper, I was told. I guessed this was the villager who helped Marjorie around the house.

'Mrs Proudlove says you ain't feeling too well,' she said in a muddy country drawl. 'I've to make sure you get some hot broth inside you. I made it myself.'

I took the candle from her and held it up. A mat of black hair tumbled untidily around the girl's large ears. A nose you could hang a towel from sprouted from the middle of her face, and front teeth stuck over her lower lip. Her eyes, however, were a bright, rich blue. They fixed on my birthmark then flitted away.

'When is the parson due back? Do you know?'

She fumbled with the front of her apron. 'Day after tomorrow.'

I examined the trencher, which she had placed on top of

205

the dresser. Wisps of steam curled up from the broth. The smell of cooked vegetables filled the room.

The girl coughed. 'Been crying have you, madam?'

'Get out,' I ordered.

A sharp tug on my coverlet dragged me from my troubled dreams. I opened sleepy eyes to find Charlotte peering down at me. Her face split into a toothy grin and a cluster of dried flowers appeared under my nose. I eased them aside and clambered out of bed. Early light leaked through cracks in the curtains. She perched on the edge of the mattress and watched as I threw on a robe and tried to brush some sense into my hair.

'I knew you would come to live with us,' she declared.

I fumbled with some pins. 'I hope we can be friends. You wouldn't mind that, would you?'

Her mouth pursed. 'Everyone is saying bad things about you.'

The hairpins fell on to the coverlet. I tried to return the brush to its place on the dresser and dropped it. Pulling up the stool, I sat beside Charlotte, fighting to keep my voice light.

'Oh? What sort of things?'

She rubbed her head with her tiny fingers and did not return my smile. 'They say you will put a hex on all the cattle, that the land will be spoiled and nothing will grow. They say you are the devil's daughter because you have his mark on your face. They are all afraid of you.'

I held her gently by the shoulders and looked down into her round face. 'The miller told you this?'

'I heard his wife say it. She was scared and crying. The miller told her not to be foolish but he was frightened too.'

I brushed away a strand of loose hair that had fallen across her forehead. 'Idle talk, Charlotte, that's all it is. Don't let it upset you. Close your ears.'

She let the posy of dried flowers fall on to the rug. 'I'll try.'

*

After breakfast had been eaten and cleared away, two visitors arrived at the gate.

'Squire Matthew and his daughter, Emma, were out riding and have decided to come and meet you,' Marjorie announced. I put down the stocking which I'd blistered my fingers trying to stitch and let her usher me down the garden path. A black hunter and skewbald mare stood on the other side of the gate, snorting and pawing the grass verge. Astride the hunter sat a pickle of a man in a feathered tricorne and bowed wig. A bright yellow riding jacket glared above striped breeches and massive silver-tipped tassels adorned his boots.

In the other saddle was a handsome slip of a girl sharply dressed in a buff riding habit. Tight black curls were neatly ribboned beneath a tall hat. She eyed me coolly as her father propped a pair of tinted spectacles on the end of his long nose.

'By God, what's the matter with that girl?' he bellowed, fixing me with a hard stare. 'Has she split her lip? Put a bandage on it. Or perhaps a sack would serve better.'

Emma stifled a giggle. Marjorie shot me a sideways glance and dipped a curtsy. 'It's merely a birthmark, Squire Matthew. A touch of powder will cover it.'

'Indeed.' He leaned forward in the saddle. 'Well, her father must have been a curious-looking beggar, no doubt of that. Girl looks as though she's dribbled raspberry jam. What have you to say for yourself, child, or has that red stain turned you mute?'

'Powder will cover the mark, just as Mrs Proudlove explained,' I replied, 'though most people I encounter are not so offended by it.'

A palpable silence followed, then Squire Matthew exploded into laughter. 'By God, barely a minute at your gate and already the girl is spitting thorns.'

'She hails from Wexborough,' Marjorie spluttered, as if that explained everything.

'Wexborough, eh?' He pulled off his spectacles and slipped them into his jacket pocket. 'A den of thieves and harlots, by God. She'll have to learn to mellow that sharp tongue of hers. What say you, Emma? How'd you fancy a vixen like this to keep you company up at the Hall? Might get you out and about a bit more if you had her snapping at your heels.'

Emma's jaw tensed. Fingers shook where her gloved hands clutched the leather reins. 'Whatever you wish, Papa.'

'Whatever I wish indeed.' He chuckled and pinched her cheek. Emma winced. He turned away from her and exchanged a few more words of idle chat with Marjorie. Then he and his daughter took their leave, wheeled their horses and cantered off up the lane, Emma's mare keeping a few paces behind her father's hunter.

'You were a bit sharp with Squire Matthew,' Marjorie accused when were back in the kitchen. 'Why did you not show more respect?'

'He was rude and his daughter hates him. Anyone with half an eye could see it. And what is this about my keeping her company? Have you not better things for me to do than pamper some spoilt featherbrain? A week ago I was a squire's wife.'

Marjorie picked up a copper pot and ran her finger around the inside of the rim. Satisfied that it was clean, she hooked it above the fireplace and lifted another from the pile by the washing tub. 'Emma is at a difficult time in her life. She doesn't often get the chance to meet girls her own age. Spending a few hours each week at Dinstock Hall will put you in good favour with the locals.'

'I will win their respect by myself,' I retorted. 'Is there anything you want from the village today, because I am going back? And I will suffer no nonsense, whether I have Squire Matthew's blessing or not.'

I was ready to argue but Marjorie was learning how to

read my moods. 'Go to the bookseller and purchase a prayer book for yourself,' she said, 'for church tomorrow.'

'I have little to thank God for.'

'Nevertheless you will go.'

The weather turned mild. Mud dried, puddles shrank. I pattered down the lane, Marjorie's basket swinging at my hip. On the village outskirts I paused and kicked the grassy verge with the toe of my shoe. The rains had loosened the soil and it came away in thick, greasy lumps. I put the biggest of these in the basket and covered them with a checked cloth. Wiping my hands on the grass, I continued into Dinstock. I strolled past the shops and houses, meeting eye for eye any curious faces that peered out. Soon I heard bare feet scampering behind me, the furtive whispers and muffled giggles.

I walked on. The first stone thumped into my spine between the shoulder blades, sending hot pain scorching across my back. I did not change pace but acted as if I was taking a leisurely walk in a town park.

The second missile struck the back of my leg. Thanks to my thick petticoats I barely felt it. However, I made as if to flee for my life and heard the triumphant whoop of my old tormentors.

At the last moment I spun around. The jeering gang of urchins almost ran into me. Jubilant cries died on their lips. Before they had broken stride I had the cloth off my basket and a good-sized divot in my hand. I hurled it at the tallest of the gang. It caught him squarely on the face, wrapping muddy fingers around his cheeks. He yelped like a scolded puppy and tried to back up but his feet ran out from underneath him and he landed on his rump. Mud dripped off his chin in thick dollops.

I did not wait to savour my success. I pelted those squealing little horrors with a rain of dirt. Some tried to return fire but I had their measure and caught them about the ears before they had time to loose any more missiles. I yelled like a madwoman. Muck covered the front of my dress. Within minutes the battle was won and I had sent my would-be assailants packing off to their mothers.

The bookseller threw a fit when I trailed mud across his shop, but he'd witnessed the battle from his window and could not be angry with me, no matter how hard he pretended. When I tried to brush the dirt from my gown and only made things worse, his face purpled with laughter. He let me have a prayer book for half price and when I went back out into the street I was ready for another fight. Not a soul anywhere except for a farmer standing by the market cross. He tugged his forelock and bid me good day. Amusement sat awkwardly on his face as if it had not known a home there for years. He would have something to talk about over supper.

I ran back up the lane, splashing through the remaining puddles and swinging the basket until my arm almost flew off. By the time I reached the parsonage, I was humming a silly childhood tune. In the kitchen, Marjorie was fussing over a brace of simmering pots packed with that evening's dinner.

'Glad you've found something to sing about at last,' she remarked over her shoulder. Then she noticed the state I was in and her own good mood turned to vapour. 'You look as if you've tipped end over elbow in a pigs' trough. Take off that filthy dress before you move another step and don't lay so much as a finger on my clean table.'

Laughing, I pulled off the gown, kicked my shoes into the corner and peeled off my wet stockings. Marjorie picked up the garments between her fingertips and tossed them out the back door. 'You can scrub those later. How did you manage to get in such a state?'

'Tripped and fell. I bought the prayer book though and it's not damaged.'

'Was there more trouble in the village?'

'No, no trouble. I doubt I'll have any again. Just a group of mischievous children, as you said.'

She wrapped a dry towel around me. 'Mr Proudlove is due back tonight. I want you as clean as an angel before you see him. The gown you brought from the manor will have to do. We can tie a strip of black cloth around the arm until something better can be found. Now go to your bedchamber and remember to brush the dirt out of your hair.'

An entire pitcher of water was needed to clean my hands, face and feet. The rattle of cutlery downstairs meant supper, so I threw on my blue gown and headed for the kitchen. Marjorie was already doling out potatoes from a copper pot. She seemed pleased with my efforts and asked me to fetch the rest of the vegetables from the stove. Through the window, I spied a black gig and mare standing idle in the lane. A scruffy young man in patched leather boots fussed around the horse. 'Has Mr Proudlove arrived?' I asked, accepting a carve of mutton. 'Will he take supper with us?'

'Nathaniel eats in the parlour. You are to go to him as soon as supper is finished and the clearing up done. Try not to be difficult, Juliana. He's had a busy day and is tired from the journey.'

The upstairs clock was striking seven when I was ready to meet my new guardian. We had previously spoken as social equals. How would he regard me now? I fingered the strip of black cloth Marjorie had fastened to my sleeve then knocked on the thick plank door. The parlour lay at the cottage's west side where the ochre stonework swelled into a bay window. It was the parson's private place and I had been warned not to go in uninvited.

A voice instructed me to enter. I had to stoop under the low doorframe. Heavy beams sprouted across the ceiling. A coarse sheepskin rug spread a woollen puddle over bare floorboards. An oak desk hugged the far wall and books

211

were piled in an alcove next to the hearth, where a small fire spluttered. A candle burned on a table beneath the window, bending to the whims of each draught.

The parson sat in a high-backed leather chair studded with round metal buttons. He still wore his clerical garb and I was scrutinised from underneath a round-brimmed hat, which he had not troubled to remove.

'Look at me closely, child.' His voice was the bough of an old tree creaking in the wind. I blushed like a timid moppet as I met that unwavering gaze. His punctured face was as rugged as a limestone quarry. Tufts of steel grey hair clung to his temples. How like a predator he looked. When he breathed his teeth ground against one another.

'Ill fortune can befall any soul, rich or poor.' His eyes were twin sparks in the candlelight. 'You have had your share of bad luck, child. By God's grace you will be a better Christian for it. My dear wife believes it is our duty to keep you under this roof. While you dwell here I will expect both obedience and honest work, as is my due.'

'Yes, Mr Proudlove.' I curtsied. He gestured ambiguously.

'I shall determine suitable duties for you. Though Marjorie will likely keep you occupied around the house we have no need of a scullery maid and you are not qualified to act as a governess for Charlotte. She would gain nothing by having you flitting around her like a horsefly. In the meantime you are not to use our family name. Though we were related by law you are no blood kin. You will answer to "Miss Juliana". Do you understand?'

I curtsied again. My knees were beginning to ache from all this deference.

'Good. One more thing. I hold an important position within this parish. Visitors will call, often at unsociable hours. Mind your manners and your business. If I am entertaining guests, draw your curtains, put out your candle and stay in your room. Ignore whatever you might hear. This house is old and distorts sound. Remain obedient and you'll have no trouble. Now get up to bed. I will see you in church first thing tomorrow.'

He perched a pair of spectacles on the end of his nose and picked up the book that had been lying open on his lap. I slipped out of the parlour and closed the door. Disquiet gnawed at me, growing as I entered my bedchamber and threw back the coverlet on my bed.

Outside, a gathering wind began to whistle through the treetops. I paused whilst undressing and stood by the window, staring into the dark woods. Only the restless chuckling of the brook added its voice to the night.

'I will be happy,' I whispered.

Chapter Fourteen

The sun peeked a bloodshot eye over the trees. Frost cracked the muddy lane and haunted shadows with glistening white fingers. I struggled to keep pace with Marjorie and Charlotte on the mile walk to Dinstock church. My black gown, freshly scrubbed, felt unwieldy, and I had to curl my fingers to stop the borrowed gloves from slipping off. I scuffed my heels, earning a rebuke from Marjorie.

Needless to say, I was in no mood for walking. I had slept fitfully, tormented by terrible dreams. A cold breakfast hadn't helped. Charlotte, sensing she would have no play out of me today, ran up and down the grassy verges until Marjorie called her back. 'No tomfoolery on the Sabbath,' the child was told. 'Stay by me and behave more respectfully.'

Mr Proudlove had already gone ahead in the gig. His church was a sagging heap of grey stone held together by ivy and cracked mortar. It lurked behind a weather-beaten lich-gate and a cluster of crumbling gravestones. Grass, knee-high in places, hid names and dates. Nothing in this rambling building matched, neither the arched door at the front, the slate roof nor the stubby bell tower.

The inside smelled of pigeon droppings and stale candle wax. Rafters of light crisscrossed the air above the pews. Every seat was empty. Prayer books collected dust in a corner. The organ lid was down, the pipes silent. In the font the water had dried up. A scum of black dirt and dead flies coated the bottom of the marble bowl.

We took places at the front of the church. Parson

214

Proudlove emerged from the vestry and began the service. His voice echoed around the bare walls. Marjorie's eyes never left her husband. I kept glancing back at the door, expecting other people to arrive soon, but not another soul entered. We sang hymns, mumbled prayers and uttered amens, our voices reedy in this dusty sepulchre.

After the service, I stood on the cinder path and sucked in lungfuls of fresh air. A coach waited outside the lich-gate. The driver informed us that we were to go at once to Dinstock Hall, where Lady Elizabeth Jane wished to see us.

'Won't take long, ma'am,' he said. 'I'll have you back at the parsonage before your husband even notices you were gone.'

The coach was fast and held the road well. Marjorie pretended to be intent on the fields beyond the window but I was having none of that. 'Why was there no one else in the church? Was it a private service?'

'Dinstock people don't attend services.'

'Are they all papists? Is there another place of worship?'

'It is a matter for their own consciences.' She turned away from the window. 'One day you will tie your head in knots with all these questions.'

Dinstock Hall sat like a red-faced bawd on a swathe of grass sliced at the back by trees. Built in Tudor times, so Marjorie had said, it was smaller than George's manor but no less magnificent. We clattered up a gravel drive lined on both sides with poplar trees. Lady Elizabeth received us in her parlour. She was lank and fat bosomed. Paper patches spotted her cheeks.

'You there,' she addressed me. 'You with the blotchy face. Come closer so I can see you better.'

I stepped into a circle of sunlight. Lady Elizabeth pursed her lips and wafted a fan beneath her long nose. 'So you are the young widow who has caused such a stir in the village.'

215

'Yes, Lady Elizabeth.'

'You will address me as m'lady.'

'Yes, m'lady.'

She turned to Marjorie, who cast her eyes down as if she was a kitchen scrubber. 'A long way for your daughter to fall, Mrs Proudlove. Mistress of the manor to a village pup.'

I butted in. 'You are mistaken, m'lady. I am only her daughter-in-law. Rodriguez is my family name.'

We were forced to walk back to Dinstock. Marjorie would not talk to me, no matter how much I cajoled her. When Charlotte tried to speak she was shushed into silence. I bit back my temper and inwardly cursed my aching feet. Lady Elizabeth's outraged face was still clear in my mind.

At the parsonage I was denied lunch and ordered to my room. Parson Proudlove arrived a little after noon and, after hearing what happened, immediately sent for me. He bolted the parlour door and drew the curtains. We faced each other in the gloom.

'You have disgraced me and shamed yourself,' he said. 'How dare you insult Lady Elizabeth.'

'How dare she insult me,' I retorted. 'Was I meant to stand and say nothing like a scolded child while she mocked me? My husband once owned land that stretched in every direction. I won't let some peahen of a woman tread on my pride. I have already had my fill of that family.'

I waited for him to say something. My breath came hard after that little speech. The parson did not reply. He stood and crossed to a narrow cupboard set into the wall beside the bookshelf. He opened the door and took out a polished stick made from some dark wood, perhaps hickory. He flicked it a couple of times. I heard a swish as it cut the air.

'What do you propose to do with that?' I demanded, backing towards the locked door.

Quick as a hawk that sights a pigeon, Proudlove snatched hold of my arm. Before I could utter another sound he bent

216

me across the table in the bay window, sending the candlestick skating across the surface. My arm was pinned behind my back and my face rammed into the polished wood. His wiry, knotted limbs felt like iron. I yelped when he lifted my skirts and tore my petticoat open.

'No . . .' The word squeezed out of my mouth. A hiss of air and the first blow screamed white-hot pain across my nerve endings. I bucked against the table. Proudlove's fingers pinched bruises into my arm as the stick struck a second time. Molten agony seared the length of my spine and into both legs.

As the stick came down again, the parson mouthed a litany of verses pulled from the pages of the Bible. Through the pain I heard his hoary voice rise in supplication to God, beseeching Him to save my damned soul. The stick cut into me a fourth time.

'Don't hit me again.' My voice was mangled, my face a puddle of sweat. 'I will do whatever you say. Please don't hit me again.'

I sensed the stick quivering in the air. Perhaps the next blow would knock me senseless, send my mind into a dark place where this man could not humiliate me any more. A second passed. Another. Footsteps crossed the floorboards and a lock clicked. I opened tear-soaked eyes. For a second, Catherine was standing in the doorway, knotted towel clenched in her hand. Her mouth was working, the words low and horrible, rasping like a sack dragged across dirt.

'You must be a good girl, Juliana. God punishes sinners. See that you behave, or your transgressions will be paid for in blood.'

The figure melted, the cream dress turning into a midnight black coat. Catherine's face sharpened. Skin wrinkled like paper turning to ashes in a hot fire. The parson stood in her place, no compassion anywhere in his stagnant eyes.

I dragged myself across the floor on my hands and knees.

217

Proudlove stepped aside. I grabbed the doorframe, hauled myself to my feet, and stumbled out into the hall. The door closed behind me.

'I cannot go back to that church.' I winced as Marjorie applied a cloth steeped in hot, salty water to my raw behind.

'You must attend services and say your prayers,' she told me, 'or you can't live under our roof.'

'I will go somewhere else. A different parish.'

'You'll go nowhere of the sort.'

I jerked again as needles of pain stabbed into my tender muscles. 'That water is too hot. You are hurting me.'

'It's for your own good. Lie still and let me see to it, otherwise we shall be here half the night and I have Nathaniel's posset to make.'

I shifted on the bed. Spread-eagled with my skirts around my waist, I must have presented a ridiculous sight. I bit my bottom lip when Marjorie applied the cloth again. The beating hadn't drawn blood, but livid welts scored my rump. Despite my defiant tone, I felt anything but brave.

'Why did you tell Lady Elizabeth that your name was Rodriguez,' Marjorie asked, rinsing the cloth in fresh water.

'Because my name is the only thing I have left.' I wiped my sweat-soaked face on the coverlet. 'Though I didn't expect to have the skin flayed from my back for using it.'

'It's not wise to anger Nathaniel. He is under pressure from the church and has many parish duties that beg his attention. It is important to maintain good relations with the squire and his family.'

'They are not *my* family. Or my masters. Taking a stick to my rump won't change that.'

'Nathaniel is your father. It's his duty to chastise you.'

'He is no such thing. I doubt any parent would put a rod across a girl's back the way your husband did to me. Don't fret, Marjorie, I know better than to cross him again. I've had my skin thrashed for the last time. I will eat my food, say my prayers and go to bed when I'm told. The next time Lady Elizabeth slaps me with her tongue, I'll turn the other cheek. But I shall never call Parson Proudlove my father.'

Marjorie dumped the cloth in the pail, splashing water over the sides. She grabbed the handle and swung open my bedchamber door. 'Supper is at eight,' she reminded me. 'Make sure you are on time.'

'Yes, Mrs Proudlove.'

She paused on the doorway, looked as if she was about to say something, then thought better of it and tramped off down the stairs. Wincing, I eased my skirts back down over my behind. I'd likely sleep on my belly for a week.

Footsteps pattered across the landing. The door pushed in and there was Charlotte, looking at me with enquiring eyes. 'Sorry,' I told her. 'No games from me today.'

She scrambled to the bed, climbed on to the side of the mattress and pushed the damp hair off my forehead with her small hand. 'Did you really steal children?' she whispered.

I propped myself up on an elbow. This child had a knack for digging up awkward questions. 'Where did you hear that?'

'Sophie told me.'

Sophie was the miller's daughter. I nodded, unwilling to lie. 'Yes, it's true.'

'Why did you do it?'

'Because certain people wanted to hurt them. I took or sent them to places where they would be safe.'

The frown returned. 'Papa steals children too.'

I gaped at her. 'What did you say?'

'Papa steals children,' Charlotte repeated, 'and takes then to the Bad Place.'

I rolled on to my knees and climbed awkwardly off the bed. My throat had gone as dry as a stream bed in a six-week drought. 'What Bad Place?'

Her small face was a pot of storm clouds, her mouth

219

flattened into a thin gash. I laid hands on her shoulders and summoned up a special smile but she did not return it. Such an expression was terrifying on a child.

'He takes them, boys mostly, and sometimes little girls like me. Babies too. He comes back with gold in his purse and a penny for me if I'm awake. He'll be angry if he knows I've told you.'

'Angry? How do you mean? Does he beat you? Does he hit you with his stick?' I was shaking her without realising it. Her face crumpled and she pulled out of my grasp. Just then her mother called upstairs. She fled the room, rubbing her shoulder. I cursed my clumsiness but a moment later her laughter burbled up from the kitchen. Relief flooded through me.

I washed my face in the bowl of water on the dresser then brushed my hair. The pain in my backside had subsided to a dull throb but putting on a fresh petticoat still took effort.

Charlotte's words ran around inside my head. She was a fanciful child, given over to a colourful imagination but I couldn't dismiss that haunted look on her face. Something was happening in this sleepy part of the country. Something bad. And for all his piousness and his pretty cottage smothered in ivy, Parson Proudlove's black heart was at the centre of it.

The following day I was taken back to Dinstock Hall to apologise to Lady Elizabeth. She waited in her drawing room as I mouthed words of contrition then dismissed me with a flick of the hand. I limped into the parlour to join Emma. My backside, after a murderously uncomfortable night, had bruised the colour of a plum.

Marjorie, who had accompanied me on this pitiable errand, returned in the parson's gig, which had been loaned for the occasion. I spent the rest of the morning perched on the edge of the parlour couch with two cushions squeezed under my rump. Emma, ladylike in her own waspish way, asked no questions. I tried to keep her entertained but she was in a restless mood. She selected a volume at random from the oak bookcase sprawled against the far wall and handed it to me. I read the first couple of chapters quickly and fluently, however Emma's attention soon wandered. We spent most of the time trying to think of something to say. I answered her questions about Wexborough and she told me something of the country. But when I asked about her parents her face went slack. Only my changing the subject breached the long silence that threatened to follow. I was relieved when the Janes' coach drew up in front of the house to take me back to the parsonage. On the way out, Lady Elizabeth handed me a note for Parson Proudlove asking me to return on a regular basis.

So it was for the next few weeks, each visit more uncomfortable than the last. I was shown round the house, the gardens, the stables. I was allowed to pet Emma's mare, Brightwater, and she suggested that we ride together. It was the first time I had witnessed a spark of interest on her face. This was quickly snuffed when I confessed that I'd never been in the saddle and did not own a horse.

'Perhaps my groom can teach you?' she offered, but I could tell her heart was not in it. We retreated to the house again and tried card games but I was too good for her and she scattered them on the floor with an angry sweep of her hand.

Then she played the spinet. I sat and listened. I had no musical skills and wasn't much of a singer either. Sewing brought on a headache and when I tried painting, the mess I left on the canvas was matched only by the one on my gown. So most of the time we walked in silence or sat indoors if the weather turned foul.

Emma's lack of curiosity proved surprising. She asked only perfunctory questions, never probing very far. Whenever I tried to volunteer anything she appeared uninterested. Her parents were out most of the time on business or social engagements and, apart from the servants, we often had the house to ourselves. I would have poked my head into every nook, explored every hallway, climbed every staircase. But no, I had to remain in the parlour trying to think of a pastime we would both find tolerable.

At the parsonage I spent much of my time reading in my bedchamber. Sometimes I would walk in the woods behind the house, a dark place of shadows where trees crammed together in a cathedral of wood. Life teemed amidst the branches and on the soft forest floor. Owls, squirrels, rabbits. Once, a deer eyed me warily from the other side of the brook where it had paused to sip the clear waters.

At other times I helped around the house, dutifully attended that empty church each Sabbath and brushed the first of the winter's snow from the front path. Charlotte had been sent to stay with a cousin in Bristol for the season. I peeked into her box-sized bedroom, fingering her rag poppets or some of the other trinkets I knew she loved to play with.

One crisp morning, Parson Proudlove went into her room and gathered everything into a sack. He took a swatch of kindling from the hearth and built a fire outside the kitchen door, feeding it with logs from the woodpile. When the flames had caught, he emptied the sack on to the pyre and stood by as his daughter's toys and scrapbooks turned to ashes. He noticed me watching from the kitchen window and ordered me into the woods with a basket to fetch more kindling. Marjorie had gone into Dinstock and it was too early for the maid to arrive from the village.

I struggled deep into the woods on the hunt for suitable fuel. Stubborn patches of snow clung to the trees and a powder of frost made every stretch treacherous. When I returned two hours later the fire had reduced to a smoking, cindered ring. The empty sack lay beside it. Tiny, black-ened faces stared out of the charred ruin. I nudged them with my foot. The porcelain heads were all that remained of Charlotte's dolls. From inside the cottage came the sound of someone weeping. I pushed open the door and stepped into the kitchen, stamping the cold out of my feet. Marjorie was seated at the table, her basket in front of her, the cover draped across the top. She stopped crying when she saw me and pounced on the kindling. 'The stove has gone out,' she said, trying to sound cheerful. 'We must get it going again else we shall all freeze.'

I didn't understand the significance of what I'd seen in the yard and wasn't willing to ask the parson. Perhaps he was clearing out before Charlotte returned from Bristol with a cartload of new things and Marjorie was just being sentimental. I did not press her on the matter. She was no friend or ally, no one I could confide in. She wanted to bend me too much to her way of thinking, almost as if she could not countenance anyone possessing a different view of the world than her own, or more accurately her husband's. I felt torn between fear of the parson, a desire to remain in her favour and a dull resentment at being pushed around like some serving wench with corn in my hair and mud between my toes.

Only in Charlotte, I believed, could I place a measure of trust, though more secrets than revelations lurked in those dark eyes. What had they seen? What had she heard in her tiny bedroom when sleep proved elusive?

'I have work for you,' the parson told me when I returned from my weekly visit to Dinstock Hall. 'Important work that I cannot spare the time to attend to. You will need to travel around the parish, for which I shall provide a carriage and driver, and be prepared to spend many hours in all weathers.'

He had been waiting in his parlour, perched on his armchair beside the hearth, a pipe stuck between his long teeth. A valise lay open on the floor. Inside were a Bible, prayer book and a thick sheaf of papers.

I curtsied and told him I would do whatever he pleased. The bite of his polished stick was too fresh in my memory. He explained that my coach would collect me at the gate tomorrow, just after daybreak. 'Be sure you are ready,' he warned. 'Many weeks of hard, Christian toil lie ahead.'

He outlined my duties, told me that I was to deliver clothes and food for the needy, collect tithes from local merchants, and hand over parish papers where appropriate. He gave me a list of hamlets and farms. 'Your driver is a local lad. He will know where to take you.'

'And my visits to Dinstock Hall?'

'Will continue.'

He grasped the arms of the chair and raised himself to his feet. I kept my head bowed. Looking the parson in the eye took more nerve than I could summon. 'Much of the work we do in the church is by necessity discreet,' he continued. 'Accept the wisdom of your betters and do not question matters that are none of your concern. Keep your attention on the work at hand. Get to know the parishioners, their families. The more we become aware of their needs, the better we will be able to serve them. Do your duty by me and I shall never have cause to punish you again. Do you understand?'

My voice was the squeak of a mouse. 'Yes, parson.'

His shadow passed away from me. I ached to sit down. Both legs had turned to water and I trembled so much I thought my teeth would shake out of their sockets. Parson Proudlove resumed his seat by the fire. Pipe smoke leaked from the hole in his cheek and curled around his face like dragon's breath. 'When you visit the farms, remember that birthing and dying are the day-to-day business of working folk. Sometimes I lose count of my flock. Keep a tally for me. I will need it when I give account to my superiors. You can do that, can't you?'

'Yes, parson.'

*

Released, and with no chores to do, I spent the remainder of the day alone among the trees. Eventually, driving rain penetrated the branches and had me running for the comfort of my bed. Daybreak caught me in a foul mood. I felt I had a lot to grumble about as I stamped my feet on the frost-cracked lane. I had slept fitfully again, poisoned by nightmares full of half-glimpsed faces that shifted in and out of focus.

My belly rumbled. Mrs Proudlove had barely put the kindling in the hearth when I'd padded into the kitchen, eyes gritty. The parson was already off on some business or other. Did he ever sleep? I pictured him stalking about his parlour in the dead of night with that one candle burning. Or perhaps other things kept him from his bed.

I blew into my hands and glanced at the leaden belly of the sky. More rain later, I suspected. I ached for bed and hot coffee. The pile of prayer books, old clothes and packets I was due to deliver today sat in neat bundles beside the gate. Marjorie had helped me out with them, puffing in the cold air.

A rumbling in the lane broke into my thoughts. I backed into the gate as a carriage hove into view. The driver, smothered beneath a heavy coat and scarf, gave a sharp whistle and brought the team of two to a halt. The coach was little better than a cart with a roof nailed on. It squatted on leather springs that squealed like trapped mice. Varnish flaked off the woodwork, the wheels looked as if they wanted to go off in separate directions and it had the damp mustiness of something that had mouldered under canvas for too many seasons. The pair of bays hauling it seemed sound enough, though they fidgeted as if ashamed to be caught between the shafts of such an ancient thing.

The driver let go of the reins and jumped down from his perch. He was short compared to most men hereabouts and walked with a slight stoop. He plucked off his cap and revealed a mop of black curls clinging to the top of his skull. Pale skin was studded by thick eyebrows, an over-long nose and a pink half-moon for a mouth. From beneath heavy lids, two bright blue eyes regarded me with curious politeness.

'Good day,' he uttered in the local drawl. 'You are Miss Juliana? Prettyman is my name, Charles Prettyman.'

'You are my driver?' I said, as frosty as the ice-hard puddles dotting the lane.

'I am that. Let me get these things on board then we can be off.'

'In that?' I gestured at the carriage, which seemed to sag further on its springs even as I spoke. 'Do you suppose it will make it to the end of the lane without falling to pieces?'

Prettyman laughed, a rich, full sound that might have come from the lungs of a sturdy labourer. 'She'll take you to Scotland and back if you've a mind to go,' he declared, slapping the wooden panel with the palm of his hand. 'She's an old carriage but she's well built and can match the Wexborough stagecoach when the roads allow. Henry Colm over at Rosecroft Farm used it for years to cart his pigs around and they had no cause for complaint.'

'Pigs?' I stared at him aghast. 'I am to sit in a carriage that has had pigs in it?'

'I've washed it out for you. Colm bought himself a new wagon and sold this to Parson Proudlove. Parson got a bargain if you ask me. Here we go now. Would you mind getting the door for me?'

A piece of rope served as a handle. I jerked the door open whilst Prettyman started picking up the books. He only used one hand to load the carriage and kept the other tucked into his coat. 'Are you injured?' I asked, once he had stacked everything on to one of the wooden seats inside.

'No, miss. I've got a withered arm. No strength in it. I'd let you have a look but it's not so pretty. I was all right as a baby but the rest of me grew and the arm didn't. I mostly keep it covered, though I'm not one for grouching.'

'Wonderful,' I groaned. 'Not only do I have to sit with the stench of pigs but also I have to suffer a cripple to drive me.'

Coloured spots appeared above Prettyman's cheekbones. His eyes lost their bright edge. 'I'm as good a man as any, more so than some. No one in the county can handle a coach better and I'd be working for Squire Matthew Jane himself if I wasn't in debt to the church.'

'Anyone can brag. Children. Wet-faced boys. Just take me where I have to go.' I reached under my shawl, took out a sheet of paper and handed it to him. 'Here is a list of places we have to visit today.'

He stared at the paper. A flush spread across his whole face. 'I can't read. Nobody ever had time to teach me.'

'No, I suppose not.' I snatched the list out of his hand. 'Little use for reading if you spend your day shovelling dung out of a stable. Well, I'll make one thing clear, Charles Prettyman. I am not here of my own choosing. All you have to do is drive this pig cart. Now help me inside then get back to your seat. A busy day lies ahead and we are already late.'

Muscles worked in his throat. He wrapped his scarf back around his face, hoisted me into the carriage, then clambered back on to his perch and clicked the horses forward. I leaned back on the hard wooden seat. The inside of the coach was scratched and bare but didn't smell of anything worse than old wood. My own carriage at last. A pig wagon.

The horses gathered speed. Prettyman could not have a more unlikely name, I reflected. He was as ugly as an old boot and spoke with the duncery of a tinker. I did not believe his boastful claims. A cripple working the stables at Dinstock Hall, in any capacity, beggared belief. Parson Proudlove must have considered it a fine jest to have such a fellow cart me around the countryside. A half-man to drive a broken-down coach. Well, I would play his game.

For four days I grit my teeth as we bumped down umpteen

muddy lanes to hamlets with ridiculous names. Sour-faced locals stared at me with undisguised mistrust as I dumped the word of God on their doorstep or handed out clothes to replace their filthy rags, garments that would likely end up peddled at Dinstock market.

I suffered their sullen curiosity, the way they sometimes plucked at my mourning gown, tried to finger my red hair or fussed over my birthmark, as if their own pox-raddled faces weren't bad enough. It was always the poorest farms we visited. Scrawny livestock scratched the dirt. Sagging thatched roofs, thick with moss, topped the tumbledown hovels in which these creatures lived. Speech was apparently beyond most of them. My missions of mercy were mostly greeted with silence or the occasional grunt.

I quickly came to hate the squalor. Faces were often scabbed with some god-awful festering that thrived on grubby flesh. Every place stank, either from the rubbish they burned in their hearths, the cow shit that plastered everything, or their own bodies. The only time anyone seemed to enjoy a wash was when obliged to step out into the rain. I hated them and they resented me. I heard the thunk of a rock against the carriage door after delivering a sack of potatoes to a starving family. Their own crop had shrivelled in the waterlogged fields because no one had the wit to drain the ground properly.

Prettyman kept an old pistol tucked into his belt. Not loaded, he assured me. 'This gun ain't fired a shot in nearly fifty years,' he explained, waving the relic in front of my face. 'But it'll put the fear of God into any who've a mind to forget their place.'

'Who are you to talk about place?' I snapped back. 'And don't point that thing at me again.'

By the end of the week the hem of my gown had frayed, along with my temper. I couldn't get the mud off my shoes or the shit from my hands. My clothes were permanently damp from wading through puddles or having to stand in the infernal drizzle that had bled out of the clouds these past few days.

Every night, after my rounds, the parson called me to his parlour. I stood in front of his armchair like a scolded child and related all the details of each visit. He listened, brows pinched, posing occasional questions, which I answered as honestly as I could.

'They accepted the clothes you offered?' he asked.

'I don't think anything was likely to be refused. Even toddlers' garments could be patched into something bigger.'

'Hmmm, no matter. A starving belly makes friends easily. You will gain their trust in time.'

It was with relief that I paid my weekly visit to Dinstock Hall. Clouds overhead had thickened. They hung over the landscape in slabs of grey, innards broiling with storms. The wind picked up as Prettyman took the coach along the exposed road towards the Hall. Gusts whooped across the fields and stripped twigs from the bare branches of the few trees lining our route. The canvas blinds flapped against the carriage windows, throwing chips of desiccated varnish over my skirts. Damp patches crept across the roof.

Eventually the drizzle turned to rain. Prettyman shouted something to the horses, voice muffled under the scarf. The carriage swayed in the wind, the wheels losing themselves in waterlogged ruts. Thunder grumbled in the distance.

By the time we pulled to a halt outside Dinstock Hall, the rain was scything across the lawns in vicious sheets. A footman appeared with a parasol, which was instantly snatched out of his hands by the wind and sent tumbling over the rose beds. I ran past him and shivered into the house. Emma greeted me in the hall, mouthing empty remarks about the state of the weather and my bedraggled appearance. She took me by the hand, her fingers warm against my chilled skin, and seated me in front of the parlour fire before ordering tea.

I was too miserable to notice the flush on her cheeks, or the way she danced around the room, hands fluttering like birds' wings. Her eyes kept wandering towards the door as she spoke in a voice that was a little higher than usual. She chattered non-stop about the latest fashions, the news from Bristol and London, in fact anything and everything. Her fingers drifted to her necklace or her earrings as if they were magical charms.

Emma had always been well dressed but today she'd chosen an especially fetching gown. Rouge tinted her cheeks with soft rosebuds. The parlour air was thick with her cologne. Jewel-studded rings formed glittering dewdrops on her hands.

I poured hot tea down my throat and sighed as its warmth spread through my belly. Emma could not sit still for more than five minutes and was soon at the window peering into the gloom. 'Is that your coach?'

I put down my teacup. 'I'm afraid so. It was the best the parson could find for me.'

'Your driver is standing in the pouring rain. He should go round to the kitchen. Cook will give him a stool by the fire and some hot broth. The wretch looks half-drowned.'

'The horses are skittish from the thunder,' I replied. 'He must remain with the carriage and see they do not bolt.'

'Our stable lad can take care of your horses. There is plenty of room in the yard for the coach. I will send my footman back out to tell your driver.'

'There is no need . . .'

'I don't want that ugly thing in front of my house.'

Before I could splutter another word she pulled the bell sash and sent the servant out into the downpour. A minute later, my carriage rumbled away from the windows.

Emma returned to her place by the fire but still could not settle. Her eyes drifted to the door then the mantel clock, which showed a quarter past the hour. Her tea lay untouched in its cup.

'Do you want me to go?' I asked. 'It seems you have other things on your mind. Perhaps we can resume our pastimes another day?'

Emma flushed and pressed her hands to her cheeks. 'Forgive me. I must seem a terrible hostess but I cannot keep it a secret any longer.'

'Secret? Is it to do with hiding away my battered old carriage?'

She laughed too loudly and leaned forward in her chair. Her eyes were like a child's, bright with excitement. She glanced again at the clock. Now her voice was a whisper. 'I have a beau,' she confessed. 'Can you believe it?'

She caught the look on my face and giggled like a girl half her age. Her fingers scurried up and down the chair arm as if she had no control over them. 'He is the most divine fellow,' she declared, as if challenging me to disagree. 'A gentleman of fine talents and not inconsiderable wealth. I do believe I am in love. I know he loves me.'

I goggled at her. Now it was the turn of my tea to grow cold in its cup. I thought any man would have to be struck very hard about the head with a spade to fall for Emma Jane. 'He told you this?' I gulped.

'No, not directly, but men have a way of showing their feelings without putting them into words. 'Tis all part of the game. A gentleman would not be so forward as to declare his intentions outright, any more than a lady would bare her heart without first savouring the thrill of the chase. You will come to understand these things should you ever fall in love yourself.'

'Indeed?' I wondered what colour my face had turned. Emma favoured me with what I supposed was a kindly smile.

'I am sure it will happen before too long. Perhaps a prosperous farmer will catch your eye, or a merchant.'

'Emma, I am already a widow. Had you forgotten?'

Her eyes returned to the clock. I could have been talking

231

to the rug for all the attention she paid me. I sat, jaw muscles clenched, whilst she described her new lover's carriage down to the last detail, even though she confessed to never having ridden in it, and his taste in clothes – surely the finest in all Europe. He was striking and debonair, a master gambler and an expert swordsman. When at last she had to pause to take a breath, I asked her where she had met this paragon of manliness. Emma explained that she had been introduced at a private ball in Wexborough. Her family had been invited through a colleague of her father's. Whilst he had slipped off to discuss politics with the gentlemen in the smoking room, the new light in his daughter's life chose that moment to put in an appearance.

'I could have danced with him until my feet dropped off,' she declared. 'The town women were staring at us, their faces sour with envy. I felt like a queen. It was the happiest night of my life and I never wanted it to end. Afterwards, he gained Papa's permission to call at the Manor. I would have died if it had been refused. All this week he has showered me with gifts, each delivered by his private messenger.'

I tried to shrug off the beginnings of a headache and sat patiently while she showed me the trinkets this mysterious lover had bestowed. Pretty baubles, sure enough, and expensive looking, but I did not care for anything. Not the gilt bracelet, or the porcelain figure of a stallion, or even the satin and ivory choker, though it looked beautiful on her and I said as much. These gifts had no sense, no order, as if they had been selected at random and packed off without thought.

I did not let Emma know what I was thinking. I doubted she'd listen. The place this 'love' had taken her lacked any door or window to the real world. I took the scone she offered and munched on it whilst she poured me a fresh cup of tea.

'What is your beau's name?' I asked, mouth a ring of

crumbs. 'I attended many functions during my marriage to George Proudlove. Perhaps I have met him?'

She laughed. 'I doubt someone like you would have made the acquaintance of such a gentleman. In any case you *shall* meet him. I have decided. He is due within the hour.'

I mumbled excuses but Emma brushed them aside. The headache lingering at the back of my brow finally burst across my skull. I had no heart to argue. Emma droned on about the new dress she had bought to impress him and the picnics they planned to take by the river when winter finally thawed to spring. I mouthed a silent prayer of thanks, hypocrite that I was, when the sound of horses on the drive stopped her chatter. Emma squealed, clapped her hands and ran to the door, leaving me with a pot of empty tea and a plateful of broken cakes.

I rubbed sore eyes, wishing I could leave. The rain and the bumpy road now seemed preferable to this neat parlour with its gleaming ornaments and too-clean hearth. A man's voice rumbled in the hall, followed by Emma's shrill laughter. Footsteps approached the parlour. The door breezed inwards. The rich scent of cologne mixed with tobacco carried into the room.

I frowned. That cologne. I had smelled it before. I opened my eyes. Emma's new love stood before me, mud caking the soles of his boots and raindrops sprinkling his powdered wig like diamonds. He held out a gloved hand. Amusement shone in his eyes. 'Charmed,' he said in that cat-purr voice.

It was Adam Fairchild.

Chapter Fifteen

I don't know how long I stared at him. I was on my feet though unable to remember getting up from my chair. At some point I had knocked over my teacup and spread a brown stain across the carpet. In the background, Emma's out-of-focus face smiled and said something, though I couldn't hear what. Adam Fairchild and I regarded each other and nothing else in the room was real. His lips moved. 'A pleasure to meet you again.'

I was vaguely aware of Emma's smile faltering. She asked a question and Adam turned to speak to her, breaking the spell between us. 'I was an acquaintance of Mrs Proudlove's late husband,' he explained, 'and our paths crossed once or twice before that.'

Doubt lifted from Emma's face. Adam sprawled out on the sofa, planting his boots on the tea table. He lit a pipe with a taper from the fire and blew smoke rings into the air. Emma perched on the end of the couch, hands clasped in her lap, face like an eager dog expecting a reward after performing some trick or another.

I remained standing, unable to put myself to any purpose or conjure any sense out of my mouth. I might have spent the rest of the day like that if Lady Elizabeth hadn't breezed into the parlour in a cloud of perfume. She greeted Adam with a kiss as if he was a favoured child, then plucked me out of the room and along to her private chambers at the rear of the house. After closing the door, she yanked off her wig and tossed it on to the dresser. For one insane moment

I thought her hair had come away too. Sunlight reflected off her bald, pink scalp. The skin was puckered with bug bites and old scabs.

'I've worn wigs since I was three years old,' she explained, catching my expression. 'When you spend all your time scratching like a tinker's cur it makes sense to lose your locks. So many lice inhabit that burdensome head-dress I am surprised the thing does not jump off its stand and flee the room.'

I shot a look at the door. What were Adam and Emma doing? Were they talking about me?

'My cousin's hair fell out before she was forty,' Lady Elizabeth continued, seating herself on an embroidered divan. 'She refused to wear a wig. Eventually she refused to wear a dress and took to turning up at the house in hessian robes. Our gatekeeper mistook her for a tinker and, thinking she had come begging, refused her entry to the grounds. He was mortified on discovering the identity of this mysterious visitor.'

I glanced at the door again.

On the table beside the divan was a slim wooden box. Lady Elizabeth opened the lid and plucked out a long-stemmed clay pipe. She stuffed in a small wad of fresh tobacco and pushed the end between her teeth. She talked around it while coaxing a spark from her tinderbox. 'Don't look so shocked. I take snuff too. Why should men have all the pleasure in life, eh?' She patted the cushion beside her. 'Would you like to play cards, perhaps a hand or two of whist? I hear you are quite good.'

I shook my head. She took a long draw on her pipe, savouring the taste before releasing a cloud of blue smoke into the hot air. 'Mr Fairchild has taken lodging at Dinstock inn, and will remain in the district for the next month. You will curtail your visits unless summoned and remain discreet on the matter of their courtship.'

'She has known him barely two weeks and already you

are calling it a courtship? You must be aware of this man's reputation?'

Lady Elizabeth tapped her pipe out on to the table.

'His exploits are familiar to every household in the county,' I persisted.

She sighed and glanced out of the window. The rain was still hammering down outside. 'He is a charming man, perfectly charming. Every gentleman of worth garners a reputation with the town gossips and scandal is usually born of jealousy, both among peers and members of the fair sex. If nothing else, bawdy behaviour is a symptom of exuberance and does not mean every male should be tarred as a libertine. Mr Fairchild's company is agreeable. Certainly he does not seem to be the lecher he is painted.'

A smile flitted across her lips. Her eyes took on a faraway look and she brushed her cheek with her fingers. She was thinking about him, the way I had thought about him for weeks after that first meeting at the Wexborough ball. Even now if I let my guard slip far enough, I could find myself thinking that way again. 'You are prepared to overlook his sins because he makes you forget you're not a girl any more,' I accused through clenched teeth. 'This is how he works, don't you realise that? He is using Emma for his own ends and putting you off the scent with sweet talk and idle compliments. While he has you distracted he will fill your daughter's womb with bastards and starve her of decency the way a leech sucks blood.'

Outside, a rip opened up in the clouds and threw sunlight across the floor. It carved Lady Elizabeth's face into light and shadow. 'Sit down,' she told me. 'Sit down you little fool before you hurt yourself.'

I panted like a dog after a fast chase and had squeezed both fists hard enough for my nails to cut my palms. I sat on end of the divan.

'That is better,' she continued. 'There is bitterness on your face, plain for all to see. I accept that you have had some

236

contact with Mr Fairchild but I do not wish to know what has passed between you. Whatever part he played in your life must remain in the past. You will not in any way compromise my daughter's happiness, do you understand? This is the second time you have crossed me, but I am prepared to overlook it. You are young and obviously hurt. I have known that pain myself and realise how it can twist one's thoughts.'

'I don't love Adam Fairchild.'

'No, of course you do not. And if I ever hear of you bringing his name into disrepute I will speak to Parson Proudlove and you will not be made welcome at Dinstock Hall again.'

I imagined the bite of that polished stick on my back and kept my mouth closed. The hall clock chimed the hour. A minute later I heard the parlour door open. Chuckling voices, words too soft to discern, drew claws across my imagination. I pictured Emma's love-soaked face, Adam's amused, slightly contemptuous charm. Then a pause, as if the entire house held its breath. In my tortured thoughts, he placed a kiss on her long fingers whilst she blushed and her head brimmed with dreams of marriage and children.

I rose from the divan and scurried to the door. Worse things than bitterness existed. Anger. Jealousy.

I thought Lady Elizabeth might try to follow me but she had confidence in her own power and her expression was warning enough. She refilled her pipe whilst I pulled open the door and gusted along the hall. Emma and Adam were standing by the open front door. Both turned to look at me as I clattered, cack-legged as any infant, across the tiles. How graceful Emma was, how elegant in her poise and mannerisms. Beside her, I felt a clumsy old widow. I tried to say something but my tongue made a hash of it. Emma giggled.

'My dear,' Adam addressed her, smile still playing across his lips, 'I fear I have left my gloves in the parlour. Would you be an angel and get them for me?'

She glanced at me then happily went to fetch them. Alone with Fairchild, I felt the air tighten around my throat. Every nerve in my body burned. 'Why?' I demanded. 'Why Emma Jane? What does she possess that you could want? You have taken and ruined richer, more amusing creatures than her. Why muddy your boots for an empty-headed country girl? What dark game are you playing?'

A nest of vipers hissed behind his teeth. 'A game you would dearly love to join in.' He leaned forward and, before I could or would stop him, brushed my lips with a kiss. I heard a strangled gasp. Emma stood in the parlour doorway, brown leather gloves gripped in her hand. Her face was the colour of ashes. She threw the gloves at Adam. He caught them, tipped his hat to both of us and strode out the front door in a gust of damp air. I watched as he clambered into his carriage, cloak flapping about his legs. A moment later the driver set the team galloping up the drive.

Emma's fingers closed like bony pincers around my arm. 'So, widow, you seek to become a rival under my own roof?'

I shrugged free. 'Fairchild is a womaniser who will kiss any pretty face he sees, whether that face is asking to be kissed or not. I did not invite his attention, nor was it welcome.'

'He is mine. Do not forget it.'

'Take him then and don't expect me to be around after he has left you broken-hearted and mewling for your mama.'

I stormed out of the house, dragging my shawl around my shoulders and cursing like a common thief. Prettyman was in the stable yard, seated inside my carriage, supping a mug of hot broth presumably begged from the kitchen. I yanked open the door. 'Out,' I commanded. 'Get back on the driver's seat.'

He climbed out and tipped the remains of his soup into the dirt. He left the mug on the kitchen step before climbing on to the carriage roof and picking up the reins. He did not utter a word, which suited me fine. I clambered inside and closed the door. 'Take me back to the parsonage,' I ordered, leaning out of the window. 'See if you can coax enough life from these nags to get there before the rain returns.'

Prettyman's face was pinched above his woollen scarf. He nodded and snapped the reins. I was flung back into my seat as the horses jerked forward. They took the drive at a fast canter. As we passed the front of the house I spied Emma watching from the parlour window. Neither of us waved. I suspected Adam knew what he was doing when he placed that serpent's kiss on my mouth.

Leather springs groaned as the carriage lurched into the waterlogged lane. I spotted a figure walking along the verge with three sizeable dogs straining on a leash. Swaddled in coats with a shovel hat crammed on his head, the figure stopped wrestling the animals long enough to look up. I recognised Squire Matthew. What was he doing outside the grounds of Dinstock Hall?

'Prettyman, stop the coach.' I banged on the roof until the carriage rattled to a halt. The moment I stepped out, the hounds were sniffing around my skirts. I tried not to wince when I felt their black button noses push into the folds. I was ignorant of dogs and did not know the breed, seeing them only as hairy bundles of fangs and scrabbling claws. One jumped up on its hind legs and slapped a warm, wet tongue across the back of my hand.

'Get back there,' Squire Matthew yelled, clipping the beast's ear with the end of the leash. It yelped and bounded out of the way. 'Back off I say.' Raindrops showered off his coat. He jerked the leash again. All three animals fell back, pawing the dirt around his boots. 'Rot my teeth, it's the young widow,' he declared. 'It gladdens me to see you, Miss Juliana, though that mourning sack makes you look like a sour old maid, let my legs turn putrid if that's not the truth.'

'Squire Matthew, I must speak to you.'

'Can't it wait for sweeter weather?'

'No.'

'Well, out with it, girl. These curs get lively when they want feeding.'

'That man who is calling on your daughter, you must not let him past your door. Forbid Emma to have any contact with him. Lady Elizabeth will not listen and Emma herself is too taken with the fellow to see any sense.'

He frowned. 'Adam Fairchild of Wexborough? Mighty impertinent of you, young widow, to dictate to me whom I can and cannot admit into my own home. What complaint could you have against him?'

'He is not all he seems.'

'Is that why you stopped that pile of wooden bones? To warn me that he is a rake and lecher? That he will wreck my daughter's happiness and bring her to ruin? That he would fritter away her possessions on drink, whores and card games?' He smiled at my look of astonishment. 'Climb back into your carriage and go home to the parson and his wife. I'll finish walking my dogs and we shall forget we spoke today.'

The sky closed up and threw down a fresh flurry of rain. One of the dogs cocked a leg and piddled on the wheel of the coach. The others sat scratching on the wet grass. I tried to think of something else to say. Squire Matthew waited me out, his coat buttoned tight to the neck, his eyes regarding me from under his hat brim.

'You hate her so much that you would stand by and let this man destroy her?' I said finally.

He wiped his face and glanced at the sky. 'On the contrary, I love her dearly, but her lack of respect has become burdensome. Oh, she does as she's bid, I'll grant her that, but everyone has noticed the way she looks at me and heard the things she mutters when my back is turned. Rather than a daughter, I find myself lumbered with an intolerant scold who has no ear for anything I try to tell her. 'Twas only a matter of time before some purse-hunting rake hooked her by the heart. It may be a hard lesson she learns, but a lesson none the less.'

He gestured at the hounds. 'See these dogs, I love them like my own sons. One scrap of disobedience, however, and they feel the end of my boot. Now if you'll mind out, Miss Juliana, the beasts are itching for their kennels and I want some brandy inside me before this infernal weather has me down with a fever.'

The dogs immediately burst into a fresh chorus of barking. I jumped aside as a snarling maw lunged at my legs. Squire Matthew laughed and pulled the snapping creature away. I waited on the verge until he'd crossed the lane and turned into his drive, whistling and calling his hounds to heel.

I clambered back inside the coach and closed the door. Prettyman clicked the reins and sent us rumbling back towards the parsonage. Outside, swollen clouds blackened the horizon. Everything went dark.

At the cottage gate, Prettyman climbed down and opened the door. He waited in the downpour, felt hat knocked out of shape by the rain. I sat huddled on the end of the seat with both arms wrapped around my knees.

'I did not care for the way that man spoke to you,' he said, 'or the way he handled his dogs.'

I unfolded myself. 'He is the squire. He can do as he pleases and it is no concern of yours.'

'If he had allowed those animals to hurt you . . .'

'Then what would you have done? A cripple against a man with two good arms and three dogs spoiling for a fight? Your heroics would get you hung if the hounds did not carve your throat out first. Then who would drive this wreck around the countryside?' I did not wait for an answer but climbed out and pushed past him to the gate. I felt his gaze on my back all the way up the front path.

I lost count of the weeks as winter bit deeper into the land. On the bitterest mornings I awoke to find icicles hanging icy fangs from the window ledge. Sometimes the brook froze and I had to break the ice to draw water. On Christmas

Eve our village help became afflicted with some malady that kept her at home. I found myself doing her work as well as running Parson Proudlove's errands.

From before daybreak until after dusk I laboured non-stop, grateful that I was too busy to even think. Half-dead with fatigue, I tumbled into bed each night and was instantly asleep. No nightmares. No Moses Cripps. I believed him gone, out of the county, overseas perhaps, and the documents with him. Better that way.

No summons arrived from Dinstock Hall, and Charlotte, I was told, would not be home until the following spring. Snow had blocked the Bristol road. 'The parsonage in winter is no place for a child,' Marjorie said. I carried out my chores with no complaint. Even the parson was satisfied enough to invest in a new shawl to keep me snug during those bitterly cold mornings.

Every day, Prettyman waited in the lane with the coach, never late, never grouching. Whichever way I looked at it, the carriage still resembled a battered collection of driftwood. During those mornings, with the frozen land resembling a cracked china plate, I delivered the sacks of food, threads of clothing or Bibles as required. I no longer cared if the locals scratched themselves or stank of piddle. Questions were always answered with blank stares so in the end I gave up asking.

'I will never understand these people,' I confessed to Prettyman in a moment of candour. 'They take our Bibles but refuse to attend the local church. Every Sabbath that place is like a tomb.'

'Bibles make good kindling,' he replied. 'As for the church, look there after dark. You might see lights. Candles flickering in the dead of night when not a soul is awake. Everybody is scared. That place is tainted.'

'I don't understand.'

'Ask the parson. Or, if you've not the courage, try asking his wife. It'll take more than luck or persuasion to get a reply, I'll wager. Mrs Proudlove is like the rest of us, more frightened than a rabbit with its head in the snare.'

At the farms, I quelled resentment with the sheer frequency of my visits and the willing offer of hands, both my own and Prettyman's, whenever wood had to be fetched or fires stoked. Working evenings at the parsonage had given me a good touch in the kitchen and more than one flustered wife was grateful for my skills.

'You must not indulge these people,' Marjorie rebuked when I tried to beg an extra jar of preserves. 'They are always dirty and sickly and try to take advantage of our charity.'

I did not argue, but slipped out with a pot of treacle when her back was turned. I also saved some of that night's supper in a square of muslin hidden within the folds of my gown. Next day I took it to the widow who, I'd heard, lived in a squat, white-walled cottage further up the brook. Here, the water spilled in a large pool overhung with willow trees. Prettyman told me her husband had died in the fields, dropped dead under a hot sun with his face muscles twisted into a horrible grimace. But she had a son to look out for her, a strapping lad of thirteen who was already a man before his time. He sometimes brought fish to the table as well as rabbits poached from the woods on the other side of the stream.

'Squire Matthew doesn't much mind,' Prettyman explained. 'Turn a blind eye and you might get a bellyful of rabbit stew for your kindness.'

Betty Hendy was the widow's name. She was digging stones out of a vegetable patch and rose to her feet at the sound of the carriage. Wiping her hands on her apron, she waited whilst Prettyman reined in the team. I stepped out to meet her and immediately wanted to step back in again. For a moment we faced each other across a strip of lawn.

'What's the matter?' she said finally. 'Aren't you going to cover your eyes and run?'

A net of scars cut Betty Hendy's face into ragged squares. Old burns puckered her cheeks like patches of mouldy pastry. Most of her top lip was missing, her teeth a row of stumps squatting in her pink gums.

'No,' I replied. 'I am not going to run away.'

'You're that girl I was told might come calling. A widow like me.'

I nodded, taking in the small, neat garden. Beside a log pile a boy in white shirt and breeches eyed me. He was chopping wood with a handmade tool fashioned from a sliver of plough blade and a stout branch. He swung the implement above his head and brought it down on a chunk of wood, slicing it in two.

Widow Hendy untied her apron. 'You'd best come inside. I have lemonade, or a spit of ale if you've the stomach for something stronger.'

The front door opened on to a square, low-beamed parlour, sparsely furnished but clean and cosy. I was offered the best seat in the room – a polished oak chair with a tall back. After pouring two mugs of ale, Widow Hendy pulled up a stool for herself. 'You want to know why my face looks as it does,' she stated, surmising my thoughts. 'You're wondering if someone did this to me.'

I sipped the ale. I'd had it before on my trips around the farms and found the flat, bitter taste agreeable. I eyed the widow above the rim of the cup. Her hair was bunched up on top of her head in a knot of brassy curls, but a bare, poached-egg patch of scalp clung to the side of her skull. She fingered it absently. 'Nothing has grown here since the accident. The sun gets to it if the day is hot. Mostly I keep it covered.'

'The accident?'

Widow Hendy nodded. 'I suffer convulsions. Have done since I had Peter, my son. I threw a fit and fell face first on to the fire. Peter pulled me off but not before the flames did their work. No great loss. I was always a plain-faced wench. I've got worse scars.'

'You were lucky not to be blinded.'

'I daresay.' She took a long draught of ale. 'Throwing a fit in public is a humbling thing. You piss in your petticoats, choke on your own tongue, have everyone standing around gawping at you. I scared everyone near to death the first time it happened. People thought I was possessed. Not a day passes without my being petrified that I've passed whatever ails me on to Peter. I'm all right so long as he's here to mind me. He knows what to do.'

I took another sip of ale. The yeasty liquid slid easily down my throat. 'Have you no friends?'

Betty set her mug on the stone floor beside her chair. 'I used to go about with a towel over my head. "Ghost-face" the local children called me. That's when they weren't chucking stones. And then I thought: why should I hide? I've no cause to be ashamed of myself. So I walked into the taproom of the inn, and this after the Tuesday market when it was packed to the rafters. I strode right up to the bar, in front of everyone, and told Bill Wheedon, the landlord, to pour me a jug of ale. After he'd stood and stared at me for a minute or so, I asked again and put my money on the counter. I got my beer and took my time drinking it. I never had to buy any more after that. I can't have proper friendship so I've settled for respect. Now I don't hide any more, though I won't normally let strangers into my house.'

'Why did you invite me?'

'Because of that mark on your face. I reckon you know what it's like to be stared at.'

I handed her the packet I'd brought. 'Here are some preserves for you, compliments of the parish.'

'Hmm. Marjorie Proudlove makes these herself. She ought to go into business. 'Tis a more honest trade than being a parson's wife.'

I wanted to ask what she meant by that remark but Peter kept flitting in and out of the cottage. No matter how many jobs he had to do, he was always careful to stay near his

245

mother. Chopping more wood, fetching water in two round-bellied pails, gutting a scrawny chicken – even when stoking the fire his eyes flitted across the room to where she sat and followed her as she crossed to the window or poured hot water from the kettle on its hook above the stove. His muscles were always tense, as if he was ready to pounce. Even whilst I sat with her, he did not relax but prowled catlike around Betty's modest parlour. When I spoke he did not look at me but at his mother, as if afraid something terrible would happen in the split second it took for his eyelids to drop into a blink then rise again. I began to wonder if he was mute but when Widow Hendy offered him a drink he said, 'No thank you' in a thin voice. Mostly though, he let his busy hands do the talking.

Betty was generous with her odd, half-chewed smiles. We joked and swapped stories. I let her treat Prettyman to a mug of ale. She had brewed the drink herself using bits gleaned from the fields when the harvest was finished. Parson Proudlove was never mentioned even when I handed over the clothes he wanted her to mend. I felt disinclined to talk about my guardian. Although I never said as much, I guessed that Betty knew I did not care for him.

'Peter is growing strong,' she remarked, glancing at her son. 'He has talked about starting a farm. My cottage isn't big enough to hold his dreams and he aches to feel his feet on the land. "I'll look after you, mama," he says to me. "I'll take a wife and you'll come and live with us. Together we'll run the farm, have bacon from our own pigs and bread from the wheat I'll grow."'

A shadow crossed her face. 'For all that, he is still a boy and does not realise how deeply into debt he would have to go.'

A tardy spring left the land gripped in a fist of cold all the following week. Parson Proudlove turned his ankle when he slipped on the icy church step and a surgeon was fetched from Wexborough to bind the limb. 'Local quack will bleed you white,' Proudlove flustered. 'If my throat was cut he'd open a vein in a bid to fix it.'

He retreated to his parlour. Marjorie and I helped him into his chair and made sure he had a blanket and bottle of brandy. He snapped at us like an irritable old hound and called for the trunk containing his books and papers, which he spread across his lap. We were ordered to leave and not return unless summoned by the brass hand bell he placed beside the chair.

The night spat out a stranger on to our doorstep. He had come on foot, stumbling along the rutted lane from Dinstock, his way lit by a bleached moon. Mrs Proudlove let him into the kitchen. He stood in front of the fire, blowing life back into his chilled hands. I was at the table finishing a dish of hot oatmeal. Was I supposed to say something? Greet him? Brew coffee? He didn't even glance at me. His face was a rock fall of deep lines and pox scars. A long nose stabbed the air above his thin lips and a tuft of greying beard clung to his chin. Mrs Proudlove went to inform her husband. I kept my eyes on my bowl. Logs cracked open in the hearth, puncturing the silence.

Marjorie returned and beckoned from the doorway. The visitor swept out of the kitchen. Despite the roaring fire, cold clung to his garments as though it had stained the coarse wool. He glanced at me before stooping beneath the doorframe, as if noticing me for the first time.

I finished the oatmeal and put down my spoon. Pleading a headache, I took to my bed. Marjorie gave me a posset and candle before returning to her needlework. She had been trying to persuade her tired fingers to mend a rip in the parson's coat. The needle strayed all over the material and the stitches would have to be unpicked in the morning, but she kept pushing the sliver of metal in and out, in and out. She did not look up when I bid her good night.

In the hall, a flickering strip of light bled from underneath the parlour door. I set the candle down and inched closer. After checking the kitchen door had closed behind me, I pressed an ear against the thick oak and strained to listen. The wood turned the voices beyond into mumbles and a metal flap on the other side of the keyhole thwarted curious eyes.

Frustrated, I picked up the posset and candle and climbed the stairs. Charlotte's room lay above the parlour. I slipped inside like a thief and blew out my light. Kneeling, I pulled back the rug and spread myself out on the floor, laying my head against the bare boards. My years at the Butter House had turned me into an expert eavesdropper. Now I could hear the crackle of the hearth, the rustle of paper and the bump of a chair. Voices ghosted into the room, filling the space with threats and curses.

'You will have to get the girl to do it.' The stranger's voice, spitting daggers. 'We won't stop now just because you can't keep your feet on your own church step. I don't have the men to spare and Ironjack needs the boy before the end of the week. We've lost enough money as it is, Nathaniel. I don't like an empty pocket.'

The clink of a glass, then Parson Proudlove spoke. His throat seemed full of old leather. 'I'll trust her to deliver sacks of potatoes to those beggars in my parish but my gold is a different matter. I've already had cause to put my stick across her back. Now she scrapes to me like a serving wench but her eyes say different. Get a man from the tavern to do it. Some will sell their wives for a shilling.'

'Aye, and flap their tongues to the justices for a crown. Won't look good to have a parson dancing from a gibbet. We need the girl. If things turn sour then she gets the blame. None in these parts would question her guilt.'

A door opened in the hall downstairs. Footsteps padded across the floor. I scrambled up, retrieved the dead candle and crept on to the landing. Marjorie was caught in the light spilling from the kitchen. Her face was lost in shadow but her head was tilted as if she was also trying to hear what was being said beyond that locked parlour door.

I tried to slip back into Charlotte's room. My foot stubbed against a protruding floorboard. I stumbled against the door. The candleholder tumbled out of my fingers and clattered on to the landing.

'Who's there?' Marjorie called up the stairs, voice twittering like a frightened sparrow. 'Juliana, is that you?'

I flattened my back against the wall. Marjorie shuffled along the passage, gown rustling like moth wings. The bottom step creaked. I could sense her peering into the gloom. I pressed harder against the cold stonework and closed my eyes. The silence of the night returned to the dark landing.

Marjorie waited for a few moments then made her way back along the hall. The kitchen door closed. Snatching up the candleholder, I hurried to my room and lay on the bed, not bothering to pull the curtains across the window. Voices whispered through the walls from the parlour. Too faint. The landing clock chimed then chimed again as the night ran its course. Below, the men continued talking.

I huddled against the bedpost with the coverlet drawn around my legs. The last of the season's frost drew patterns across the window. My breath plumed into the moonlit air.

At last the parlour door groaned open.

Daybreak found me hungry. Muscles ached, drums pounded inside my head. I hurried into the freezing kitchen and crammed some cold oatmeal down my throat before coaxing fresh life out of the embers of last night's fire. Marjorie appeared a few minutes later, puff-eyed and shrouded in her night attire. She placed a cup on the table in front of me. The dregs of my posset. 'I found this in Charlotte's room,' she said. 'What were you doing in there?'

I picked up my shoes and started scraping off the dried mud. 'I miss her. I was searching for a keepsake.'

'I miss her too, but I don't want you going in there again.'

I dropped my shoes on to the floor. 'Who was that man? The fellow who marched into this house last night as if he owned it? He eyed me as if I was a harlot, when he troubled to notice me at all.'

'He was a man of the cloth come to discuss parish matters with Nathaniel.'

'No vicar comes calling in the middle of the night, and no church business would keep him talking until cockcrow. He seemed more cut throat than cleric. I could not sleep for his rantings.'

Marjorie paled. 'What did you overhear?'

'Nothing. Just voices.'

'Did my husband not warn you to mind your business?'

'Yes, he did. I still have the marks on my back to remind me.'

'Then be sure to do as he says.'

She picked up the cup and tipped its contents into the slop bucket. 'Nathaniel has other work for you today. Go and see him.'

The parlour was a sour pit of stale pipe smoke and spilled brandy. In the hearth, the fire had choked on its own ashes. Dried soup crusted a bowl. Papers spilled off the table and littered the rug.

The parson waved me to a stool in front of his chair. He fingered his throat whilst I seated myself. His clothes were crumpled and dusted with pipe ash. He coughed as if the rotten air in the room was strangling him.

'No farm rounds for you today,' he began. 'This evening you will go to Eastleigh and fetch a lad whose parents have died. You must take him to his uncle, who is lodging at the Rose Inn. 'Tis a long journey across the length of my parish but there is no one else to look after the lad. Once you've delivered him return directly here, do you understand? Don't stop. Speak to no one on the way.'

*

250

'The Rose Inn?' Prettyman frowned. 'I've heard that name before. Many times. Why are we going there?'

'What you might have heard is of no concern to me,' I said, climbing into the coach. 'We are going because Parson Proudlove wishes it. I have no choice in the matter.'

Six miles outside Dinstock one of the horses threw a shoe. Prettyman cursed like a tinker as he clambered down from the driver's seat and fished the shoe out of the mud. He tried to knock it back on with his boot heel while the animal snorted and kicked. I sat on the carriage step, trying not to laugh. The shoe slipped out of his hand and he had to scrabble in the dirt for it. 'Get a move on, you oaf,' I called. 'I would like to get this business done and go home.'

The sun kissed the horizon and dark clouds brewed in the west. My behind ached from trying to keep its place on the seat whilst the bad road took its toll on my patience. My belly was grumbling too. I had nothing but a slice of cheese with which to pacify it.

'We need a smithy,' Prettyman said. 'This shoe will come off again within a few miles.'

'We will continue on our journey. You will have to fix the shoe as best you can. I cannot spare the time.'

'The animals will need to be fed and watered. There is a smithy in Morley, a village not two miles from here. Otherwise this horse could go lame.'

'Then make sure it does not, otherwise I will put you in the harness and you can haul the carriage. Now finish your work. I want to collect our charge before those clouds decide to split above our heads.'

Red circles cut into his cheeks. He held the horse's leg firm as he knocked the shoe back into place. The hammer head broke as the last nail went in. He threw the pieces into the ditch and wiped his hands on the side of his coat. Moisture glistened at the corners of his eyes as if the rains had come early and washed his face with their cold, relentless touch. 'Why don't you like me?'

251

My face was as harsh as the winter and my heart without a spark of warmth. 'I was a lady once. Even before I married George Proudlove I enjoyed a good roof over my head. You remind me too much of what I've become. In many ways I'm just as poor, just as crippled as you.'

I climbed back into the coach. 'You can be a lady again,' he whispered.

The storm sniffed us out like a hunting dog. Thick curtains of rain swept along the road and pounded the carriage as if it was a ship on a wild ocean. I thrust my head out into the screaming wind. Hair slapped about my face. I screwed up my eyes and peered into the murk. There: a smudge of light within the grey. Eastleigh. Three miles short stood the crossroads where we were due to collect our charge. It was marked by a hand post that pointed splintered fingers to the four points of the compass.

At first I thought the place was deserted. Prettyman brought the horses to an untidy halt. A figure shifted beside the dyke and staggered to its feet, huddled against the driving rain. Prettyman had lit the carriage lamps. In their doleful light stood a boy of about ten, soaked through despite the heavy coat that shrouded him and shivering fit to crack his teeth. 'Is no one with you?' I shouted, my words snatched up and flung across the encroaching fields.

He shook his head and pulled the coat tight across his chest. I opened the carriage door. It took all my strength to stop it being wrenched out of my fingers. The boy walked like a drunken rooster, both feet sliding on the mud. Before Prettyman had a chance to come and help I caught the lad by the collar and hauled him inside. For the next few moments I battled with the door while the wind howled around my ears. It closed with a thump and I fell back on my seat in a flurry of raindrops. Prettyman immediately set the horses on the road to the Rose Inn.

The boy huddled in the corner with his arms wrapped

252

around his legs, watching as I tried to tug some order back into my hair. He touched the corner of his mouth with one finger and traced a line to his chin. I managed a smile, though Lord knew it was hard. I had enough water down the front of my dress to give myself a bath and my ears were stinging with the cold. I rubbed my chin then held up a clean finger.

'A birthmark,' I told him. 'Nothing more.'

Six miles separated the Eastleigh crossroads from our destination and the boy said nothing, not a word, for the entire journey. Instead he sobbed into his thin fingers like an old man while his sodden clothes spread a puddle of dirty water across the floor. When offered a handkerchief he cringed and covered his head with both arms.

Outside, night swelled like an inkblot across the storm-cracked sky. Open farmland gave way to clusters of trees, branches whipped into a frenzy by the gale. Sometimes the boy ceased his bawling and stared out of the window at the dark-ening countryside. He'd be a fair-looking lad if all the crying hadn't made red sores of his eyes. Under the coat, his breeches and jacket were of a fine cut, and his hands were free of the calluses that marked the Dinstock farm men.

'Why don't you speak?' I prompted. 'You know I'm not going to hurt you. Even your name would be a start. It's not much to ask, is it?'

He went rigid with fright. I felt like shaking him, to knock a response out of those cold, puckered lips. Immediately I felt ashamed. This boy had lost his parents. He was an orphan like me. Little wonder he burrowed into the corner of the coach and tried to push the world away.

At some point I fell asleep, dragged under by sheer exhaustion. I awoke to darkness and an anxious silence. I sensed the boy staring at me from his corner, though it was too dark to see his face. Some time in the night the storm had died, the clouds squeezing out the last of their rain before moving on.

We had stopped. I poked my head out of the window. Prettyman was struggling with one of the horses, a lantern flickering at his feet. He heard me and looked up. Sweat streaked his brow. 'So you're awake,' he said. 'This animal has thrown its shoe again and this time I can't fix it back on. You should have listened to me. Now I'll have to walk the horses to the Rose Inn and hope I can get a shoe there.'

I yawned and rubbed my eyes. My body was a sack of aches and pains. I wanted hot soup and a warm bed. 'How far is it?'

He dropped the horse's leg, pocketed the broken shoe and wiped his hands on his coat. 'Can't be much more than a mile.' He glanced at the sky. 'It won't rain again tonight. If I can get the horse shod at the Rose you can be back in the parsonage before dawn. Best get back inside and see to the lad.'

I pulled down the blind and the carriage crawled forward. It seemed we had not been underway for more than ten minutes before we halted again. My patience in tatters, I opened the carriage door and jumped into the mud. I got soaked to my ankles for my trouble but I was too angry to care. I wanted this accursed journey finished and that silent, staring boy in the hands of someone better able to care for him.

Prettyman was up front with the horses, lantern shielded behind his hat. He stared up the road at a cluster of lights and waved me to silence when I tried to speak. 'Can you hear it?' he asked, as I stood and fumed. 'That sound on the air. Like screaming, only worse.'

I listened. There it was, like a cat chorus only deeper and far more threatening. A mixture of voices, human and animal, carrying through the night. I forgot to be angry and I was sorry that I had left the carriage. 'Those lights,' I whispered, 'is that the Rose Inn?'

He nodded, his face a horrible pallor in a loose sliver of lantern light. 'Now I know why I've heard the name before, and what that sound is. I shouldn't have brought you here.

254

Get back inside the coach and I'll take you home. We'll just have to suffer the horse going lame.'

'What is that noise? It is like the devil screaming.' I shivered, wishing I had brought a thicker shawl.

'Dogs, fighting to the death. Behind the inn is a killing pit. A circle of sand, or maybe sawdust. Animals are tossed in to battle it out. Sometimes when the bloodlust gets them they'll chew each other to pieces. The ground turns red with spilled blood. Sit at the front and a torn limb might hit you in the face. The beasts are bred to die in the ring. The place stinks like a flesher's stall.'

'Cockfighting took place each week at Wexborough market,' I pointed out. 'It drew a fair crowd.'

He snorted as if I was an ignorant child. 'Cockfighting's too clean for the sort of men that haunt the Rose. Why would your parson have dealings with such a place?'

'Should a man of the cloth not be found amongst sinners?' I countered. 'The boy is to be delivered to his uncle, nothing more.'

Prettyman strode back to the carriage. He held up the lantern, illuminating the interior. I ran after him and peered over his shoulder. The boy shrank further into his corner as if trying to burrow into the panelling. Both hands shielded his face.

'Look at him,' Prettyman growled. 'He's like a rabbit in a fox's jaws.' He put the lantern on the carriage floor and held out his good hand. 'Talk to me, lad. Tell me whom this uncle is you're going to meet.'

The youngster turned his face to the woodwork. 'Satisfied?' I demanded. 'Now you have upset him even more. How am I going to get him out of the carriage when he clings there like a tic on a cur's back?'

Prettyman picked up the lantern and held it in front of my face. 'For all your bluff and bluster, you're just as scared as he is. Let me take you home. I'll speak with the parson. This boy can't go anywhere.'

'Proudlove will thrash the skin from your back and throw you into the ditch. My guardian is not a man who listens well. I know that more than most.'

His eyes hardened. 'How do you know? Does he beat you? Tell me, Juliana. Has he taken his stick to you? Or worse?' I tried to push past him but he caught my arm and spun me around. 'Tell me.'

'Get off.' I pulled free. 'Don't ever touch me again. Drive the last mile or I shall walk. The boy goes with me even if I have to carry him.'

Prettyman climbed back onto the driver's perch. As soon as I was back inside he urged the stumbling horses up the lane. But the fight had not gone out of him yet. Some minutes later the coach clattered to a halt outside the Rose Inn. He caught me at the door as I stepped out. 'Let me go in with you,' he said. 'I'm a better man than I look. My good arm is strong and I can kick like a donkey. This is no time to turn proud on me. The Rose is no place for a woman. You can see that, surely?'

'You have to find a shoe for the horse, you said so yourself. Besides, the coach and team might get stolen. If the customers are spoiling for a fight you will only make matters worse. You're a cripple, whether you like it or not. Don't give anyone an excuse to make sport of you.'

I reached back inside the carriage and grasped the boy by the collar. Exhaustion had put him into a whimpering sleep and he was limp in my arms as I hauled him outside. The chill air brought him round and he remained sullenly obedient whilst I buttoned up his coat and led him towards the inn.

It was going to be another frosty night, the clouds having split apart to reveal the cold mercy of the stars. The air was pregnant with the sounds of barking dogs and yelling men. We both shivered. Glancing back over my shoulder I saw Prettyman standing with the horses, the carriage whip gripped in his hand. Get a shoe, I mouthed, but if he noticed he didn't let on. I thought I'd smile to reassure him but there was no smile to be found inside me.

The Rose Inn presented a square, brooding face, light spilling out of its eyes and open mouth. I'd be two minutes, no more. I gritted my teeth and pulled the boy along. The door hung askew on its hinges like a drunkard. I banged my head on a low wooden beam. Cloying heat smothered me. Pipe smoke, thick as a fog, swirled between the dozen or so tables. Men sat drinking or gambling with dice, pausing only to lean over and spit on a packed earthen floor littered with dirty straw. Grease and tobacco stained the walls with long brown fingers and a huge fire coughed sparks from a fat stone hearth.

As I edged towards the bar, some men turned to eye me. Others were beyond seeing anything. They sprawled across tables, waxen faces lying in puddles of spilled drink and vomit. A woman giggled in a darkened corner, a coarse, guttural sound, followed by a man's drunken jeer. At the back of the room an open door led outside, presumably to the killing pit. This close, the noise was like a gaggle of howling demons.

Someone pawed my behind as I squirmed between the tables. I jerked away, knocking over a mug. A leering hulk of a man blocked my path, his face cut from ear to ear by a puckered white scar. A gap-toothed grin split his mouth open like a rotten apple. 'A shilling for you,' he growled. 'And two for the boy.'

'Let me through,' I demanded. 'I have business with the landlord. This boy must be delivered safely into his uncle's hands.'

'Uncle is it?' My tormenter snorted. 'I think you and I have other business to settle first.' He reached for my bodice. I braced myself, ready to stick a knee into his crotch. But a well-muscled arm batted his hand away. A thick voice rumbled through the noise and stink of the room.

'Leave her be. She's doing the parson's work. We've

257

enough whores in here, enough even for you, Jimson. Go and see to your dogs. Leave this matter to me.'

Jimson grumbled under his breath, pulled a felt cap down over his matted hair and took himself outside. I turned to face a stout, bald-headed man with a moustache that curled in a hairy grin. A leather apron hung from his neck, stained with spilled ale, dollops of fat and dried blood. He scratched his ear and regarded me with quiet amusement. Despite coming to my rescue, no friendliness lived in his round, rheumy eyes. 'I'm the landlord,' he declared. 'Was I right in thinking the parson sent you?'

I pushed the boy forward. He'd pulled his head down into his coat collar as far as it would go. 'This is the lad from Eastleigh. I will leave him with you and be on my way. Are there any papers to sign?'

The landlord scooped up a bag from the counter and tossed it at me. It jingled when I caught it. 'There's your "papers". See the parson gets 'em.' He laughed and some of the men at the tables joined in. Ears burning, I picked my way back to the front door. Risking a last glance at the boy, I saw him fetch a cuff around the ear before being bundled through a curtain on the other side of the bar. Then the night embraced me. I ran towards the carriage. Behind the inn, the unseen fight intensified, as if a hundred snapping dogs were spilling their lives into the blood-soaked dirt of the killing pit.

Prettyman tried to catch me as I scrabbled for the door. I dodged his outstretched arm and threw myself into the comforting darkness of the coach. 'Take me home,' I ordered. 'Get me away from this filthy place.'

'I couldn't find a shoe. The stables were full of dog pens. The beasts are half starved.'

'I don't care. We'll just have to risk the horse.'

He hesitated, his boot on the mounting step. 'Where is the boy?'

'Where he belongs. Now get on the road.' Still he

wouldn't move. 'Do it, Prettyman. A word from me to the parson and you'll never work or hold lodgings in this parish again.'

He reached up and tugged his forelock. 'Yes, Miss Juliana. Whatever you say.'

The door slammed. I sank back on to the seat, low sobs slipping out of my throat like blood oozing from a wound. The reins clicked and the carriage lurched forward, the shoe-less horse trotting unevenly between the shafts. The sounds of savagery faded with each slow, painful mile.

About half an hour later the coach drew to a gentle halt. The bag I had collected at the inn felt heavy in my lap. I pulled open the drawstring and tipped it up. A welter of coins tumbled into the hollow of my gown.

The door opened. Prettyman's face appeared framed within a starlit rectangle of night. 'I need to know what happened back there,' he said. 'If some ill had befallen you it would be my head in the stocks.'

He held up the lantern, swallowing the stars in a yellow halo. I squinted at him, saw the blood drain from his haggard face as he stared at my lap. Gold glimmered in the folds of my dress.

'That child wasn't adopted,' he whispered, and I could be Judas himself for all the accusation in his words. 'He's been bought. And you made me take him to that godawful place. I hope the parson rewards you well.'

The door shook on its hinges as he slammed it on my stupid, sinning face.

'Charles . . .'

But he had already clambered back on to the driver's seat. A second later the carriage trundled forward again.

Chapter Sixteen

A hand pummelled my shoulder. 'Wake up, Juliana. Hurry and put some clothes on.'

The coverlet was pulled off the bed. Cold air swept across my legs. I opened a bleary eye. Marjorie's taut face hovered above me. 'What's wrong?' I mumbled.

Already she had my wardrobe door open and was tossing garments on to the bed. 'Lady Elizabeth has taken ill. She asked for you. We are to go at once.'

I swung my legs over the edge of the mattress and rubbed sleep out of my eyes. The curtains had been thrown wide and the sun was a yellow eye stabbing me with daggers of light. 'What ails her? Can her surgeon not deal with it? I thought she paid a handsome fee for the ministrations of some local quack?'

In one deft movement, Marjorie snatched the hem of my shift and hauled it over my head. Despite the bright day outside my bedchamber was an ice pit. I dressed as quickly as I could, fingers struggling with some of the fastenings.

'At first they thought it was a fever, one of those seasonal things that has you sneezing into a handkerchief for a week,' Marjorie explained. 'But something has gone bad inside her. The doctor is at a loss. She has been desperately ill for hours and Squire Matthew fears for her life. With my husband away and the vicar of Eastleigh laid up with gout it falls on us to offer what spiritual succour we can.'

My clothes felt stale and clammy. I crammed my feet into a pair of shoes.

'The messenger from Dinstock Hall was sick with worry,' Marjorie continued. 'Squire Matthew is beside himself. Elizabeth is very dear to him.'

I combed the tugs out of my hair. The looking glass was turned to the wall. I did not care for the reflection it gave – a haggard peasant girl with tired red hair, a gaunt, haunted face and bruised-looking eyes. My birthmark stood out in a livid welt against my pale skin. With no rouge, I pinched my cheeks to bring the blood up and tied my lifeless hair with a scrap of ribbon.

We journeyed to Dinstock Hall in my old carriage driven by Charles Prettyman. I had no heart for this errand. Too many people in the surrounding farms were already sick to the gills for me to feel much sympathy for the squire's wife. Though I still made occasional visits to local smallholdings my duties had been restricted since the night of the Rose Inn. 'We have given all we can for the time being,' the parson said. He had been furious with Prettyman over the shoeless horse. As feared, the animal had gone lame and was useless for weeks afterwards. If not for his own injured leg, Proudlove would have taken his stick to my hapless driver. And it was my fault.

The parson was now on the mend. The local blacksmith had bound his leg and fashioned crutches for him to hobble around on. I made no more night-time visits to the Rose.

The bell tower of Dinstock church slipped past the carriage window. 'I can't imagine what Lady Elizabeth wants with you,' Marjorie remarked, examining her nails. 'You're hardly schooled in church matters.'

'Perhaps it is for Emma's sake,' I suggested.

'Emma has Mr Fairchild to look out for her. You haven't visited Dinstock Hall for some time. She'd be better served in the company of a man who loves her rather than a sour-faced widow.'

'Sometimes women need each other.'

'Mr Fairchild gives her all she needs.'

'I am sure you are right, Mrs Proudlove.'

I'd had my fill of Adam Fairchild. Marjorie slipped his name in to conversations as easily as she might comment on the weather. She talked about the happy couple over dinner, at the fireside, on the way to church. I was force fed stories of Fairchild's charm and gallantry, of how a country girl like Emma was lucky to land such a fine catch. When I mentioned that he was the scandal of Wexborough society my words were wasted in the air.

These days I saved my breath and let the paragon remain on his pedestal. Since leaving Dinstock Hall in near disgrace I had not set eyes on Fairchild. Talk was rife in the village – not the idle gossip of farmhands or milkmaids, but dark snatches of conversation whispered above gin mugs and behind bolted doors. Our maid was being courted by a cellar boy who worked at the inn and he liked to scare her with tales of what went on behind the Tudor façades of Dinstock Hall. Lazy as the girl often was, her tongue could never keep still. She passed on these rumours whilst I supped with her in the kitchen or we collected kindling from the woods.

'Miss Emma Jane has taken the devil himself to her bed,' she told me in the silence of the trees. 'He likes to hurt her, do unnatural things that ain't fit for a man and woman. Mary Clark, who delivers bread to Dinstock's kitchens, says she saw Miss Emma lying on a pile of straw in the stable like she was dead. Marks covered her face and neck, like one of the dogs had got her. 'Tis said that Fairchild fellow has bewitched Squire Matthew and Lady Elizabeth and that he won't stop his perversions until Miss Emma has split her womb birthing him a trough of bastards.'

'Your country superstitions sicken me,' I told her, gathering up some deadwood. She laughed, nudging twigs into a pile with her bare feet.

''Tis also said the more Mr Fairchild hurts Miss Jane, the more she likes it. I've heard he's ridden her like a mare across her own parlour carpet. He's tupped Lady Elizabeth too – took her whilst the squire was out and her daughter asleep in the room next door. I'm thinking there'll be bastards born on all sides at Dinstock Hall.'

'Don't think. You are not very good at it.' I picked up the last of the kindling and tramped back to the house. Behind me, the maid's mulish laughter echoed through the woods.

Outwardly, Dinstock Hall had not changed. The carriage halted at the front steps. No footman scuttled out to welcome us. Squire Matthew himself opened the door. The stink of grief hung around him, a tired, wasted smell that clung to his clothes. Loose skin sagged from his neck and jowls. 'Thank God you have come,' he said.

We kept silent as he led us to an upstairs bedroom. Lady Elizabeth lay in a sprawling four-poster, her small frame shrouded beneath an embroidered coverlet. The windows were shut tight, the curtains closed. A candle sputtered yellow light over her face.

'No servants,' Squire Matthew flustered. 'Lizzie won't allow anyone in except the surgeon and myself. But she keeps asking for the widow girl.'

Lady Elizabeth eyed us from within a mountain of white pillows. Her eyes were cold ashes staring out of a pinched mask. Lips split apart into a worn smile. She tried to lift a hand in greeting.

'Lie still, m'lady. This is a very delicate business.' A man in a sharp coat and white-ribboned wig leaned over her, his nose clutched by a pair of spectacles. He had opened a vein in her arm and was letting blood pour into a porcelain bowl. On a table beside the bed was a leather wallet glittering with metal scalpels and a tourniquet fashioned from a strip of linen.

Marjorie scurried to the other side of the bed and took Lady Elizabeth's free hand in her own. The surgeon secured the tourniquet and laid the bowl, brimming with crimson, next to the wallet.

'I am dying,' Lady Elizabeth whispered. 'Nothing this oaf can do will prevent it.'

Her voice was like a sigh on the wind. She did not move her head as she spoke, as if even that small effort was too much.

'A fever, m'lady, nothing more.' Marjorie clucked. 'This changeable weather has us all out of sorts. The winter was greedy. It didn't want to let go. Now we are left with headaches, sour bellies – all sorts of devilments. Rest and prayer will have you on your feet.'

The surgeon looked up and frowned. I dithered at the foot of the bed, trying not to gag at the fetid smell thickening the room. Every puff of air Lady Elizabeth exhaled carried the reek of decay.

'We have prayed for you,' Marjorie continued, stroking that flaccid hand. 'God will help.'

Lady Elizabeth gave a dry, bitter laugh. 'God was driven from this house months ago. We drove Him out with our avarice and let the devil take his place. Why should He return to help me now?'

'You don't mean that. The fever is talking through you.'

The hand was pulled free. 'You are a worthless fool, Marjorie. Let me speak to the widow girl. She has intelligence, a spark of fire, everything you lost as a girl. Get away from my bed.'

Stricken, Marjorie stumbled away from the four-poster. Lady Elizabeth beckoned me to her side and clasped my hand in her cold fingers. Four words were whispered into my ear.

'Emma is with child.'

She was in the parlour with her lover, her swelling womb pushing out the waist of her loosened gown. Hair hung in lank, greasy strands around her cheeks. She resembled a rug that someone had pegged up and beaten the life out of.

Fairchild was reading a newspaper. A half-empty glass of port lay on the table beside him. He folded the paper and consulted his pocket watch. 'Ah, a reluctant visitor,' he said, noticing me for the first time. 'How fares Lady Elizabeth?'

'She has fallen asleep,' I replied. 'The surgeon is still with her. Do you intend to marry Emma?'

His cheeks were powdered the colour of white marble, his mouth a scarlet gash that cut a tooth-ringed hole into his face. A bleeding heart had been painted below his temple. Gold and silver rings glinted on his fingers. A green velvet coat topped a pair of sharp riding breeches and soft leather boots gripped his calves. A dandy dressed for the hunt. 'Fetch me another fill of port,' he said. 'I have a thirst fit to crack my throat.'

'I am not your servant.'

Emma stood behind him. She leaned over and circled his neck in lace-wreathed arms and rested her cheek on the crown of his head. Adam regarded me with glittering shark's eyes.

'Port,' he repeated. 'Now.'

Marjorie found me sitting at the bottom of the staircase snorting tears into a handkerchief. I told her I was upset over Lady Elizabeth. 'Go home,' she instructed. 'I'll stay here with the squire and his family. Nothing more can be done for m'lady. You'll be sent for if she wakes and asks for you again.'

I dried my face and waited outside whilst Marjorie sent a footman to fetch my driver. In the lifetime it took for Prettyman to bring the coach around from the stable yard, I spied Fairchild and Emma watching from the parlour window. Her arms were still draped around him. She smiled at me then smothered his face in elaborate kisses.

'But I have a secret, Emma,' I whispered, as a sudden gust caught my hair and spun it into windmills of copper. 'I know your lover. I've heard the lies he's woven. You won't wear that smile for much longer. Not once you've seen what's behind those eyes.'

This house was sick. A poison had wormed its way under the doors and through the windows. It had knocked Lady

Elizabeth off her feet and turned Squire Matthew into a flustered, finger-kneading ploughboy. No contagion this, but a malady of the heart, and it was burrowing into Emma.

The sun fled. Clouds rolled over the sky in a dark wave. Raindrops spat on the white gravel and smeared the tall windows of Dinstock Hall. A drumming of hooves and the carriage drew up. Prettyman scrambled from the roof, bad arm flapping at his side. 'Don't bother with the step,' I told him. I tried to hoist myself inside but my skirts caught on something and I stumbled back on to the drive. He made to catch me with his good hand but I shrugged him off.

'You've been crying again,' he said.

'Just take me home.' I pulled myself inside at the second try and slammed the door.

Rain. Another unrelenting downpour. I gazed dismally at the wet curtain swishing across the open fields. The carriage slid and bumped along the exposed lane. The horses seemed to be crawling. Each yard felt like a mile. I stood up and banged on the roof. 'Hurry up. I want to be home before I drown!'

'The road is treacherous,' Prettyman shouted back. 'The ruts have filled with water and I can't tell how deep they are. We could get bogged down, or one of the horses might catch a hoof in a pothole. They're struggling as it is.'

'Then I will get another horse. And perhaps another driver.'

Prettyman slapped the reins and our pace increased a notch. I plumped back down on the seat and folded my arms. He was a fool. An ignorant cripple who tried to put himself on equal terms with other men.

The carriage lurched. Springs groaning, it listed like a sinking ship. I thrust my head out of the window. Swirling mud was only inches from the bottom of the door. We had ground to a halt, the horses snorting as they pulled on their harnesses. Prettyman threw down the reins and jumped into the lane. He checked all around the carriage then splashed over to my window. 'We're buried to the axle. I warned you this could happen.'

I ignored the rebuke. 'Can you free us?'

His head slipped out of sight then reappeared. 'The axle itself looks good and I don't reckon the wheel's broken. If you climb on to the roof and work the reins with me pushing from the back then we might get her out.'

'I am not going to suffer a drenching just to save you a bit of work. There must be another way. You're the driver, think of something. It's what you are paid for.'

'I ain't paid a penny for what I do. Remember that next time you don't want to get your feet wet.' He checked the lane. Our route crossed a high point in the surrounding farmland. 'I can see a thicket of gorse about half a mile ahead. If I can break some off it'll go under the wheels and give better purchase. This mud is treacherous. I can't do any more until the rain's eased.' He glanced at the sky. 'The clouds are breaking up over to the west. This downpour won't last but the blackest cloud is right above us.'

As if to confirm his words, the rain intensified into a hammering sheet that beat against the carriage with a million tiny fists. Prettyman pulled open the door. A shower of freezing water shivered around my feet. He tried to climb inside. I caught him with my heel and shoved him back into the lane. 'You're not to come in here. Find another place to shelter. Go and crawl under one of the horses.'

He rubbed the top of his shin. I grabbed the door, ready to slam it. He reached back inside, grabbed my sleeve with his good hand and pulled. I tumbled out of the coach as if I weighed nothing and landed on the verge.

He's going to hit me, I thought. Self-control seemed to have fled Prettyman's face. His fingers curled into a taut fist. His teeth were bared, his neck muscles bunched like knotted rope. He tore off his hat and threw it into the mud with a savagery that made me flinch.

'I won't take you any further, Juliana Rodriguez, Mrs

267

Proudlove or whatever you want to call yourself. Not another inch. Though it might cost me the only job I've ever had I'd sooner sleep in a barn and eat with pigs than stand your company another mile. You cut my peace to ribbons with your poisoned tongue.'

Rain plastered his black hair to his scalp and streamed down his face. He held his hand out as though pleading. 'What happened to make you so bitter, to give you such a hateful, twisted view of everyone? Nothing can pull a smile from your sour face. What dark things haunt you? How can I ever drive them away?'

My gown was already drenched, my own hair hung in tangled knots. I faced Charles Prettyman and wished him into his grave. 'I wanted love and got hatred. I longed for kisses but received bruises. Instead of truth I was lied to, instead of being cherished I was abused. No one cares, cripple boy. Does that answer your question?'

'You won't let anyone care. You shut yourself up inside your head and spit at the world. I've never knowingly crossed you, yet you curse me to my face and trample over what little pride I have left. Did you expect me to thank you for that? Did you expect me to like you?' He shook his head. 'Something ails you that's beyond the help of any preacher or surgeon. I pity you.'

'Pity? From a servant?'

'Yes, a servant. Not a slave to hatred. You can walk back to the parsonage and if you drown or break your leg in a rut it's no longer any concern of mine. I'll unharness the horses and ride back with them. Someone can fetch the carriage once the rain's eased off.'

He walked away. His figure soon blurred in the downpour. His name was on my lips before I knew what I was doing and when he did not stop I said it again. My eyes were full of water. He paused, looked over his shoulder. Then he came running back. But when he reached out I pulled away. I could not bear his hand on me. Not yet.

'I don't know who I am,' I whimpered. 'Or where I come from. All I have is a name and a story told to me by a sailor that may or may not be true. Everyone wants me for their own ends as if I have no right to choose for myself what I want to do with my life. I am worse than a dog with a rope for a collar.'

'You've called me an oaf, a fool and a cripple,' he said. 'That last part is true. I'm ignorant about a lot of things but that's different from being stupid. I've been foolhardy more times than I dare count. Sometimes I've made the right choices. Whatever happens, this is the life I've got and I don't moan about it.'

He hooked my sleeve with his finger. 'Come inside the carriage. You don't belong out here in the mud. The rain will stop soon and then I will take you home.'

'The parsonage is not my home. It's just a place where I live.'

'Better than nothing, Miss Juliana. For now.' He slid his good arm around my waist and lifted me back inside. I didn't protest when he climbed in after me and closed the door. Dirty water pooled on the floor. But the coach offered a haven out of the downpour. We could hear one another's breathing even through the ceaseless hammering on the roof.

I shivered like a petrified rabbit. My gown clung to me in a shroud. Charles tucked himself up against me and warmth seeped into my drenched skin. We both laughed at our dripping wet hair. From somewhere inside the folds of his coat he found a strip of clean linen and wiped my face while I sat like a child. He brushed my face with his fingers. I flinched again.

'No,' he whispered. 'I won't touch you that way, I promise.' He shifted on the bench. His leg pressed against mine. 'Are you scared because I want to be kind to you?' he continued. 'Afraid that my kindness will unbar some of those doors you've locked yourself behind? Maybe you need to let a bit of fresh air into your soul.'

269

'Listen to you,' I teased. 'A country sage in muddy boots.'

'My mama said I had to speak well or not at all.' He stroked my forehead, a gesture that would earn us both a beating if Parson Proudlove ever got to hear of it. 'There must be someone who knows about your past.'

I shivered again. 'There is.'

During the last days of Lady Elizabeth's life, I was called back to Dinstock Hall to help Marjorie attend her. Since my guardian had no authority over the Hall staff, she took to ordering me about. I fetched towels, water by the bucketful and took soiled linen down to the kitchens where it was boiled in a big metal tub.

The surgeon bled his patient white and filled her throat with vile concoctions. At night her bedchamber was filled with whispered prayers. She smelled of death. I covered my ears whilst she screamed for hours at a time. Her arms flailed as whatever badness was killing her ate up her insides. Squire Matthew hung around her bed with a face like a crumpled blanket, muttering, 'Oh dear, oh dear,' until the surgeon, in irritation, ordered him from the room.

Emma was not at her mother's bedside when she died. Adam Fairchild had taken her to a ball in Wexborough. She had bought a new gown for the occasion and had filched Lady Elizabeth's best necklace from her jewellery box.

Three days after the internment in the Jane family vault, I resumed my visits to the district farms and hamlets. Everyone was full of talk. They treated me as if they could scent death clinging to my skirts.

'You were at the house the night she died,' one farmer's wife said. 'You there and her daughter gone off with some rake. 'Tis not right.'

'I had no say in it.'

'I've heard Squire Matthew is a broken man,' the old clod persisted. 'The estate could be sold off and us along with it. The church has already put in an offer for the land. My

270

husband's worked this farm all his life, as did his father before him. I've a right to be afraid.'

I gave her a sack of flour and some parish clothes, then left.

Last call of the day was to the Widow Hendy. I was in no hurry to return to the parsonage, especially as I had not seen the widow for some weeks. Charles Prettyman whistled a merry tune as he eased the carriage down the narrow track to her cottage. His good spirits lifted my gloom.

Spring had been forced into retreat by a cold north wind but no smoke drifted from the cottage chimney. Widow Hendy always favoured a generous hearth, even on the milder days and Peter more often than not would be outside chopping logs.

The garden was empty, the vegetable patch churned up, the seedlings trampled. Wheel tracks rutted across the square of lawn that was the only luxury the widow and her son had enjoyed.

Charles stopped whistling. A face peeked out from behind drawn curtains. I climbed out of the coach and picked my way across the garden. Battered plants littered the grass. Hoof marks crisscrossed the path. Muddy footprints trailed back and forth from the front door. Careless damage wrought by men who had other things on their minds than looking out for a few vegetables. Broken glass yawned a jagged mouth from one of the window frames. The front step was a swamp of dried muck. I banged on the door. Charles had settled the horses and was already hurrying across the lawn.

The door groaned open. Betty Hendy's face was a broken mess of lank hair, tear-streaked cheeks and bloody eyes. A plum-coloured bruise hugged the left side of her face and her dress was ripped in several places. Even with the fresh air at my back I caught her stink and the parlour behind her looked cold and dusty, even with the curtains closed.

'What do you want?' she demanded, clutching her tattered bodice.

'Betty, what has happened? Were you robbed?'

'Robbed, yes I was robbed.'

'Where is Peter?'

She covered her face with her hands. 'My son is gone.'

'I should not have let you in. I should have shut the door in your face and put the bar across it. You live with that man, eat food from his table and sleep under his roof. You're as guilty as he is and I'd curse you to your face if I did not think it could mean more trouble for me.'

I shifted on the squat wooden stool. Widow Hendy paced the rug, anger and terror fighting for control of her face. Cold ashes had turned to powder in the hearth and a half-eaten plate of mouldy food drew the first of the season's flies. 'What trouble? You are talking in riddles, Betty. I am your friend.'

She rounded on me, finger stabbing the air. 'I don't want your friendship. I want Peter back and if you had a spit of influence over that devil you would not have let him steal my son away.'

She started walking again, wiping her mouth with her sleeve. 'Where were you when the men came with the parson at their head? Where were you when this mighty pillar of the church violated me, slapped my face and called me a slut before taking the only thing I had not been willing to give him?'

'The parson did this? But he is in Bristol on church business.'

Contempt dripped from her voice. 'You really are the innocent, ain't you? His cut-throats put a rock through my window because I tried to bar the door. Then he ploughed me the way a farmer turns over a field. I bit and scratched and kicked. All I got for my pains was a black eye. "Cause trouble and we'll have the rest of this hovel down about your ears," that's what I was told. I daresay I should be grateful they didn't all take turns with me.'

'Betty . . .'

'Proudlove ended up going to Bristol, right enough. A merchant lives up in Clifton, a man with no son of his own. He'll pay handsomely for a strong boy like Peter. I had to sign the papers – sign my son away. I'd no choice. I've not an ounce of courage or a strip of pride left. I can't go to the magistrate. Everything has been done legally. Who'd doubt the word of a parson against the likes of me?'

'He sold your son?'

'Sons, daughters, infants – he sells them all. But I never thought he'd touch a village child. "Ill-bred peasants" is what he calls us. Peter is strong with a good head on him. Too tempting for that whoreson.'

'Perhaps Peter will find a way to return home. He's bound to try.'

'If he does he'll be flogged and me along with him. Proudlove threatened to take his stick to me if I ever tried to fetch him back. You're scared of the parson too. It's on your face. You must have felt his anger, seen what he can do. I'm frightened. More frightened than I've ever been in my life.'

'My driver will light a fire and clean up your house.' I gestured at her torn dress. 'I've one or two garments left in the coach that might fit you.'

'Keep your leftover rags along with the rest of your charity. I used to spend the evenings with my son beside that hearth. No fire will burn there again.' I reached for her hand but she pulled away. 'Don't touch me.'

'Why, Betty?' I asked, knocked stupid by the things she had told me. 'Why did he do this to you? Why not just take the boy and go?'

Her eyes spat hatred. 'Because I am in debt to his church. This plot of land, the house, everything is his. He charges rents I can't pay and if I tried to move out his bailiffs would have my chattels sold and both of us in the debtors' prison. I was only twenty-five years of age when I became a widow.

My man was barely in the ground before Proudlove came debt collecting. He took me on my own bed, the bed I'd shared with my husband, while I was still wearing my mourning gown. I've been paying debts ever since.'

'Did your son know about this?'

'Of course not, otherwise he would've tried to do something stupid and got himself hung.' Her lips pulled back from her teeth. 'Perhaps Peter is better off where he is, where he won't see his mother's shame.'

On the way back to the parsonage I tapped on the roof and had Charles halt the coach. I climbed out to meet him as he jumped down from the driver's seat. 'Why do you work for Parson Proudlove?' I asked. 'A good, strong-witted coachman can surely find work elsewhere, bad arm or not. There's more able-bodied men have less skill with the reins and less chance of persuading a stubborn horse to pull a carriage out of a rut.'

'I have to work for him.' Charles took off his hat and mopped his forehead. 'I'm in debt to his church.'

'You are in debt to him?'

'That's right, near enough the whole county is.'

Mrs Proudlove was in the kitchen cutting vegetables. Through the open window came the maid's tuneless whistling and the swish of a broom on the back step. 'You're late,' Marjorie said, slicing a fat turnip in two.

I slipped off my shoes and placed them beside the hearth. 'What happens to the children?'

'What children?'

'The ones that get taken away?'

'Away?'

'Yes, to the Rose Inn.'

She chopped the turnip into cubes and dropped them into a pot. 'The winters are always hard and sickness is rife. Many children are orphaned, in fine houses as well as the

274

farms. Last year Mrs Yelland – daughter of a local parliamentarian, no less – took sick and withered like a bloom without water. She left two young sons. With no surviving relatives, a husband at sea for five years and a father in his grave for two, other homes had to be found for her children.'

The pan hissed as she hung it from the crane and pushed it over the fire. 'Sometimes whole families are buried in a single plot. The soil is barely turned on one unfortunate before another is laid to rest. These are harsh times, despite Nathaniel's good work. Now go and find a clean apron and help me with the dinner.'

I did not move from my place at the table. 'It seems that mothers don't have to die to lose their children.'

'Whatever do you mean?'

'Falling in debt to the church seems cause enough. Don't feign ignorance, Marjorie. Sons and daughters are sold like cattle. Peddled to wealthy merchants, ladies with barren wombs or titled men who cannot father an heir. 'Tis not God's work your husband is about but a trade in flesh. That is why he sent Charlotte away. She knew about the Bad Place, the Rose Inn, where the children are taken and sold on. I've carried the parson's blood money in my own hands.'

Marjorie slapped a side of beef down on the tabletop and began sawing with a knife. Sweat prickled her brow. She grunted like an old woman climbing a steep hill. 'Charlotte will return within the month, when the weather is kinder.'

'I doubt you'll see your daughter again, not while the parson runs his errands in the night.'

'He wouldn't harm Charlotte.'

'No, but he would sell her. You too if there was an extra shilling in it.'

A sound trickled out of the back of her throat. Hair caged her face in limp, greying strands as she bent over her work. The meat had been hewn into ragged strips. Not even a dog would find that mangled food fit to eat. I leaned over to see her face. Her mouth was carved into a grimace, the eyes shining.

'You have been listening to the gossip of farmers' wives,' she said. 'Those women are idle and dirty – too stupid to live any better than the scrawny animals they rear. They don't deserve to be mothers. Other women are more fit for the task.'

'You knew it was going on,' I accused. 'You have always known.'

The knife cut into the tabletop, gouging brittle splinters that showered on to the floor. Finally, the blade snapped. The edge sliced into her palm. 'See what you made me do,' she cried, dripping blood on to her apron.

'You did it to yourself. God knows what other harm you've done.'

'I did my duty by my husband, which is more than you can say, you spiteful wretch. I want you out of this house. Pack your belongings and take yourself to the church stables. Nathaniel will deal with you when he returns.'

I fled the kitchen and ran upstairs. Working quickly, I spread my belongings out on the bed. More than my one small bag could carry. I chose what I thought was essential, stuffed the bag to bursting and fastened the straps.

Downstairs I paused in the hallway. I could hear Mrs Proudlove moving around in the kitchen. I opened the front door, spat on the knob, then slipped outside. The walk to Dinstock was the longest mile of my life. Charles was in the church stables, grooming the horses. He spotted me standing in the open doorway, scuffed bag in my hand. 'Mrs Proudlove turned me out,' I explained. 'I can't say I'm unhappy about it.'

He put down the brush and grinned. 'That tongue of yours never stops getting you into trouble. Well, you can stay with me if you want. No doubt the village scolds will have plenty to say but any bed is better than the ditch. But first there's something you need to know . . .'

Chapter Seventeen

'Someone has been asking for you in the village. He wouldn't give his name. I heard it from the wheelwright, Tom Bryant. He says the fellow was poking around the inn, a man with muscles like knotted rope and scars around both wrists. He wanted to know where you lived. Tom said that as far as he knew you were still at the parsonage with Nathaniel Proudlove and his family.' Charles eyed me from beneath the brim of his hat. 'Any notion who this fellow is?'

'Perhaps it is one of George Proudlove's old creditors,' I replied. 'My husband left a debt far bigger than his fortune when he died but no doubt there are those who believe he did not entirely leave me penniless.'

Charles was silent for a moment. He led me along the cinder path that skirted Dinstock church to a low roofed stone hut that squatted by a rusted gate set into the wall. The building had a graveyard for a garden and a door of oak panelling stripped from a carriage. 'My palace,' Charles announced, taking out a heavy iron key and shoving it into the makeshift lock. ''Tis as old as the church, built from broken pieces of stone and leftover timber. Gravediggers used it for some years but they have cottages in the village now and there wasn't any sense in letting the place stand empty.'

He nudged the door open with his boot and gestured me inside. I had to stoop under the sagging lintel. It took a few moments for my eyes to adjust in the thin light seeping through the shuttered windows. A square room with a stove in the corner. A chipped wooden dresser, a bare stone floor and narrow bunk. Everything was makeshift but clean. A scent of dried herbs tinted the air.

Charles breezed in after me, lifted the bar on the shutters and swung them open. Daylight pierced the murk. Slivers of old stained glass, along with a few bottle pieces, had been used to patch up the window. It mottled everything in hues of red, green and brown. 'I've a kettle and packet of coffee,' he said. 'Or if you prefer, a nip of ale is tucked away in the bottom drawer of the dresser. You can draw water from the butt beside the door. The baker gives me his leftover bread and I've laid rabbit snares in the strip of woodland that runs alongside the churchyard.'

He thumped the wall with his fist. 'Two feet thick. Stove only needs a couple of logs chucked in to keep this place hearty. Dinstock Hall it ain't but you can have all the peace you want. No one ever comes here, not nowadays.'

'What about the church?'

'The door's always locked and the parson has the key.'

'And the lights you mentioned?'

'I don't see them.'

'Why don't you see them?'

'I look the other way. I've been looking the other way for the past three years. Like I told you, I'm scared.'

I sat on the bed. The straw mattress shifted under my weight. 'You are not going to tup me, Charles Prettyman. I will make that clear now. I'll live under your roof but I won't share this strip of a bed.'

'You think I'd want to, do you? Think I've never had a woman before, that no one would be interested in a cripple?' He laughed. 'Ain't nothing wrong with me where it counts, as some have found to their joy.'

He tossed the door key on to the woollen bed blanket. 'I'll sleep in the stables. Should be warm enough now that spring is coming. The horses will keep me company.'

I fingered the key. 'I will have to face the parson.'

'He won't beat you, I promise.'

'You haven't felt that stick across your back.'

'That may be, but I won't stand by and let him hurt you again.'

'You are in debt. You said so yourself. He could have you thrown into gaol. How can you stand up to Proudlove if you are afraid of a few flickering lights in a church in the middle of the night? He's got you, Charles. Like he almost had me.'

Prettyman sat down on the bed beside me. His bad arm was tucked inside his coat and the other rested on his knee. 'Some might say I ought to be grateful to Proudlove. He took me in after my parents died and gave me what I have now in exchange for menial work.'

'That was very charitable of him.'

'Charity?' Prettyman laughed bitterly. 'He kept me only because I couldn't be sold on. Not even a sweep would take me as his boy. Now I am the parson's dog to fetch and bark as he sees fit. But I promised it wouldn't be for ever and that's a vow I aim to keep.'

I slipped my fingers into his hand, felt the hard flesh and rough edges of calluses. 'My father was hanged. I don't know who my mother was. Chances are that I am a bastard. I am no better than you, Charles. I know what it's like to be unwanted.'

'You're better than a queen,' he said, 'and prettier than an angel.'

I laughed and let go of his hand. 'An angel? Clothed in a homespun mourning gown with a cherry-coloured birthmark running down my chin? There are those who would call me a witch.'

'Are you?'

I wasn't sure if he was teasing me. He rose, donned his cap and lifted the door latch. 'Fresh kindling is in the box by the fire, the log pile is underneath the window and you'll find water in the jug on top of the dresser. I'll see if I can get a scrap of beef and some milk. This is no lady's parlour but it's yours for as long as you want it.'

'Here.' I handed back the door key. 'I won't lock you out of your own house. I trust you.'

He stared at the key then looked up, mouth tight. 'If that's so, why did you lie to me?'

'Lie?'

'Yes, when you said you didn't know anything about the stranger who's been asking about you in the village.'

'Why do you believe I wasn't telling the truth?'

'You wouldn't look at me, and your voice was all wrong. A child could've seen it.' He tossed the key back on to the bed. 'You don't trust me enough.'

A pounding on the door woke me from a troubled sleep. Dawn poked a bleary eye through a chink in the shutters. I shivered in the cool morning air.

The hammering continued. Urgent, demanding. Yawning, I threw back my patched coverlet and padded barefoot across the stone floor to the window. Opening the shutter a fraction, I peered outside. A young woman stood at the door wearing a bonnet and shawl. Distress pinched her face.

I shoved my arms into an old overcoat and unlocked the door just as her fist rose to beat another tattoo on the wood. 'What do you want?' I demanded, rubbing the sleep out of my eyes. 'Charles Prettyman is not here. You will find him at the church stables, if he is not already out on the day's work.'

'Beg your pardon, madam, but it's you I'm after.'

I frowned. She looked familiar but a hundred such faces could be found around the county. Behind her, the last of the morning's mist seeped into the ground.

'I'm from Dinstock Hall,' she continued. 'I was Lady Elizabeth's maid. I'm here to tell you Miss Emma's baby is coming.'

'It can't be. Not so soon.'

The girl nodded. 'Two months before its time. Miss Emma was with child long before she told anyone. Turns out she was hiding the signs. Even though, the baby's still early.'

'Well, it is a matter for the surgeon or midwife, not me. Is Mr Fairchild not present?'

She grimaced. Dampness clung to her clothes with shivering, clammy hands. 'He's there, right enough, and I pity Miss Emma all the more for it. I remember you from your visits to the Hall. You were kind to her, tried to be friends when she hadn't a friend in the world.'

'That was a long time ago. I am not wanted now.'

'Please go anyway. The housekeeper will let you in.'

'What of Squire Matthew?'

'Off in Bristol. He doesn't care about his daughter. M'lady's death has broken him.'

'How am I to travel? Did you bring a carriage?'

'No, madam. Squire Matthew has the coach. Lady Elizabeth's gig has a broken axle and no one knows where Mr Fairchild's driver has gone.'

'So I am to trek three miles there and another three back?'

The maid shrugged. 'I'll walk with you, madam. It's all I can do.'

I arrived at the Hall muddied, footsore, and with a temper that could slice marble. The maid had jabbered incessantly into my ear until I'd threatened to throw her into the ditch. It was all 'Miss Emma' this and 'Miss Emma' that and 'isn't Mr Fairchild such a terrible fellow?'

The housekeeper met us at the front door and ushered us inside. 'Miss Emma has had a daughter,' she told me. 'An easy birth, praise God. The midwife has already left.'

'Where is Emma?' I asked. 'In her room?'

The housekeeper nodded. 'Mr Fairchild is with her. You may wait in the parlour until she is ready to see you.'

'No, I won't wait.' I kicked off my muddy shoes and ran

up the stairs in my stockings before the flustered servant could gather her wits. Emma's bedchamber door stood ajar and Fairchild's voice purred within – calm, persuasive and utterly chilling.

I pressed my body against the wall and peeped through the crack. Emma was sitting up in her grand four-poster. Bedcovers were gathered around her legs in a knotted heap of soiled linen. She resembled a doll with most of the stuffing pulled out. Her pale, moon face was a pathetic picture of hope and trust. Poor, silly woman. She still believed that Adam would look after her, that he'd forsake everything for their bastard child, even as he stood at the foot of her bed and told her that he was leaving and wouldn't return. She asked if he would write. He chuckled. When she started to cry he laughed openly. She gestured at the crib beneath the window but he would not go near it.

Finally, Adam Fairchild walked out of Emma Jane's life as quickly and brutally as he'd pushed his way into it. He pulled open the door and strode right past me as if I wasn't there, Emma's parched voice calling after him. He descended the stairs two at a time, slapping his riding gloves into his open palm.

I stepped into the room. Emma's head was cradled in her arms. My shadow fell across her and she looked up, her eyes like shattered windows. 'Come to gloat?'

'I have better things to do.'

She wiped her nose with a damp kerchief. 'Why are you here then?'

'Lady Elizabeth's maid fetched me. She thought you might need a friend. I was the nearest thing she could find. A desperate choice.'

'You have every right to hate me.'

'You are too foolish to be hated. As foolish as every other empty-head Adam Fairchild has bedded from here to Wexborough and beyond.'

'I thought he loved me.'

'Did he ever say that? Did you once hear those words pass his lips? No, I thought not.'

'Have you come to take my baby?' She drew the tangled sheet over the tops of her white, swollen breasts. 'I've heard talk about you. Some say you stole newborns from women who did not deserve their children.'

'No, Emma. I will not touch your child. You must play the part of a mother with as much passion as you have played the fool. You will grow up at last, just as your father wanted.'

'I will get a nurse.'

I shook my head. 'No respectable wet-nurse or surgeon will tend you or your bastard. I'll wager the midwife was some wise woman lured out of the woods with the promise of a shilling.'

Emma's face turned grotesque with horror. 'But I don't know how to look after a baby.'

'You will have to learn.' I glanced at the crib. 'Listen, the child has started to cry. She's hungry. Better get used to those tears. Especially when she starts teething, when she falls over, and when her heart is broken for the first time. Think about what you will say when she asks where her father is, or for that matter, who he is.'

Emma pressed her fists against her forehead. 'I want to die.'

'You can't afford to die. Your daughter needs you. Do what's right for her. In the end you'll have her love if nothing else. More than I have ever known in my life.'

I turned away and made to leave the room. A pillow flew past my head and struck the wall. 'I hate you,' Emma cried. 'You are a witch. You are doing this out of spite because Adam came into my bed instead of yours. You wanted him as much as me, don't deny it. Yes, he's gone, but I have something of his that you'll never have, and you cannot bear it can you, child stealer?'

I slipped into the passage and closed the door behind me.

*

I was heartily footsore by the time I arrived at Dinstock church. Walking lopsidedly, I skirted the tombstones until I found the cinder path to Charles's hut. Peace had settled over the churchyard. I paused a moment to savour the simple pleasure of it. Ahead, the door to the gravediggers' hut stood ajar. Light glimmered in a hundred facets from behind the unshuttered window. Inside, I found a warm fire crackling in the hearth. The stone floor had been swept and my bed was made – the woollen blanket smoothed out and neatly turned over at the top. Bread and a round of cheese lay on a trencher on top of the dresser.

I smiled. Charles would be wondering where I'd gone. Perhaps he was looking for me even now. Even as that thought occurred to me a shadow filled the door. I turned, grinning widely. 'You make a good housekeeper, Charles, I . . .'

The smile fell off my mouth. A figure lumbered into the hut and closed the door. A smell of old sweat filled my nostrils. I felt all four walls draw in on me like the sides of a coffin.

'Greetings, my little kitchen queen,' said Moses Cripps. In the firelight I could see the twisted muscles of his arms, the hard gristle ringing his neck, and his chest, like rough bark, caught in the V of his open shirt. He had all the brutal savagery of an animal on the run.

'So you lost your husband.' He spoke with a loose, tooth-broken mouth that turned each word into a snake hiss. 'And now you have a new fancy man. You always were a sharp one. I followed him here. Then I waited, as I've waited these past months.'

'Where is Charles? Have you hurt him?'

'No, he's gone to see to his horses. I made sure before coming back here. Maybe he'll return, maybe he won't. Makes no difference either way.'

He stepped forward. I stepped back. 'They'll catch you,' I warned. 'You'll be hung for sure.'

Laughter burbled out of his throat. 'I'm bound for Ireland. Got a horse waiting and a boat to carry me across, once my business here is done.'

He flicked my dress with his forefinger. 'You've gone up and down in the world. Suffered a bit perhaps. But not like me. It took a while to track you down but I'm able to bide my time. Prison taught me that. It took away my dignity but I learned patience. I've hidden in barns and ditches, grubbing food out of pig troughs and running like a fox with dogs nipping at my heels. The winter nearly did me in. My fingers swelled with the cold but the thought of meeting you again, my pretty young betrayer, kept me alive. You who wrecked my life just to save yourself a bit of shame.'

He plucked at his shirt. 'Like my clothes? Better than those prison rags.'

'Stolen I suppose?'

'Just like you to think that. I worked for a tinker to earn them. I was an honest man before I met you. I aim to be an honest man again.'

'After you've murdered me?'

'By God, you've a neck on you. Aren't you afraid at all?'

'Yes. Afraid for my life. I knew you were coming. I heard about the stranger asking after me in the village but I had no intention of running away. Better to be frightened now and get it done with than spend the rest of my days seeing your face in every corner, jumping at every shadow or squirming at every piece of gossip my imagination might link to you. I won't be hunted.'

He grinned again but something melancholy lay in his expression. 'I can live with Blake's death on my conscience because he was a bad 'un and got what was coming to him. I won't add your life to that tally, worthless as it may be. It'll be a new start for Moses Cripps.'

'So why did you come here?'

'To finish things properly.' He rummaged in the belt of

285

his breeches and pulled out a sheaf of papers. The pages were soiled and the wax seal had flaked off so that only a red stain remained. But I recognised them at once.

'I know who you really are,' Moses said. 'I know everything about you. These have been in the safekeeping of a friend all the time I was imprisoned. Yes, even I, murderer and criminal that you made me, still have friends. This one learned his letters as a lad. Told me what's written here. It's quite a tale.' He dangled the papers in front of me. 'How badly do you want to learn the truth? How much does it mean to you?'

'What is your price?' I demanded. 'There *is* a price isn't there, behind all this teasing? If you're not here to kill me then say what you want and get out.'

'How much are you willing to give?'

I stared at the papers dangling a few inches in front of my face. Cripps was ready to snatch them away in a twitch. While he held that bundle, my life would always be in his hands.

'Everything,' I whispered.

He laid the documents on top of the dresser next to my uneaten supper. 'Still ready to sell the world in order to get what you want? Thank you for making it easy to let you go.' Cripps spat on the floor and left. The makeshift door shook in its frame as he slammed it. His footsteps crunched on the path then silenced to a whisper as he cut across the grass. I wrenched the door open again, squinting into the weakening afternoon light. But he was gone, disappeared into the churchyard as though the tombstones themselves had swallowed him up. Crows wheeled overhead, their raucous cries like laughter in my ears.

I stepped back inside and closed the door. The bundle of papers lay on the dresser where Cripps had left it. With shaking hands, I picked up the documents and sat on the end of the bed. I remembered how they had once looked – the paper crisp, the wax seal a vivid red against the cream-coloured sheets. In my haste, I broke a fingernail trying to snap the binding. Infuriated, I pulled the string off with my teeth. The bundle fell apart in my lap like a dropped egg. A stale, musty smell, like leaves rotting on the ground in early winter, clogged my nose. But I could see Mr Littlejohn's handwriting, remembered how he used to sit at that big oak desk in the shipping office, the surface a clutter of papers and ledgers, and enter the day's business. Each line flowed and looped so that the words seemed to be chattering to themselves. The sentences in front of me were faded, the writer's hand unsteady, but there was my name at the top of the first page.

'My dear Juliana,' it began.

Charles was in the stables when I tumbled in with the sun climbing up my back and the village yawning awake. He put down the bucket he was holding in his good hand and grinned. 'Sorry I couldn't see you last night,' he said. 'I got called out to help Francis Bryson with his dray. Damn thing got its leg caught in a gate. It's the only nag he's got to pull his milk cart and he can't afford it going lame. He sent his lass, Betsy, to tell you where I was. I take it from the look on your face that she did no such thing.'

I shook my head.

'Thought not,' he continued. 'She probably met a sweetheart on the lane. Damn girl's head is full of butterflies. Well, don't be too hard on me. There's no harm done and the beast will recover.'

'I had a visitor right enough but it certainly wasn't Betsy Bryson. I need to talk to you, Charles.'

I related my encounter with Cripps. At some point Charles picked up a brush and started grooming one of the horses in long, hard strokes. The animal flicked its tail and snorted at the rough treatment.

'Moses Cripps gave me back my past,' I finished. 'The one thing I wanted more than anything else. I wrecked his life. He had every right to wring my neck if he chose.'

Charles put down the brush. 'Well, Juliana Rodriguez, it seems you have finally found what you were searching for. I hope it was all worth it.'

'You are my friend, the only real one I've ever had. Those papers Cripps left me won't change that.'

He picked up a blanket and threw it over the horse's back. 'I don't want to hear it. You've had fair use out of me and I shan't begrudge that. But friends trust one another. They don't cut the truth up into snippets and hand them out as they please. You know this Cripps fellow better than you've cared to admit. Escaped prisoners don't stalk a young woman for weeks just to hand over a bundle of papers.'

I didn't know what to say to that. Charles waited for a few moments then shrugged. 'You can stay in the hut as long as you want, or until the parson throws us both out. I promised he wouldn't beat you and I'll hold to that. I'll go on driving your carriage if I must but you shall not have anything more from me.'

'You are a stubborn fool,' I blurted, and was sorry the moment the words were off my lips.

His expression was chipped out of flint. 'Aye, but even fools have pride.'

The night was mild but I held a blanket around me in a shroud whilst staring at the patterns made by the crackling flames. I could not let the fire die, despite the kind weather. I needed its comfort too much in this restless graveyard. Owls and other creatures of the night kept their homes and hunting grounds amidst the tombstones.

My mind was a cauldron of confusion and self-reproach. It robbed me of sleep as a thief might rob a traveller of his purse. My eyes were sore with crying. I could not guess the hour. Time seemed to crawl, prolonging my misery. From where I lay I could see the bundle of documents that I had left on a fold-down table beside the hearth. How easy it would be to slip out of bed and throw them on the fire, watch as the pages blackened and curled before bursting into orange flame. In the morning nothing would remain except ashes.

I sighed and sat up on the edge of the bed. Moses was gone. Even if I burned the papers I already knew the truth. In a way, I resented poor, murdered Mr Littlejohn for confirming all my suspicions, for spelling them out on those neatly written pages.

'I wiped my eyes. "Mother . . ." I whispered.

Sound was amplified in the night, carried on the spring air. Footsteps in the churchyard. They hesitated then crunched uncertainly towards the hut. I had left the shutters open in the hope that Charles might see the firelight and come in to warm my heart, to forgive me, to embrace me and most of all understand.

I hurried to the window and peered through the glass. A figure, lit by a bobbing lantern that hung in the air like a ghost light, picked his way along the cinder path. Every few paces he halted and held up the lantern. I sensed him peering into the darkness, trying to follow the path's course as it wound between the broken monuments to death and decay.

It was not Charles. This man, wrapped up to the eyes in a cloak with a tricorne cocked on his head, was too tall. Prettyman could have bounded across the graves in the blackest of nights without the aid of any light. I waited, more curious than afraid, as the figure drew closer. He made no effort to conceal his movements. Here was no robber or rapist. I stifled a giggle as he stumbled on the half-buried stump of an ancient headstone. His cloak breezed open to reveal a coachman's liveried jacket. What brought another servant to my door at this deathly hour of the night? Not more trouble at Dinstock Hall, surely?

When he arrived, brushing the mulch from his coat, I was ready. The bottom drawer of the dresser had conjured up a threadbare cloak. I pulled this around my shoulders before slipping my bare feet into a pair of coachman's boots.

I opened the door on the first knock. The coachman started back in surprise. Confusion scrawled across his features. He held up the lamp to get a better look at me. 'You, wench,' he growled. 'I have come for Mistress Juliana. Is she somewhere in this hovel?'

'Nearer than you think,' I replied, 'and I'll have less of your impudence. Now what is so important that you have to drag me from my bed?'

He squinted. Dark spots pricked his cheeks. 'I beg your pardon, madam. I have brought a visitor from Dinstock Hall. The carriage is in the lane. I am to take you there at once.'

I frowned. Squire Matthew must have returned from Bristol. No doubt he'd be curious about Adam Fairchild. Visiting a disgraced widow in daylight hours was out of the question and he wouldn't want me at the Hall where Emma would get to hear of it.

'Very well,' I sighed, 'but let me carry the lantern. This is consecrated ground and you've blackened it with enough profanities. Follow me and try not to end up on your rump.'

I set off across the graveyard at a brisk pace, the coachman scuttling to keep up. Two bay mares stood snorting between the shafts of a chaise drawn up outside the lich-gate. The coachman was obviously keen to be away from this place and ushered me into the lane. He opened the carriage door and gestured at the dark interior. I handed back the lantern, wrapped the cloak tightly around me and clambered inside. The door closed with a soft 'click'.

I sensed movement, heard the rustle of blankets. 'Squire Matthew?' I whispered. 'You would have words with me?'

'Sit down, Juliana.'

I thumped on to the coach seat. The figure shifted. A face pushed into the soft bleed of light from the carriage lamps outside. Emma Jane's face, cold and bleak, her features drawn into an ugly visage. 'You must help me.'

Her voice was low and horrible. Old woman's words. Something was desperately wrong. The chill weight of fear pressed me back against the seat. 'What has happened? Why are you not at home with your daughter?'

She pressed her fingers against her cheeks. Tears gushed out of her eyes.

'My child is gone,' she said.

Chapter Eighteen

Emma's tears spread a damp patch across the front of my shift as I cradled her head. She wiped her face on the edge of a coach blanket. I waited while she gathered her thoughts. Some night creature scuttled through the grass bordering the lane.

'My child is gone,' she repeated. 'When Papa returned from Bristol, Parson Proudlove was waiting in the library. Whilst I slept, Papa paid the parson a hundred guineas to take my baby away. I didn't wake up for another three hours. A servant told me what happened. Papa was drunk out of his wits. No sense could be coaxed out of him. I came to you because you know where my child has been taken. I don't care what becomes of me. I can suffer your disgust and my father's contempt. You were right, my daughter is my life now.'

'What would you have me do?' My mind was in a whirl.

'Steal her. Fetch her back from that evil man who profits from his parson's garb. As for Adam Fairchild, I was a fool to think I loved him. I will never doubt your word again, Juliana, I swear.'

Easy for her to say, I thought, as if you can sacrifice everything for someone and then throw him out of your life. I doubted whether Fairchild would show his face at Dinstock Hall again but whether Emma pined or prospered as a result of that would depend on just how strong a character she was. Either way, the matter had been out of my hands for some time.

For now, it seemed as if I was back in the Butter House larder with a sleeping baby in my arms and a minute to decide its future. Emma spoke the truth. I knew where the baby would have been taken, at least for tonight.

'If I fetch it, where will you go? Return to the Hall and your father will merely hand the child back to the parson. Proudlove runs a trade in children and will spirit yours out of the county at the first opportunity.'

Emma sat up. 'Mama put aside a large sum for me in the event of her death. I daresay she always suspected Papa would buckle at the seams. Any ties that bound me to him were severed the moment he placed my child into Parson Proudlove's hands. I will lodge with some acquaintances I made in Brussels during my tour of the Continent a couple of years ago. The letter has already been drafted and I know they will not ask too many questions. It is the only future I can offer my child for now.'

'You will travel alone?'

Her dark hair was a shadow within shadows. 'My coachman will accompany me.'

'Have him take me to the edge of the common land, then go to the church stables where you will find my driver, Charles Prettyman. Wake him if need be and tell him I sent you. He will keep you safe until I return. I hope to have your child before daybreak.'

'Where are you going?'

'A place where someone like you doesn't belong. I could be risking my life for you, Emma. I hope you realise that.'

'What do you want in return? Money? Name your price.'

'I'll need cash for bribes, true, but I want no payment for myself. Nor do I want your friendship or gratitude. In fact, after this week I don't ever wish to see your face again. Now, let's make haste.'

The gypsy fires were burning high on the dark circle of the common. I was taken to the stone bridge spanning the boundary stream, the same one that chuckled so merrily past the back of the parsonage. Now its waters shimmered black and cold. Swollen with rain, they gushed around exposed rocks and splashed into flooded pools. In the distance, behind the caravans where the firelight could not reach, dogs barked above the wheezing melody of a hurdy gurdy.

'Shall I go with you, madam?' the coachman asked. 'A gypsy camp at night is no place for any man, let alone a young woman.'

I unhooked a lantern. 'People come to the gypsies after dark for favours they don't dare get when the sun is up. Find Miss Emma at the church stables and wait there with her.'

'I ought to wait for you.'

'This is not something you need get involved in any further. You will be of more use to Miss Emma. It is safer this way, for everyone.'

I stood by the bridge until the carriage was out of sight then took my courage in my hands and set off across the common, stumbling over clumps of wild grass and bracken. Half a dozen bow-topped caravans were spread in a loose semi-circle, the horses grazing a short distance away. Camp fires spat orange sparks into the deepening night, the smoke caught in a cauldron of hot air and sucked up into the blackness.

They sat beside the largest fire, the dark-skinned men and women. A pot suspended over the flames filled the air with the smell of cooking meat. Stew, probably made from rabbits poached off Squire Matthew's land, and potatoes hooked out of the earth whilst a farmer was having his fortune told. Or perhaps his eyes were turned by some lithe gypsy girl with a love potion in one hand and a blade to cut his purse in the other.

I showed them Emma's gold and explained what I wanted. They glanced at one another, speaking a silent language with their eyes. A nod was given and one of the women slipped away on silent feet to a caravan, returning with a bundle that she dropped on the grass.

Their leader, a big man who reeked of incense and nameless herbal concoctions, nudged the bundle open with the toe of his leather shoe. 'You will become one of us now,' he said in an accent that called no county its home.

I put on the bright gypsy gown. I stripped my feet bare and rubbed cinders into my hair. When I saw my reflection in the bowels of the moonlit brook, I looked as wild as any Romany woman born on to an unforgiving road.

Pietre, the gypsy leader, took me to the fireside and examined my hands in the blazing light. 'You've done work,' he said, tracing the outlines of old blisters. 'Hard work.'

Fetching wood, scrubbing the parsonage floors, hauling bales of clothing into my old carriage. Yes, I had earned those marks. Pietre grinned and cuffed my shoulder when he caught the look on my face. The men with him laughed before drifting off into the fire-spiked darkness.

We took two wagons, filled them with muzzled dogs and laughing young women – the prettiest in the camp. Before we left I had my face painted. A swirl of pagan colours hid my birthmark. I sat next to Pietre on the driving seat of the leading caravan. Behind us, crammed into the cluttered interior, the Romanies immediately fell into a pin-drop silence. Even the three dogs, held in a pen on the floor between the gypsies' feet, caught the mood and subsided into a watchful stillness.

'We do business at the Rose once, sometimes twice a year,' Pietre quietly explained. 'Ironjack, the landlord, will likely try to sell me cheap on the dogs. I of course, will argue. I will point out what fine beasts they are and explain that the paltry sum he is offering is not worth my effort or the wear and tear on my wagons. It is a game we always play and it can go on for an hour or so. That should give you the time you need. There's never less than thirty or forty men in the taproom or killing circle any night of the week, but most will be too drunk to cause trouble, and my girls will keep them distracted. Ironjack himself is the one who always needs to be watched. Never touches a drop when the inn is open for business.'

The gypsy pursed his lips. 'I've had the better of him in the past – beat him at arm wrestling a few times and won shillings off him in a fistfight. But he's slippery – keeps an old hunting gun in an empty barrel behind the counter. If you get caught watch your back because, woman or not, Ironjack will put a lead ball between your shoulder blades.'

'I have promised you more money . . .'

Pietre shook his head. 'The Rose needs my dogs. Ironjack could get animals from elsewhere but not the winners I fetch. He owes me too many favours to bear a grudge. He'll wait until autumn when I return from Bristol with new animals smuggled in on the slave ships. Slave dogs are vicious killers. Not too bad to sell to a gypsy though.' He winked and clicked on the reins.

The wagons joined the high road as it rose above the sleeping village and cut a path across the moorland beyond. The bright moon made for easy driving and Pietre pushed the horses into a fast walk. Apart from the creak of wood punctured by an occasional snort from one of the dray animals, it remained a hushed procession that moved along the weary miles.

I tried to swallow down my growing unease. Pietre caught me mopping my face for the fifth time in as many minutes. He fumbled beneath the seat with his free hand and plopped a small earthenware jug into my lap. 'You're afraid,' he said. 'Can't let my dogs get the scent. Ironjack will notice too. A nervous lass always gets his lust up. Drink some of that, no more than two mouthfuls.'

I eased out the rag stopper, put the mouth of the jug to my lips and took two draughts of the warm liquid. My tongue recoiled at the mix of oil and spirits but I gulped it down. Replacing the stopper, I handed back the jug. 'What's in it?' I asked, spluttering.

'Courage mixed with a bit of gypsy magic. Tonight will seem like a dream to you. Your mind will dance a little but your body will stay sharp, your wits keen and your mouth silent.'

His silver tongue was persuasive. It sounded like a tale to pamper the ears of the gullible. But tonight, on the winding moonlit road with a breeze gusting over the moors and uncertain trials waiting ahead, I was prepared to believe in a little gypsy magic.

The Rose Inn sat like a fat spider in a web of light. Doors and windows were flung wide, noise spilling out of the open portals in a raucous tide. Laughter, oaths, a screeching dirge torn out of a badly tuned fiddle. And the dogs, always fighting, spilling their lives on to the stained sand of the killing pit.

My senses heightened by the gypsy brew, I smelled blood on the air, heard each snarl and snap of those vicious jaws. It set my veins on fire. Fear, excitement, the taste of violent death in the night. The animals behind me caught it and snarled, only to be silenced with a sharp word from Pietre. He drew the caravan to a halt in the yard. The second wagon rolled to a stop a few feet away. Someone loitering outside the tavern door shouted a greeting and ran over. Words were exchanged – rich-sounding gibberish in some foreign tongue. Pietre jumped off the driver's seat and slapped the fellow on the back. Then he waved towards us. The dogs and the women were brought out to murmurs of approval.

My feet weighed nothing, my head danced along with the music. I followed everyone inside the inn. Tables were shoved aside and the dogs' cages were placed in the middle of the floor for inspection. Ironjack stepped out from behind the counter. The same gore-encrusted apron was tied loosely around his waist. His chin was blue with stubble. 'You're two days early,' he told Pietre.

The gypsy shrugged and thrust an empty tankard into Ironjack's fingers. 'I'm leaving Dinstock. There's no more money to be had. The local land grubbers have all dried up. Give me a drink and let's do business. My tongue is like dried wood.'

Ironjack shook his head. 'I can't bid high, not tonight. My takings are poor. The fighting's not much better. I don't know what's got into those animals tonight.'

'So I take what I can get and come back with more beasts in the autumn. Tonight you get a bargain. Now give me some ale.'

Ironjack filled the tankard and the two men started haggling. The gypsy girls spread from man to man, lap to lap, kissing, teasing, caressing dirty faces and laughing as shillings dropped down the front of their bodices. The driver of the second caravan plucked the violin out of its owner's hands and started up a wild, ear-jangling tune. Pietre's own daughter clambered on to one of the tables, hoisted her skirts above her knees and began a lithe dance that had the drunken, leering rabble falling out of their chairs.

I glanced towards the curtained door behind the counter. Ironjack had not recognised me. I edged towards the gap in the bar. The room whirled. Smoky lights, jeers and laughter, the stench of vomit and alcohol tainted my senses with giggling demons. My head pounded, my throat tightened until I thought I would suffocate. Hands, always hands wherever I went. Groping, slapping. I grinned stupidly at everyone and pecked their cheeks with sweet gypsy kisses.

Ironjack crouched with his back to me. He baited the dogs, encouraging them to lunge at the bars of the cage. I allowed myself to be pulled into another ale-sodden lap. A face framed with matted whiskers swam in front of me. I nibbled at the scarred ear and laughed like a simpleton when breath, fouler than the deepest cesspit, blew lecherous promises into my face. I wriggled loose and cupped the chin of another purple-nosed drunkard. 'You. I like you better.'

This one was as ugly as the first but to a chorus of cheers I fell on him, smothering his cheeks with my mouth. My former admirer mouthed an oath and grabbed my legs. I kicked him away. He pulled my hair and I tumbled on to the floor. Bone crunched as a fist smacked into my assailant's face. Blood gouted from his nose. He responded with a boot to the other fellow's crotch. Both men fell in a writhing heap, limbs flailing, curses colouring the air. Drunken friends joined in. Jugs smashed, tables were overturned. The music stopped in mid-note.

And I was alone.

I crept around the edge of the counter and slipped through the frayed curtain into a narrow passage. I straightened and fumbled along the wall. The place smelled of stale piddle and rancid meat. I tripped over a huddled shape that groaned and shifted. Whoever it was muttered something unintelligible then settled back into a drunken stupor. I let out my breath and carried on.

So little time. Already Ironjack's voice was calling the rabble to order. A moment later the music started up again. I reached a dimly outlined door at the end of the passage. Behind it, a child was crying. I pressed my ear to the wood and thought I also heard laughter but I couldn't be sure.

Mouthing a prayer, I felt around for the latch, lifted it and pushed. The door swung inwards on well-oiled hinges. Beyond lay a cramped, low-ceilinged room bloated with ale barrels and sacks of animal feed. A stained blanket littered with crusts hugged a far corner. The floor was slippery with grease. Moonlight bled through the half-shuttered window puncturing the opposite wall. On top of a pile of crates, a gasping lantern threw streaks of light across the plaster walls.

Three women sat on a makeshift bench in the middle of the room. Toothless witches straight from the pages of *Macbeth*. I ducked behind a row of barrels and peered through a chink. One of the trio spat on the floor and scratched herself. Another poured something down her throat from a cracked earthenware jug.

The baby girl was passed around like a gin bottle, each taking a turn to press her tiny mouth against one grubby tit and then the other. She wailed morosely, cheeks plum red with effort. The women handled her as they might a bundle of dirty linen. These were the kind of whores not even the lowliest brothels would take. Wet-nurses selling their milk for a penny a time. Wexborough was full of them.

Noise from the passage behind me. A groan followed by a curse. The woman holding the baby scratched and jerked her head. 'Sounds like old Merrow's come to,' she cackled. 'He'll be wanting more gin, otherwise he'll be back to pester us.'

'He thinks your tit's wasted on a baby,' one of her companions laughed. 'Sixpence for a suck is what he once offered me.'

'He ain't got no more 'n' tuppence to his name. Only way he'll ever get his paws on me is if he digs up my dead body and I hope I'm smothered in quicklime just to spite him. Wait now, and I'll go and see if I can shut him up. There's enough row already with this brat bawling its gums off.'

She hauled herself off the box and set the baby down in a crate lined with tangled straw. After she'd disappeared into the passage, the other women continued drinking, gin slopping down their chins. I edged around the back of the barrels until a few feet separated me from the child. A shuttered window lay directly at my back.

The women looked strong. Old scars crisscrossed their cheeks, necks and arms. Surprise was on my side but I doubted I could overpower them both. Their companion would return within moments.

I fumbled along the top of the crate. My fingers curled around the base of the lantern. I picked it up and hurled it on to the floor, splitting open the cheap brass and setting the candle to the tinder-dry straw. The fire caught quickly, devouring this new-found fuel with hungry tongues of blue and orange. Fiery fingers spread out in a web of heat, locking the barrels in a searing embrace.

The women screamed. The jug fell out of their hands and smashed open. Gin added venom to the blaze. A burning carpet swept across the floor. Running to the window, I hauled open the shutters and tried the catch. It wouldn't budge. The frame had been painted closed, sealing the prison. In desperation I picked up a box of dog meat and hurled it at the glass. The window splintered outwards, showering the night with jagged shards of glass. I scooped up the baby and tucked it inside my gypsy shawl.

Footsteps pounded along the corridor. I kicked over the makeshift crib, adding more straw to the fire. Both women had retreated to a far corner and were beating at the flames with their bare arms.

I eased out of the window. Broken glass scratched my arms. A sliver cut through my scalp and I squealed in pain. Worse waited outside. My bare foot landed on a glittering lawn of broken glass, but the cool air was a blessing compared to the inferno I had created inside. I hauled my other leg over the sill just as Ironjack appeared in the doorway and stared at me over the top of the flames. Recognition coloured his features. Then rage. 'That's no gypsy,' he bellowed. 'It's her, the parson's foundling. He's double dealt us.'

I dared not try to find Pietre. I fled into the enfolding arms of the night, the baby pressed against my chest. Perhaps it caught my terror, because it wailed all the louder. Behind me, the inn flared like a beacon, its old walls succumbing to the surging flames.

Exhaustion weighted my limbs and my bleeding feet sent screams of pain up both legs. I sought a refuge amidst the maze of lanes leading away from the Rose Inn. Above the crackle of the fire I heard an angry mob baying for my blood. Then the vicious snarl of the dogs. The beasts would run me down in no time. If I hid they would sniff me out.

The child would be just another piece of meat between their jaws.

I halted, gasping, in the road and tried to get my bearings. Ahead lay a black expanse of moor. To the right, water glimmered under a fugitive moon. A lake squatted like a silver shilling in the coarse grass. So be it. With my last ounce of strength and the dregs of my courage I would walk out into the cool, soothing waters. Better we both drown than let our blood be spilled on the dirt.

I opened my shawl and gazed at the tiny life nestling in my arms. She had quietened. Her round eyes peered up at me.

'I am so sorry,' I whispered. 'I hope your mother will forgive me.'

The stampede of horses, of wheels thundering down the lane. Not even enough time to lose myself in the bowels of the lake. I waited and hoped that death, whether under a wagon or at the blood-slavered jaws of fighting dogs, would be mercifully quick. But a coach hove into view from the opposite direction – out of the stomach of the black moor. Perched on the driver's seat was the unmistakable figure of Charles Prettyman.

Harnesses jangled as the carriage squealed to a halt. 'Juliana, get up here,' Charles yelled. I scrambled one-handed up the ladder and squeezed next to him on the wooden seat. Providence smiled on us. The lane here was wide enough to turn the carriage. We were soon galloping back the way we had come. Behind us, the inn was an orange welt on the horizon. A hot wind churned out of its burning innards and rained cinders around us.

'We won't get away.' The swirling air plucked the words from my mouth. 'A coach cannot outrun men on horseback.'

Charles leaned across and shouted into my ear. 'Dinstock wood lies ahead. 'Tis a rabbit warren of old drovers' roads and foresters' tracks. I spent my whole childhood exploring them. I know this area better than any man. Hold tight.'

The carriage lurched as he made a turn. Immediately the stars were lost above a canopy of branches. Charles ordered me to extinguish the lanterns. It was as if we had fallen into a black pit with sides we could not see. He pulled on the reins to slow the careening horses. 'Keep the child from bawling if you can,' he said. 'Those dogs won't give up easily and I want to put at least five miles between them and us.'

They chased us into the dawn but their hearts were not in it or their animals too weary. We clopped into Dinstock as the first blood-red fingers of the new day groped above the treetops.

'Why did you come after me?' I whispered. My throat was parched. A grey film of ash covered the coach roof and the backs of the horses. Falling embers had singed my hair in places. Charles looked like a ghost.

'That Jane girl warned me not to follow you,' he said, hands limp on the reins. 'When she told me you had set off after her child, I knew you were bound for the Rose. I would've left at once but the parson's wife turned up with young Charlotte. Mrs Proudlove's face was black and blue and the child was screaming. She begged me to take her to her cousin's house in Wexborough, claimed the devil had a hold of her husband and she feared for her life. I tried to explain that I had pressing business. She nigh went berserk, used curses I'd never heard before and set about me with her fists. In the end she collapsed in front of the stables. I had to get the Dinstock coachman to take her and the girl up to the Widow Hendy's. I'd have been after you sooner were it not for that.'

'Betty Hendy? Was that a good idea?'

His cheeks coloured. 'I've been keeping an eye on her. I lit the fire in her hearth, cleaned her house and made sure she had something to eat. Having someone else to look after for a bit will take her mind off her boy.'

'Well, it seems I wasn't the only one keeping secrets,

Charles Prettyman. We owe you our lives, myself and the baby, but you may have damned yourself in coming to our aid. I saw where they kept the children at the Rose. I burned the place to the ground but not before Ironjack recognised me. Chances are he escaped the fire. Whilst others turned a blind eye to the goings on in this county, I have blundered in and learned enough to have them all hung in chains. They will want my life for it, I am sure, and yours too for helping me. The gypsies cannot help me now. I must go to the magistrate in Wexborough.'

Charles's face was grim. 'You'll do no such thing. Look at yourself, Juliana. You're half-dead with exhaustion.'

'I daren't go back to the cottage. Or to your hut. The parson is bound to learn what happened.'

'Once we have delivered the baby to its mother I will take you to a place where you can rest safely for a while. Five men could barely have managed what you did alone tonight.'

I was too tired to argue, or laugh at the ridiculous compliment. The baby had cried itself to sleep and my arms ached holding it. But I would not give it up and Charles knew better than to ask. We pulled up outside the church stables just as a distant cock started screeching at the dawn. I fought to keep my eyes open. Charles clambered down and hurried inside. When he returned, Emma was with him, running like a demented thing. I buried the baby in my shawl. I wanted to pick up the reins and snap the sweating horses into a gallop. I would leave Charles, leave Dinstock and all its sins behind me. I would flee until the horses dropped, then I would run on my bare, bleeding feet. I had nearly died for this child. It was mine as surely as if I had carried it in my own womb.

'Give her to me,' Emma squealed, clapping her hands as if applauding me, as if I was an actress in a travelling show who'd performed some pleasing drama. Two seconds of eternity passed. I sat without moving, staring down at her with more loathing than I had felt for any human being in my life. Uncertainty slipped across her face. The baby woke and started crying again.

'Juliana . . .' Charles said gently.

I passed the child down to the woman who had borne it. I would not call her a mother. It felt too much like some vital organ had been wrenched out of my body. I had no right, no right at all. But Emma would not have rubbed cinders in her hair and travelled with the Romanies. Pretty Emma, who spent her life wrapped in silk and muslin, would not have faced the flames, or the dogs, or the rage of the mob. If not for me she would have sat and wept, and let this precious child be taken away for ever.

'Bless you,' she smiled, nuzzling the baby's head against her face. Her coachman reached into his coat and tossed up another bag of jangling coins. He had to leap aside when I threw it back. The bag burst and scattered coins across the packed dirt of the stable yard.

'Feed the child,' I said, 'then go to Belgium and don't come back.'

Charles drove the coach down a narrow track to a place where the brook formed a series of large pools overhung with trees. The crumbled remains of a mill, its waterwheel long ago plundered for wood, hugged the bank. A dense patch of woodland kept the area hidden from the road.

Charles made up a bed on the carriage seat and let me rest while he unhitched the horses and led them to the water's edge. He kicked off his boots and waded into one of the pools to tickle trout, which he did expertly with his good hand. Within half an hour two good-sized fish lay flapping on the bank.

He kindled a fire and built it in such a way that it gave off almost no smoke. While the trout were sizzling, he washed the ash and cinders from the carriage. The horses had drunk their fill and wandered off to crop the lush grass

305

sprouting between the walls of the ruined mill. My breakfast was brought to me on the end of a stick and washed down with a flask of bitter ale.

Charles waited until I had licked the grease from my fingers and drained the flask. 'What'll you do now that you've changed both our lives for ever?' he asked.

'I will go to Wexborough and see the magistrate,' I repeated. 'Then I have affairs of my own to attend to. My papers . . . oh!' Realisation, followed by despair, hit me like a rock. 'I have left them in your cottage. I must fetch them before going to town.'

Charles put his feet up on the seat and settled back against the window. 'Yes, the papers. What's in them? What could be so important that even now sees you willing to risk more? I know you tried to tell me and I wouldn't listen. I'm listening now.'

'I do not wish to talk about it, not any more.'

'This is my business too. You've brought me along this road with you, Juliana Rodriguez. I want to know where we're going and what lies at the end.'

'I've involved you enough. I don't want to pull you in any further.'

'You didn't want to give Miss Jane her child back either but it was her right to take it, just as it's my right to demand a reason for not returning you to Parson Proudlove, as my duty requires.'

'You would not dare.'

Prettyman picked at his teeth with a fingernail. 'I'd dare. I'm only a humble, half-crippled coachman who does as his master bids. I was not recognised on the road last night and I didn't put the Rose Inn to the torch. If you want your papers, you'll need my help to do it.'

'So, now I have to pander to you? How many other people do I have to satisfy? I do more running around than a scullery wench.'

He sat up and clasped his hands as if in prayer. 'Is there

still room for nothing but bitterness in your heart? You spit at life, yet you save the children of strangers, of people whom you owe nothing. Why do it? Are you seeking glory? Or salvation?'

'I want those children to have a life, a right to their place in the world.'

'What about your place? Who are you really, Juliana? What made you the way you are?'

I pulled off the coat he had spread over me and sat opposite him. Our faces were only inches apart. 'Did Emma tell you about her lover, that same lover who went on to ruin her? Did she mention that she stood with her arms draped lovingly around his neck whilst he humiliated me? That child was worth much more than the purse of money her coachman tried to offer me. I daresay I was trying to prove a point. My father would have been proud.'

'Your father?'

'Oh yes. I have his blood in my veins, right enough.'

'Juliana, you're talking in riddles.'

I prised his hands apart and took hold of his fingers. 'Do you really want to learn about me, Charles? Very well. You can decide for yourself whether my past has turned me into what I am. It is quite a tale, full of romance and tragedy.'

'As long as it's the truth, I don't care.'

I squeezed his knuckles. 'I am the daughter of Manuel Rodriguez, an executed cut-throat who plagued the southern seas.'

Charles gawped. 'A *pirate*?'

I squeezed out a bitter smile. 'Officially he was no criminal. A letter of marque from the Spanish king gave him the right to plunder English ships, which he did so mercilessly, often butchering the crews and hanging their corpses from the rigging. Any women and children travelling as passengers were sold as slaves or concubines. One ship he raided carried the daughter of a wealthy merchant who had interests in the West Indies. She was sailing to join her father, in a place called Antigua, and her fiancé whom she planned to wed within the month. A renowned beauty respected for her wit as well as her looks, she warmed the heart of this butcher-seaman. He threatened to kill any of his men who mistreated her.'

I stared at my lap and the pink knot of my clasped fingers. 'Forgive me for asking, but are your parents still alive?'

'Sorry to say they're not. Fever claimed them both. Bowled them off their feet like a pair of wooden pins and put them in the ground in less than a week.'

'Did you know them well?'

'Here, look at this.' He reached into his shirt and pulled out a leather cord with a ring attached. A semi-precious stone was set in a lead band that moulded itself to the finger.

'I always wear this around my neck. I made it for my mother the year before she died. I was only eleven years old. When I was born my da wanted to wring my neck. Said he wouldn't suffer a cripple for a son. Ma warned him that if he tried it he'd have to throttle her too. He loved her, the old bastard, and so I lived.'

'I don't know what I can tell you about my mother. Was she fair or dark? Brown eyed or blue? Tall and thin or short with a rounded face? No sketch or etching was included in the papers. I've no memory of her touch, her scent, or if she smiled when she saw me for the first time.'

'She gave you up?' Charles asked gently.

'It was her husband's wish. She probably had a notion what would happen to her if she were returned to her family – what would happen to me. The marriage would likely be annulled. I'd be branded a bastard and spirited off in the night. My mother saved me, and I never even knew her.'

'I take it this was the girl on the boat, the one who met the pirate?'

I nodded. 'A bargain was struck. She offered to become his wife if he spared the other passengers and crew. Manuel agreed. Though he could have taken her like any cheap whore, he recognised the treasure he had found. In any case, this fresh young girl, straight from England's green heart, was captivated by him in turn and became a willing spouse, turning her husband from murder.'

'Then what happened?'

'One of Manuel's men, who lived for blood and booty, was not happy with this new-found tenderness in his captain and betrayed him to the British. Manuel had suffered a death sentence on his head for many years. The authorities tricked him, hooked him and threw him in gaol. His wife was already big with child. A daughter was born while Manuel rotted in his cell awaiting execution, a little girl with her father's blood-red mark staining her mouth. Me.'

I swallowed. It felt like a pebble was stuck in my throat. 'My mother was to be returned to her family who had almost died of shame, for word of this bonding had spread quickly around the islands and beyond. I was never spoken of. A wet-nurse, or someone like that, would take me away. I would not be seen again.

'Manuel thought only of his child. He saw me just once, through the bars of his cell. A maid smuggled me in. The prison was also used as a storehouse for rum and other goods bound for England. A young man whose business was in shipping came to inspect the cargo. His name was Richard Worledge. Manuel watched as the young Englishman played cards with the clerks and cargo master. He had a fair hand for the game back then and quickly stripped them of their stakes. Manuel seized his chance. As soon as the Englishman was alone, Manuel offered a hidden cache of Spanish gold as his stake and challenged Richard to play.

'All night the cards turned, Manuel goading the English gentleman, pushing him into higher and higher stakes. Richard found himself owing a small fortune and without a farthing in his pocket. "Why should I consider myself in debt to a criminal," he said, "when you are due to be hanged?" But the Spaniard challenged his honour, dared him to default and still call himself a gentleman.

'"From the gallows I will tell everyone that you would not honour your dues," he warned. "Even as they put the rope around my neck I shall shout it to the crowds. Thousands will be there to see Manuel the Bloody executed. They shall all know of your disgrace."

'Richard bluffed and blustered but in the end Manuel forced a payment. I was the price. Richard was to take me to England and raise me as his own until the day I wed. Manuel made him swear to do so. "Give her what Christian name you will," he said, "but she is a Rodriguez and that part of her must not be taken away." The next day he was hanged.

'So there I was, a nothing child, raised not out of love but to honour a debt. Catherine, Richard's shrewish wife, discovered through his business associate that a large amount of Spanish money had been put in trust to me. I was forced to marry George Proudlove, the parson's son. George was an oaf in life and a fool at the card table. He owed money to some very dangerous people. I was his guarantee, even though I would not come into my inheritance until my twenty-first birthday. Not even a broken neck absolved my husband of his debts. His estate was plundered and I was taken in by the parson.'

Charles stroked my cheek. I did not move away. 'Have you found out what became of your mother?' he asked.

'Taken off to the madhouse. Her wits shattered along with her heart. Perhaps she is still alive. Perhaps some day I will find her.'

He cupped my chin and looked into my eyes. 'Those papers told you all this?'

'Enough for me to piece the rest together. Quite a tale, isn't it? Richard's colleague was always a shrewd man. Catherine and her incestuous lover would have come in for a big bite of my fortune. That was the bargain they struck

310

with George. I was sold like a dray horse and Mr Littlejohn was murdered.'

I rested my head against Charles's shoulder and grasped his coat sleeve. It was his withered arm but he did not seem to mind. 'I have the knowledge about my past that I always craved. I have money, I have the evidence to bring Proudlove down. I ought to feel elated but I don't. I have looked inside myself and found nothing. All those people who have helped themselves to a part of my life – I think they have taken too much.'

He placed a kiss on the crown of my head. 'We'll get your papers,' he said gently, 'but now we must rest and wait until nightfall. They'll be looking for *you,* not your documents. Your past will be safe enough for the next few hours.'

'The children,' I sighed. 'All those children.'

His lips brushed my ear. 'I think it's time you had a child of your own, don't you?'

I pulled away. Heat rose in my cheeks. 'What do you mean? That was a foolish thing to say. Don't laugh at me.'

'It's what you want,' Charles said, grinning. 'It's what you've always wanted. I saw the look on your face when you held Miss Emma's baby, remember? You were wrong, Juliana Rodriguez, when you said no one ever loved you. I adored you from the moment you first tumbled into the lane in that black dress and started ordering me about like a peasant. I love you still and would gladly be a father to any child of yours if that was the only thing in the world that could make you truly happy.'

He touched my lips with his fingers. I kissed them, savoured their taste as if they were drenched in sweet wine. 'You are beautiful beyond words,' Charles whispered, 'and I will spent the rest of my life fighting to win you.'

'Love me now,' I said, 'and the fight is already won.'

He shook like a frightened child but his touch was as gentle as a whisper. We held each other. I wanted nothing more than to see pleasure on his face and see my own delight

311

reflected in his eyes. He gave instead of taking and I gave in return. When it was over we sat together, Charles with his good arm wrapped around me, and slipped off into a comforting sleep. We woke after sunset. Night enfolded the carriage in a soft black glove.

We slipped along the lane like a pair of brigands and ducked behind the hedge bordering the churchyard. Charles peeked over the top and declared the place deserted. He took my hand and helped me through a gap. We fetched up against one of the larger gravestones and waited. The church was a dark sepulchre of mossy stones, silent against the stars.

'Wait here while I check the hut,' Charles said. Before I could protest, he crossed the intervening space with the stealth of a poacher stalking game. His figure appeared briefly at the cottage door then he crouched to peer through a chink in the shutter. Satisfied, he slipped inside.

I set off across the churchyard. A few yards felt like a hundred miles. I imagined snarling dogs waiting to pounce, grizzled men with clubs, or Ironjack, face black with soot, rising from behind one of the stones with a pistol clutched in his hand and a shot bound for my heart. I stifled a squeal when a rat scurried out of my way. When I stumbled through the hut's door, Charles was waiting for me. He'd lit a candle stub and his face was tense. 'Where did you say you hid those papers,' he whispered. 'I've looked where you've told me, but nothing's there.'

I fell to my knees and pulled open the bottom drawer of the dresser. Old clothes spilled out on to the floor. I scrabbled around inside but the documents were gone.

'Someone's been here,' Charles said, sniffing the air. 'Perhaps just one man, I can't say for sure.'

I rose to my feet. I could smell it too. A faint whiff of tobacco, a hint of ruby port hugging the stale air inside the hut. A familiar smell, teasing my nerves like a nagging ache that wouldn't go away.

The parson.

Chapter Nineteen

A light glimmered in the parlour window.

'D'you suppose he's there?' Charles whispered in the dark tunnel of the lane. 'The curtains are open, but I don't see anyone moving around.'

'The rat always returns to its hole,' I replied. 'With Iron-jack and his company of cut-throats at large, Proudlove will likely want to lie low. I doubt any of that mob will dare to show their faces this close to the village.'

We waited half an hour to make sure but nothing stirred either in or around the silent house. 'He may be asleep,' I said at last, 'either in his armchair or upstairs in bed. He is an old man, for all his wiry strength. Sometimes he naps for hours.'

'I say we slip through the kitchen and take our chances,' Charles ventured. 'I'm not keen on the front door. It's too near the window. Besides, if we're caught we can always run back out into the woods. D'you know if the parson keeps a gun?'

I climbed out of the hedge and tugged the hood of my woollen cloak over my head. 'I never noticed any weapons, if you don't count his stick.'

'He's handy enough with that,' Charles admitted, 'but I learned a few tricks from a bare-knuckle fighter. Taught me how to use my good arm to do the work of two.'

'I would rather not meet him. Who knows what he might keep locked up somewhere.'

'Suppose he's out and the house is locked. I'll have to force a window.'

'The kitchen key is on a small ledge above the lintel.'

'That settles it then.' His hand sought my own and squeezed it. Together, we scurried across the garden into the shadow of the woods. The back door latch lifted on the first try and we crept into the empty kitchen. Stuffy, oppressive. Utterly quiet. The hall door hung open. The clock on the upstairs landing had stopped. I listened for sounds of life – breathing, snoring, floorboards creaking as someone crossed the room, or perhaps the squeak of leather as the parson shifted in his chair.

Nothing. Yet I was sure we were not alone. The parlour door, always closed when Proudlove was at home, hung ajar. Through the crack I spied his armchair. Unoccupied. The fire had crumbled into a pile of dead embers. Charles pushed the door wide. A brace of candles flickered on the table beneath the bay window. They had burnt down to stubs. No one was in the room, nor any sign that there had been for some hours.

'Take a look inside that trunk,' I whispered. 'I think it's where he keeps all his important papers.'

Charles crossed the parlour, pulled out the trunk and rattled the heavy padlock binding the lid. 'I'll have to drag this outside and get an axe to it.'

'There's one by the woodpile, but search the room first. I will check upstairs.' I turned to leave and was fetched by a pistol poked into my stomach. Adam Fairchild grinned, his face a mask of teeth glinting in the half-light. Behind him, the front door stood wide open.

'Back inside,' he ordered.

I backtracked into the parlour, not taking my eyes off the gun. Charles was fussing around the bookcase and did not realise something was amiss until I bumped into him. His face blanched when he set eyes on Fairchild.

'So, two rabbits caught in a snare,' Adam purred.

'No longer pretending to be a swordsman?' I enquired. 'Or a gentleman?'

314

'What have you done with the brat?'

'Oh?' I raised an eyebrow. 'You mean your newborn daughter?'

'A hundred guineas is what I mean,' he snarled. 'That's how much I was due for poking the Jane bitch. Only half of what the parson would receive for selling the child on.'

'So you too are part of this trade in flesh?'

He moved further into the room, the pistol still aimed squarely at my belly. 'Well-bred babies fetch a tidy sum when our lords and ladies can't manage to make their own, or when it dies in the crib and they can't wait for another. But this particular child is missing, stolen by you I daresay, and the parson won't pay. Clearly he failed to keep you on a tight enough leash. Old Fortescue was prepared to pay two hundred guineas to be rid of the bastard I put in Cecilia's belly. A couple in Exeter would have bid another two hundred to take it. Instead you got a fancy gown and we were left with nothing. Not even marrying you off to that imbecile George Proudlove was enough to curb you.'

'You were paid to get women pregnant?' I was awestruck. 'I underestimated you, Adam. I thought you were driven by lust and a desire to notch up conquests. I had not thought you capable of such a scurrilous business arrangement. How many unmarried girls, how many wives of men fighting in America have you charmed into compromise, only to have Parson Proudlove conveniently arrive when there was a child to be rid of?'

'Mostly what we did was within the law,' Fairchild retorted. 'Papers were signed, or we had witnesses to say the babies died. There's not a courthouse or country assizes would send me to gaol. Did you get signatures when you stole babies? You're the thief, not I.'

'What about Catherine Worledge? Was she involved, or was she trying to imitate you? The baby I stole from her was going to be killed. I know that for a fact.'

Fairchild gestured vaguely with his free hand. 'Sometimes, if there is too much involved, too much risk of a scandal, other measures have to be taken.'

'Murder?'

'No. Correcting errors.'

'But you were the one putting their daughters with child.'

'I did not force them into bed. If their lack of morality opens up opportunities for sharp-minded businessmen to make a little profit, then who is to blame?'

'And George?'

'Wanted your fortune to pay off his debts. No need to look surprised, we all knew about your Spanish plunder. As your husband, everything you owned would become his. Catherine would fetch a healthy slice as a reward for putting you into his hands. We would stave off George's creditors until you came of age, with perhaps a child or two as security.'

'You would have taken my children?'

'So many little ones die before their first year. A little invention and you would have been none the wiser. Unfortunately, George seems to have proved somewhat deficient in that respect.'

'This is all too clever for you, Fairchild. You are nothing but a male harlot. All your talent lies in your breeches.'

'Your tongue will prove less sharp with a rope around your neck. You were seen burning down the Rose Inn and making off with a child. One of those crimes alone would be enough to send you to the gallows.'

'The baby has gone abroad with her mother. You won't see either again.'

'Fairchild shook his head. 'No matter. I am done with this business. You've stirred up too many hornets with your prodding for things to remain comfortable. Tell me where the parson keeps his money and his papers. I might decide to let you both make a run for it.'

'Proudlove will find you,' Charles broke in. 'His henchman, Ironjack, will feed you to his dogs.'

316

A smile played across Fairchild's mouth. 'I daresay you guessed what happened to old Littlejohn. Other men came too close to the truth, or became greedy and tried to take more than their share. The parson is a possessive man. As he sees it, you are his property but in betraying him you have lost your value. He will see you do penance. When it is finished, you will pray for the comfort of a hangman's noose. Turning king's evidence will save me. Proudlove can hang alongside you, 'tis your choice. You have lived with him, been inside this very room I don't doubt. Tell me where he keeps his papers.'

I spread my hands. 'I don't know. We came here tonight to recover my property. You are welcome to anything of his you find.'

His smile never faltered. 'You are a cunning vixen. I admire that. However my patience is not inexhaustible. Remain stubborn and I will kill the cripple.'

The pistol shifted and aimed at Charles's head. Fairchild cocked the hammer. A rash of sweat broke out on his face. His eyes were twin mirrors full of death.

A clap of thunder. A stench of hot gunpowder. Blood sprayed across the front of my cloak. I screamed. A trapdoor of wet flesh flapped open on Adam Fairchild's skull. The life had already gone out of his eyes before he crumpled on to the rug. He twitched once, twice, his hand still gripping the pistol, which miraculously had not discharged. The dregs of his final breath rattled in the back of his throat. Beside me, Charles cursed softly.

Another figure stood in the doorway. Death in a shovel hat, the night clinging to his black clerical garb. He tucked a smoking gun into his belt and cocked another with the ease of one accustomed to dispensing misery. 'My traitorous friend was correct in one respect,' Parson Proudlove said, nudging Fairchild's carcass with the edge of his foot. 'You are a clever witch. An element of risk was always involved in bringing you under my roof.'

Without taking his eyes off us, he swooped down, pulled off Adam's rings and pocketed them. An engraved snuffbox was plucked from a waistcoat pocket followed by a gold fob watch. Fairchild's purse was emptied on to the rug, the parson taking the sovereigns but leaving the rest to be swallowed up by the spreading pool of blood.

'Not content with murder?' I accused. 'Now you must rob the dead?'

To my horror, he slipped his tongue through the hole in his cheek and licked his jaw free of some irritation. 'I have taken back that which belongs to me. Even his garments are mine by rights. When a dray horse turns sour and the farmer must slaughter it, he will keep the harness, for what does it profit him to lose that as well?'

'I don't understand.'

'But my child, it was you who correctly surmised that Fairchild was not a gentleman. In fact, his father was a cooper spending a second year in a debtor's prison. The mother was a whore. I found Adam working in the same brothel, catering for patrons with special tastes. Such a charismatic lad. I clothed him, taught him to speak well, put the rings on his fingers and threw society at his feet. What well-bred filly could resist him?'

'Did you pick his women with care?' I spat. 'Did you wait until they were at their most vulnerable before sending in your lackey with his oily charm? Even their husbands, in debt and humiliated could do nothing after Fairchild had stripped them at the card table. Only now with a gun aimed at my head can I fully appreciate what you have done.'

'You are young and healthy,' the parson continued. 'I could squeeze a dozen children out of you. Such a waste.'

'So I am still to die, after escaping Fairchild's gun?'

'You are already dead. After setting fire to the Rose Inn, you fled into the night. You have not been seen since. Perhaps in the dark you wandered into the nearby lake and drowned. Or you blundered out on to the moors and fell to your death over an escarpment. At any rate you will never be seen again, you or your lover.'

'Ironjack will get you. He believes you tried to use me to turn a trick on him.'

'Any misunderstanding can be cleared up with enough money. I could build him a dozen pigsties like the Rose. Now,' he waved the pistol at the door, 'it is time to go to church and make your peace with God.'

We had no choice but to do as he wanted. He marched us down the lane to the stables. Charles and I stumbled along in silence. No carriage or horseman passed us. The parson was eerily surefooted, as if moving through the dark was second nature to him. At the stable door, he ordered Charles to pick up a spade before shoving us both in the direction of the church. Once through the lich-gate, Proudlove gestured at a patch of weed-covered ground next to one of the older tombstones. 'Start digging,' he said. 'Make it a deep hole, deep enough for both of you.'

'I'll not dig my own grave,' Charles growled. 'You'd be as well to kill me here and now.'

'Don't try to be noble. There are many ways to die. Defy me and I'll shoot the wench's belly out. A slow, painful death, and I won't miss. I've been knocking the wings off sparrows since I was a boy.'

'What kind of clergyman are you?' I whispered. 'You wear the cloth whilst delighting in the works of the devil. If you like to inflict suffering, why not go with the army and vent your black passions in America? A battlefield is the place for a butcher, not a church.'

He laughed. A hideous expression on his mutilated face. 'For such a clever one you have the sense of a donkey at times. I fought in wars before your father spat you out of his loins. I was a mercenary prior to becoming a clergyman, back to the Seven Years' War and earlier. 'Twas not the pox that put this hole in my face but a French musket ball. With his own bayonet I gutted the man who tried to kill me.

However, the ways of the church were to my liking. A parson's collar can open more doors than a scarlet uniform and who would question a cleric who wishes to travel the county visiting his flock?'

He gestured with the pistol. 'No more talking. You girl, get on your knees and help him dig. Use your hands.'

Footsteps crunched on the cinder path, the sound amplified in the still air. Proudlove snapped around. Marjorie stood on the path, burning torch in hand, her face a wrinkled grey blanket. 'No more killing, Nathaniel.' Her voice was barely more than a whisper. 'No more sin.'

'Ah, the prodigal wife returns to lecture me.'

An expression of terrible weariness hung in the folds of her face. 'I was not always your wife. I had pride once.'

'Go back to the house and shut the door,' Proudlove told her. 'Better still, crawl into your miserable bed and forget you saw anything tonight.'

'As I had to forget the day of my father's funeral? When you ripped the fastenings on my mourning gown and took me with tears of grief still wet on my cheeks?' She turned to me. 'When I found out I was carrying his bastard I wanted to die. I could not accuse him. He had weasled his way into the minds and pockets of all the fine households and dispensed terror from the pulpit to bring common men to their knees. He needed a wife for respectability. What choice had I? The rest of my family would have disowned me for birthing a child out of wedlock. I faced ruin.'

Marjorie took a deep breath. 'I should've embraced the gutter with open arms. When George was born he wanted to sell him to a couple in Somerset and tell everyone that the child had died in his sleep. I swore that if he touched the boy I'd denounce him, no matter the consequences. Let me raise the lad myself, I said, and I'll hold my tongue. I will turn my eyes away and close my ears. That was the pact I made.'

She held up a strand of grey hair. 'Do you know how old

I am, Juliana? Forty-eight years I've suffered on this earth, yet I have the look of a crone. His evil has sucked the life out of me.'

'You turned barren and it soured your temper,' Proudlove retorted. 'You made a martyr of yourself.'

'Birthing Charlotte tore me up inside. I could have no more children. After the surgeon told me, I cried for weeks. I couldn't bear to be touched. Nathaniel took his pleasure elsewhere, tumbling the farm girls because their fathers could not pay a tithe to the church. He keeps his money hidden in an altar to a God he has no respect for. His church is tainted with the cries of stolen children. He has desecrated the entire county.'

Proudlove paced up and down the path, pistol swinging. 'Don't shed any tears over that rabble. They are no better than flies. They proliferate without thinking of the consequences. Women have four, five, six brats in the knowledge that at least half shall die. Their foul wombs are breeding pens for hordes of hungry mouths. Throughout their lives they spread filth and disease. Even in death they blight the earth. Paupers' graves are scattered everywhere like boils.'

'Nathaniel, for years I've kept my peace. I played the pious wife, sitting quietly in that empty church each Sabbath while you laughed up your sleeve at the ignorance of your parishioners. Now you would murder these two for depriving you of a few sovereigns. It can't go on.'

'Then tell me, wife, what you propose to do about it.'

'Drive your gig to Eastleigh and tell the constable. He's an honest man who won't be bought with your liar's gold.'

Proudlove gestured at Charles and myself. 'Is this really what has turned you from a sheep into Judas? An orphan-widow and a crippled farmer's boy?'

'You sold Betty Hendy's son. That brute from the Rose, the one called Ironjack, came prowling around Dinstock. I saw him leave the tavern and caught him in the street. The fellow was burned about the head and babbling like an idiot.

He told me you sold Peter Hendy to a merchant in Clifton. Ironjack planned to keep the money because you tricked him and put his inn to the torch.'

'Criminals spout nonsense the moment they scent the gallows. Talk, talk, talk, as if making speeches could prevent their deaths. That sort will say anything to earn a few extra moments of life. They don't care whom they sully with their lies.'

Charles muttered something. The parson rounded on him. 'Did you say something, cripple-boy?'

'A light is burning in the church,' Charles said. 'It's getting bigger.'

A huge crash sounded from the building's east wall. The tall window exploded in shower of glittering splinters. A tongue of flame thrust out of the shattered mouth. Melting lead spread gunmetal fingers across the blackening stonework. We all stared as a tunnel of smoke spiralled into the sky. Strips of ash wafted on to the ground like dandelion seeds.

It seemed like the end of the world. Another window shattered, raining glass on to our heads. Instinctively we ducked, the parson shrouding himself in his black cloak. A shard sliced into my cheek. I felt warm blood slither down my neck. Another split Charles's good hand open. He stuffed it inside his coat, staring in horror at the blazing church.

We ran around to the front, the spade left abandoned by the tombs. A terrible sight greeted us. Beyond the open door, the church had become an inferno. Rivers of pitch entwined the pews like black ivy. Prayer books lay scattered on the floor, their innards gutted and ripped into white shreds. The pulpit was a tower of fire, the roof a sheet of orange flame. Rafters cracked and dropped blazing splinters into the christening font.

'This is your doing, wife,' Proudlove roared. 'You and your ignorant friends will have to work all the harder to pay for it. I shall have it out of your blood if need be.'

He lunged towards her. Marjorie thrust out the torch and caught him on the side of the face. He howled like an injured cur and backed away, clutching his temple. I could smell singed hair. 'If you've robbed me . . .' he gasped.

'I have taken nothing,' Majorie said. 'Your hoard is still inside. Enough money for fifty churches. Lives can't be bought back, Nathaniel. Not for all the sovereigns in the country.'

A livid welt blackened the parson's head where she had branded him. Hatred simmered beneath his chiselled brows. He shoved Marjorie aside and ran into the furnace, a black, flapping figure like a huge crow. He managed to pull a brass-studded box from behind the burning pulpit and crammed it inside his cloak. Cinders rained from the ceiling. On the way out he lost his grip on the box. It smacked on to the floor and the lid burst open. A welter of coins rolled into the fire.

Marjorie blocked the door. He raised a fist to strike her. She shook her head. 'You can't kill us all.'

'I won't be hung,' he growled, 'not by a gaggle of peasants.'

Fire licked at the hem of his cloak. The pitch-sodden material blossomed into flame. He threw his arms wide and backed into the church. Through the colours of his own destruction, the parson's face melted like a wax candle. He screamed something, the words unintelligible. His cloak was now a shroud of fire.

Charles leapt forward and pulled Marjorie away from the door. My senses swam with the mixed stench of burning pitch and wood. I prayed that I would pass out on the ash-caked grass, begged for darkness and relief. But I could not close my eyes, or cover my face and run.

The roof caved in and the fire swallowed itself up. Three of the church's walls collapsed in a rumbling cacophony of dust and shattered masonry. Smoke swirled around the gravestones, gritting our eyes. We fought not to choke on the scorched air. The sky had turned the colour of blood and everything was tainted.

Footsteps pounded up the lane. Men's voices cried out in alarm. Too late to do anything. Charles's arm slipped around me. I pushed myself deeper into the nest of his comfort. We slunk away, Marjorie in tow, and hid inside the hut whilst the church burned to the ground. Villagers stood in a loose circle, no one making any effort to quench the flames. Afterwards, when the morning sun revealed a blackened, smoking husk, Charles went to tell everyone that the parson was dead.

As if a spell had been broken, a rowdy mob of village men gathered outside the tavern. They streamed out of Dinstock by cart, on horseback or, if no other transport could be found, on foot. Returning at dusk – grim and unwilling to talk – they shut themselves behind their doors and drew the curtains across the windows.

Later, I heard that members of the parson's unholy gang had been rounded up as they tried to seek refuge in the countryside. Some were garrotted, others strung up from the nearest bough.

Ironjack was dragged, still babbling, from the barn in which he'd been hiding. The following morning a miller from Eastleigh found him lying face down beside the brook. His skull was caved in. A bloodied rock lay nearby.

For Marjorie's sake we slipped away to the Widow Hendy's. There was no telling what the mob might do to the parson's wife. She clung to Charlotte, quietly sobbing into the girl's hair. Meanwhile a spark had returned to Betty Hendy's eyes. She stoked the hearth, made coffee from a packet hidden under her bed and fussed and clucked around everyone.

That night, the parsonage was looted and put to the torch. An orange glow lit up the treetops. In the morning we made our way to the church stables. The parson's gig had been pulled to pieces and scattered across the cobbled yard. His charcoal mare was missing. The other horses, though badly frightened by the carnage, had not been touched.

We smuggled Marjorie out of the village in my old coach, Charlotte seated on her lap. My papers were tucked into her gown. Knowing where they were hidden, she had smuggled them out of the parsonage before coming to the church. After long hours on the road we arrived, bedraggled and exhausted, at her relatives' house in Wexborough. The family received us with great kindness and bid us stay as long as necessary. Whilst in town I settled my legal affairs and swore a statement for the magistrate. News of events in Dinstock was already beginning to filter through. The coffee houses were all buzzing with it, I was told.

On the way back, my hired chaise passed the Butter House. The windows were boarded up, the front door nailed shut. Weeds poked green heads between the cracks on the front step. The lawyers handling my inheritance had explained that the property was for sale at a bargain price but no one wanted the house of a madwoman.

Catherine was indeed committed to Bedlam. They kept her bound, as much to avoid her hurting herself as others. Each night she cried out for her dead brother. Her lover. Sometimes my name tumbled out of her mouth, though most of what she said no longer made much sense.

I came into my father's money but found I couldn't live easily with the trappings of wealth, or the kind of society it bought me into. Some declared that to look deep into my eyes was to see a hundred stories simmering away like a pot about to blow its lid. Others suggested that many scars lurked behind my tucked-up smile.

But my days of telling stories were done and my sleep no longer haunted by nightmares. My smiles were real enough. I had much to be glad about.

I knew what love meant now and held it dearer than any other treasure. Much of my new fortune rebuilt the lives of those the parson nearly destroyed. Dinstock received a new vicar, a humble, devout man who held services on the common land when the weather was kind. Sometimes the gypsies, when camped there, listened to his sermons.

The widow's son, Peter Hendy, was found bedraggled and hungry on the Bristol road. His would-be purchaser, getting wind of a scandal, had ordered his coachman to dump the boy on the outskirts of town. Peter had tramped miles, begging food and snatching nights in barns when the chance arose. Betty was transported with joy. It was a new beginning, and we all hoped more would follow.

Meanwhile the old church remained a charred ruin in the middle of the neglected graveyard. No one ever went there. In the days following the burning, a group of village men poked among the rubble. All they found were blackened coins and a brace of twisted candlesticks. Nobody wanted the money. Not even the poorest in the parish would touch it. A curse lay upon the place and mothers frightened unruly children with tales of the parson swooping through the night to snatch babies away.

They spoke too, of the child stealer, who brought Miss Jane's baby back from the Bad Place. With each telling the story grew. One child saved became ten, then a hundred.

But such tales were nonsense and would fade with time. I was content with what I had. I heard that Marjorie married a banker and moved to a fine house in Wexborough with her daughter. Charlotte was growing fast and would become a young woman to reckon with before long. Neither returned to the ruined parsonage. The bones of Adam Fairchild lay undisturbed.

Charles still travelled to Dinstock, usually on business. He turned into quite the horse dealer, my husband, with a haggling skill and eye for a bargain that would put the Romanies to shame. We bought a smallholding five miles north of Eastleigh that boasted a modest but comfortable house, excellent stables and a few acres of good land. Our business prospered. Though Charles could squabble like a woman sometimes, we loved each other very deeply. I treasured every moment of my normal, ordinary life.

Spring was painting the land green again when I felt the first stirring of life within my womb. Our daughter, Mary, was born just before Christmas, a healthy, bawling child weighing all of seven pounds. Charles lifted her up and laughed as if he had cracked open the world and found it lined with gold.

I could never forget looking down on her face for the first time as she pressed against my breast. White, all white save for the dark lashes and tiny, rosebud lips. A tuft of coppery hair was my bequest, but those round, enquiring eyes could only have come from her father. Her skin was as pure as a fresh sheet of linen. She did not bear the red smear that had marked me out all my life. Manuel's legacy ended here. Charles's blood flowed in her veins as well as my own. She was a part of us both. Our child.

And no one would steal her away.

The Gallows Girl

Melanie Gifford

Isaac and Harriet Curtis are in trouble. Their Hampshire coaching inn, Green Gallows, is threatened by the rumours of a new turnpike stretching from London to Portsmouth. The new road will leech all the important trade away from the inn and ruin Isaac's plans for expansion. All will not be lost if they can still succeed in landing a titled – and wealthy – husband for their eldest daughter, Lucy. No expense is spared in grooming her for a better life; while their youngest daughter, Rachel, is little more than a servant.

Rachel cannot help but envy her sister her pretty dresses and the easy admiration she wins from stable hands and gentlemen alike. But while Rachel's world seldom stretches beyond the stable yard or taproom, she little dreams that Lucy would give anything to trade places with her.

For when their father's business plans crumble he does not hesitate in trading Lucy's virtue to pay his debts. But neither sister will submit to her fate without protest, even if it will be left to Rachel to pay the price for her sister's final act of defiance. And it will be Rachel too who seeks the ultimate revenge . . .